TADE THOMPSON

ROSEWATER

orbit

www.orbitbooks.net

ORBIT

First published in the USA in 2016 by Apex Publications
First published in Great Britain in 2018 by Orbit

1 3 5 7 9 10 8 6 4 2

A CIP catalogue record for this book
is available from the British Library.

ISBN 978-0-356-51136-8

Typeset in Sabon by M Rules
Printed and bound in Great Britain by
Clays Ltd, Elcograf S.p.A

Papers used by Orbit are from well-managed forests
and other responsible sources.

Orbit
An imprint of
Little, Brown Book Group
Carmelite House
50 Victoria Embankment
London EC4Y 0DZ

An Hachette UK Company
www.hachette.co.uk

www.orbitbooks.net

For David; welcome home

Chapter One

Rosewater: Opening Day 2066

Now

I'm at the Integrity Bank job for forty minutes before the anxieties kick in. It's how I usually start my day. This time it's because of a wedding and a final exam, though not my wedding and not my exam. In my seat by the window I can see, but not hear, the city. This high above Rosewater everything seems orderly. Blocks, roads, streets, traffic curving sluggishly around the dome. I can even see the cathedral from here. The window is to my left, and I'm at one end of an oval table with four other contractors. We are on the fifteenth floor, the top. A skylight is open above us, three foot square, a security grid being the only thing between us and the morning sky. Blue, with flecks of white cloud. No blazing sun yet, but that will come later. The climate in the room is controlled despite the open skylight, a waste of energy for which Integrity Bank is fined weekly. They are willing to take the expense.

Next to me on the right, Bola yawns. She is pregnant and gets very tired these days. She also eats a lot, but I suppose that's to be expected. I've known her two years and she has been

1

pregnant in each of them. I do not fully understand pregnancy. I am an only child and I never grew up around pets or livestock. My education was peripatetic; biology was never a strong interest, except for microbiology, which I had to master later.

I try to relax and concentrate on the bank customers. The wedding anxiety comes again.

Rising from the centre of the table is a holographic teleprompter. It consists of random swirls of light right now, but within a few minutes it will come alive with text. There is a room adjacent to ours in which the night shift is winding down.

"I hear they read Dumas last night," says Bola.

She's just making conversation. It is irrelevant what the other shift reads. I smile and say nothing.

The wedding I sense is due in three months. The bride has put on a few pounds and does not know if she should alter the dress or get liposuction. Bola is prettier when she is pregnant.

"Sixty seconds," says a voice on the tannoy.

I take a sip of water from the tumbler on the table. The other contractors are new. They don't dress formally like Bola and me. They wear tank tops and T-shirts and metal in their hair. They have phone implants.

I hate implants of all kinds. I have one. Standard locator with no add-ons. Boring, really, but my employer demands it.

The exam anxiety dies down before I can isolate and explore the source. Fine by me.

The bits of metal these young ones have in their hair come from plane crashes. Lagos, Abuja, Jos, Kano and all points in between, there have been downed aircraft on every domestic route in Nigeria since the early 2000s. They wear bits of fuselage as protective charms.

Bola catches me staring at her and winks. Now she opens

her snack, a few wraps of cold moin-moin, the orange bean curds nested in leaves, the old style. I look away.

"Go," says the tannoy.

The text of Plato's *Republic* scrolls slowly and steadily in ghostly holographic figures on the cylindrical display. I start to read, as do the others, some silently, others out loud. We enter the xenosphere and set up the bank's firewall. I feel the familiar brief dizziness; the text eddies and becomes transparent.

Every day about five hundred customers carry out financial transactions at these premises, and every night staffers make deals around the world, making this a twenty-four-hour job. Wild sensitives probe and push, criminals trying to pick personal data out of the air. I'm talking about dates-of-birth, PINs, mothers' maiden names, past transactions, all of them lying docile in each customer's forebrain, in the working memory, waiting to be plucked out by the hungry, untrained and freebooting sensitives.

Contractors like myself, Bola Martinez and the metalheads are trained to repel these. And we do. We read classics to flood the xenosphere with irrelevant words and thoughts, a firewall of knowledge that even makes its way to the subconscious of the customer. A professor did a study of it once. He found a correlation between the material used for firewalling and the activities of the customer for the rest of the year. A person who had never read Shakespeare would suddenly find snatches of *King Lear* coming to mind for no apparent reason.

We can trace the intrusions if we want, but Integrity isn't interested. It's difficult and expensive to prosecute crimes perpetuated in the xenosphere. If no life is lost, the courts aren't interested.

The queues for cash machines, so many people, so many

cares and wants and passions. I am tired of filtering the lives of others through my mind.

I went down yesterday to the Piraeus with Glaucon the son of Ariston, that I might offer up my prayers to the goddess; and also because I wanted to see in what manner they would celebrate the festival, which was a new thing. I was delighted with the procession of the inhabitants; but that of the Thracians was equally, if not more, beautiful. When we had finished our prayers and viewed the spectacle, we turned in the direction of the city ...

On entering the xenosphere, there is a projected self-image. The untrained wild sensitives project their true selves, but professionals like me are trained to create a controlled, chosen self-image. Mine is a gryphon.

My first attack of the day comes from a middle-aged man from a town house in Yola. He looks reedy and very dark-skinned. I warn him and he backs off. A teenager takes his place quickly enough that I think they are in the same physical location as part of a hack farm. Criminal cabals sometimes round up sensitives and yoke them together in a "Mumbai combo" – a call-centre model with serial black hats.

I've seen it all before. There aren't as many such attacks now as there were when I started in this business, and a part of me wonders if they are discouraged by how effective we are. Either way, I am already bored.

During the lunch break, one of the metalheads comes in and sits by me. He starts to talk shop, telling me of a near-miss intrusion. He looks to be in his twenties, still excited about being a sensitive, finding everything new and fresh and interesting, the opposite of cynical, the opposite of me.

4

He must be in love. His self-image shows propinquity. He is good enough to mask the other person, but not good enough to mask the fact of his closeness. I see the shadow, the ghost beside him. Out of respect I don't mention this.

The metal he carries is twisted into crucifixes and attached to a single braid on otherwise short hair, which leaves his head on the left temple and coils around his neck, disappearing into the collar of his shirt.

"I'm Clement," he says. "I notice you don't use my name."

This is true. I was introduced to him by an executive two weeks back, but I forgot his name instantly and have been using pronouns ever since.

"My name—"

"You're Kaaro. I know. Everybody knows you. Excuse me for this, but I have to ask. Is it true that you've been inside the dome?"

"That's a rumour," I say.

"Yes, but is the rumour true?" asks Clement.

Outside the window, the sun is far too slow in its journey across the sky. Why am I here? What am I doing?

"I'd rather not discuss it."

"Are you going tonight?" he asks.

I know what night it is. I have no interest in going.

"Perhaps," I say. "I might be busy."

"Doing what?"

This boy is rather nosy. I had hoped for a brief, polite exchange, but now I find myself having to concentrate on him, on my answers. He is smiling, being friendly, sociable. I should reciprocate.

"I'm going with my family," says Clement. "Why don't you come with us? I'm sending my number to your phone. All of Rosewater will be there."

That is the part that bothers me, but I say nothing to Clement. I accept his number, and text mine to his phone implant out of politeness, but I do not commit.

Before the end of the working day, I get four other invitations to the Opening. I decline most of them, but Bola is not a person I can refuse.

"My husband has rented a flat for the evening, with a view," she says, handing me a slip of paper with the address. Her look of disdain tells me that if I had the proper implant we would not need to kill trees. "Don't eat. I'll cook."

By eighteen hundred hours the last customer has left and we're all typing at terminals, logging the intrusion attempts, cross-referencing to see if there are any hits, and too tired to joke. We never get feedback on the incident reports. There's no pattern analysis or trend graph. The data is sucked into a bureaucratic black hole. It's just getting dark, and we're all in our own heads now, but passively connected to the xenosphere. There's light background music – "Blue Alien" by Jos. It's not unpleasant, but my tastes run to much older fare. I'm vaguely aware that a chess game is going on, but I don't care between whom. I don't play so I don't understand the progress.

"Hello, Gryphon," someone says.

I focus, but it's gone. She's gone. Definitely female. I get a wispy impression of a flower in bloom, something blue, but that's it. I'm too tired or lazy to follow it up, so I punch in my documentation and fill out the electronic time sheet.

I ride the elevator to street level. I have never seen much of the bank. The contractors have access to the express elevator. It's unmarked and operated by a security guard, who sees us even though we do not see him or his camera. This may as well be magic. The elevator seems like a rather elegant wooden box. There are no buttons and it is unwise to have confidential conversations in there. This time as I leave, the operator says, "Happy Opening." I nod, unsure of which direction to respond in.

The lobby is empty, dark. Columns stand inert like Victorian dead posed for pictures. The place is usually staffed when I go home, but I expect the staff have been allowed to leave early for the Opening.

It's full night now. The blue glow from the dome is omnipresent, though not bright enough to read by. The skyline around me blocks direct view, but the light frames every highrise to my left like a rising sun, and is reflected off the ones to my right. This is the reason there are no street lights in Rosewater. I make for Alaba Station, the clockwise platform, to travel around the edge of the dome. The streets are empty save the constable who walks past swinging her baton. I am wearing a suit so she does not care to harass me. A mosquito whines past my ear but does not appear to be interested in tasting my blood. By the time I reach the concourse, there is a patch of light sweat in each of my armpits. It's a warm night. I text my flat to reduce internal temperature one degree lower than external.

Alaba Station is crowded with commercial-district workers and the queues snake out to the street, but they are almost all going anticlockwise to Kehinde Station, which is closest to the Opening. I hesitate briefly before I buy my ticket. I plan to go home and change, but I wonder if it will be difficult to meet up with Bola and her husband. I have a brief involuntary connection to the xenosphere and a hot, moist surge of anger from a cuckolded husband lances through me. I disconnect and breathe deeply.

I go home. Even though I have a window seat and the dome is visible, I do not look at it. When I notice the reflected light on the faces of other passengers, I close my eyes, though this does not keep out the savoury smell of akara or the sound of their trivial conversation. There's a saying that everybody in Rosewater dreams of the dome at least once every night, however briefly. I know this is not true because I have never dreamed of the place.

That I have somewhere to sit on this train is evidence of the draw of the Opening. The carriages are usually full to bursting, and hot, not from heaters, but from body heat and exhalations and despair.

I come off at Atewo after a delay of twenty-five minutes due to a power failure from the North Ganglion. I look around for Yaro, but he's nowhere to be found. Yaro's a friendly stray dog who sometimes follows me home and to whom I feed scraps. I walk from the station to my block, which takes ten minutes. When I get signal again, my phone has four messages. Three of them are jobs. The fourth is from my most demanding employer.

Call now. And get a newer phone implant. This is prehistoric.

I do not call her. She can wait.

I live in a two-bed partially automated flat. Working two jobs, I could get a better place with fully humanised AI if I wanted. I have the funds, but not the inclination. I strip, leaving my clothes where they lie, and pick out something casual. I stare at my gun holster, undecided. I do not like guns. I cross the room to the wall safe, which appears in response to signals from my ID implant. I open it and consider taking my gun. There are two magazines of ammo beside it, along with a bronze mask and a clear cylinder. The fluid in the cylinder is at rest. I pick it up and shake it, but the liquid is too viscous and it stays in place. I put it back and decide against a weapon.

I shower briefly and head out to the Opening.

How to talk about the Opening?

It is the formation of a pore in the biodome. Rosewater is a doughnut-shaped city that surrounds the dome. In the early days we actually called it the Doughnut. I was there. I saw it grow from a frontier town of tents and clots of sick people huddling together for warmth into a kind of shanty town of hopefuls and from there into an actual municipality. In its eleven years of existence the dome has not taken in a single outsider. I was the last person to traverse it and there will not be another. Rosewater, on the other hand, is the same age and grows constantly.

Every year, though, the biodome opens for twenty or thirty minutes in the south, in the Kehinde area. Everyone in the vicinity of the opening is cured of all physical and some mental ailments. It is also well known and documented that the outcome is not always good, even if diseases are abolished. There are reconstructions that go wrong, as if the blueprints are warped. Nobody knows why this happens, but there are also people who deliberately injure themselves for the sole purpose of getting "reconstructive surgery".

Trains are out of the question at this time, on this night. I take a taxi, which drives in the opposite direction first, then describes a wide southbound arc, taking a circuitous route through the back roads and against the flow of traffic. This works until it doesn't. Too many cars and motorbikes and bicycles, too many people walking, too many street performers and preachers and out-of-towners. I pay the driver and walk the rest of the way to Bola's temporary address. This is easy as my path is perpendicular to the crush of pilgrims.

Oshodi Street is far enough from the biodome that the crowd is not so dense as to impede my progress. Number 51 is a tall, narrow four-storey building. The first door is propped open with an empty wooden beer crate. I walk into a hallway that leads to two flats and an elevator. On the top floor, I knock, and Bola lets me in.

One thing hits me immediately: the aroma and heat blast of hot food, which triggers immediate salivation and the drums of hunger in my stomach. Bola hands me field glasses and leads me into the living room. There is a similar pair dangling on a strap around her neck. She wears a shirt with the lower buttons open so that her bare gravid belly pokes out. Two children, male and female, about eight or nine, run around, frenetic, giggling, happy.

"Wait," says Bola. She makes me stand in the middle of the room and returns with a paper plate filled with akara, dodo and dundu, the delicious street-food triad of fried beans, fried plantain and fried yam. She leads me by the free hand to the veranda, where there are four deckchairs facing the dome. Her husband, Dele, is in one, the next is empty, the third is occupied by a woman I don't know, and the fourth is for me.

Dele Martinez is rotund, jolly but quiet. I've met him many times before and we get along well. Bola introduces the woman as Aminat, a sister, although the way she emphasises the word, this could mean an old friend who is as close as family rather than a biological sibling. She's pleasant enough, smiles with her eyes, has her hair drawn back into a bun and is casually dressed in jeans. She is perhaps my age or younger. Bola knows I am single and has made it her mission to find me a mate. I don't like this because ... well, when people matchmake, they introduce people to you whom they think are sufficiently like you. Each person they offer is a commentary on how they see you. If I've never liked anyone Bola has introduced me to, does that mean she doesn't know me well enough, or that she does know me but I hate myself?

I sit down and avoid talking by eating. I avoid eye contact by using the binoculars.

The crowd is contained in Sanni Square – usually a wide-open space framed by shops that exist only to exploit visitors to the city, cafés that usually cater to tired old men, and travel agents – behind which Oshodi Street lurks. A firework goes off, premature, a mistake. Most leave the celebrations till afterwards. Oshodi Street is a good spot. It's bright from the dome and we are all covered in that creamy blue electric light. The shield is not dazzling, and up close you can see a fluid that ebbs and flows just beneath the surface.

The binoculars are high-end, with infrared sensitivity and a kind of optional implant hack that brings up individual detail about whoever I focus on, tag information travelling by laser dot and information downloading from satellite. It is a bit like being in the xenosphere; I turn it off because it reminds me of work.

Music wafts up, carried in the night but unpleasant and cacophonous because it comes from competing religious factions, bombastic individuals and the dome tourists. It is mostly percussion-accompanied chanting.

There are, by my estimate, thousands of people. They are

11

of all colours and creeds: black Nigerians, Arabs, Japanese, Pakistani, Persians, white Europeans and a mishmash of others. All hope to be healed or changed in some specific way. They sing and pray to facilitate the Opening. The dome is, as always, indifferent to their reverence or sacrilege.

Some hold a rapt, religious awe on their faces and cannot bring themselves to talk, while others shout in a continuous, sustained manner. An imam has suspended himself from a roof in a harness that looks homemade, and is preaching through a bullhorn. His words are lost in the din, which swallows meaning and nuance and shits out a homogenous roar. Fights break out but are quashed in seconds because nobody knows if you have to be "good" to deserve the blessings from the biodome.

A barricade blocks access to the dome and armed constables form up in front of it. The first civilians are one hundred metres away, held back by an invisible stanchion. The officers look like they will shoot to kill. This is something they have done in the past, the latest incident being three years back, when the crowd showed unprecedented rowdiness. Seventeen dead, although the victims rose during that year's Opening. They were ... destroyed two weeks later as they clearly were not themselves any more. This happens. The alien can restore the body, but not the soul, something Anthony told me back in '55, eleven years ago.

I cough from the peppery heat of the akara. The fit drives my vision briefly to the sky and I see a waning gibbous, battling bravely to be noticed against the light pollution.

I see the press, filming, correspondents talking into microphones. Here and there are lay scientists with big scanners pointed finger-like towards the dome. Sceptics, true believers, in-between, all represented, all busy. Apart from the classified

12

stuff about sensitives and the xenosphere, most information about the dome is in the public domain, but it is amazing that the fringe press and conspiracy theorists have different ideas. A large segment of the news-reading population, for example, believes that the alien is entirely terrestrial, a result of human biological experimentation. There is "proof" of this on Nimbus, of course. There are scientists who don't believe, but they take observations and collate data for ever, refusing to come to conclusions. There are those who believe the dome is a magical phenomenon. I won't get started on the quasi-religious set.

I feel a gentle tap on my left shoulder and emerge from the vision. Aminat is looking at me. Bola and her husband have shifted out of earshot.

"What do you see?" she asks. She smiles as if she is in on some joke but unsure if it's at my expense.

"People desperate for healing," I say. "What do you see?"

"Poverty," says Aminat. "Spiritual poverty."

"What do you mean?"

"Nothing. Maybe humankind was meant to be sick from time to time. Maybe there is something to be learned from illness."

"Are you politically inclined against the alien?"

"No, hardly. I don't have politics. I just like to examine all angles of an issue. Do you care?"

I shake my head. I don't want to be here, and if not for Bola's invitation I would be home contemplating my cholesterol levels. I am intrigued by Aminat, but not enough to want to access her thoughts. She is trying to make conversation, but I don't like talking about the dome. Why then do I live in Rosewater? I should move to Lagos, Abuja, Accra, anywhere but here.

"I don't want to be here either," says Aminat.

I wonder for a moment if she has read my thoughts, if Bola matched us because she is also a sensitive. That would be irritating.

"Let's just go through the motions to keep Bola happy. We can exchange numbers at the end of the evening and never call each other again. I will tell her tomorrow, when she asks, that you were interesting and attentive, but there was no chemistry. And you will say . . . ?"

"That I enjoyed my evening, and I like you, but we didn't quite click."

"You will also say that I had wonderful shoes and magnificent breasts."

"Er . . . okay."

"Good. We have a deal. Shake on it?"

Except we cannot shake hands because there is oil on mine from the akara, but we touch the backs of our hands together, co-conspirators. I find myself smiling at her.

A horn blows and we see a dim spot on the dome, the first sign. The dark spot grows into a patch. I have not seen this as often as I should. I saw it the first few times but stopped bothering after five years.

The patch is roughly circular, with a diameter of six or seven feet. Black as night, as charcoal, as pitch. It looks like those dark bits on the surface of the sun. This is the boring part. It will take half an hour for the first healing to manifest. Right now, all is invisible. Microbes flying into the air. The scientists are frenzied now. They take samples and will try to grow cultures on blood agar. Futile. The xenoforms do not grow on artificial media.

In the balcony everyone except me takes a deep breath,

14

trying to get as many microbes inside their lungs as possible. Aminat breaks her gaze from the dome, twists in her seat and kisses me on the lips. It lasts seconds and nobody else sees it, intent as they are upon the patch. After a while, I am not sure it happened at all. I don't know what to make of it. I can read minds but I still don't understand women. Or men. Humans. I don't understand humans.

Down below, it begins, the first cries of rapture. It is impossible to confirm or know what ailments are taken care of at first. If there is no obvious deformity or stigmata, like jaundice, pallor or a broken bone, there is no visible change except the emotional state of the healed. Already, down at the front, younger pilgrims are doing cartwheels and crying with gratitude.

A man brought in on a stretcher gets up. He is wobbly at first, but then walks confidently. Even from this distance I can see the wideness and wildness of his eyes and the rapid flapping of his lips. Newcomers experience disbelief.

This continues in spurts and sometimes ripples that flow through the gathered people. The trivial and the titanic are equally healed.

The patch is shrinking now. At first the scientists and I are the only ones to notice. Their activities become more agitated. One of them shouts at the others, though I cannot tell why.

I hear a tinkle of laughter from beside me. Aminat is laughing with delight, her hands held half an inch from her face and both cheeks moist. She is sniffing. That's when it occurs to me that she might be here for healing as well.

At that moment, I get a text. I look at my palm to read the message off the flexible subcutaneous polymer. My boss again.

Call right now, Kaaro. I am not kidding.

15

Chapter Two

Rosewater: 2066

Now

It's the middle of the night when I arrive at Ubar. I come off the last train and there's a car waiting for me. Ubar is an area between the North Ganglion and the widest part of the River Yemoja. We drive along the banks before turning away into empty roads between dark buildings. The driver stops in front of imposing iron gates, waits for me to get out, then drives off.

I walk into a facility that belongs to the Ministry of Agriculture. From the outside it is a simple two-storey building with ordinary signage showing the Nigeria coat of arms covered in dust. Inside there's a reception and an open-plan office. There are framed photographs of the president on one wall and Rosewater's mayor Jack Jacques on the other. Mundane. I'm buzzed through all of this without delay and my implant's RFID is logged sure as cancer.

I go straight to the elevator down to the sub-levels. These are used and controlled by Section Forty-Five, or S45. Most have never heard of this obscure branch of government. I have only heard of them because I work for them. Before that, I was a finder and a thief.

Part of my job with S45 is interrogation. I hate interrogations.

It is 0300 hours and we are in a dim meeting room. There are two agents in black suits standing on either side of a prisoner, who is naked and tied to a chair. The prisoner is blindfolded. The agents don't speak and I do not know what information they need. I don't bother trying to read them because the organisation would not have sent them if they knew anything. This is part of some bureaucrat's idea of keeping the subject's mind uncontaminated with expectations. What they want is for me to copy all the information from the subject's mind, like making a backup of a hard drive. This is ridiculous and not possible, but no matter how many times I've written memos to the powers-that-be, this continues to be the manner in which they request interrogation. I continue to do it my way.

Data does not spool into or out of the human brain like a recording.

The man in front of me is black, unbruised, breathing in ragged hitches, and muscular. From time to time he says "please" in Kanuri or Hausa. He tries Igbo and Yoruba sometimes, but I am not convinced he speaks any of the languages fluently. I am uncomfortable and stay two feet away from him. I connect to the xenosphere. I first establish that he is not a sensitive. His self-image is the same as the man in the chair. That's good – it means I will not be here all night.

There is violence in this man's head. I see two men beating a third in what looks like a back yard. The two men alternate kicks and punches between them while their victim tries to stay upright, using his forearms to shield himself as best he can. The victim is bruised, dirty, and bleeding from the mouth and nose. He does not seem afraid. If anything, he appears to be mocking his tormentors. His attackers are uniformed, dark-skinned, with berets and sunglasses designed to make them seem identical. They do not look like the Nigerian police or army, at least not by the uniform. Looking closer, the uniforms seem homemade, like from one of the militias. They have no weapons holsters, but one has a pistol stuck in a belt at the small of his back.

Something else that is odd: I cannot smell the yard or taste the dust that the three men kick up. I have neither the taste of blood in my mouth as the victim should, nor the pain of impact on my knuckles as the perpetrators should. Instead, this image is associated with the taste of food and drink, specifically kuli-kuli and beer. I also keep getting snatches of music from a cheap keyboard.

I briefly emerge from the xenosphere and inspect the prisoner. I walk around behind him and check his bound hands. His knuckles are dark, callused. You get this from knuckle push-ups and punching a hard surface like a wall or a wooden man in order to remove sensation from the area, to make you a better fighter. I know this because I have done it. None of the participants in the prisoner's memory seemed trained in hand-to-hand. He is not one of them.

Did he order the beating? From where did he witness it?

Then it hits me.

"Oh, you clever bastard," I say.

I re-enter the xenosphere. The "memory" is staged. The prisoner watched it in a movie on repeat and was probably eating and drinking at the same time. He probably found a lesser-known Nollywood film, which accounts for the cheesy music and the poor production values. He is not a sensitive, but he knows we exist and that he might be exposed to one on arrest. What it means to me is that he does have something to hide. I probe at the edges of the memory, which is like trying to peel off the adhesive label on a packet. I need to find purchase. I fix not on the image or the sound, but on the other senses. Touch, smell, taste.

"Hello, Gryphon."

It's the same woman as earlier in the night while I was at the bank, playful, curious, ephemeral. The interruption breaks my concentration and I see the beating looping around and around. I search for a linked self-image but all I can find is the noise of the general xenosphere. Random mentations. Useless. I am irritated, but my training kicks in and I focus my will on the matter at hand.

The sensation associated with the beating is gentle pressure on the buttocks, and food, which tells me he was seated in some living room watching the scene on a widescreen TV or a hologram. I discover the smell of cigarette smoke. The scene shifts, wobbles, dissipates, and I'm in a smoke-filled room with five other men, all of whom are intent on the screen. Nobody speaks, but they drink beer, they smoke, and they chew the snacks laid out on a tray.

I don't like interrogations, but I'm good at them. I feel proud of myself when I solve a puzzle, and then I feel disgust. I try to think of myself as a lawyer, operating within certain parameters that do not include morality. Focus on the task.

I pull out and say to the agents, "I need a forensic sketch artist. Now."

*

I am debriefed by my boss, Femi Alaagomeji. Videoconference, of course. Nobody in the security services would ever knowingly be in the same room with me. I know for a fact that they are not even allowed to form relationships with sensitives and are required to report the occurrence of sensitives in their families. The last time I breathed the same air as Femi was six years ago, but the time before that was eleven years ago, when she shoved me into S45, just before my training, when the dome was new and Rosewater was nascent.

Femi is the most beautiful woman I have ever seen. She is physically perfect in so many ways it hurts. In a sterile room, with a secure link, I videoconference with her. Today she wears burgundy lipstick. I happen to know she has a burgundy convertible Mercedes-Benz. She must have driven it to work.

"Kaaro," she says.

"Femi," I say.

"Call me Mrs Alaagomeji."

"Femi."

This is an old dance that we dance. She is not really irritated and I am not really impudent. We play the roles all the same.

"Who is the prisoner, Femi?"

"Classified, need-to-know, all that good shit. What do you have for me?"

"Faces. Five of them. The artist did well and is running them through the system right now. She's also looking at the location, the brand of the electronics, everything. That's all for today. I'm tired and it's almost time for my day job."

"It's not a job. You contract. This is your job."

"Fine. My other job."

"How long will it take?"

"I do not know. If you told me his name—"

"No."

"—or what he's done—"

"No."

"Then we do it the hard way, inch by inch. I discover information, I stop, I let the artist know, we start again."

"So be it."

"Can I go home now?"

"In a minute. How are you, Kaaro?"

"I'm fine."

"You're lonely."

"I am alone, not lonely. It's solitude, but that doesn't have to be a bad thing. I'm keeping up with my reading. I'm going to learn to play the oboe."

"What are you reading?"

"Chomsky."

"All right. Are you really learning the oboe?"

"No."

"I don't know why I bother asking. Go home."

"Goodnight, Femi."

I'm barely able to keep my eyes open by the time the S45 car drops me at home. The night has lost the battle with the day and soon Rosewater will rise and go to work. The city wakes up in layers. Food comes first. Long-haul drivers bring in crops from Oyo, Ogbomosho, Ilorin and Abeokuta. Cassava, corn, yam flour, millet, rice from Thailand. Not a lot sourced locally any more. These are delivered to the many categories of bukka, the mama put, the food-is-ready. Cheap, local, and essential for the unskilled workers, who need a hearty carbohydrate bomb before tackling their less-than-minimum-wage jobs where they use their biceps, triceps and spinal columns to lift, hew, saw, join, shave, slaughter and clean. The aroma draws out the first tier of office workers: clerks, secretaries, juniors. Over a two-hour period, the middle-class professionals of Rosewater will arrive at their offices, surgeries, law chambers, accounting firms and, of course, banks.

I will be joining them, but I need a shower and breakfast, perhaps strong coffee. I live in the middle floor of a three-storey in Atewo. An eight-digit code opens my flat, but there is an override key.

A series of phone messages come through as if the signal just became strong enough. I seriously consider skipping the bank, pretending to be sick and sleeping all day. I want to find out who is trying to reach me across the xenosphere. I strip and walk naked into the shower. I try that trick of using warm, then cold, then scalding hot water, but it does not refresh me. In the mirror my eyes look bloodshot and baggy, like they're from a pervert's mug shot.

"You look like an idiot," I say to my reflection. "You *are* an idiot. Your life is meaningless."

I put on boxers and pad into the living room without getting fully dry.

"Miles Davis, 'So What'," I say to the sensors, and the bass plucks out on the speakers.

"Phone, messages."

I sit. I close my eyes. I listen.

My accountant wants to discuss my taxes.

The National Research Laboratory calls. They want three days of my time. They will pay. I will ignore them. I have worked for them before and I don't want to any more. They're in Lagos and they want to know about sensitives. I hate going to Lagos, and the NRL scientists stare at me as if they want to open my brain while I'm still alive.

A message from Aminat, her speech stopping and starting like musical chairs. "Hello, Kaaro. I know. I know, we were only going through the motions. But I find myself thinking of you and I wonder what ... " (laughter) "Oh God, this is so ... Okay, call back. Or not. I'm not as needy as I sound."

She has me smiling.

A television producer who has been hounding me for two years offers me money and fame if I will appear on *Nigeria Is Talented*.

"Hello, Gryphon."

I first think the person has left me a message on my phone but that's not it. I open my eyes and a shoal of mackerel, oku eko, fly past my face. Miles still plays the horn, but it sounds distant. I am in a place of shifting colours and shadows. I look down at my hands and they are gone. Instead, there are feathers.

This shit hasn't happened to me in a long time. I am in the xenosphere – asleep and in the xenosphere. It's easy to see how. Warm shower, sleep deprivation.

"Gryphon."

"Who are you?" I ask, against all of my training.

"I like your plumage," she says. "Can you fly?"

"Anybody can fly here. Who are you?"

The fish are beginning to bother me. The air has the consistency of water. I hear an under-hum of voices and thoughts of others at low signal. I cannot see this woman although I hear her clearly. No self-image?

"I am an individual," she says. "I am a one."

"Yes, but what's your name? *Ki l'oruko e?*"

"Must I have one?"

"Yes."

She is silent for a time. I try to scratch my face, but I tickle myself with feathers instead. I stretch my wings and it feels better.

"My name is Molara," she says.

I snap up one of the mackerel in my beak and break its back, then drop it to the floor between my forepaws. It twitches and lies still.

"Show yourself," I say.

"I don't know how," says Molara.

Definitely a wild strain. I speak, echoing the words of my instructor.

"Think of something you love, something you hate, something you fear, something disgusting or beautiful. Something you find impressive."

Fire trucks of all sizes and descriptions stream past, none of their lights flashing. Some of them are toys. Behind each one a red masquerade runs, tiny Lilliputians for the toys, giants for the full-sized.

A butterfly flowers in front of my face. It unfolds lengthwise with a fourteen-foot wingspan. It is black and blue and its wings move in a majestic slow beat.

Then I wake, jarred out of the xenosphere at the same time by the phone. I am confused for a moment. The phone stops, then starts again.

"Yes?" I say.

"You're meant to be here," says Bola. "You sound hungover. Are you hungover?"

"Oh, shit."

*

24

I am monstrously late.

My grooming is sloppy, but better than the metalheads', so I'm fine. The customers surround the bank like ants feeding on a child's dropped lollipop. The day after the Opening is always extra busy because people want to see their doctors and get laboratory tests to confirm their healing. The Rosewater medical community is not very robust and comes alive only at this time of year. One would think they would be out of practice.

The firewall is up without me. Two of the metalheads are absent, likely hungover, and Bola tells me the wild sensitives are quiet – perhaps they too have been celebrating Opening Day.

The team are reading pages of Tolstoy. I sit in the break room and rub ketoconazole cream on my exposed skin to keep me out of the xenosphere. It's the busiest banking day of the year and I do not want to fatigue myself further. I drink horrendous instant coffee by the cupful to keep myself awake, a benched striker.

Interlude: Mission

Lagos: 2060

It is unbearably hot, but still I wait. I feel rivulets of sweat dripping down my back, in between my butt cheeks. I can just about breathe, but the close, oxygen-poor air threatens to make me black out. There are mothballs here waxing aromatic in my nose and mind, whispering fact and fiction about my wife. I can barely keep still. The clothes in the closet caress my back. Down around my feet there are shoes crowding, jostling for space. A dangling belt tinkles with my movements, made loud by the silence. My left hand rests against the warm wood of the door, my right by my side, weighed down by the knife.

I wait.

Any moment now.

I hear a door slam from elsewhere in the house. I hear the beep as the door autolocks, and giggling that makes me see red. Literally, red flashes across my eyes in the darkness, like a surge of blood, just for a second. I can feel my heart driving the blood through my body, demanding that I move. I wait.

26

There are bumps and mistakes as two people wind their way through my house, through our house. The door to the room swings open. I imagine them standing there kissing. I hear the sucking sound of their lips. My fist tightens on the handle of the blade.

"Stop," says my wife, but she is laughing.

"Okay. No means no," says the man, with mock seriousness.

Her perfume reaches me now. I hear the adulterous rustle of her clothes falling to the carpet.

"Really?" says my wife.

Now the blood sings in my ears. My head feels larger and my mouth is completely dry. I feel my scrotum constrict.

Lydia, Lydia, Lydia.

I do not know if I am thinking this or if her lover is repeating her name, but her first gasp of pleasure is my cue.

I break out of the closet. The first few seconds are free, because they do not hear me in their passion. I am at the bed. She is naked, supine, legs apart. He is between those legs, his hand buried in her sex, his head beginning to turn.

I cut him first, side of the neck, one stroke. The blood spurts, but I ignore it and shove him by the right arm. Lydia screams. Her eyes are rather comical circles, the whites larger than I have ever seen. For spite I drive the knife into her left eye, withdraw it, then stab her throat. I look at the man, who is holding his neck and wetting the carpet with his blood. His shirt is soaked. His movements lack direction and he will die soon. I turn back to Lydia, who is gurgling now.

I take my time to . . .

I vomit.

I fall to all fours and spew yellow-green slime. "Oh fuck. He did it," I say.

Ohfuckohfuckohfuck.

"Are you sure?" asks Femi. "No hair, no DNA, no physical evidence."

I cough. "Holy fucking shit, Femi, if I say he did it, he did it. He did it, okay? I fucking did it."

"Kaaro, calm down." She places a hand on my back, but I shrug it off.

"I did it. I bought a gene grub and let it feed on me, then let it loose in the room after I killed them both. An elegant drone hack removed traces of me from surveillance cameras. I paid the hotel staff for their blindness. I drowned them in a river of foreign currency. They will go to their deathbeds denying that they ever set eyes on me."

I dry-heave.

"Kaaro, you mean *him*, right?"

Oh fuck, the revulsion. Oh fuck. Ori mi. *Help! Lydia! Lydia!*

Why the fuck does it feel like ... Why am I guilty?

"Help me," I say. "Help me."

I crawl into a corner. I cannot stop shaking; I cannot stop seeing my arm rise and fall, the wide eyes, the gurgling ...

"Overidentification," says the doctor. I forget his name, I do not like him.

Three months since the assignment. I am sequestered, back in from the cold, as they say. They stick me in a mental joint, for field agents who go over the edge, and I most definitely went over the edge.

He continues. "You identified too strongly with your subject. Ego boundaries blurred and you lost the integrity of your self. You thought you were him."

"I know that here," I say, pointing to my head, "but not in my heart."

He laughs. "That's an improvement over when you first arrived. If it's in your head, your heart will follow."

I am not so sure. I am not so sure who I am. I mean, I know I am Kaaro, and I work for S45 and I was trained by Professor Ileri and Rosewater is my home and ... but ... but I *remember* how Lydia sighs after fucking, just before she demands that I get her a glass of water. I remember sliding the ring on her finger the day we got married. The biodome is a mixture of cerulean and vanilla in the background of our wedding photos. I remember her cooking. I remember opening a saucepan to see the stew bubbling, gurgling, like the froth from her neck when I ...

I feel a tear roll down my cheek. "Doc, I miss her," I say. "If I never met her, why do I miss her so much? Why do I feel guilty?"

"Maybe you feel guilty because there is someone you, Kaaro, have an unconscious desire to kill. The murder of Lydia fulfilled that desire. Down under the surface of our mind lie the demons and gremlins of our base instincts, struggling for expression." He checks the screen in front of him and asks, "Have you been taking the meds?"

No.

"Yes."

No. They make me impotent.

"This is the third antidepressant we've tried. I've never seen such a strong reaction. Ileri thinks it's because your ability is more acute than any other."

"My wife is dead. I should be sad, right?" I ask.

"Kaaro, you have never been married. You never even met

Lydia. You spent time in her homicidal husband's mind. The experience was so intense that you can't disconnect. The pills aren't working. I'd like to try something else."

He slides across consent forms for shock treatment.

I walk out of the building.

I really want a cigarette, even though I have not smoked for a long time. It feels right that I should be smoking at a time like this.

Nine months. I have lost enough time to have a baby.

A drone descends to read my identity, then flies off.

I get a phone call. It's Femi, so I ignore it. Great service to your country blah blah put the man in jail for life blah blah sacrifice sacrifice sacrifice blah blah.

I cannot remember everything that happened, gaps in my memory. A part of me thinks perhaps there is a reason for the gaps and that I really do not want to know.

There's a sorrow in me, though. I do not know why, but I feel it.

Whatever they pay me is not enough.

I look for a taxi.

Chapter Three

Rosewater: 2066

Now

When I arrive home that evening, there is a reanimate at my front door, the second one of the night. I encounter the first on the 18.15 anticlockwise to Atewo.

There is a curfew enforced by the Nigerian Army Special Detachment the week after the Opening. The NASD is strictly an execution detail that exists for the sole purpose of killing reanimates and disposing of the remains. Everybody must be home by 1930 hours or risk being shot, electrocuted or burned.

I am slightly late and sprint to the platform. I'm breathing heavily when I enter the carriage, just making it before the train starts moving. My plan is to sit and gather in peace to myself. The banking district is in Alaba. There is only one other stop, Ilu-be, before I disembark in Atewo. The trip takes twenty minutes when the ganglion is working.

A child walks down the aisle selling water, oranges, nuts, soda and some other shit. She balances herself by having one hand on the grab rails on the seats. I don't buy anything. There are four other people in the car. One man stands, back to me, facing a window and wearing a grey suit. His head is bowed. It's an old carriage. The seats are covered in brown faux leather. It smells stale, but not bad. Six years ago we had old trains imported from Italy – I suspect they were World War II era – but they were replaced with these new ones, which look better but are rather basic, like the template from which all modern trains are made rather than a unique entity in and of itself.

Above the luggage racks there are posters on the side panels, mostly showing Jack Jacques. He gives us a thumbs-up and smiles, shooting the whiteness of his teeth at us. Rosewater's status in Nigeria is dubious, but the mayor is the head of what passes for local government. I have met him; he's a narcissist, a demagogue and a sycophant to the president. The dome is ignored, the unspoken city. The House of Assemblies declared seven years ago that the alien is not a legal entity. We like to pretend it's a natural formation, like a hill, or Olumo Rock down in Abeokuta.

The train's seats are uncomfortable, but it is possible to doze off, which I do. I come to with a start because I hear snarling.

The suited man who had his back to me now stands over a couple. His right flank is to me, face in shadow from the overhead light. The woman is hitting at him with a rolled-up magazine, ineffective, laughable even. With her other hand she cradles her man, who appears to be hurt. The growling man sways with the vibrations of the train.

"Hey!" I say, and stand up.

Suit man looks towards me. His head is abnormally long, and one of his eyeballs is missing, the empty socket gaping like a toothless second mouth. The head is also flattened in a way that accounts for the length, looking like it has been incompletely crushed. The nose is twisted as if the bottom half of his face wants to go one way while the top chooses the other. His left ear hangs by a thin thread of human tissue. Yet with all this there is no bleeding and he is not in obvious pain.

He is three, four feet away, and he charges towards me. When the dome brings a body back to life, sometimes it simply drools. And sometimes, like this guy, it wakes up angry. Scientists haven't worked out what makes them go one way or the other – me, I think it might have to do with temperament, some people being more aggressive than others. Or maybe, like this guy, how they die. He didn't give up the ghost peacefully in his sleep.

Other than the grey suit, he's wearing white gloves, a fake carnation in his lapel, white shirt, blue tie. I wait for him, breathing out, then side-kick him in the middle of his chest, aiming for the blue strip. It's a good hit. I hear the expulsion of fetid air from his lips. He is still standing, so I hit him again with the other foot. He staggers back, hits the centre post, which rings dully. A part of my mind notes the couple leaving the carriage. I do not blame them.

The reanimate bounces back at me. I have nothing to kill him with. I do not like to fight. In fact, I'm a coward. When I used to steal for a living, I was a sneak thief, not a robber, and I ran away from every physical confrontation until S45 recruited me. Basic hand-to-hand training based loosely on karate and Krav Maga changed my view on violence very little. I'm not good at it, but I'm okay. I can't fight multiple opponents like in a kung-fu flick, but one reanimate I can handle. Maybe.

The overhead lights flicker. I grab a hanging strap with each hand, lift myself up and kick him in the head. He falls but gets up again. I hope the couple have raised the alarm, but I think not. The train would have braked, although the driver could have just left his cabin and abandoned ship.

The reanimate swings at me. I raise both forearms like I've been taught, catch his clumsy blows. He bleeds where I've broken his face, and there is some pink fluid leaking from his left ear. I jab at his face and belly, trying to buy time and control my breathing and fear. There is nothing in here, in this carriage, to use even as a non-lethal weapon. The windows are double-glazed shatterproof glass. I wonder if I should just run and wait for the authorities to deal with him at the next station, but I'm in an end car and he's blocking the exit.

The train hits a bend and the two of us are flung right. I grab hold of a seat and just stumble, but the reanimate goes flying into a window. The window does not break, but there is a smear of blood at the impact point. A two-inch-square sticker says, *Are YOU ready for JESUS?*

The reanimate is lying across two seats. The middle armrest must be digging into his midsection as he thrashes about to reorient himself. This is a great opportunity to run away.

His hand is in an awkward position hung over the next seat. I stamp on the shoulder joint where arm meets torso. I feel it give. He falls further, the limb flapping uselessly. He does not cry out.

He works his way up with one arm. He still tries to hit me with the working arm, but it's rather pathetic and perhaps funny. I do not fear him any more. I punch him again – a straight right with all my weight from the hip. His head rocks and I feel the counter-force in my fist, but he's still standing. Why can I not knock this fucker unconscious?

I keep punching and kicking till his face is a mess of red and brown. I am still striking him when a man with three stripes on his army-green shirt walks into the carriage and puts a bullet in the reanimate's head.

"It says here you're licensed to carry a concealed weapon," says the Special Detachment guy.

"Yes," I say.

He waits, expectant.

"I *can* carry a gun. I do not. I choose not to."

We are in the stationmaster's office at Atewo for a quick debrief. It is not yet curfew, but the SD units are gathering. This sergeant was on the train and saw the attacked couple. The driver is a bit annoyed that we have soiled his train with blood spatter.

There is a glass of something fizzy and orange in front of me. The sergeant has a sick mother at home and a disabled older brother. He joined the army to cater, to help. I get this information quickly, in seconds. The fight, the exertion, it has all made me sweat off the antifungal cream. I am open to the world. Or open to the mind of the world. I just want to go home. This soldier boy thinks he's helping, but he's not.

"I'll have to file a report and this will go to your supervisor," he says. He inclines his head like he's apologetic, like he feels bad about it.

I shrug. "Can I go?"

"I've uploaded a curfew pass on your implant just to ensure you get home on time without harassment from other SD units."

"Thanks."

"*Esprit de corps.*"

I walk home and there, at my doorstep, is another reanimate.

*

I'm not in the mood for a second fight. I consider other options. I could wait it out, but I don't want to be outside. I have a few friends, but none close enough for me to consider calling them under these circumstances. The reanimate bounces her head against the door. She looks like a schoolmistress, wearing a skirt and blouse and sensible shoes. She is getting blood on the finish. I expect the other tenants can hear the knocking but ignore it. I am behind her and she has not noticed me yet.

On a whim, I call Aminat.

It rings once, then there is a loud hissing and I pull the phone away from my ear. It stops and I hear her voice.

"Hello?" she says.

"What the hell was that?" I ask.

"Kaaro! Don't mind me. I'm cooking. How're things?"

The reanimate hears me speak and turns.

"This will sound odd and forward of me, so I'm going to apologise in advance—"

"Yes."

"I haven't said what I want to—"

"You can come over."

"How did you—"

"Be quick. There's a curfew on." She gives me her address.

I leave just as the reanimate decides to investigate me.

Aminat plays "Top Rankin'" and hums it to herself as she drops my drink on the side table. She is barefoot, wearing rolled-up jeans and a vest without jewellery, a carefully casual look.

She has a house in Taiwo, one station clockwise from me, closer to the North Ganglion. It's a more affluent area, with cars in every garage, barbed wire and security systems being common features. They have the kind of high-octane satellite technology that used to be the domain of spy thrillers.

I'm slightly embarrassed to be there, but Aminat is so natural about it that any discomposure fades quickly. There is warmth and twentieth-century reggae and light incense on the air. She takes me to the bathroom and I think I'm going to get mothered, but she gives me cotton wool, water, soap, plasters, disinfectant, iodine and a smile. She tells me she'll be out in the living room when I'm done washing the blood off my face and hands. When I'm half decent, I join her and she plants the drink beside me, leaving a wake of jasmine. She sits opposite me, still mouthing Bob Marley, and stares.

"Are you some kind of warrior poet, then?" she asks.

"Nothing even remotely as glamorous as that," I say. "I can't fight and I don't do poetry."

"And yet your knuckles bleed. Who are you, Kaaro? Is that a first or last name?"

"It's just Kaaro."

"Are you Yoruba?"

"I am."

"So your name means 'good morning'?"

"Yes and no. My full name is Ile Kaaro o Jiire, which can be transliterated to 'good morning, you've woken up well', but is a term that means 'all Yoruba-speaking peoples or lands'."

"That's a strange name. Your parents called you that?"

"Yes. My father was an idea man."

"He told you not to use a surname?"

"No, that was my idea."

"How do you get away with that in a bank?" She crosses her legs and takes a sip of her own drink. There is a shadow of agility in her movements, the ghost of an athlete's drills.

"What exactly did Bola tell you about me?" I ask.

She laughs. "She said she knew the right guy for me. Good-looking, single, has a reasonable job and is not a dog. She didn't seem to know or care if we have anything in common."

"Do you know what I do at the bank?"

"Counter-fraud, isn't it? You combat 419 scams, same as Bola."

The temptation to look into her head is overwhelming, but I resist. This is one of the reasons I do not date. Once you've been in the xenosphere, you get used to rapid familiarity. You scan quickly and know that the person in front of you is hiding a second wife or has a secret vice. The usual mutual self-disclosure, which regular people do, is plodding and inaccurate, but this equality is necessary for a real relationship. Patience.

The sound of automatic rifle fire rises above the music for a few seconds, making Aminat flinch.

"The cull," she says.

"Tell me about yourself," I say. I have no sympathy for reanimates, but something in her voice tells me she does. "How do you know Bola?"

"She's my sister-in-law."

"You're Dele's sister?"

"No, her first husband. Dominic."

"Oh? I didn't know she was married before."

She rises, goes to a display case and returns with one of those digital frames that changes photographs every few seconds. This one cycles through photos of the same man in different places and circumstances.

"That's Dominic Arigbede," she says. "Was."

He is thin, reedy even, with hollowed-out cheeks in the

manner of a congenitally underweight person rather than a starving or sick one. Slightly fair-skinned, like Aminat. His eyes are warm and expressive. Here he is receiving a qualification in something. Here he is in a suit. Here he is getting married to a painfully young Bola.

"When did they split up?"

"They didn't. He died."

"I'm sorry to hear that."

She shrugs and takes the photo frame out of my hands. "I see him in dreams sometimes. He always asks me to tell Bola to come see him."

"And you?"

"What about me?"

"Well ... why are you single, with your good taste in shoes and ... erm ... magnificent breasts?"

"Just garden-variety divorced, I'm afraid. My ex wanted someone more fecund."

"Again, sorry. I'm a magnet for bad topics tonight."

"No need to apologise. He's generous. I got the house and a good alimony. It affords me a lot of freedoms. What about you?"

"I never married. It just never happened."

"Children?"

I shake my head.

"Why?"

"It just never happened for me."

"What did your parents say?"

"I don't know. I hardly talk to them."

"Can I ask how old you are?"

"Older than forty, younger than fifty."

"Why no last name? Are you a criminal? Are you

dangerous?" Conspiratorial tone now, one eyebrow up. There's a linear indentation on both temples that suggests she wears glasses.

I walk over to her.

"I am not dangerous."

She stands. "We'll see."

While we make love, in our moisture and our hunger I lift into the xenosphere.

I'm still thrusting when I see the butterfly, Molara.

She stares, wings slowly flapping, antennae twitching here and there.

Go away, I think at her.

She does not.

When I climax, her wings spread fully and my whole world is full of the blue and black pattern.

Chapter Four

Lagos: 2032, 2042, 2043

Then

Being a sensitive is difficult to explain. There is no omen at birth, no weather phenomenon, no annunciation to herald my arrival. I am a normal child by all accounts, with five fingers and toes, nappy rash and cradle cap.

The first time I find something, I'm eight or nine years old, skipping along our street, trying to get home before it's dark. Even though it's Lagos, my neighbourhood is safe for kids. I get a sudden urge to investigate a garbage can. I don't know why. When I open it, there's a baby, a girl. She is bloody, surrounded by trash, but alive, awake and calm. She looks at me and blinks. I lift her out. I remember being fascinated by her size and the way her hands move, almost like an experiment, and the way her whole body responds with a startle every few minutes.

I plan to take her home and keep her. I have no siblings, and to my childish mind this is the solution to everything. I carry her along, but an adult stops me, a woman wearing a wrapper and head tie.

"Whose child is that?" she says, accusation heavy in her voice.

"She's my sister," I say. At this point the baby starts to sniffle.

"This one is your sister?"

Seeing as the baby looks nothing like me and is filthy, the woman's suspicions are understandable, but not to me at eight.

"Yes. I'm taking her home."

"What's her name?"

"It ... it's ... I mean—"

"She's your sister and you can't remember her name?"

"I—"

"Give that baby to me."

The baby starts crying at this, attracting a small crowd. The woman takes her from me and cradles her. Soon the police arrive. When I protest, they scuff me behind the head.

I shout, "She's my sister! She's mine, she's mine!" until my mother comes to get me. She assumes that I must have heard the baby crying. She is not angry with me, however. Her eyes are soft and moist as she orders me to take a bath. Later, I find out that a house girl a few streets away had become pregnant, hidden her figure, delivered, and thrown the baby and placenta into the bin. This is the first time I hear the word "placenta" and I am disgusted when I look it up.

Time passes. I grow a bit.

School is uneventful. I don't hate it or love it; I don't distinguish myself in any way. I'm neither sporty nor brainy nor cool. I stay out of trouble. At home I see very little of my father, who works all the time. My mother and I drift apart emotionally over time. Not that there is hate; it's more like we are going through the motions of being parent and child. Memory is always distorted by time, but I think this distance starts with the baby girl whom I find but cannot keep.

I'm seventeen. I get a vacation job in a paper factory while considering university. It's boring and clerical. I am the youngest person in the entire complex, and everyone is bemused by my presence. I make enough money to pay for my travel and lunch, but nothing else. I am surrounded by old, uninteresting people. There is a guy in my office who is forty years old!

One day I am looking for a taxi in Lagos, at a bus stop in Ikorodu Road, late for work, about to spend money that I do not have, when I get this feeling. It is like déjà vu, almost remembered from when I was eight, but not. It is like knowing two plus two is four without having to learn it. It is a certainty, not just a conviction, the way believing in God is a conviction but believing in gravity is a certainty.

My body seems to know it faster than my mind, because I leave the bus stop. I walk along Ikorodu Road for seven minutes. I stop and wait for seventy seconds, just as a taxi disgorges a gaggle of students. I get in and give the driver a destination I have never heard of and have no intention of reaching. I am calm when I do all this.

I tell the taxi driver to stop after he has driven for fifteen minutes and eight seconds. I pay him and exit the vehicle. I pause and turn around. There are street traders and face-to-face bungalows. The road is untarred but strangely lacks potholes. Each car raises a cloud of dust when it passes. There are no storefronts or street lights.

I am in the middle of a street, so I start to walk north. I arrive at a T junction. Kehinde Street, perpendicular to Ago Street. I wait. Nobody stares at me or wonders why I am standing still, neither do I feel uncomfortable. A bolekaja rolls by, all the passengers glaring at each other. A bolekaja is a modified Mercedes 911 truck used for mass transit. The word means "disembark so we can fight" because the passengers are tightly packed and always aggravated.

When they write about this kind of thing, or make movies about it, they always make it seem like a seer will hear voices or see visions, but I now know they are wrong. There are no voices, no visions. There is only knowledge.

People start to turn up and stand next to me, odd, disharmonious individuals with whom I would not ordinarily be seen. I am dressed for work in black trousers and a white shirt with a tie, two pens in my pocket, one blue, one red. The first person to appear is an old man, completely bald, bespectacled, about four feet tall, face lined and cracked. He stands to my right, leaning on a walking stick. I know his name is Korede, though I've never met him. He is followed by a slender girl, maybe four or five years older than me, sweating in her cotton blouse and out of breath, although not because of exertion but because of some condition, perhaps sickle cell. She has a long face and the whites of her eyes are discoloured, a tinge of yellow. She smells of pineapples and tobacco. This girl stands in front of me, blocking my view of the road, but I am not angry. Her name is Seline.

Another person joins, then another, then another. Despite the fact that I have never met them, I do not feel unfamiliarity. This is sometimes called *jamais vu*. I know that they know me too, these people. I wonder what we are all waiting for.

"A truck," says Korede, although I did not speak aloud. "Or a bus."

"Van," says Seline.

I know Seline is right, but then so is Korede, even though he is wrong. The van pulls up, trailing a gigantic dust cloud. We all get in, but the van does not start moving.

"One more," says the driver, and this is right, I think. Seline looks at me, puzzled.

"It's his first time," says Korede. "He does not know."

"He's the youngest," says Seline.

"*Omo t'oba m'owo we, a b'agba jeun,*" says Korede. The child who knows how to wash his hands will eat with the elders.

And what is so great about eating with the elders? They speak about matters of which I know nothing, and some of them smell. I think this to myself, but Korede picks it up and scowls briefly. His fist tightens on his stick.

Nobody says anything, and I am on the verge of asking a question when the door to the van slides open and a portly man enters. His name is Iyanda. The van continues and I lose track of the winding paths it traverses. *The hand never gets lost on the way to the mouth,* says someone. Or perhaps they think it, I do not know, but it is meant to comfort me.

After about forty minutes, the van swirls round a roundabout in a town called Esho, unfamiliar to me. We come to a stop in front of the most prominent structure, a clock tower with no clock. There is a painted-on clock face.

"It's odd here," says Korede. "Every hour someone climbs the belfry and paints the correct time. There is no bell in the belfry, but a rod with a loop of wrought iron marks the spot where one might have hung. There is a strict rota for this, adhered to quite rigidly by the townsfolk."

Old people know shit and like to share. I'm just not fond of listening.

The van parks directly under the painted clock and the

ground is spattered with old and new paint. I find this more interesting than the clock itself. It is like an art installation, a living explosion of myriad colours rioting in the early-afternoon sun. We all pile out and orient ourselves.

The Esho townsfolk ignore us, by and large. Footprints lead over and away from the paint puddle. Hundreds, maybe thousands of shoeprints, some fresh, some faded, some mere ghosts of impressions of the living and the dead. I know that Iyanda has a brief notion to buy the town a new hall and a clock that works, but I also know that the town is not poor. I can see that there are cars, that the Mercedes count is high, that there are no beggars in the town square. That people are dressed well enough suggests affluence. No, this painting behaviour is there by design. This is tradition.

The building might be a town hall, might have been a chapel in the past, but I know it does not matter. There is a man waiting outside the double doors, which are open. Inside, there is a coffin. I disembark with the others from the van and as one we avoid the paint. Iyanda is idly doing sums in his head about the cost of paint over a one-year period multiplied by the probability of falls. Seline wishes he would stop seeing things in monetary value all the time. "We are here for our brother," says Korede. "We should focus on him."

We surround the casket and I know who the dead man was. I have seen dead bodies before, even of family members, but none affects me as much as this man, whom I have never seen before but who is not a stranger. He is bearded, with scattered grey and white hair. His face is scarred, as if he ran through an entire warehouse of razor blades. His eyes are sutured shut, although the thread is small and I only see it because I am interested in such things. There is perfume, but also the faint whiff of formaldehyde underneath it all. I feel deep sorrow and surprise myself by being on the verge of tears.

Korede sidles up to me.

"You don't always use your cane," I say.

"I'm all right for short distances," he says. "How are you feeling?"

"Upset. Why do I feel I know him when we've never met? Why do I feel sad?"

Korede sighs. "You're upset because you feel the absence of a person like you, different from others but not in a visible way. You feel like you know him because people like us are always aware of each other, but not in a conscious way – and he was one of the greatest. Thus we come together to mourn. It's like breathing. Most of the time you don't know you're doing it, but try holding your breath and I bet you'll miss it." He laughs, a short bark. This close I can see all of his pores. I cannot believe this ageing will happen to me some day.

"Will we come together when you die?" I ask.

"If I'm notable, but I'm not. My time has passed. I'm almost at the end of a journey you're just starting. I envy you."

"Who are we?"

"We are people who know," says Korede, as if that explains it. But at least I know this gathering doesn't happen for everyone.

I look at the corpse. "It feels like he's not dead."

"That's because he isn't. His spirit is in the air somewhere. This man was homeless, a vagrant. The one we mourn only took refuge in this body. He has moved on."

"I don't know what you're talking about."

"You will. I saw him once, you know. It was the most frightening day of my life. Pray you never encounter him."

47

Before I can ask what he means, Korede drifts away.

There is no eulogy, and no biological family attends. There are drinks, there is music and dancing, and none of this seems odd to me. I mean, yes, they're playing Clayton's "Requiem for a Dead Superhero", which is both shit and appropriate, but they seem to like it. Old people are funny that way. At some point during the revelry, while I am slightly tipsy, Seline corners me and tells me I am a finder.

"Nothing will be lost, and nothing will be hidden from you."

Like Korede, she does not explain, neither does she need to. I know. I see the world differently. The physical objects are all the same: the cheap finish on the casket, the linoleum floor of the room, the dingy chandeliers, the booze, the music, the body odour of some of the people with me, and the sensation of fan-generated air on my forearm skin. But there is more, as if an organ or gland that was closed off is now functioning and I can sense an extra dimension. It's like one of those console games where items of value glow when the player comes into proximity.

I am pondering this when the homeless man is buried. The name on the headstone is Ryan Miller, but I know from my people that that is not his only name, just his modern one. Even though the body goes into the ground, I can feel him somewhere out there, in the air, as Korede says. I tremble and feel goose flesh spread over my skin, but this passes.

It's dark when we all enter the van and return to the junction of Kehinde and Ago. Each goes their own way, and I never see them again. Well, that's not entirely true, but it is virtually true. Almost true.

By the time I get home, a lot of the knowledge is gone, as if being together in the same place with Korede and Seline enhanced whatever was nascent in me. It seems like a dream by the time I slink into my room, avoiding my mother.

Because I am curious, I look up Esho on Nimbus, trying to find out about the painted clock. I find out that Esho is the anglicisation of the old name "Eso", and that the clock-painting tradition has been going on for centuries. In the late 1700s, the village was under threat from marauders, mixed Portuguese and Zanzibar slavers, although the accounts vary. A white priest called Father Marinementus, who plied his trade in Eso, came up with the idea of building a fake clock tower in order to fool the marauders into believing that the village was already an outpost of some European empire. As the village was never attacked, the people of Eso thought it had worked and kept doing it.

All those years, painting fake time to fool scouts bearing telescopes; faking time to stay alive.

From that day I begin to find things for people. It is an obsession, compulsively done, with a strange, erotic need for completion. I find car keys, memories, heirloom brooches, squirrelled-away money, PINs, mobile phones, photographs of loved ones, mathematical formulae, and spouses. There are always women looking for errant husbands, and cuckolds locating wives. This does not end in violence as often as might be imagined.

I do not plan to become a thief. It just happens naturally. I go with my parents to my uncle's house and the valuables burn like coals in my mind. It irritates and draws my attention while we converse and sip Star Lager and eat pepper soup. I cannot concentrate and I make excuses – not completely false; I do need the toilet.

After I empty my bladder, I wander into my aunt's room. I find her gold and diamonds in a box under the carpet in a false floor. I know the key is on her dresser, hiding in plain sight. I know my uncle has thousands of dollars in cash in the ceiling space. I also know they have a vermin problem and that he is worried about rats eating the notes. I take an indeterminate wad and stick it in my waistband, then I take a golden crucifix from the jewellery stash. I know, in the same transcendental way, when my cousin Eliza is about to come looking for me. I know when and where to hide from her to avoid discovery. Eliza is puzzled when I get back to the main party before her. She will later die in a horrific car crash at Ore with four of her school friends.

That night, in my room, under the covers and with a torch, I stare at my swag, rotating the cross so that it catches the light and counting the money. I feel powerful, and not because of my emergence as a sensitive, which I do not even recognise, but because I can buy things without having to ask or justify to my parents. I would like to say that I use my power for good, dispensing gifts and food to the poor and living happily ever after, but that would be untrue. I use it to purchase junk food, premium pornography, alcohol, lap dances, drugs, alcohol, clothes, shoes, alcohol and other dissipations.

Stealing is unlike anything else I have ever experienced. Our people say: *stolen meat is twice as sweet*. I say: stolen anything is a hundred times as sweet and fulfilling.

Until you get caught.

For one year, I am the Rat, the Termite, the Eater of Wealth, the Still One, the Quiet. We live in a nice area where there is a low incidence of robbery and families have known each other for up to three generations. Things consistently go missing and nobody can explain it. Some say there is a spirit, and there is some precedent of emere assisting the possessed person to find items of value. Pentecostals pray and cast out demons to no avail. Some preach with foghorns, stating how it's biblical to kill thieves according to Exodus 22, and it's true that in many parts of Nigeria we tend to go Old Testament on those caught stealing. Thieves are generally beaten within an inch of their lives and necklaced. No thief ever believes this is their destiny until there is a tyre around their neck and the petrol is wetting their hair, fumes choking their ability to cry out for mercy. Babalawo cast spells, leave curses and lay fetishes. I am immune to all this but afraid in the forty per cent of my mind that might believe in the supernatural.

I can't stop, though. I have a lifestyle now, and I tell my parents with absolute credibility that my holiday job and gifts from grateful people fund my parties and clothes and night-life. My father snorts, wavers. My mother is the first to put it together, finding and stealing. If you can find anything, will you have the moral fortitude to stay honest? She looks at me and thinks not.

At this time I know nothing of the xenosphere or my connection to other sensitives or regulars. I do not know the ability is alien – I think it is a mystical thing, spiritual or juju-based. It does occur to me that the objects and valuables I find have to belong to someone. I am useless in prospecting for gold or oil, for example.

The day I am caught, a specific song plays on the radio: Fela Kuti's "Mr Follow Follow", a song I cannot hear without nausea any more. It rings through the house on the primitive hi-fi my father insists on. I have a sort-of-girlfriend called

Fadeke, who is the epitome of materialistic Lagos. She is bought and paid for from her extensions to her stilettos, a razor-blade sisi eko trophy. She is the woman who asks for money without irony or shame. She is coming over and I don't have anything for her because I spent everything the night before. I am slightly hungover, but I have a strong sense of cash in the neighbourhood, which I know is because it is the end of the month and people have their pay cheques.

The strange thing is, I do not steal from my parents normally. I know where the house valuables are, of course. My intention is to borrow from my mother's stash and return it when I have done some scavenging. She puts some of her money in the bank, some sewn into out-of-fashion clothes deep in the recesses of her wardrobe. I have a switchblade now; I carry it for this very purpose, since many people do what my mother has done. Nigerians do not really trust the whole digital-money, cash-you-can't-see palaver.

I'm slicing and dicing when I hear her.

"What are you doing?" says my mother.

There is no explanation that makes sense, so I just stand there with her ripped clothing in one hand and a knife in the other. I can feel the weight of the cash, the exact weight of the truth. In my pocket my phone vibrates and I know it's Fadeke. My brain freezes, and not only can I not think of a lie, I cannot think *anything*. I am afraid that I have been damaged by my actions or a curse or the hand of God. You hear about that kind of thing happening to those who deserve it.

My mother's entire face scolds me in that combination of surrendering the curve of her mouth to gravity and her eyes to moisture. She spreads out her arms and looks up to heaven and says, "*Aiye me re,*" which means "this is my life".

"Mummy—" I start.

"Do you know why you are my only child?" she asks.

"No, Ma," I say, using the more respectful form to try and butter her up. I put the jacket with the ruined lining down.

"When you came out of me, you ripped so many blood vessels that I bled and bled. They took me to Igbobi and transfused and sewed, but nothing helped. At one point my blood stopped clotting. The surgeons had no choice but to take my womb out."

Her voice is calm and I don't like that. I want hysterics, but this emotionless delivery bothers me. She is usually incontinent of anger and distress.

"No more children after that, of course. But your father and I, we lavished all our love on you. He did not take another wife, though he could have. Maybe he has other children outside, I don't know, but he has never paraded it in front of my face. You were everything to me."

She sits on the edge of the bed, two feet or so from me.

"I love you, but you are a thief, and I didn't bring my child up to steal. You cannot be my child."

This is good. Melodrama I can deal with. I am about to launch an explanation when I see her hand go to the whistle that every family in the neighbourhood has.

"Mummy, what are you doing?"

"*Ole!* Thief!" she screams. She blows the whistle and I vomit with fear and disbelief.

In Lagos, the whistle is a tool of the community watch. One blast at midnight means all is well. A sustained note at any time of day or night means there is trouble and the blower needs help. People will come running.

I run, out of the room, down the stairs, out the front door, into the waiting crowd. They do not seize me, because they think I am fleeing from whatever the danger is. I am halfway down the street, passing a startled Fadeke, who is driving towards the house, by the time my mother has updated the vigilantes.

Because they hear her shout my name, the mob turns on Fadeke.

Chapter Five

Rosewater, Lagos: 2066

Now

It is a Saturday, so neither Aminat nor I need to rush away. I know I still have an interrogation to continue, but I feel so languid that nothing exists for me outside this room. When I open my eyes, the first thing I see is the spine of a book on the display case titled *How to Listen to God*. There is a ceiling fan with three blades, static.

The night before, we never made it to the bedroom and there is minor disorder in the living room. I am lying on the carpet, one leg on the sofa. Aminat's head is on my shoulder, arm flung across my chest. Parts of me are numb, but pleasantly so. I am getting unfocused psychic noise from Aminat and I wonder if she is dreaming. With sheer force of will I resist entering the xenosphere to find out.

Through the gaps in the blinds I see that the sun is out. Mid morning. I hear the songs of people hawking breakfast foods. Despite the air conditioning, I can smell burned flesh. Faint, but definitely present, from the bonfires of reanimates that the Special Detachment put down over the course of the night.

They will miss a few here and there, and for the next four months reanimates will keep turning up in the oddest places. Teenagers will spend their aggression on some before finally killing them. The reanimates will kill some people themselves, mostly elderly or babies, those caught by surprise, those who are not vigilant. There will be brief public outrage and indignation, which will last a week in the dailies. It will then go quiet until the Opening next year.

I nudge Aminat. She shifts her limbs and mutters something. "Loo," I say.

She mumbles and points in a general direction away from her. I get up and explore. A door leads me out of the front room to a short corridor adorned with landscape watercolours and beige paint. At the far end there's a kitchen, a flight of stairs going up, and a door on the left of that. A house this big has two toilets at the least, but I do not need to snoop. I do my business in the small one, staring at a line drawing of a small boy pissing into a stream. There are foreign and domestic magazines in a rack next to the toilet. The foreign are British, and English-language Chinese publications. There is an old American magazine dating back to 2014, which is not even yellowed. It should really be in a museum or at least preserved in some fashion.

I make some tea in the kitchen, then return to the sitting room. Aminat is still asleep, lying curled up on her left side. She has some stretch marks on her hips, but otherwise has a long, toned body with pear-shaped breasts. A ten-centimetre scar runs along the line of her ribcage on the right side. It's surgical and I remember that she was ecstatic on the night of the Opening. She is strong like an athlete; I remember feeling that during the night. I sit opposite her and watch her sleep while I drink. My bruises are tender and the reanimate must have tagged my mouth, because the tea hurts. I wonder if I can get away with turning on the television.

I read *How to Listen to God* until she yawns, stretches and sits up.

"Hi," she says.

"Hi," I say.

"I thought you might be gone."

"Why?"

She shrugs. "I've been with men who have not been impressed with me come sunrise."

"Then they're stupid."

She smiles. "You're sweet." She leaps to her feet, puts on her panties and walks out, dodging me when I try to grab hold of her. I hear a door close and sounds of her gargling water before she emerges.

She leads me by the hand to the kitchen and shoves me into a seat at a small, square dining table. She now has a long white T-shirt on. She empties a percolator that looks like it cost the earth. The dead coffee goes in a bag, and then in a bin.

"Coffee then food for me. You?" she asks.

"I'll have what you're having," I say.

"Good, because I have excellent taste. I'm going to make yam and eggs."

I do not think I am hungry, but I am sure I will eat. I want to eat for her.

"What do you normally do on Saturdays?" she asks. She adds beans to the percolator. One falls to the counter and she hands it to me. I smell it and pop it in my mouth. It has the smell and taste of tobacco and wood.

"Depends. I work if I have a freelance job on the go. If not, I visit the hospital."

"Why? Do you have a sick relative?"

"No, I just go to ... help out." This is only partially true. I go to hospitals for perspective. "What about you?"

"I usually go to Lagos to see my family." She adds water and flips the switch. "Mum, dad, younger brother."

"Every weekend?"

"Most. I just help supervise the house girl, plait my mother's hair, that sort of thing. My mum thinks the girl is a witch. Which, who knows? She is rather slothful."

"How long have you been in Rosewater?"

She cocks her head to the left. "How do you know I haven't always been here? It's not that old."

"Because I *have* always been here, and I would have noticed someone as striking as you before now."

She laughs and takes the basket out, empties the grounds. "Flatterer. I've been here three years."

"Why leave Lagos? More money, more jobs ... better class of men. Or women."

"Pfft." She pours two black coffees into identical mugs that sport yellow smiley faces with a linear red smudge at the eleven o'clock position. She opens a cabinet under the sink and selects a large yam, hairy with rootlets and gnarly with clumps of soil. She washes it, places it on the kitchen top and starts to cut it into slices. From her phone she activates the hi-fi, which starts playing "Woo-woo", and she makes a face. Everybody claims to hate the song, but it continues to climb the charts, and insipid lyrics or no, fans are listening to it. She turns the music off.

"I was sick."

"I figured. I saw how you reacted at the Opening."

"Yeah, I'm grateful. I love the biodome and what it does for us. What it's done for me."

"What was wrong with you, if you don't mind my asking?"

"I don't mind. I enjoy spreading the story, you know? About a year after my husband left, I got this persistent cough, low-grade but really irritating. Two months, I took every pill or cough mixture under the sun. Nothing. When I started losing weight, my doctor did a sputum test. I had tuberculosis. TB. Consumption."

"Sorry to hear that. Must have been rough."

"It was. One of my lungs collapsed and I had a thoracotomy to release it." She raises her T-shirt, revealing the curve of her buttocks, stretch marks on her thigh and the merciless curvilinear scar that I saw earlier. "This was a big problem for me. I did long jump and triple jump in school. I hated this weakness, the inability to function. Plus, as a bonus, I found out that the reason I got TB in the first place was because my immunity was down. My immunity was down because the bastard gave me HIV."

"Fuck."

"Don't worry. I did the tests after my healing and every three months since. All gone. No TB, no HIV, no nothing." Using a paring knife, she works the skin off each yam slice in one long peel, then drops them in a basin and turns on the tap. "Are you scared, Kaaro?"

"Of?"

"Catching plague." She concentrates inordinately on her task, washing the pieces before placing them in a saucepan. The moment is pregnant.

I push the chair back and stand, coming up behind her. I turn her around and kiss her on the lips, as wet as possible. "I am from Rosewater. In this place, we do not fear pestilence."

I kiss her again and insinuate myself under her T-shirt.

The knife clangs into the basin.

*

59

We decide to spend the day together. I feel up to a trip to Lagos, anything to get away from the baked-flesh smell that will cling to Rosewater over the next week. She insists on driving and I don't argue the point. It takes two and a half hours to get there and the journey is stultifying sameness punctuated with police checkpoints. We are stopped seventeen times and give money at each before we are waved through. There are automata behind the policemen at some places. They are stumpy, tank-like moving turrets that are seven feet tall. They are old, ten, maybe twenty years, and ill-maintained; repurposed American gear abandoned in conflict zones. If you look closely, you can see the embossed Stars and Stripes, even when painted over with the green-white-green Nigerian flag. I have never seen them in action, and I wonder at times if these are rolling hulks with flashing indicator lights and no active ordnance.

Driving south always nauseates me. I feel like I should be wanted by the police because of my youth as a thief. I know I am not, but something in my soul thinks that is unfair for me to be free.

Each time the traffic slows, we are besieged by young boys and girls trying to sell us something, mostly snacks, fizzy drinks, "pure" water, magazines, joss sticks, almanacs and religious stickers. This happens in Rosewater too, but it is not as frenzied. Aminat enjoys these as opportunities to socialise. She is wearing dark glasses and a sleeveless black top with oversized silver circles for earrings, and perhaps looks like a movie star to them. She buys everything and chats with the children whenever she can, cajoling and teasing. They, in turn, love her and smear her car with their fingerprints, which she does not seem to mind.

I like cars. When the windows are up and the air conditioning is on, I am cut off from the wider xenosphere and can have relative quiet without having to use antifungal creams. Aminat does not know, but I manage to find some clotrimazole in her bathroom cabinet before we leave her house, which quiets the xenosphere a little.

There is a fight in the street where one car has scraped another. We are sealed in, but I can see straining neck muscles, open mouths and silent caterwauling. A small crowd gathers, some people to encourage violence, others as peacemakers. There will be pickpockets, but I cannot identify them. Passing vehicles blow their horns. Lagosians love a good fight.

We move on when the traffic speeds up again. We break free from Ojota, shoot up Ikorodu Road, and leave it behind as we head for Oworonsoki, close to the lagoon. This place is alien to me, but Aminat powers through with confidence. I get a good chance to study her profile. She has high cheekbones and a slight overbite. Her neck ... As we come to a loopy slip road, an army-green jeep cuts us off and comes to an abrupt halt, forcing Aminat to brake.

"*Ekpe n'ja e!*" she yells at the jeep.

Two young men step out and come to each of our windows. Their movements are synchronised and they wear suits and dark glasses. I notice the deformity of their jackets over concealed weapons.

"Be still and quiet," I say. "Can you do that? Please?"

"Do you know these people?"

"In a manner of speaking," I say.

The man on my side taps on the window. I open it.

"Kaaro," he says, "I have a message for you. Step outside, please."

"No," says Aminat. Her breathing has changed and her eyes are wider.

"It's all right," I say. "Just do what I said. You will be safe."

I read the man – no malice, no tension. He means me no harm, so I open the door. He takes off his glasses and hands them to me. We are causing an obstruction and tailback, but the usually aggressive Lagosians don't even yell. When I don the glasses, Femi is there on the screen.

"What are you doing in Lagos, Kaaro?"

The training kicks in automatically and I cover my mouth to stymie lip-readers.

"Hello, Femi."

"Answer the question, yam head. Why did you leave Rosewater?"

"It's a social matter."

"You only have the social matters that I choose for you, Kaaro."

"I wasn't aware that I was under house arrest or in exile. Am I not allowed to move around?"

"You're the man on the ground. You always have been. There's an ongoing interrogation, remember? You can't leave that half done. And what are you doing with Aminat Arigbede?"

"Excuse me?"

"She has a history. Her family—"

"Stop. I don't care. Also, I'm taking a day off. I haven't had any leave. I need a break."

"I didn't authorise—"

"I wasn't asking your permission, Femi." I take off the glasses and carefully collapse the temples. I make as if I will hand them back to the man, who reaches, but I drop them and stamp down. "Oops."

He is furious, but I don't give a shit.

"Get your jeep out of the way before I make you swallow your tongue and gouge your own eyes out," I say. I don't even know if I can, but I will try until I succeed or burst a blood vessel. The other man is standing on the driver's side. I open the passenger door and say, "Get the fuck away from my girlfriend."

I settle in, aware that Aminat is staring.

"You okay?" I ask.

"Yes," she says. "So. I'm your girlfriend?"

I shrug. "You got me acting all protective."

"Are you military? State security?"

"Not exactly. But I sometimes work for the government."

I have never had a girlfriend. Not a real one, at any rate. I do not know why I said that about Aminat. The truth is, I would not know what it means. Most of the sex in my youth was meaningless and my felonious lifestyle precluded intimacy. Still, this liaison with Aminat has exposed a vein of possessiveness and aggression that I did not know was in me.

The jeep revs too loudly and spins tyres before speeding away. An arm reaches out of one window, middle finger extending from the hand.

Children.

Aminat's family house is one of those three-storey buildings built in a moderately deprived area that was part-gentrified in the 1980s. The government at the time gave it various names, like Gbagada and Phase Two, but it remained a residential area for working-class and poor Lagosians, with an incongruous scattering of overblown, architecturally suspect cocaine-millionaire mansions.

Western sociologists and criminologists will tell you that crime, particularly violent crime, concentrates in this boundary of the rich and poor. Nigerians can be different in that regard. We celebrate and venerate the rich, especially the criminal class. The non-white-collar criminals, the armed robbers and sneak thieves (ahem), prey on the helpless. Rich folk have razor wire, illegal alien life forms, and bootleg turret bots that will vaporise your average AK-47-wielding home invader.

I do not know what Aminat's parents used to do, but the house stinks of depleted money. It has a massive compound with decorative palms interspersed with almond trees, and a gardener toiling away. There are two wings at right angles to each other and a portico marking the entrance. The columns have complicated capitals with angel heads and curves.

Closer look: the gardener is old, gaunt, and wears no uniform. The paint on the house is faded and peeling. Green algae stains the wall where it meets the ground and weeds sprout like pubic hair here and there.

"This is my father's white elephant," says Aminat. "The house I grew up in was built on this site. It burned to the ground when I was a teenager. Daddy cleared the land and built this."

"Do you have a large family?"

"No. It was a mid-life crisis. Some men buy big cars; my dad built a big house." She waves to the gardener, who does not respond. I think, unkindly, that it will take him a week to realise he needs to wave back.

Aminat has a key, and inside it is quiet. The air is not processed but isn't fresh either. The decor is baroque, with golden filigree on the tips of the ceiling fan blades. It rotates at a lazy pace, providing no air current whatsoever.

"Hey! I'm home," Aminat yells. "Sit here. I'll get you something. What do you want?"

"Erm ... water," I say.

She leaves the room and I sit, sinking into an overstuffed armchair. The air I displace is dusty. I feel for the xenosphere. The entire house is a black hole. I cannot even sense Aminat. I wonder how that can be. The xenosphere conduits are everywhere, although you can create sterile rooms if they are airtight.

I hear dragging. Something solid sloughs and rattles along the floor. I am uncomfortable without access to the xenosphere. I wish I had my gun with me. I examine my phone. I have both charge and signal, so I dial Aminat's phone. I ignore the many notifications for messages that no doubt come from my boss.

"Hello," says a voice.

I look up. A tall, muscular, fair-skinned boy stands in front of me. He is handsome in a way that brings pain to my heart, a being of perfect symmetry and regularity of feature. His muscles are straight out of an anatomy textbook. He has small black eyes fixed right on me and shining with unblinking benevolence. He is shirtless and wears khaki shorts. Not a scar, not a single mark on him. Zero body hair. I want to touch him to make sure he is not a hologram. On his left ankle there is a single manacle, to which is attached a thick silver chain that trails off out of the room, into the corridor and on to parts unknown. I have seen something like this before.

"Hello," I say. Then, "I'm a guest."

He smiles. "Obviously."

I stop trying to call Aminat. It's difficult to concentrate with that beatific face shining down on me, combined with the great silence from the xenosphere. His voice sounds rich, educated and welcoming. Next to him I sound like the braying of a donkey. I am thinking of what to say when Aminat returns with a tray holding a frosty glass of water containing a slice of lemon.

"I see you two have met," she says.

"Sister!" says the boy.

She places the tray on an occasional table next to me and squeezes her brother.

"Kaaro, this is my brother, Layi. Layi, Kaaro's my friend from Rosewater."

I stand up to shake hands, but he initiates a warm hug so I reciprocate. He is as hard as a machine, his muscles cordy, taut, not just for show.

Aminat kneels, examines Layi's ankle, which has a callus and looks chafed from the manacle. Not as scar-free as I imagined. She tuts.

"You haven't been looking after this," she says. She leaves again before I can speak.

"You're from Rosewater?" says Layi.

"Yes."

"Come with me. Let me show you something, Kaaro. Kaaro. Hmm." He looks up and seems to taste the word, turning the sound over in his mind. "Your name means 'good morning'."

"And yours means 'wealth turns'. So what?"

"Unusual name, that's all."

"All names were unusual once."

"This is true." He seems satisfied with that and takes me to his room, dragging the chain. The people who live here must be used to the sound. I find that the chain is moored to an iron ring that projects from the floor off to the side near the door of his room. Outside the door there are two fire extinguishers and a sand bucket.

Layi's space appears massive and is surely composed of

several rooms with the walls knocked out. The west wall is lined with bookshelves from end to end, about twenty metres. The windows are barred. There is a skylight, which is also barred. The far end of the rectangular space has weights, a free-standing punchbag, and a cross trainer. There is a work-station with a display sphere. I've never seen one of those outside magazines. It's a translucent plastic sphere with an opening to allow computer users to step in. The entire concave inner surface is the display. Users claim it's better than a holo field. There are other iron rings sunk into the floor at various points in the room.

Layi's lodgings are neat to the point of neurosis. Not a speck of dust anywhere. Everything is in its place and we are the only sources of disorder as we move about. He opens a cabinet and rifles around until he finds an old, damaged pink mobile phone. The screen is broken, but all the pieces are in place like a solved jigsaw.

He hands it to me. "I bought this off Nimbus."

"You got four-one-nined. It won't work. This tech is from 2040 or so."

"I did not buy it to make telephone calls. I just wanted to show you where I got the video footage from."

"What footage?"

He activates a remote, and a plasma field forms in the air in front of us. It's black, and an image resolves. A moving image. The area it's shot in is one I know.

"There is no timestamp, but I am sure you have seen this before," he says.

The camera shows an external scene, daytime but near dusk. The area is undeveloped land except for a single tarred road and a lonely row of poles bearing electric wires. There is a downed and smoking black military helicopter, but the crowd is strangely uninterested in this. The crowd itself is odd itself because of the stillness of the people who make it up. They are watching something out of shot. It's shaky amateur footage, but I know what is missing. My heartbeat tells me I'm getting nervous.

The camera jerks and pans rapidly towards the object of the crowd's attention.

The dome is rising, growing into the sky like a blanket of flesh. There are gaps in the sheet, but they close at the same pace as the vertical ascent, rapidly, like time-lapse wound healing. In the gaps one can glimpse ephemeral, indistinct movement of people-shaped blurs.

The dome seals itself and the fluid in the membrane swirls and diffracts the light. There is a ganglion poking into the sky, mushroom grey, like a tree trunk reaching to the same height as the dome, with a ragged tip crackling with electric current and menace. Ninety-two people will die before we recognise it for what it is: a power source from a generous deity.

The frame freezes.

"This is the day, isn't it? The first day of Rosewater. History made."

"It wasn't incorporated as a town until—"

"And I know why you seem familiar to me."

"I didn't know that I seemed familiar."

He points to a young man in the crowd. The man is not looking at the dome or the helicopter. He is looking in the other direction and the expression on his face is not indicative of awe. I know this for a fact.

"That's you, Kaaro."

Chapter Six

The Land That Would Become Rosewater, Maiduguri: 2055

Then

"There is an explanation," I tell Femi. "I demand to be heard first."

"What explanation, you moronic amateur?" says Femi. "You had one task. It did not involve violence or force of any kind, because we all know how cowardly you are."

We are in a field office in the place that will become Rosewater. Literally a field office. It is a tent on a field with liberal scatterings of horse and cow dung. The soldiers around me and the S45 agents who have their guns trained on me are covered in dust. Most other people in the camp are walking wounded. The air is full of a low-level electric hum, which is coming from the dome and ganglia. Femi manages to be immaculate, as if the dust and grime refuse to stick to her. She looks and smells delicious.

"I have had no training in talking to or negotiating with extraterrestrials, Femi."

"Mrs Alaagomeji to you. And you said you could do it."

"I said I would try. Not the same thing. It's not like you sent me in with a squad of soldiers or anything, not that it would have made a difference."

"The executive body of S45 – all dead and gone or comatose."

"How is that part my fault? They went in hostile and the alien responded in kind. I went in after that, remember?" I resist the temptation to point out to Femi that this means she is in charge, something she has wanted for a very long time. She stands in a tight red suit with high-heeled shoes. Who comes to a refugee camp wearing that? Or smelling of ... whatever that divine fragrance is? "Look, I fucked up, okay? I am not too proud to admit my failings, but I'm not one of your agents. I am not trained. You framed me for a crime to get me here."

"It isn't framing when you actually commit the crime, you yam head."

"Whatever. Entrapment, then. Just pay me my fee and I'll be on my way."

Femi actually laughs. With mirth.

"There's a termite in your skull eating away at your brain, Kaaro. You should see a doctor or an exterminator or somebody."

"Fine. Don't pay. Fuck you very, very much, Mrs Alaagomeji." I move to leave but the soldiers block me. I look into the eyes of one of them and there is nothing there. No love, no hate, just bland, unfeeling obedience. He is a flesh robot, not human at all. This scares me, and my eyes slide away from his face. I focus on a vein throbbing in his neck.

"Your freelancing days are over, Kaaro," says Femi.

I turn to her. "What do you want from me?"

"You join Section Forty-Five and work with us to unfuck this fuck-up as much as is possible."

"No thank you. I've had enough of this freak show."

"You join us or you die in jail. I will send you to Kirikiri right now. Today. No trial, no saying goodbye to your parents."

At that moment, an aide taps her. "The president."

She takes the phone, covers the microphone. "What's it to be? Don't worry, we'll train you. You can have all the payment owed up to this moment, then you'll be on the payroll. Which is generous. I'm doing you a favour, Kaaro."

At this moment I experience perfect hatred for this most beautiful woman. I want to kill her even though I am not a violent man. My silence is assent. Femi nods and an agent grabs my arm just as Femi starts talking to the president. Her gaze stays on me till I leave the tent. "Yes. We'll say it's an experiment in sustainable energy and clean living within a biodome. We're all very excited with how Nigeria is leading the world ..." Her words are a lie that will not last beyond the first Opening Day.

I phone Klaus from the army base where I'm receiving basic training. I ache all over and my jaw hurts. Despite this, I'm fitter than I've ever been because of the running. My belly is flat, my arms are toned and my knuckles are raw from hitting a mu ren zhuang.

"I hate the hand-to-hand shit," I say.

"You never did like fighting. Remember that time in Idi-Oro when we got into that brouhaha over a hooker?"

"She wasn't a hooker, Klaus."

"I paid her."

"How many times do I have to tell you that the women here sometimes ask their boyfriends for money?"

"But why? Are you paying them to love you or something? Are they on retainer?"

"Klaus . . . "

"Okay. Anyway, I had to do the fighting. An old man like me."

"You're not old, Klaus." I pause. "You do understand what I'm saying here, right?"

"You're saying our partnership is over because of those bastards."

"And bitches. Don't forget the bitches. Or *the* bitch."

Klaus is my agent of sorts. He finds me assignments and I carry out the work. Flat fifteen per cent fee. He is much more, though. He has been my father since my parents finally kicked me out. He taught me a lot and changed me from an unfocused psychic teenager to a slightly focused bootleg psychic adult with money. Both of us, he and I, are liminal, on the edge of civilisation at all times.

"It's okay. I made a lot of money on this last deal. You negotiated it with them, you can keep it," I say.

"No. You earned it. I'll keep it in a fixed deposit. When you survive the training and you're back in society, you can pick it up."

"I don't want it, Klaus. I . . . What's the point?"

I really don't want the money. I am on autopilot, an automaton. An essential part of me, the *élan vital*, died when the dome came up. I miss Oyin Da, and she's in there, out of reach for ever.

A bell sounds. "I have to go, Klaus," I say.

"Pavlov's dog," says Klaus. "Keep your chin tucked in."

"I will." I hang up and trot along to the gymnasium with others like me.

*

I am in a classroom. I haven't been in one since for ever.

There are only ten students including me, and I am the oldest. They are kids, male and female, irreverent. I know I am kin to them, and they know the same, but it is not like when I discovered my own gifts as a youngster, where I found a sense of family and acceptance with Seline and Korede. Here there is the *tabula rasa* of indifference. It is like attending a family gathering and realising that you are old and the new generation does not give a fuck about you or your experience. I know where they hide their money and music and love letters on their phones. I know what they value and how to get at it, and they know that I know. I am the only finder among them. Like before, being among them enhances my abilities.

There is a whiteboard and it has the word "mycology" written in upper case and underlined. A slight, bespectacled man stands in front of the word and looks down at us like God, judging us.

"My name is Professor Ileri. I'm a mycologist. I know fungi and my job is to make sure you do too," he says.

"Why do we need to know about fungi?" says a girl.

"You failed A-level biology." A boy from behind me insults the professor. I get the knowledge at the same time he does. Ileri isn't bothered by the revelation, though. No discomfort from him. No anger.

"Do you think you're the first cohort of sensitives I've taught? Here's the first lesson, child: it does not matter what you did not know in the past. What matters is what you do know now. So you can waste your time reading off random facts from my mind, trying to embarrass me, or you can let me teach you how to be better at what you do."

"But why fungi?" I ask now, with no irony. "Seriously, I hated this shit in school."

Ileri flicks his eyes to my ID and smiles. "Have you heard of Tokunbo Deinde?"

None of us has.

"How about ectoplasm?"

Blankness.

Ileri sighs. "People don't read any more."

He flicks a remote and a plasma field fires up. There is a projected black-and-white photograph of some white people around a table. They all focus on one woman in black who appears to be regurgitating a white cloud. Within the cloud there are faces. The woman has her hair tied into a bun and pulled back. She seems uncomfortable. The exposure isn't great, but the people around the table seem impressed.

"Spiritualists, psychics, mediums, sensitives, clairvoyants, clairscientists, mystics, witches, necromancers, telepaths, empaths, shamans, aje, emere, iwin, occultists, diviners, psychomancers. These are some of the names you might have been called in the past, and may be called in the future. This photograph is from nineteenth-century England. It shows a medium spurting ectoplasm. It was a common practice in the day and it impressed the customers. Ectoplasm was supposedly spiritual material that manifested as a physical substance through which random ghosts could become visible in the world."

He cycled through a few more slides showing ectoplasm emerging from the nostrils, ears, mouth, and in one photo from between a woman's legs.

"They were all frauds. The Society for Psychical Research investigated them and discovered that they did it with ingested textiles, clever lighting and the very best four-one-nine spirit."

The class titters, but mostly they are attentive. I can hear the silence in their minds. We have become a hive, absorbing and sharing as one.

"Now, the babalawo, the witches, the sensitives, the Victorian mediums, all were considered frauds of some kind. No credible scientist believed in psychic ability until after 2012."

The mention of the year 2012 sends a surge of recollection through our collective consciousness. You are not a sensitive and will never experience this, but raw data surges blunt information with errors, which are slowly refined like the process of chiselling out a sculpture from a block of marble. Corrections nudge the data towards truth, or at least truth as the ten of us know it.

In 2012, an alien landed in London. It was the size of Hyde Park and immediately grew underground like an amorphous blob. Her Majesty's Government cordoned off the entire M25 area and it took close to a decade to stabilise the economy. At the time it was thought to be first contact, and global media reported it as such, but the Americans later revealed what might be evidence of three earlier landings. This was before America went dark.

There was no spaceship in London, just a rock enclosing a large sentient being. It turned out this sentient being had seeded the entire biosphere with new macro- and microorganisms as a result, although it took decades for us humans to find this out. One biblically minded BBC reporter nicknamed the being Wormwood, and the name stuck. No one was sure if these organisms were stowaways, or an invasion attempt.

"Tokunbo Deinde was a microbiologist fresh out of Unilag, a Youth Corper in Nsukka. Like most Corpers, he wanted to serve out his year quietly in the dozy town. He heard tell of a powerful soothsayer in one of the villages. A hundred per cent accuracy, he was told. Curious, he visited, paid his money and waited. During the visit, the soothsayer vomited, but it was a strange fluid that turned to vapour and persisted temporarily. Then she told him everything he was thinking and about a large part of his childhood. He was astonished.

"Tokunbo stayed with the soothsayer, eventually taking samples of the ectoplasm and analysing it. It was made of the neurotransmitters dopamine, serotonin and noradrenaline, and what he initially thought was a fungus.

"What we at S45 call the xenosphere, the psychic link that you are all able to exploit, is made up of strands of alien fungi-like filaments and neurotransmitters. We call the xenoform *Ascomycetes xenosphericus*. It is everywhere, in every environment on Earth. These delicate filaments are too small for the naked eye to see, and they are fragile, but they form multiple links with the natural fungi on human skin. They have an affinity for nerve endings and quickly access the central nervous system. Everybody linked to this network of xenoforms, this xenosphere, is uploading information constantly, passively, without knowing. There is a global store of information in the very atmosphere, a worldmind that only people like you can access."

"Bullshit," someone says, but we all think it. Our abilities might be weird, but alien? It's beyond belief. One girl does not even accept the Wormwood landing as real – she has clearly been reading too many conspiracy theories on Nimbus.

Ileri laughs. "You don't believe me? What are the limits of your abilities? Have you noticed that your powers work better outside in the open air than inside enclosed spaces? That when it rains, they may become unreliable or conk out? Do you wonder why, or do you think it's just a joke God plays on you?"

Ileri tells us no one is sure why some people can manipulate the xenosphere. The information is bidirectional for us, instead of unidirectional. There are theories that we sensitives have a separate unidentified infection on our skin that allows us some control over *Ascomycetes xenophericus* growth patterns.

Under his guidance, we experiment. Rubbing an antifungal cream all over the body suppresses the xenoforms and stops our abilities, but only temporarily. They respond by increasing their growth rate exponentially. A room without windows that is disinfected has no xenoforms and our abilities are knocked out. We can block other sensitives if we flood the xenosphere with data, like reading a book.

"Good," says Ileri, once he is sure that we have accepted the nature of the xenosphere. "Let's talk fungi. The word comes from the Latin *fungus*, which means mushroom. Mycology is derived from the Greek *mukes*, which means fungus, and *logos* which means knowledge ... "

This is hell.

Here we are in Yerwa, in fucking May, the warmest month of the year, in full military gear, wading through swampland. In many ways it is the perfect training ground.

Maiduguri is perfect. It has been a military outpost since the British were here in 1907. It's got the Ngadda river, which leads us right into the Firki swamps. One grand hike, which, if we go all the way, will lead us to Lake Chad.

Mosquitoes are plentiful. We won't get malaria because of subdermal implants, but nothing stops those shits from biting.

Our trainer, Motherfucking Danladi, tells us to imagine we are those heathen British explorers of yore. "You can't go back, because to quit means to disappoint your queen. *Pax imperia regina*, lazy fucks! To quit means to shit on the memory of Livingstone. No, no, we will crack on, lazy fucks, crack on into the arsehole of history!"

Jesus Christ. Motherfucking Danladi is insane. I wish I had a fragmentation grenade – I'd bake him a shrapnel pie.

As usual, part of my brain asks me what the fuck I'm doing here, and I cannot say.

Motherfucking Danladi's favourite phrase is "splinter group". All his combat examples come from when he fought this or that splinter group. My class gave him his nickname after he made us taste the dust of our parade ground. Now we have to be careful we don't say it in his presence.

The sun is right overhead, baking us. Motherfucking Danladi has us singing "Wade in the Water". We wade. Blackflies join the mosquitoes. My exposed forearms are dotted with bites and weals, but they are also bumpy with muscle. Fair trade. We disappear into the xenosphere, leaving our bodies on a kind of autopilot, singing the Negro spirituals that Motherfucking Danladi seems to favour.

The shared mindspace is, unsurprisingly, filled with swamp flora, as if our imaginations cannot stretch too far from the hellish reality our bodies inhabit. I spread my wings, stretch my forelimbs, extend my claws and indulge in a cat yawn. The lion part of the gryphon takes precedence at times. Without Ileri to guide us, we do what we like. The vegetation is polka-dotted, blue and yellow, with black flowers and pollen drifting into the air like smoke from a burning oil well.

Temi's avatar is a serpent, although it seems more like an air-swimming eel, with lateral fins that undulate when she takes to the air. She is relatively twelve feet long, although dimensions are difficult to gauge in the xenosphere.

John Bosco presents himself as a man, a monk with his cowl pulled up and darkness where a face should be. The avatar trails a ghost image of his real self – a rookie mistake, or indicative of the humble size of his talent. He is a god at Krav Maga, though.

See that man all dressed in white.

I am thinking we need new music. I let this thought leak and I feel the agreement of my peers.

Drake is a puddle of peach-coloured liquid that flows in rivulets around all of us. He dissipates into vapour and re-forms with dizzying speed.

God's gonna trouble these waters.

Temi swims close to me, coiling around the gryphon. If I beat my wings I will hurt her, so I stay still, groom myself with my beak as she frolics.

Ebun becomes completely conceptual in the xenosphere. She is an idea from infancy, the non-verbal stage. There are no words with which to understand her form, and there is no image. We are aware of her presence, but it is extremely abstract. The idea is her own, from her own early life. Even she does not fully understand it, but she can pull it out of lost memories and use it. She is safe. It is an elegant solution that I wish I had thought of.

The dark pollen from the flowers coalesces and form clouds. Someone is upset, or sad. We all feel it. I hate this hive-mind shit.

"Lazy fucks!" Motherfucking Danladi breaks in. The clouds are from him, I think, and someone agrees.

He is stationary, and ahead of us, looking into the bush. He turns back to us, and says, "Hide." His face is fixed, set, focused. He moves ahead.

We melt into the undergrowth, covering ourselves with mud as we have been trained. More bites from more creatures likely. We dare not breathe.

Motherfucking Danladi is gone for twenty-five minutes, and when he reappears, he is breathing heavy and his fatigues are bloodstained.

"Let's go, lazy fucks. We've taken too long already. Must get to Alau Dam by nightfall. Get up, get up, get up! This water isn't going to wade in itself."

We do what we are told, cautiously. He does not speak of what transpired, so I look into his head. We're not supposed to, and we are told the instructors have been protected, and this is true to an extent. None of my classmates can get through the ... protection. I can. It's difficult, but I can. I have not told anyone this.

Motherfucking Danladi stalks and comes across three insurgents, a scouting group bearing light arms. He bursts among them with speed I can only follow because I am in his memory. He kills all three with his bare hands before they can get a single shot off. It is as if he is not human. With a single punch to the temple he cracks the skull of one, then holds him up, unsheathes the insurgent's knife and buries it in the neck of the second. The third is still turning toward the commotion. Motherfucking Danladi sweeps the man's feet from under him. He follows the body to the ground and, almost gently, smashes the insurgent's head against the terrain, twice.

I am in awe, and perhaps this makes me careless, because he is staring at me, and he knows that I know, but says nothing.

When we return to base the next day, he puts me on latrine duty for the next two weeks.

*

Professor Ileri sits down after his talk. I do not know how one person can contain so much information and wisdom, but it seems to pour out of him casually, without friction.

He says, "It is now time for you to show me what you have done. Time in the xenosphere is like sex. You can pick up some nasty diseases, so protection comes first. Let us see what you have built. Temi, you first."

Temi is nervous, but we all are. She takes us into her mindspace easily enough. The classroom drops away and we are standing in front of a stone wall thousands of feet high, thousands wide, so that there is no end. We cannot see around it, and the blocks look formidable. There is a door, but this is locked with a padlock. On the other side of this barrier lie Temi's secrets and vulnerabilities. Ileri has been teaching us to place defences in our minds.

"This is a nice effort, Temi, but it shows a lack of imagination, and stultifying conventional thinking. Stone, door, padlock? The first thing anybody attempting attack will think is that no matter how hard, stone can always be broken. Have you not read Shelley? Oyzmandias? *Round the decay of that colossal wreck, boundless and bare, the lone and level sands stretch far away.* A door is weak around the hinges. Padlocks have keys. You are announcing to your visitors that this might be hard, but there are solutions." Professor Ileri tuts.

"But I thought—" says Temi.

"Do it over." He turns to me. "What do you have?"

I feel for all the minds around me – my class, my professor – and lift our awareness from Temi's mind straight into mine. I feel the surprise flow like smoke through them. Nobody has ever done this to them. Usually they passively enter the mind of a student who wants to demonstrate.

I have grown several feet, and distorted. I have feathered wings, an eagle's beak, a lion's body. My space is a tall, hedged maze, with cloud formations in the sky and complex combinations of wind, breeze, light and dark. There are rotating sequences of sounds from seagulls, bats, dogs and crickets. I beat my wings and rise into the maze, and to demonstrate, I negotiate the maze through the single multisensory line. Taking a wrong turn, pausing when you should move or moving when you should pause, would cause the entire construct to collapse and lock the mind from an invader. I pirouette in the air and fold in my wings to relinquish my ride on mental thermals. I drop back to the class.

Fuck me.

Wow.

I am so dead. I've done nothing like that.

Ileri smiles. "Ladies, gentlemen, Kaaro has just jumped forward a few lessons. Finally he has shown us that he is the oldest in the class. Impressive work, Kaaro. Tell me, why did you see the need to transmogrify?"

"I don't know what that means," I say.

To change, to transform, you illiterate. Good-natured ribbing.

"I don't know. I was reading about Egypt and the Sphinx and this led me into gryphons. I liked the idea of a creature like that."

"Yes, Kaaro, that was your choice. But why change at all?"

"More difficult to identify me if I don't look like me, right?"

"Indeed," says Ileri. "Indeed."

I return us to the classroom.

Show-off.

Teacher's pet.

Bastard.

Making us all look bad.

"New assignment. Any student who successfully breaks into Kaaro's mental fortress will immediately graduate to field agent. Who's next?" says Ileri.

I endure many attempts on my mind, some while I am awake, some while I am sleeping, some in the open, others surprises.

Nobody ever gets through.

Every day for a year I stand outside the dome for as long as I can spare away from training, lots of jaunts between Rosewater and Maiduguri. I hope that I am being watched from within. I hope that someone will come out and let me in.

Nobody comes.

The tents change to lean-tos and wooden shacks with corrugated tin roofs. Two-wheel ruts become dirt roads, and when signs go up, I realise that there is a village growing around me. My soul dies in fragments.

I'm in Maiduguri for endurance training. We walk for miles without food or water but carrying full infantry kits. I do not know why they make me do this. It's not as if I'll be fighting in a war. I go to the S45 liaison and talk to my boss.

"Stay there," says Femi over the secure line. A soldier keeps watch outside the tent.

"It's a shithole," I say.

"Which is why you're going to stay there. Around the dome."

"As punishment?"

"No, as assignment. The place has legs; they're calling it Camp Rosewater."

"You guys call it Camp Rosewater. Down here it's the

Doughnut. And no, it does not have legs. The hooples will go home. The dome isn't going to open."

"It already did."

"What?"

"It opened for some minutes last night while you were in Maiduguri."

"How is that information not on Nimbus or in the news? Nobody's talking about—"

"We blanketed it. There were some odd effects."

"What do you mean?"

"Some general said he got cured of prostate cancer by breathing the 'fumes' from the pore."

"That's bullshit."

"Maybe, or maybe the prostate cancer was misdiagnosed in the first place. Either way, Rosewater has legs. More people arrive each day. We've got some professor from Lagos tapping into the electricity from the ganglia. Builders are coming in. I need you as eyes and ears there. You are going to stay."

I am not listening to her. It opened. Did it open for me? Did it close because I was not there?

When I return from Maiduguri I head straight for the dome. No sign that it ever opened. I try to walk around it, but after an hour and three litres of bottled water, I concede that it has grown since I last tried to circumnavigate it, and I'll need a vehicle. I don't know why I'm looking – the surface is one overwhelming sameness. It is definitely wider in circumference, and the margins show where it shifted the soil and uprooted shrubs. There is dust and movement everywhere. Every motorbike has a passenger. Military personnel and men in black are ubiquitous. Cyborg hawks criss-cross the air, though many of them litter the ground, dead, decaying, burned. Whatever controls the biodome does not wish to be observed.

I have been either too self-absorbed with grief or too tired from the fucking training, but I see that Femi is right about the Doughnut.

I hire a motorbike and ride around the dome, hugging the driver's midsection. This is a cross-country ride and we bound over clumps of grass and mounds of earth that the motorcycle was not designed to tackle. There are schools and eating joints and prayer meetings. These people are here to stay. When we arrive at the North Ganglion, there is a smell of burned flesh on the wind. This is not unusual – some poor fool gets drunk and staggers through the warning stanchions, electrocutes himself – but it is different. First of all a soldier type, a Hausa boy, tries to order me back. I show him my S45 ID, and he reluctantly backs away, though he won't let my driver through. I pay the man to wait.

I walk past the screens put up just a few yards from the dome. There are perfunctory biohazard symbols, but nobody is wearing protective gear more complicated than a handkerchief across the lower half of the face. I have of course seen burning bodies before. Immolation is the punishment of choice used by vigilante mobs and political rivals nationwide. I have almost been burned myself. What I have never seen is mass burning of dozens of people.

I see where they have been killed. The streaks of blood, the drag marks on the ground, the pools of blood. Strangely, there are no flies. I am by now inured to most suffering, but what I see here shakes me out of complacency. In that bonfire of human firewood, *there is movement*.

It's odd that I did not notice this before. Most of the limbs are twitching, writhing. Are they ... alive? Are those mother-fuckers burning them alive? But ... no screams. There is an eye detached from a head, but it stares at me. I see the pupils change size. An unblinking, detached eye focusing on me. It sees. It sees me.

Perhaps I've been wound up too tight, or I have a death wish, but I start shouting at the nearest soldier. I do not remember what I say, but I remember the glint in his eyes and the curve of his lips.

Then he hits me and I black out.

I spend two days in a hole before Femi retrieves me.

"Are you insane? These are death squads," she says.

"They were burning people alive, Femi."

"Not people, and not alive."

"What do you mean?"

"Remember that general with prostate cancer? The healing was real. Everybody who was here at that time was healed. We think that when the dome opened, it released some xenoforms that healed people in the vicinity."

"That means the alien hasn't quite given up on humanity."

"Yes," says Femi.

"What's that got to do with the burning people?"

"The xenoforms worked too well. Most of the graves around the camp are shallow."

"They raised the dead?"

"No, not like Lazarus. They are more like reanimated flesh. Healed, hearts beating, eyes open, bodies warm, but no ... life. No memories, no soul, no recognition of what they used to be. We had to kill them all over again, and death didn't come easy."

"Do they contain the xenoforms?"

"No. Our analysis shows the xenoforms just heal and leave. The scientists theorise that they returned to the biodome before closure."

Femi steps into a jeep, leaving me filthy in the crowded shanty town. She gives me cash, a tent, a certificate of non-impedance coded into my implant, a Smith & Wesson automatic, a supply of ketoconazole cream and a handshake.

There is a shack offering haircuts and shaves. That's where I start.

Chapter Seven

Lagos, Rosewater: 2066

Now

I look at Layi, this beautiful boy, and I can't think of anything to say. I usually lie to get myself out of situations like this. In Rosewater, there are a few people from the early days who know me of old. A lot of people have a vague idea that I am significant, but I keep a low profile and there are any number of big-breasted starlets to occupy the imagination of the public instead. Occasionally I'll be at a football match or a concert and someone will stare for a while. A few times I've been accosted, but never with Layi's certainty.

Aminat comes in. "Is he telling you his conspiracy theories?"

She kisses me and Layi mimes vomiting. "Stop. I don't want to see that." He turns to me. "You were at Rosewater from the start."

Fuck it. "You're right, I was. That is me in the video clip."

Layi smiles. "I knew it as soon as I saw you."

"Really? You were a supplicant?" asks Aminat.

Supplicant is the name the rest of Nigeria gave the settlers of

Rosewater. Since most of them were ill with AIDS and terminal cancers, the name is not one of good connotation.

"Well, no. I was there on business."

"What was it like?" asks Layi. "I've read everything, all the memoirs, blog posts, letters and declassified documents. I've listened to every broadcast about it. You are the first person I've met who has been there."

"What about me?" asks Aminat.

"From the start. I mean from the start. So, Kaaro, what was it like?"

"Pretty feculent."

"What do you mean?" asks Layi.

"He means it was shitty," says Aminat.

"Yes, I know what the word means, but I think he means it literally."

"I do. The predominant smell was of shit. At first it was animal stuff because there was a farm close by, but it quickly became worse. There was no sewerage system. People used to just dig shallow holes, do their business and cover it up. Sometimes they would not bother digging holes. Then it was impossible to step anywhere because, you know, shit happens. Then the banks of the Yemaja became the place. There was a hanging shelf over which you could do it and the water would carry it downstream. For a while. A series of dysentery and diarrhoea outbreaks took its toll on the children of the camp. We got together, had a few town meetings. It's awkward when the place is circular. You have to send town criers all around the dome, and that takes ages. We bribed the army to bring an Engineers Corps digger and built some soak-away systems and salanga. That helped a bit, but it was still a long time before the federal government asked wolewole to inspect us. The fragrance of Rosewater was terrible. For a long time, in front of my tent, there was a dead horse. It got swollen, then maggots burst out of it, then it dried up and stopped smelling. And, of course, there were the bodies of the reanimates."

Aminat squints. "So when we say Rosewater ..."

"Exactly," I say. "We mean the opposite. Actually, the real name is Omi Ododo, which is 'flower water'. It stank."

"Do you like it there?" asks Layi.

I pause, then I say, "It grows on you."

I wander the grounds for a time. I feel odd inside the house because of the chain, and because I cannot sense the xenosphere. Layi seems to think I am off to smoke and I do not disabuse him. The boy has an intense benevolence to him that I need a break from. There is a gravel path and I take it away from the back of the house, crunching stones underfoot, walking towards the east wall. I feel the connections come back gradually. I feel the gardener first, signal strong like an act of parliament. He is called Bernard Okoye. I see his dreams. He is a young man in his dreams and his mind's eye. He loves someone called Cecilia. In the past he was not able to woo her. He started studies, but his father—

"Hello, Gryphon."

The words knock me out of the afternoon in Lagos and into a field. A light shower cools me. The elephant grass is waist high. There are red-brown hills all around, and the field is sunk in the valley. No trees anywhere. I turn around and there is Molara.

"Hi," I say.

She is different again. She still has butterfly wings, blue with black margins and speckles. The wings flutter, but she no longer has an insect body. She is a woman now. She is stocky in build, a stout, muscular woman with a tight round belly and small, jutting breasts. Her face is angular: sharp chin, crisp cheekbones, flat nose, large eyes. She has a dark copse of pubic hair.

The rain is no longer cooling. I am hot and wet. Her body glistens with seriousness and sensual intent. I think she will never fly with those wings – they won't carry her body weight. She turns away, drops to all fours and pushes her posterior in my direction. I get behind her.

As we rut, the field around us fills with butterflies of different colours and sizes. I read somewhere that they do not fly in the rain, and I cannot ever remember seeing one. My claws extend and dig into Molara's flesh where I am holding onto her shoulders. I gouge my curved beak into her neck for more traction. Blood wells up, but is washed away in the rain. The blue gossamer wings rip to shreds with the force of our copulation. I cannot help myself; I stretch and flap my own wings. Conjoined, we take to the air together, surrounded by butterflies.

A tremor runs through her. She is frightened. There is lightning, but the thunder is lost in my climax. Between the orgasm, her sweat and the slick of rainwater, I lose my grip. She falls, turning head over heels, shredded wings beating like it could make a difference.

I return to Lagos, to Aminat's family house. I can feel the wetness in my boxer shorts. Bernard stands a few feet away from me, staring, a strange expression on his face. I look down, but there is no wet spot on my trousers. I mould my face into a smile, but then worry that it'll seem like an orgasmic glow. Wouldn't do for my brand-new girlfriend to think she's attached herself to a pervert. Hmm. Am I a pervert for doing this? I try not to think about it.

After cleaning myself up, I go inside and find my way to the living room. I am ready to go home, and spending Saturday together does not seem as exciting as it did when Aminat and I awoke in the morning. Again, the muting of the xenosphere inside the house. Not something I wish to endure for long. The paradox, of course, being that I hate it when I'm in the full xenosphere. Maybe I just hate everything.

Aminat is seated on the floor at Layi's feet. She smears cream on the skin of his leg, around the ankle where it makes contact with the metal of the manacle. The skin on both legs is darker and rugose in that area. Layi grins when he sees me. After a little while, Aminat can tell that I wish to leave; she mouths, "Five minutes."

"Will you return to see me, Kaaro?" asks Layi. "I like you."

He says this with such openness and a lack of irony. "I will," I say, and I mean it.

On the way back, the sun is low, almost extinguished. The radio is on, on 98.5, playing oldies, currently Otis Redding with "Hard to Handle", but also Marvin Gaye, the Seekers, the Temptations, and a host of other Afro-sporting Motown-like crooners, some great, some flashes in the pan. The DJ keeps interrupting with his idea of commentary, but his English is horrendous and we wonder who he bribed to get the job. We are singing along where we know the lyrics and making up the parts we don't. We laugh at our own inventiveness at filling in the gaps and we start to create deliberate mondegreens. When we tire of this, we listen silently for a time.

"Your brother," I say.

"Yes," says Aminat.

"The chain."

"I know. You didn't mention anything to him, did you?"

"I didn't. It seemed the polite thing."

"Thank you for that. He can be sensitive about it with people he's just met."

"Aminat, it's a fucking chain."

"I know."

"You could have warned me."

"I know. I'm sorry."

"That's not an explanation. He's chained in his own house."

"He's not captive."

"Then why?"

"So he won't fly away."

"Okay." I think of Layi's living space, the richness of what he has there, the gilded cage. I wonder why Aminat took me home at all. She must know it is bizarre to have a grown man chained up. Unless she wants me to see this part of her life, giving me an opportunity to flee.

"Every year on Christmas Eve he goes out for the fireworks. The rest of the year he's home. He's exceptionally fragile, Kaaro. He cannot tolerate the world, and has not been able to do so since he was a child. We home-educated him."

This is not as unusual as it may seem, although "fragile" may mean Layi is mentally unwell. Not all psychiatric patients go to doctors or hospital in Nigeria. At times people are kept at home so as not to tarnish the family name. I know of one household where the oldest daughter was tied up with hemp rope and kept in the boy's quarters behind the property because she had screaming fits. It is not polite to probe under these circumstances, so I drop the matter.

"He's quite striking," I say.

"Everybody loves Layi," she says.

It is dark when Aminat drops me at home. We kiss through the car window for an eternity.

"I like you," she says in a husky voice. "I'm in like. Are you in like?"

"I am in like," I say.

She nods and drives off. I can feel the smile on my face.

The reanimate who was at my doorstep is no longer there. I am aglow from the encounter and this blunts my vigilance, but as soon as I enter my flat, I know I am not alone. This is not going to be pleasant.

"I know you are here," I say. "Tell Femi I'll come quietly. I have no wish for violence."

Two intruders, one male, one female, dressed in dark body suits, masks, goggles, armed with pistols. No skin visible. They are prepared to subdue a sensitive.

"Get your shoes off my rug," I say.

"Kneel," says the female. "Cross your ankles and put your hands on your head."

I obey, although I know they will not shoot me.

"I am about to search you. Are you carrying a weapon?"

"No."

"Are there any sharp objects in your pockets?"

"Well, there's my prick. Sometimes I can reach it from my pocket."

"*Alawada*. Keep joking, see what happens," says the man.

There is an edge to his voice that suggests to me that he might be emotionally involved with his colleague. The xenosphere is devoid of their presence. The female searches me with rough hands.

"I am about to inject you with something to relax you. If you move, my associate will shoot you."

"You're not going to kill me," I say. "Femi would—"

"I said nothing about killing." She speaks this sentence in English.

I feel the jab in my deltoid. I soon get slightly woozy. I tip over backwards, but the woman catches me efficiently and lowers me to the floor, straightening my legs. When she is sure I can breathe, she rolls up my sleeve, ties a tourniquet and takes a blood sample. The male holsters his weapon and produces a scanner device from a pouch. It looks like a magic wand. I've seen the like before. It scans implants, downloading telemetry and other stored data. There is a short beep, which I assume means the scan is complete, then they both step away from me. I hear only the hum of my refrigerator and the blood speeding through my veins. I feel slightly euphoric, but that's whatever drug they gave me. I'm on the floor for a while – I lose track of time.

The man kicks me. "Sit up."

They position a small box close to me and activate a plasma field, which floats up to eye level. Even before it resolves, I know she can hear me.

"This is home invasion," I say.

"You're still not carrying a gun," says Femi.

"I forgot."

She's casually dressed and has one of those Bluetooth devices clipped to her ear. No earrings, and minimal make-up. She is also at home, judging by the kitchen behind her. I can tell, because I have been there.

"Kaaro, you've been delinquent."

"I have, but I was young and foolish at the time."

"You know what I mean."

"I was off duty."

"You're always on duty."

"Then maybe that needs to change."

"Maybe it does," she says in a softer tone. "But we will come to an agreement about that instead of you running off willy-nilly."

"I've never taken time off."

"I know. But you're in the middle of an interrogation, remember? We lost a whole day, and that can be critical. I also need to know where you are."

"That's what the implant is for."

"It needs an upgrade."

"The implant is fine."

"You can't see that woman. Aminat."

"Why not?"

"Her family is ... problematic. Did you see the chained man?"

"Yes. He's sweet."

"He is dangerous. Just stay away, Kaaro. Can you do as you're told for once?"

"For once? I always do as I'm told."

"Call me Mrs Alaagomeji."

"I almost always do as I'm told."

"Be careful. That entire family is bad news. I'm too busy to explain, but Aminat has an ex-husband—"

"I know."

She sighs. "You were easier to manage when you were an outlaw."

"S45 has other sensitives. Go bother them."

She is silent.

"Femi, you *do* have other sensitives, right? I've met them in training."

"A few."

"What? What do you mean?"

She frowns. "Don't get alarmed, but some sensitives have died. The rest are sick, and one or two have lost their skills."

I sit forward. "When were you going to tell me this?"

"There was no reason to tell you. You are operating fine and show no signs of deterioration. We think the *xenosphericus* is killing some of your people. You are the oldest active sensitive we currently have on record."

I am speechless. I think of Molara.

"I have to go," says Femi. "There's a thing I have to deal with. A guy washed up in Lagos, says he's from America."

"There are many Americans—"

"Last week. He said he left America last week. Be careful, Kaaro. I prefer you predictable and boring. Go back to the fucking interrogation."

Chapter Eight

Lagos: 2043

Then

My mother probably thinks Fadeke is my accomplice. Either that, or she thinks seizing Fadeke will make me stop running. Both are faulty assumptions and do not take into account the selfish mind of the thief, or the desultory nature of my relationship.

I watch from the end of the street. One of my shoes is gone, but I barely register this. The mob drags Fadeke out of her car and starts beating her. A youth climbs onto the roof of the car and bounds up and down. They pull her hair and kick her in the stomach. The mob breaks in two and one strand makes its way towards me like a malign tentacle. The roil drowns out Fadeke's screams. It is like a football match. *Ole!* is the chorus and I do not like the tune. I am ashamed to say that self-preservation trumps my affection for Fadeke. I run. Past the church, past the sawmill that doubles as a bus stop, past the fake spiritualist, past the bolekaja, which almost hits me, all the passengers swearing at me, past the swineherd.

Four people with clubs cut me off. More people stream out of doorways and alleys. I see Jeff Norton, the Englishman, staring from his veranda, smoking, calm. He is a bank robber, or so they say. He spends the whole day getting sunburnt and inhaling carcinogens. I have never intuited anything of value in his house.

I sense the blow before I feel it. It is from a housewife with a wheel spanner. I lose my footing and someone sweeps my feet out from under me – known as "clearing" in local parlance. I take the hits. I have no defence and I know I am about to die.

"*Lo mu ibon mi wa!*" Go get my gun.

I close my eyes and protect my genitals. Death by bullet won't be so bad.

The mob rips my clothes. My unshod foot bleeds. I know what comes next. Tyre around the neck, wood, dry grass, kindling, and someone with a match and a lighter. I have seen it before.

I mentally search for my brothers and sisters. The kinsmen. The ones like me. I have never done this before, but desperate times, etc. In my mind's eye I can see my thoughts as white waves against a black background, the darkness of solitude.

My distress call goes out and I endure kicks, punches, clubbing and fear. I am doused with petrol. I start to choke on fumes. I open my eyes and the petrol gets in, stings me; I squeeze them shut again.

Brother, I see you, but I cannot come to you.

Help! Fucking help me.

Do you see the swine?

What?

Pigs. Do you see the pigs?

I open my eyes again. A steel-toed boot lands on my lower jaw, adding dirt to the blood I already taste. I blink to clear my vision. The pigs, the pigs.

Where?
Your left.

I see them. Grey, long snouts, hairy, some spotted on the back, unbothered by the commotion, rooting in rubbish.

Wait, wait, wait. Go! Now! They are distracted looking for a tyre to burn you with.

The herd is stationary because there is something to eat at this spot where the mob has found me. I crawl into a puree of moist garbage and night soil. The stench is overpowering and must make the mob hesitate. I move faster. I hear the squeals of swine as they complain. I gag and dig further into the shit. I am at the edge of a deep ravine. What happens is people throw their rubbish off the edge, turning it into a landfill site. The problem of course is that some people throw better than others, so that over time half of the street has become a tip and only one lane of traffic is open rather than the two it is designed for. I dive into the pit. I'm trying to dig a hole and hide while I think of my next move. It works for some seconds, then I am sinking deeper without effort. I slide into a pathway of mud, and start to fall in an ersatz avalanche of faecal sludge mixed with refuse.

I lose my sense of up or down and am banged on outcroppings, broken pipes and pieces of timber. A brief flash of pain signals what I find out later to be a dislocated shoulder. I fall for ever and land on the roof of a rusting VW Beetle feeling no pain at all. There is a mile of filthy incline between me and my tormentors, who hurl insults and missiles at me, but this is half-hearted, as if they have grudging admiration for my escape. I am covered in shit, but already my nose has accommodated. It smells like fucking freedom, and that's always sweet. I run along the floor of the ravine. I know there is a streamlet close by and

I aim for it. The bobbing of the run alerts me to the dislocation, but there is nothing I can do but hold the bad arm with the good.

The stream is sluggish at this time of year, but it is water and it flows and is therefore good enough for me. I wash. I cannot get clean without soap but I fear infection because of my bruises and cuts. I also need a doctor to set my arm. I don't know when they arrive, but I look up and two men are there staring at me on the other bank of the stream. They are casually dressed and stink of otherworldliness. I know I can trust them.

"Come with us when you're done," says one.

"No hurry," says the other. "I don't want that stink in my car."

One of the men makes me stand naked in a courtyard and hoses me down. It is cold, and surrounding taller houses have windows that look down, but I have no choice, and only the living, the free and the honest deserve modesty. I am a thief and therefore beneath contempt.

"Raise your hands," the man says.

"I can't." I point to the dislocation.

He aims the jet of water at my armpits all the same. When this ends, I wait in the cold, shivering. He brings talcum powder and clothes. The trousers are small, the T-shirt too big. There are red thong slippers, which I slip on. The man makes me sit on a wooden bench and I wait some more. It is dark now and there have only been two power failures all evening. I hear a church bell somewhere – midweek service. A television blares out of a window. Just within earshot a couple argue violently. I smell pepper soup and smoke. I am hungry, but I do not wish to ask for food because my hosts have been kind enough. I wonder about my mother and Fadeke.

"They killed her," says one of the men. I do not know how he came within inches of me without me knowing. "Fadeke, not your mother. They locked her in the car and set it alight."

"Jesus."

"Fire purifies," he says.

"Fadeke was a money-grabbing serpent, but nobody deserves to die like that."

"I agree." He looks at my shoulder. "We'll have a doctor look at that in a minute. What are your intentions?"

"I don't know ... I thought I'd go back home when my mother cools down."

"Don't do that unless you want to spend time in prison. She is absolutely convinced that the best thing to do is to deliver you to the mob. She thinks she has failed to teach you morals."

"It's not her fault."

"She thinks it is."

"It's no big deal. I didn't steal a lot."

"You think a little stealing is all right?"

"Oh God. You're not Jehovah's Witnesses, are you?"

"No. We're like you, heard your call. This is my house and you are welcome to stay as long as you need to find your feet. Call me Alhaji."

"Is the other guy your brother?"

"You mean Valentine? No, he's my lover. The absolute love of my life."

This is a tricky confession to make. I have nothing against homosexuals and I have seen and interacted with enough of them at nightclubs to know we are all the same, but it's a criminal offence to be gay in Nigeria. Being arrested is the better outcome if one is discovered. Usually the flames are reserved for thieves, witches and gays. That's the way it is.

I decide that being caught here is likely to complicate matters further.

"I understand," says Alhaji.

"I'm grateful that you helped me, but I do not like how you read my thoughts."

"I'm sorry, it's just that I spend so much time pretending not to. How do you control your gift?"

"I do not read thoughts."

"Yes you do."

"No. I find things. I can hear the thoughts of people like us, but that's it."

Alhaji laughs. "And how do you think you find things? You think an angel shines a divine light that shows you the way? People think about the things they value a lot. You trace the thought pathway. It is reading thoughts; you just have not paid enough attention to your gift."

I ponder this briefly, but then the doctor arrives and my world becomes pain for a time.

Although I have seen her posters, Alhaji is the first person to talk to me about Bicycle Girl. He tells me because he is convinced that whoever she is, she is one of us sensitives. He is wrong, but neither he nor I can know this.

I am twenty years old and on the verge of leaving the sanctuary that he and Valentine have given me. I steal, but more carefully than before. I do not stockpile any more, for example. I steal what I need for a week. Alhaji will not accept ill-gotten wealth as my contribution to the household, so I get a job loading items at a shipping company and give him one hundred per cent of my wage. He is still benefiting from crime, because there is no way I can afford to give him all of it, but he does not know, so no harm. Loading hardens my muscles into the kind you cannot get in a gym.

I do not steal from the needy. I get a sense of the household and give many a pass. I take a small amount from a number of different people to spread the liability, taxing them in a way. I mostly steal from those who can afford it. At some point – I can't say when – I decide to take from those who have surplus and break into the homes of the needy to leave something there, minus my cut. This is not altruism. I simply become more aware of widespread deprivation and it makes me uncomfortable. Giving makes me feel better about being able to buy what I want.

I learn to screen myself from Alhaji. He smiles and is happy when he can no longer read me. When I am not partying, I try my own experiments in hearing thoughts. These do not yield much, but I become better able to tell which women are willing to sleep with me. Motivation, I suppose.

I drink copious amounts of beer and Jack Daniel's.

I think about my parents, but there is no seismic emotion attached. I hate my mother for about five minutes. I am not a good son; I cannot blame her. If I were a good son I suppose I would be better able to muster resentment. The fact is that I do not miss my parents at all. My father only cares about and attends to his business, his chain of shops where he sells grain and other foodstuffs to the Nigerian lower-middle class, who buy in bulk. He is reasonably successful and gives my mother and me a reasonable life. Not rich, but not in want, and respected in the community. He has been indifferent to me since birth.

Because I am fickle and young, I stay with Valentine and Alhaji only until I get irritated by their mentoring overtures. I resist Alhaji's attempts to foist Heidegger on me. A few of my neurones are firing and I know he is trying to improve me, but at that age the hormones speak louder than neurotransmitters, and the blood flow to my brain is always compromised by my erection. I start to go out again. I steal more, but not anywhere near the home. I buy alcohol and drugs and lap dances.

"Have you ever heard of Bicycle Girl?" says Alhaji one day.

I'm watching the football. The Black Stars of Ghana are trashing the Green Eagles of Nigeria. Valentine is fussing about Alhaji's head with an implant scanner. There is a rumour that government agents have cracked the encryption used by homosexuals to hide the identification signal they use to recognise each other in public spaces. Alhaji just had the signal removed and Valentine is checking to be sure the removal took. Valentine never speaks. He is younger than Alhaji, though older than me. It is difficult to tell what he is thinking, because his face is smooth and expressionless most of the time. When they make love, one of them makes pleasure sounds that spread through the house, but I do not know which.

"No. Who's Bicycle Girl? Is she an athlete?" I ask.

I say this without thinking, but I remember being handed a pamphlet in the market once or twice. I have also seen the police take down posters.

"She is an activist. She speaks against the government and takes willing people with her to a new society that she has formed."

"And why does the government allow her to live? Or her society of perfection to persist?"

"That's the problem. Nobody knows where it is. They say she lives and operates from a travelling village called the Lijad."

"Not Lijad? *The* Lijad?"

"Yes."

"That sounds like bullshit, sir," I say.

"I know it does. I think there is some truth within the myth. She is like us, I think. Sensitive to and manipulating thoughts."

This does not interest me and I turn the television up so I can catch the commentary of the football match. Alhaji does not bring it up again, but I see her one day, this Bicycle Girl. At least, I think I do. I am drunk and stagger out of a nightclub to vomit and make myself decent enough to go home without detention by the constables. Around the corner I see a woman raise a defiant fist and turn into a shimmery . . . gap in the air. There are seven people standing in front of her as if listening to a speech. When the gap disappears, they notice me. I finish vomiting as they disperse. One of them hands me a leaflet that says: IS LIFE BETTER IN THE LIJAD?

I do not tell Alhaji.

A week later, I meet Klaus, the mad Belgian.

Chapter Nine

Rosewater: 2066

Now

Interrogation involving sensitives has a protocol.

The subject never sees the sensitive. There has to be a continuous environment between subject and sensitive. There should be no involvement of the sensitive in the inducements and encouragements. Inducements and encouragement usually means beatings and electrocutions. The protocol means I don't contribute to the physical side of the interrogation. The torture. I can't ask questions either. I can, however, give the agents a list of words to read out. They are hooks, trigger words that summon thoughts.

I have already established that this subject has something to hide and that he is aware of the use of sensitives. His counter-measures prove pathetic, but their existence means knowledge.

Trigger words work best after a period of sensory deprivation. At the very least, white-noise headphones should be in place for an hour. This subject has been wearing them for twenty-four hours, because I was jaunting with Aminat in Lagos.

I have never been dedicated to my job at S45, but I have

never neglected my duties. I am indifferent to them. This is an improvement. I used to despise them. It is okay to put up with working for S45 when I have nothing else to live for. Aminat is a change in the equation, an imbalance.

I'm in the Department of Agriculture in Ubar. Level minus four. A smaller room than before.

He, the subject, is seated opposite me. One agent sits between us, facing neither, back to the wall, able to shift her gaze between us. She holds a sheet of paper on which I have written trigger words. She has her hair cut short and wears glasses. She is tall, though not in the upper torso, all legs and trouser suit. She smoothes the paper and has done so seven times by my count. It means she is nervous.

I try not to yawn and wonder what Aminat is doing.

The subject is naked, on a plastic seat, hands cuffed behind him. He is sweating because a heating lamp is trained on him. They use a female agent to increase the embarrassment factor. He has cuts all over and his face is as bumpy as the last time I saw him. I'd guess they beat him daily.

The agent looks at me and I nod.

"Mother," she says.

The subject twitches and a face appears in his mind, a middle-aged woman, corpulent, smiling, big bright eyes, hair in braids. The emotion around the image is overwhelming love of the Madonna variety. She might as well have a halo. There is a house, four other people whom I guess are siblings. The forensic artist will have a lot of work to do. I do not recognise any of the locations, but I memorise the details. This is easy; I've been trained to do this.

I nod, and the agent says, "Father."

Weak. Bastard.

It comes out as words and the smell of ... honey? Yes, honey.
And physical pain – sharp pain, not agony. An image accompanies the words: a man, bearded, harsh, works with his hands
as a labourer? Some kind of manual worker. The mother image
intrudes every fraction of a second. This is normal. What
happens is that when people experience or think of something
difficult, painful or uncomfortable, they insert happy memories automatically, a mordant. We all do it.

"Latin," says the agent.

Natus ad magna gerenda, the subject thinks.

This is a sneaky one, but devised entirely by me. Most
Nigerians do not read or know Latin, with the exception of
their school motto. The first and usually only Latin phrase in
their thoughts can be traced back to their alma mater. From
there, identity and known associates is easy. Femi commended
me when I shared this technique.

More words follow.

*God. Boko Haram. Death. Bible. Jihadi. Business.
Overwhelming. Victory.*

Biodome. Jack Jacques. Presidential.

Ulterior.

Nimbus.

America.

Homosexual.

Fair and unfair options. It is war. A secret war that has
existed since before civilisation, amplified by the Twin Tower
bombings. The rules of polite society do not apply.

My questions are racist, homophobic, and offensive in every
way. This is my job. My real job. I read minds for the government. The bank thing is an aside. A way for me to make extra
money while keeping tabs on untrained wild sensitives.

Later, I write the report up at a secure, non-networked terminal. The information is divided into degrees of confidence. This is not an exact art. People often do not think about what they mean. They deceive even their own selves. I have to sift through all of that. My report is at least sixty per cent true. Twenty per cent is highly likely to be true. The rest is so random as to be useless.

His name is Tolu Eleja. His surname means "fish-seller" or "fisherman" in Yoruba. He is either twenty-three or thirty-three, the first of four children. He is educated to primary-school level. He, like his father, did some shitty manual work. Something happened, I don't know what – buried too deep – then he joined a group. There were firearms involved.

That's all I know for now.

I am not curious. I want to leave. This thing I do is not beautiful. It is filth.

Monday. The bank.

Bola captures me in the break room.

"I hear you really took to Aminat. Tell me. Tell me."

I say nothing, drink my tea.

"You're smiling! You never smile."

"What did she say about me?" I ask.

The overhead light glints in her eyes. "Girls don't tell."

"Just tell me if she likes me."

"Do you like her?"

"Yes." I don't have to think about it.

"Good."

"Well?"

"What?" she says, all innocence.

"Does she like me?"

"She said you're very intense."

"Is that good?"

"It could be."

"I can read your mind, you know. I can read her mind too."

"You're joking now as well. Jokes. Humour. You must really like her."

"She told me you were married before."

"I was."

"You don't have to discuss it."

"I'm fine. It was a long time ago. I was young and beautiful."

"You're beautiful now."

She nudges me. "You're quite the flirt when you come out of your shell."

"In my youth," I say.

"*Playa!*" She flickers her fingers and I do the same, touching her tips with mine.

"For sure." I'm grinning now, lost in indistinct memories. "So, your husband?"

"He was murdered. At least I think he was. We were on our way north to see my sister and her husband. It took too long. Dominic was really bad at maps and directions. We stopped over in some tiny, nameless village and spent the night in the local hotel. I remember we fought that night over nothing, then went to bed sulking. That was the last time I saw him alive.

"Let me give you some advice, Kaaro, never go to bed angry at someone you love. You'll never forgive yourself if something happens to them. I woke in the middle of the night, turned over, noticed that he wasn't in the bed. I called his name, but when he didn't answer, I thought he was still angry and I went back to sleep. I remember the next morning was a particularly beautiful day, drenched in sunlight and birdsong. I searched in vain with a steadily rising panic. The villagers seemed sympathetic, but they all spoke Hausa and I didn't get much help. His body was never found. Some blood-smeared grass about five hundred yards away from the hotel was all we found. It matched his DNA."

"I'm sorry," I say.

"Long time ago. No longer painful."

"Aminat said she still dreams of him."

She smiles, but it is the shade of a grimace. Then she inclines her head as if she is testing the truth of her thoughts, or what she is about to say. "I'm told it's normal to dream of those you lose. For the first six months or so, anyway. I see Dominic in dreams every week. Not on the same day, but ... "

The Yoruba say "*o d'oju ala*" when someone dies. I will see you in dreams.

"He doesn't age." She rubs her belly as she speaks. The baby must be kicking. "The age he was when he died. He begs me to stay each time. Every time. He says he's trapped and can't find his way back out."

"Does he know he is dead?" I ask. "Is he a ghost?"

"It's just a recurrent dream, Kaaro. It happens. Guilt, unresolved sexual whatyoumafuckit."

It's not an unreasonable question. Ghosts exist. I'm not saying that the spirits of the dead return to haunt the living. That's absurd. I am saying that the xenosphere contains some persistent patterns. Some people leave their imprints and they remain to be discovered. They are mostly fragments of habits or personal tics or phrases. I know of at least one dead person who not only has a complete personality in there, but has on one occasion "possessed" a living body. But this is not her story.

Our break is over.

We return to the firewall, where we read Ayn Rand. I fucking hate Ayn Rand.

"Have you ever paid for sex?" Aminat asks.

This is a difficult question to answer. While I haven't paid for sex the real enquiry is, have I ever had sex with a prostitute, and the answer to that is more complicated.

Is it sex with a prostitute when you do not know the person to be a commercial sex worker? When does intent come into it?

"No," I say. I think this is consistent with the spirit of her question. "Have you?"

She laughs. Aminat has two laughs. A tinkle, which she uses when she's slightly nervous, and this heavy guffaw, which amuses me to no end.

"I paid for a lap dance once," she says. "Does that count?"

"It depends on if you came or not."

Silence.

"Well, did you?"

In the dark I cannot tell, but I feel she is laughing.

I shut her up with a kiss.

Afterwards, it is images of Molara that run through my mind. The strangeness of the situation makes me look up the butterfly she uses as an avatar. It's an African bluewing, *Charaxes smaragdalis*, navy-blue variety. Strong wings, can travel up to forty miles per hour, which is impressive for a butterfly. Tropical old-world butterfly. Spotty wing markings, iridescent blue. Two horns on the hindwing.

Why did she choose this? As soon as I contemplate this, I . . . know something. This is something I have picked up from the xenosphere, from Molara. It's an image, not of a bluewing, but something similar in design. It is mechanical, made of alloys and plastics, with a telescoping proboscis. There are too many limbs, sixteen, filamentous and constantly moving. The wings do not flap and this butterfly does not flutter. It hovers, not using the wings for propulsion. The body is full of memory space and a data-checking processor. It plugs into a server and runs a data-integrity check, and then rises, only to alight on another server adjacent. There are servers as far as the eye can see, extending over the dark horizon. Other butterflies rise and fall from them.

What the fuck? Science-fiction film? Art installation?

"Hello, Gryphon," she says. Her wings are folded in front of her, the way a butterfly would never be able to do.

"Who are you? In reality, in real life, who are you?"

"You know who I am, Gryphon." She spreads her wings, and I am again distracted. "I am a friendly friend."

Chapter Ten

Lagos: 2045

Then

I love dancing.

Not the professional kind, where you have specific forms or have to wear funny costumes. Just regular hip-hop, R&B dancing in clubs.

I am dancing at the Cube. It is trendy now and will remain so for the next five years, after which it will burn down in a freak fire that the police will attribute to insurance fraud but never prove. All the local Nollywood stars and low-level military officers and drug barons come there, but they take their special tables and trophy women and chill with them. I'm here for the music. I am surrounded by friends of the fair-weather variety. I spend money freely, therefore I have people around me.

I see a cluster of fine boys around a woman. This in itself isn't unusual. Maybe she's new, or exceptionally beautiful. I don't go for such women myself. Still, I look. I appreciate beauty, though I am generally more interested in the body shape. That's just me, my preference. I inch away from my dance partner, smiling, nodding, signalling termination of the dance. She turns to another, no harm done. I approach the group of about six and see the woman. She is old and wizened. Her hair is grey and patchy and she is dressed casually. Her spine is curved forwards, giving her a gaunt look. And yet she holds forth and the young men hang on her every word. She looks at me while laughing and holds the gaze. By now, I'm so puzzled that I've stopped dancing and the laughter fades from her eyes.

You can see me.

Yes.

Shit.

It's fine. I won't tell anyone.

It's not fine. I'm self-conscious now. Go and wait for me outside. I'll meet you in a minute.

I've not finished my drink.

Go outside right now, child.

I do as she says. I have a car that I hide from Alhaji and I lean against it. I wonder what glamour she is using, what the horny young men see when they look at her.

"Why do you have scars?" she asks.

"Mob. Narrow escape from being necklaced."

"Hmm." She lights a cigar, which smells foul, but I don't say this because truth be told I am a little afraid of her.

"They call your kind a shift. A finder who steals."

"Sometimes. Sometimes I steal."

"A lot of the time," she says.

"What about you?"

"I am neither a shift, nor a thief. I was once a kind of prostitute, until I got bored."

"Kind of prostitute?"

"They thought they were having sex with me, even though they weren't. They paid." She shrugs.

"And tonight?"

"I am blowing off steam."

"Aren't they a bit young?"

She snorts. "If I were a man, you would not bat an eyelid. So I manipulate their perceptions. So what? I am entitled to a little warmth in my senescence. You, though, you can see me." *I can make you see what I want, grandchild.*

"No need," I say. "I respect you, Ma. Go in peace."

"Don't call me Ma. My name is Nike Onyemaihe." *I'm dying.* She suddenly seems vulnerable.

"Do you want a lift home?" I ask.

When Nike gets into the car, the young men seem envious and hoot. Jealous, because they think I have what they want. I can't say I know what I'm doing. Nike radiates some anger, some darkness, but I feel sorry for her. I sense she is at the end of something that I am just starting. We drive in silence, with her occasionally thinking something at me, or feeling dread and fury. I know where she lives from my own ability to find. It's better than having an onboard navigator.

"Grandchild, you are not using the full extent of what you are capable of," she says. "You are as lost as America."

"I'm happy with what I have," I say.

"Then you are a fool." Nike says this without derision; just another fact, like gravity and rain. "When it comes to talent and ability, you must always seek more. Get better today than what you were yesterday."

"My talent works fine, Ma. It does what I want when I want it to. It gets me money."

"For now. Do you not think that I have told myself that

when I was in full bloom? You should listen to your elders when they speak, Kaaro. They know more than you."

"I am sorry if I have offended you, Ma." I am not sorry and she is experienced enough to read it in me. I am young and I don't care for platitudes or unsolicited advice. I want to get back to the club, truth be told.

When we arrive at her house, she appears weaker than before. I have to help her out of the car and am obliged to walk her in.

"There you are. I've been looking all over for you," says a man's voice from within. Foreigner, judging by the accent.

He is tall, well over six feet, a white man. He is shirtless and shoeless, wearing worn jeans. I would have taken him for one of those refugee Americans if not for his accent and the expensive watch. His skin is loose, but that could be age, because there are muscles underneath. He is one of those anthropologist-type white people with their fearlessness and leather toughness. He does not look at me, focuses entirely on Nike. I wonder if they are lovers, but it's not that kind of look.

"Help me with her," he says to me.

Between us we get her into the house, past a gateman who does not even hide his sleepiness. There are at least three luxury cars, which I casually note as I walk by. At this age, the trappings of wealth and taste are important to me. The man leads me into a room that smells of sickness and death, but not in my nostrils.

"You can go now," he says.

"No, let him stay," says Nike. She grasps my forearm with a weak grip.

Is this your husband?

No, it's Klaus. He's my employer.

A look passes between them and I know she is communicating something to him but keeping me out of it. He snorts, glances at me and leaves the room.

"Child, listen to me."

"Is this advice? I don't want any. I—"

"Shut up. You will never grow old this way."

I mutter something.

"What?"

"I said, I have no plans to grow old."

"Neither did I."

"I do not want your advice!" I yell. "Why does everyone want to improve me? I do not give a fuck. Grandma, I'm sorry you are dying, but I'm leaving. Goodbye."

"You are such a fool," she says.

I am flooded with sensation. Nike seems to push into me, into my mind, and there is light, heat, sound and experience. There is her marriage, which ended in the natural death of her husband. There is her as a prostitute. I feel every degradation, every jibe. *Ashewo.* She has been to America in her youth. Disneyland. Florida. Way back before. She has known violence and tenderness. She remembers the world changing – Hyde Park on the news, aliens among us. Nobody who didn't live through it can understand the frisson that passed through every self-aware human at the realisation that we were not alone in the universe. Humanity was no longer the only child of an indifferent chaos goddess, but one of many siblings. Nike remembers the look on her own great-grandmother's face when describing her first aeroplane. Horse-drawn carriages to automobiles to the Wright Brothers, same generation.

She remembers her world changing, slow but definite, the

new abilities she discovered. The finding. The stealing. A thousand and one spliffs and one thousand more. Semen leaking out of her after a broken condom. Abortions. Many, but all the same. Faces, make-up. Sisters of the night. Death, destruction, decay. Thoughts, not as words, but as circles, discs, intersecting spheres, concentric, radiating outwards. Inconstant shapes. All gathered from within the womb and wasted at the point of death. All her pain and ecstasy, all mine, and all for nothing. Her life and mine, meaningless. Church. Praying to a silent God, hoping for an answer but knowing in her core that none is forthcoming. A litany, confessions, a liturgy in her mind, access to forgiveness. Hope? Love, laughter, haemorrhoids and lost teeth. Cocks and money stretching into for ever. The minds of the many open to her. To me. This is how it is done. She has fucked this knowledge into me, into my mind, and I am crying. I can feel the wetness of my tears mingled with that of her blood.

When it is over, I am alone, sitting on the floor of the room. Nike's body is still and somewhat diminished. She is gone. I am exhausted and sweaty. Klaus is standing at the door.

"Is she dead?"

"Yes," I say, because I cannot hear her thoughts any more.

He walks to the bed and covers her body.

"You better come eat something," he says.

"I'm fine."

"You're not. You have been in here for three days."

"*What?*"

"I guess it takes a long time to impart knowledge. Come on."

He watches me eat. I am famished and I demolish three eggs, four slices of bread and two oranges. All that is left are the pips and the peel. I phone Alhaji and say I am safe. I cut him off when he starts complaining.

"You okay, son?" asks Klaus.

"Not really. I feel fucked up. She stole my youth."

"What do you mean?"

"I mean I can see the futility of it all. Repetitive alcohol intoxication, repetitive going to clubs, dancing, picking up girls. Fuck. Spend money. Repeat cycle. It's all meaningless."

"Meaninglessness goes better with cash is what I say."

"What?"

"My motto: everything goes better with cash. If you must live a life without meaning, live a rich life without meaning."

I reach for the glass bottle filled with cashew nuts and tip it into my palm. The bent nuts are salted, but I hate this so I brush and blow on them before popping some into my mouth. "What are you asking me, Klaus?"

"I'm saying you should work for me. Or with me. Same thing."

"Did you hear what I just said about it all being meaningless?"

"I think you'll find that of the many things Nike regretted, working for me was not one of them." He sticks a finger in his left ear, working out some wax. "I love this country of yours. There is so much money to be made here. There is oil and gas. You have a population that is massively superstitious, including the intelligentsia. Churches and mosques exert a powerful influence on people, families and the government. You have terrorist cells, you have a paranoid executive who has a personal babalawo installed in the state house. You have laws against homosexuality. China and Russia are squabbling over who will be the new United States and everybody is scared, man. They need what you have. I have the clients and the contacts in government. I have financial savvy. What do you say?"

I take more nuts. "I'll think about it."

I already know I'll work with him.

Chapter Eleven

Rosewater: 2066

Now

A few days after the Opening, there's a parade of sorts.

You know about this. It happens every year. You have seen the photos and the almanacs and the Nimbus entries. There is even reconstruction art now. The healed are miraculous, the deformed a tragedy and the reanimates a horror, but the reconstructed are perhaps comedy or ... whatever. The bank is closed for two hours. This is how long it takes for the parade of the reconstructed to pass. It will go all around Rosewater slowly, all day long. Closing the bank might seem unprofessional, but this is Nigeria.

We all watch from above, us bank employees. Clement is kissing my ass, bringing me coffee. I don't know why. Hero worship? I'm not that impressive. I'm suspicious. Bola has a cough, says it kept her awake the night before, seems unrested but has time to murmur, "*I send upon you famine and evil beasts, and they shall bereave thee.*"

Down below, someone drums. Not stretched goatskin. Upturned plastic containers. It begins. The lead: a man with

123

wings. He has latched hawk wings to cuts in his back and the xenoforms smoothed it over, probably built muscle and blood vessels to make it work. The wings are unimpressive but the man seems elated. I think briefly of the gryphon, and Molara pops into my mind. Not that she's in the xenosphere; just the thought of her.

A woman who might have been bow-legged or something now has knees that point backwards. She seems like a statue of Caliban or a demon. A man hobbles along with a gigantic goitre as large as a football hanging down from his neck. There are scars on it to suggest he has tried to cut it open. He probably expected it to shrink, but what I think has happened is the xenoforms have instead rebuilt it bigger and better.

There are men and women with multiple and displaced orifices, like a girl with two mouths, one above the other. The pattern of scars makes me think she tried to remodel her lips. There's a guy on a trolley dragged by two teenagers. I assume it's a guy. What's left of him is a jumble of too many limbs and tufts of hair here and there. I count five left hands and three feet. A single, desperate eye looks out from the central fleshy mass, leaking tears. I cannot theorise as to how he ended up like that. Industrial accident involving more than one person, perhaps.

Many wrap themselves up like Egyptian mummies, hiding whatever grotesque changes they have brought upon themselves. People throw them money or laugh at them. There is a periphery of the curious normal following them: kids, some police, jesters, area boys.

I get up to leave.

"You haven't finished your coffee," says Clement. His eyebrows are raised in that hopeful-expectant way. I want to pull on his metal-encrusted braid just to see if his facade of niceness will crack, but I resist. What does he want from me?

"I'll be back."

I go into the toilet on this level. I walk all the way to the end stall. There is nobody else with me. The smell of strong disinfectant mixes with that of cheap liquid soap and urinal cakes. I enter the stall, flip down the lid and sit on the seat. What I have to do is tricky, especially from here, but I need privacy and don't want to wait. I have been worried all night, thinking about what Femi Alaagomeji said about sensitives getting sick and dying. If it had occurred to me at home I would have done it there, but it did not.

I close my eyes and put out a call. It is complicated, because I have to shield the call from reaching the ears of Bola, Clement and any of the other bank sensitives. This also contravenes the agreement I signed with the bank not to carry out any personal xenosphere activities on the premises. Since I don't really give a shit about the job, I'm not concerned about what documents I may have signed.

I send a single, simple message, a broadcast.

Who is out there?

I feel it go out in a wave, and I feel it bounce off the neurotransmitter blocks I place on local distribution. I open my eyes and colours flow downwards across my field of vision like an insane Van Gogh. Someone walks in and the footsteps stop before a stream of fluid begins and there is the hiss of the automated flushing system on the urinal. He leaves without washing his hands. I close my eyes again and my query is still flowing outwards. Five minutes, ten minutes, no response. Granted, I have not had to do this in a long time, and I am in a firewalled location, but the firewall is down, all its members watching the procession of the grotesque. The problem is worse than I thought.

"Hello, Gryphon," says Molara. She has appeared and is followed by a swarm of houseflies. They do not land on her, but fly around her. Her wings are fully restored since our last ... encounter. She does not talk, but kneels in front of me and crawls under my forepaws. She folds her wings to fit, and I feel her mouth on me. It is so fast and unexpected that I gasp and open my eyes. The colours swirl and shift and it is hard to tell which is reality and which is xenosphere. Where is the coat hook on the door? There are flies everywhere, crawling over the door, orbiting the overhead light like planets, dropping into the gap between my collar and skin. I feel them just as vividly as I feel her mouth and ...

And there is a problem with Molara's self-image. It is too distinct, too together, too unified.

... and I feel each of my hairs stand on end and instead of a gentle mixture of colours in my mind it becomes a riot, a splash of one against the other without admixture. My blood is a cricket's hiss in my head.

After *la petite mort*, Molara is gone, but left in her place is a feeling of mouldering doubt. I clean myself and think.

What you think of as your self is actually many things. At the core is your true self, of which you may not even be fully aware. Wrapped around this are several false selves that are used at different times in different situations, social selves that serve the function of translating your true self to the world. We swap between these effortlessly as we grow up, but they are elaborate fictions. Or they are real but alternative selves. It depends on where you stand epistemologically, but that's irrelevant. What's relevant is that when I look into someone,

I see these shifting selves as blurred boundaries of the mental image. Molara's boundaries are too distinct. I was looking for sensitives and Molara showed up, but ...

It might not mean anything. I've met two or three autistic children with vivid self/non-self demarcations, but this is different. Molara is not just a wild sensitive with succubus tendencies.

Something else is going on here.

Later that day, I have to fight for my life.

I am walking towards the train station, wondering if having sex in the xenosphere constitutes cheating. I am not paying attention to my surroundings and essentially sleepwalk to the ticket office. The dome gives off an orange hue, which it does at times. On nights like this, there is a kaleidoscopic colour display to rival the aurora borealis.

I am on my way to Ubar to continue the interrogation, but I decide to surprise Aminat with some flowers on the way. I am waiting at her gate when two men walk up to me from a parked car. The driver remains inside, and I can see his hands on the wheel. It's not clear to me if the engine is running. The two men stay on either side of me, as if waiting for a response to the doorbell.

"Hello," says the one to my left, and I turn to him. He is slightly shorter than me, with smooth dark skin, short hair and small eyes. He is accompanied by a cloud of cologne. The other guy is taller and broader, with the look of hired muscle. A bodyguard, then.

"Hello," I say.

"Delivering flowers?" he asks.

"In a manner of speaking."

"Who are you?" he asks.

"Who are *you*?"

The man looks round the street, then back at me. "You don't know who I am?"

"Sorry, I don't get out much and I don't watch TV."

Whatever he is about to say is lost to me because I feel pain all over my body and my limbs jerk like they are not my own. The flowers fall to the ground and my head follows. I watch three petals settle before losing consciousness.

When I come to, my first thought is that I have been tasered. I've been tasered before and the feeling is similar. My muscles ache and there is blood in my mouth. I did not dream. I am in a dim room, ten, maybe fifteen feet square. I know I have not been here long because I am on a stone floor, unfettered, but the parts of me in contact with it do not feel cold. I suspect I may have been thrown here and woken on impact. I am lying on my face, and when I get up, I am relieved to find none of my bones broken. I move my jaw around, test the range of movement in my limbs. I spit into the corner. There is a window, but it is covered in old newspapers. Light makes its way through, but not a lot. I walk to it and pick at the unravelling edges of the paper. There are bars across the window and under the paper there is a dilute smearing of whitewash. I will not be escaping that way. There is a distinct smell of rotten eggs.

They have taken my shoes and I regret not wearing my gun holster, but fuck it. I've been shot before, and the hair at the back of my neck rises just thinking about it. Not sure I could do that to another person. I test the door, which is made of heavy oak. There is nothing on the floor but small pebbles and dirt. I idly wonder if I can use the pebbles: collect them, rip my clothes, make a cosh, an idea squeezed out of the layers of time dust covering my self-defence training. I've picked up three before I realise they are not made of stone. I examine them in the sickly light.

They are bone fragments.

I drop them in disgust. They are all over the floor and I wonder what this means for me and my bones. I feel for the xenosphere. In an effort to soundproof the room, the builders have limited the airflow. I can't reach anything outside it. Within the room, though, there are echoes of previous occupants. Residual neurotransmitter patterns. I relax, breathe, and taste the channels.

I feel fear, death and predation. I see snatches of faces: black, white, Pakistani, male and female, all terrified. I can feel each person reaching for images of their loved ones. I can tell that they all died in here, some begging, some unconscious, some fighting, all in fear. The last thing they saw was a pale demonic image. Distorted and different for each person, but that is normal as well. We don't all see the same thing, especially when fearful. This does not fill me with reassurance. When the images and emotions become recursive, I tune out. No new information.

The door clicks, clacks and slowly opens. I back away from it. The smooth guy and his bodyguard come in. Smooth guy has a blue rope wrapped around his right hand and it trails behind him and up, as if attached to a balloon.

"Why have you been visiting my wife?" asks smooth guy.

Oh.

"Do you mean ex-wife?" I ask.

Bodyguard slaps my face. It feels like a punch. I hate violence, especially when it's done to me. The smell of rotten eggs follows them through the open door and mingles with his cologne. It is sickening in the extreme. Someone is playing fucking "Woo-woo" at full blast somewhere in the house.

"Aminat is not yours," the smooth guy says.

I am not going to argue. I get into the bodyguard first. His thoughts are simplistic, but he has a clearer image of ... Oh fuck. Rotten eggs, bone fragments, pale demon, balloon. I know what it is. I send signals to the bodyguard's brain. I convince his brain that he is underwater. He begins to choke, and holds his breath. He thrashes about. I enter his employer's mind, but as soon as I do that, he lets go of the rope. I know what's coming next.

It sweeps through the narrow door, knocking Aminat's ex-husband down as it flies into the cell and floats to the ceiling. The rope is around its neck and it snarls wordlessly out of my reach.

It's a floater, alien fauna, kept illegally. S45 taught me all about them, but I have never seen one outside videos, simulations and photos. I'd rather not be with one right now, truth be told.

It's pale, like a white man drained of all blood. It has elongated limbs, claws for grasping prey, long, sharp homodont teeth, large compound eyes like an insect, and is mostly devoid of hair except a few strands randomly placed on its body like an afterthought. The penis between its legs is almost vestigial. It flies, but without wings. There is a gasbag between its shoulders. A chemical reaction creates gas that causes it to float soundlessly.

Oh, and floaters are carnivorous.

I assume they use it to dispose of undesirables, hence all those who died in this room. It is bony and its belly is entirely concave. It's starving. It spots us, but is deciding between me, the bodyguard and Aminat's husband. It's about four feet away and I do not wait for it to make up its mind. I run out the door. I hear screaming, but I do not look back.

I am in a boys' quarters. During colonial times in Nigeria these were slave quarters. We thought this was how all houses should be built, and so all big post-colonial homes have a satellite bungalow. I unlock the door and find myself in a compound with twelve-foot walls. It is still afternoon, and the sun bears down on me. I have no phone and no shoes. Behind me, there are sounds of violence and conflict. No more screams. *Sorry, Aminat, I may have killed your husband.*

The architecture of the main house is all slopes and strange ramparts. I cannot scale the wall, it's too high, but I can follow it to find the gate.

This is the house of a bandit and he is bound to have dozens of armed men in residence. I find an alcove and press myself into the space. I start to access the xenosphere, but I hear smashing and rending of wood and glass. The floater breaks free of the boys' quarters. There is blood on the lower half of his face and on his claws. He sniffs and looks in my direction at the same time. Floaters don't see well, but they do combine visual and olfactory stimulus with auditory input to create a devastating composite.

He charges me, the rope from around his neck flying in the air behind him like a torn umbilical cord. The inflated gasbag looks like a parachute or rucksack and the silent flight makes me underestimate his speed. He is in my face before I can react, and grips me with both fore and hind claws. As he lifts me from the ground, I ignore the needle-like pain of his grasp and place both hands under his chin, pushing back. I hope this will keep him from biting me, though the blood and the crazy jarring motion make it difficult to keep my grip. A gurgling sound and a powerful stench comes from his bladder.

We rise slowly because of the combined weight. He may just want to raise me up and drop me, dash me against the concrete to make a softer and more cooperative prey. I try to read him, and that is a mistake. I feel the raw, unknowable alien mind and it stuns me. Maybe it uses different neurotransmitters, or the direction of impulse is different, but connecting sends a shaft of pain through me. It is like a head full of broken glass. His thoughts or impulses or whatever pick at my neurones one at a time and I nearly lose my grip on the chin. He snaps his jaw and through my headache I see flecks of flesh between his teeth.

Just as we rise above the fence, the floater's head bursts into pink mush. Seconds later, I hear the gunshots. Its limbs are still jerking. The remnants of the rope fall away. The floater shits, adding a surreal and human smell to the mix. I feel the vibration of the bullet impact in my arms.

The floater is headless and dead, but I am still hanging fifteen feet in the air because the gasbag still works. I am holding onto slippery, jerking, blood-smeared dead flesh and some motherfucker is shooting at me. I am at the mercy of the wind, which is picking up. As I drift away from the property, gunshots zip by and I hear shouts. The plot behind Aminat's husband's house is marshland. I see the dome in the distance, to my right. I'm not far from Ubar and my employers will be looking for me.

I slip, reach for the floater's ankle, catch it, but am unable to hold on because of the blood. I fall and land hard on a mound of moist earth.

I don't lose consciousness, but I choose not to move. The

creature hangs in the air, bleeding on me. I am horrified, and sputter to clear my mouth, but my pain is worse than my revulsion. I stay there, baptised in alien blood. After a time, this stops. A mammal investigates me, something furry and friendly, with a cold nose, but I shoo it away. I plan to get up and run through the swamp like a movie fugitive, but I must pass out, because I am suddenly aware that the sun has moved and the shadows are longer.

"Mr Kaaro, are you there?" says a voice on a public address system. Nobody calls me that. I sit up, and fall back down. Pain.

"He's over there!"

Someone has obviously spotted me, but I cannot move or fight any more. I am tired, hurt and out of energy. Fuck it.

I feel for the minds around me, preparing for a last defence, some kind of mass-seizure effect that Professor Ileri taught me.

Aminat, what have you done?

Aside from a science prodigy in Afro puffs, you have been the most troublesome woman I have ever been involved with.

When I touch the first mind, I find it to be friendly. It is the cavalry. S45 agents have come for me, tracking my chip.

"About fucking time," I say aloud. I lie back down.

I am in hospital.

I'm not hurt that badly, no broken bones or anything, but I do need a bit of time to rest and heal. Lots of soft-tissue injury, sprains, infections where the floater's claws dug into me. Incidentally, they found a mildly raised blood pressure. Nothing major, but enough to concern the doctors. I'm not surprised. The last week has been a little more exciting than I usually prefer.

Aminat's husband is still alive.

"Is this him?" says the agent who comes to my bedside to debrief me. He shoves a photo in my face.

I nod.

"His name is Shesan Williams. He's a local criminal linked to a number of investigations, but no convictions in adulthood. He kept the unauthorised life form like a pet. The bones you found were both human and animal. They generally fed the floater pigs, but Williams may have used it for body disposal. Can't prove anything yet."

"What do you mean?"

"We can prove that some human bones are there, but not who they are. We can't prove that Williams fed the humans to the floater. At most we can charge him with keeping an illegal life form. The relevant law concerns genetically modified life forms, because there is no law about keeping extraterrestrials."

"So he'll go free?"

"We have the kidnapping charge, but that's not as straight-forward, agent. We found you outside his property and unbound. I'm not saying he'll slide, but the only witnesses were you and the bodyguard. Williams is in a coma. He's a multiple amputee and he was in shock so long that doctors don't think he'll ever recover fully. He's lost fifty per cent of his kidney function. Liver's all fucked up. I don't think that qualifies as going free."

"The bodyguard?"

"Dead. You don't want to see the body. The floater was ravenous."

The agent berates me for not carrying my firearm and leaves. There is no direct communication from Femi and I wonder why. She did say she was busy with some American thing, and now I think it must be serious, because she always calls me when I've fucked something up.

Aminat visits, looks guilty.

"I'm sorry," she says, crying, holding me in a way that, to be honest, hurts my bruised ribs but is pleasant in other ways, so I don't wince or cry out.

"Why are you sorry? You didn't set a carnivore on me or hit me with a taser."

"I didn't think Shesan could . . . I mean—"

"You are still married to him."

"Technically, yes, I'm still married to him, but not because I care about him or love him. I . . . we never got round to the paperwork. He's always been jealous but I never dreamed that he would . . . and now you're here in hospital."

"It's not that bad," I say. This is true. I actually like hospitals. On some weekends I volunteer at emergency departments and chemotherapy wards, drifting in and out of the xenosphere. The dying have wonderful insights on life and there is much to learn from them, from their regrets. A washing machine repairman dying of laryngeal cancer had only one recurring thought:

There is no excuse for making an angel cry.

I still do not fully understand what it means, but it was tinged with anguish, so I wrote it down.

"Layi said he has you in his prayers," says Aminat.

"But he can't visit," I say, remembering the chain.

"No." She insinuates herself onto the hospital bed, folding her long limbs and dropping her shoes to the floor.

I make room.

Interlude: Mission

Rosewater: 2056

Burials. One of the first customs that changes as a result of the biodome rising is burials. Coffins must be welded shut and graves are now filled with cement rather than soil. This is why.

I live in a ramshackle prefab in a place we're calling Taiwo. It is named after a gangster, a twin. The other twin, Kehinde, lives on the opposite side of the dome. They had a massive falling-out and cannot stand the sight of each other. They split the gang in two and parcelled out the crime in the Doughnut. My current assignment has been to read them both and closely document the key players of crime in the conurbation. I am in a quasi-undercover state. I hang out with them and gather information from their thoughts. I do not go on raids with them most of the time. I know, from reading Taiwo's mind, that I have their trust. They think I'm slightly kooky, but reliable, although not useful in a fight. One member of the gang thinks I might be gay.

We live as if it's a commune in a single large hall. Shared flatulence breeds trust. The ill-gotten gains are in a pit, sealed, locked. The opening is patrolled by a Gujarat-built attack construct. I have been trying to bend conversation to the bot so that I can get Taiwo to think about where he got it from. S45 wants to know. So far, no luck.

Every day I document my findings in tiny, tight hand-writing rolled up into a cylinder the size of bubble gum. At precisely 0200 hours I wake up to take a piss and one of S45's silent-running drones swoops down. I fit the intelligence in a compartment and it lifts off. All the while my head is in the xenosphere, scanning for observers. There are none, and even the Gujarat bot dreams of electric sheep.

On this day, the drone doesn't lift off and there is some-thing for me. Instructions. Coordinates I'm to go to. It must be important if they want me to risk my cover with the Taiwo gang.

I jog for a mile to an alleyway where I've hidden a stripped-down buggy. The Doughnut is slowly resembling a real town now, albeit a mostly wooden one. There is steel and concrete but it is slow. It's more like a frontier town than anything, a bit spare, a bit lawless. I feed the coordinates into the guidance system and take off over the dusty streets. There is no moon and I run into potholes frequently. I am linked mentally to one of the gangsters, and there has been no alert. He dreams of roasted corn and one of the camp followers.

Closer to the coordinates, I can see better because of the South Ganglion. It glows brighter than the biodome does, phallic, potent. There is an after-smell of those daft mother-fuckers who get themselves electrocuted. There are other cars congregated, but not as many houses. I know this place. It is where we bury the dead.

The headlights pool to form a lit area. I do not add my buggy to the illumination. I stop a yard or so before the nearest and walk the rest of the way. There are people and they seem to all be clad in night and mystery.

"I'm Kaaro," I say. "Who's in charge?"

"You're the S45 guy? You seem kind of young," says one of the shadows. "Corporal Remilekun. Army."

"Well, Corporal, why don't you tell me what the problem is?"

"Can't you just read my mind?" he says. The others laugh.

I see him better now that my eyes have adjusted. He is cocky, large, muscular, and armed with a rifle. He wears a beret. I hate him on sight. I hate him because I know him of old. He is exactly the kind of person who used to beat me up when I was a child, the kind I used to run from. Ileri's voice comes back to me.

Do not deploy your gifts frivolously. You are dangerous and not to be trifled with. Your wrath can turn humans insane. This you must avoid. Be professional and a professional at all times. But that is not to say you should not teach a lesson where one is tactically necessary. What am I saying? If someone stands between you and your assignment, do not hesitate to fuck them up.

I exhale, feel for Remilekun's mind. He is not calm. Sensitives make him uncomfortable, and his self-image is small, dwarfed by a gun that is almost the same size as he is. I isolate him. I drop him into darkness of a density he has never seen. He fires his gun, but even the muzzle flash is lost in the unrelenting black.

"Help!" he calls out. "Officer needs assistance. Is anyone there?"

Oh, you want company, Remilekun? I'll give you company.

Eyes open in the blackness. Large eyes, small eyes, cat's eyes, blank eyes, jaundiced eyes, bloodshot eyes, glowing eyes. Every kind of eye that he remembers with fear. Remilekun squeals like a goat being slaughtered, and when he is on the verge of wetting himself, I bring him back.

He drops to the ground, sits with his knees drawn up, and looks rapidly around him, trembling. His men crowd around him, unsure.

"Is anybody *else* in charge here?" I ask.

Eventually, with grudging respect, they point me at the problem. Noise in the cemetery where there should be none. Knocking, banging, screeching. Some implants from dead people appear to have spontaneously reactivated, which is what led the patrolling army to the cemetery in the first place. They have two diggers, an armoured vehicle, some jeeps, and about ten men. Nine, if you take out Remilekun.

The ganglion crackles and throws off thunder. Some night birds complain.

Accounting for the soldiers on the surface and still keeping my link to the gangster back at Taiwo, I feel for life, for living minds. Nothing, but I can't be sure it's not the dirt that blocks the xenoforms.

"Dig them up," I say. I go to my buggy to snooze while they do my bidding.

While waiting, I try to reach Anthony through the xenosphere. This is a new hobby of mine. I want to get inside the biodome. Is this praying? Am I praying to the space god? How did it come to this?

Someone kicks the door of my vehicle. I open my eyes.

"They're ready."

There are sixteen coffins. The air is full of the smell of moist soil and rot. Some of these dead people were not embalmed.

This time I see without Remilekun's distortion field. The men are not all army. Some are militia, others civilians, area boys. The land is torn up, as if ploughed. The coffins are laid out like seeds, rather than harvest. I step into a trench that drops me in the exact midpoint between all of them. There is no sound. The men stare down at me.

"I thought there was supposed to be noise," I say.

"Stopped once we started digging."

They are all relaxed, guns slung on shoulders, smoking. A stray dog wanders into the light pool, but yelps when someone throws a stone. I do not see Remilekun.

Back in Taiwo, the thug I am connected to stirs, turns, and falls asleep again.

Behind me, the South Ganglion thrums. I wonder how many charred corpses are at its base today.

I don't close my eyes.

I reach out, feel for the xenosphere ...

One of the soldiers, called Kofo, has thousands of dollars in his pockets. He won't miss a few hundred—

The din startles me right out of the trance. Each coffin bursts open, splinters flying in the night. I lose connection to Taiwo, to everything. The reanimates come for me, reaching, pushing and shoving each other. Revulsion flows through me in the wake of the fetor. I panic, and I don't know how but I incapacitate all the soldiers. I hear them shout in pain. I run. Those hands on me.

Fuck. Get the fuck off me.

My hand-to-hand training flies away. I swing my fists in blind panic.

I run. I run in the direction of the ganglion. In the direction of away from the fucking reanimates.

There are no thoughts coming from the reanimates. I can't white-noise their minds because they have none. There are too many arms holding on to me, too many bodies weighing me down, slowing my sprint. I fall to the dust.

Why do they want me?

I hear a shearing sound, that noise that is always heard at the butchers. Steel cutting into flesh and bone. Wet thuds and cleavage. I hear his mind before I see him.

Remilekun fights his way through the mindless ones. He does it because he does not want to have to explain my death to his superiors. His contempt for me is like mustard gas.

The other militants wake now and join the fight.

The reanimates die.

Again.

Later, there is a bonfire. The reanimates are burned and scattered, accompanied by Yoruba maledictions. I am quiet. They all fear and hate me, but fuck them. I drive my buggy back to Taiwo, with the biodome to my left, trying to beat the rising of the sun.

I sip my coffee, but immediately want to spit it out. These coffee beans have definitely not been partially digested by a mammal for better flavour. It smells better than it tastes, so I bring the rim of the mug close to my nose and just inhale.

"Kaaro, are you listening to me?" asks Femi.

"Yes, Ma," I say. This is only partially true. I am also watching the TV screen where Jack Jacques, a local loudmouth, is trying to convince the camera that we need Rosewater to have its own mayor. We don't have mayors in Nigeria. The guy is a lunatic.

"Your report is a mess. You almost got people killed," Femi says. She speaks from a plasma display generated from a matchbox-sized holo box. The signal is decoded by my implant. Any other person in the vicinity will see a blur and hear white noise. The coffee shop is empty apart from the tired barista anyway.

"They were soldiers," I say. "And assholes."

Femi's eyes go even narrower than before. "You fried their brains while they were on an operation."

"That was an accident."

"You ran away, Kaaro."

"I am not a tactical agent. I gather intelligence, Femi. I don't fight, I don't shoot, and I definitely want nothing to do with undead hordes rising from their graves to eat my brains."

She massages her temples. "Reanimates don't eat brains, you ignorant fuck."

"Well they weren't looking for a group hug," I say.

She sighs. "Kaaro, you have to realise that there is internal resistance in S45 to the use of sensitives. You are more accurate than most, but you seem to cause twice as many problems as everybody else. Not everybody loves you." She says the last sentence slowly, and in English.

"What are you saying?"

"An agent can't run away from a firefight. You've had the training, you have a weapon. Where the situation calls for it, you will use both. There will be unpleasant consequences if this happens again, so grow some testicles."

"Can I borrow yours?"

"Keep making jokes. See what happens when you get one person killed. Just one. Get back to that gangster and stop neglecting to check in."

The plasma dissipates. I don't know why she's angry. I told her clearly last year that I didn't want anything to do with their precious agency. I focus on the TV.

Jacques talks about how much revenue Rosewater brings to the country from health tourism alone. A lot of it goes into the federal coffers, but he feels it needs to be invested locally. The federal government taxes the pilgrims who come every year to be healed at the Opening. They also tax the people who just want to see the biodome, evidence of first contact, and the reconstructed and reanimates. Rosewater currently gets none of that revenue. The first Opening, last year, had fewer than a thousand people. This year, up to five hundred thousand thronged around the biodome. Some had to be carried there on pallets. Bus- and truckloads of AIDS sufferers came along. The mud tracks that pass for roads in Rosewater cannot cope with that kind of traffic.

"This influx should be taxed and regulated. That is the correct approach. The revenue, however, should come to us. We built this town with our bare hands. We dug latrines, cleared the bush, chased off wild dogs and suffered blackfly bites because we belong here. With the revenue, we can have good roads, transportation, modern sewerage, electricity that doesn't depend on local generators, civil defence, and every other accompaniment of basic human civilisation. This is not the Wild West. This is not a frontier town. This is the twenty-first century."

Jacques is a convincing little shit, I'll give him that.

I get up, pay my bill and walk into the mud.

Chapter Twelve

Lagos: 2055

Then

In the Seven Sons Beer Parlour, I drain my tankard, burp onto the back of my hand and seek the needed words from within my booze-soaked brain. A woman who can listen, who *wants* to listen, is rare, and I love to talk. The woman nods as if she understands what I have just said, which is doubtful.

"It's not as simple as you think," I say. "Most people, when they go looking for something, they think they know what they're going to find."

She asks me what I mean.

"Everything is changed by virtue of being lost. What you find, your object, your idea, your person, your thing, is not really what you lost."

She asks me if I will be able to do the job.

"Yes." I say this with some sorrow, but I take the money.

A wedding ring glitters on the hand that pays me. The skin is smooth, well nourished, fair. Her clothes are expensive. Her watch, her necklace, her earrings, none of them cheap. Her face is unlined, her eyes clear, her hair thick and healthy. I want to bite her cheek, not out of malice, but to see how rich her flesh tastes. She has never suffered from malaria or dysentery. No microbe can stick to her skin.

"You are a beautiful woman," I say.

"Thank you."

"It's not a compliment, ma'am. I'm saying it because being beautiful, it's likely that you are desired by someone, maybe a spouse. Now, it may be that this spouse is who you are looking for, who you want found?"

I make it sound like a question, but the woman does not deign to respond.

"Ma'am, customers who go looking for their spouses are seldom happy with the results, in my experience."

"I see."

"No, I don't think you do. Attractive customers, such as you . . . well, they have very little experience of rejection."

"I think I'll be fine," says the woman. "How do we do this?"

"Give me your hands."

I don't really need to hold her hands, but I have found that some form of participation increases customer satisfaction. Theatrics, no matter how subtle, lead to better tips and bonuses. I also want to touch her, to feel that silky skin. It does not disappoint. It feels like being held by a cloud, there and not there, with muscles that have never known manual labour. I do not even think she has ever typed on a keyboard. Every machine she has ever owned has been touch screen or holo field.

I find what she is looking for in less than a minute. The path is as clear as the whites of her eyes.

"We will need an automobile," I say.

She calls for the bill and signals to a man sitting by the bar. He nods and walks out of the bar. I do not know him, but the rich woman did not get here by taxi or bus. Klaus, the mad Belgian, just told me to be at this place at this time, and that it would be a woman. No names. The woman knows that I am an unregistered finder, or a registered finder doing unregistered finding for extra cash. Klaus has never led me wrong.

Bill paid, make-up fresher, the woman leads me out to wait for her car.

The driver parks precisely one foot from my feet. It is a sports utility vehicle, black, tinted windows. The woman gets in the back and I follow, although I should not. Nobody knows where I am, and if this is a government trap, I may spend the rest of my days in detention without trial.

"Where to, boss?" asks the driver.

In that voice I detect volumes. Education. A cultivated informality, a mask donned to put a commoner at ease. This is no driver. The depth of the register, the teeth in his mouth, the muscles on his turned neck. At the very least, this is a corporate bodyguard.

"Go west," I say.

The ride is quiet, though punctuated by my directions. After forty minutes the driver speaks.

"We're going round in circles, boss."

The woman cocks her head in response.

"You are wrong," I say. "But I forgive you. The path we are describing is called a spiral. We are winding our way inwards in curves of regular reducing radii. We are working towards the centre."

"Why can't we just go to the centre?" asks the woman.

"You're paying me for a job. Let me do it." I shift away from her slightly. "I do not know the destination, but I know the way."

The woman crosses and uncrosses her legs. The movement

146

causes a puff of perfume to tickle my nose. I have a sudden powerful erection and I trap it between my thighs so that it isn't visible.

The roads become narrower. The dark windows give the world a richness that it lacks in reality. The bleached sand looks amber rather than the usual stark beiges.

They are closer. Soon, now.

The road is bumpier. Fewer houses. Clumps of hardy weeds, industrial waste, dumped pallets. The last vestiges of civilisation are the speed-limit signs, tortured and broken up for scrap metal, then there is just dry red earth. I see in the rear window that the SUV kicks up a ten-foot dust cloud.

Hawks swirl in the sky.

Here.

"Stop the vehicle," I say.

My heart thumps. I am close. I see a meaningful look pass between the driver and the woman, but I do not or cannot care. I am caught in the ecstasy of a hunger that I cannot define, but that I have felt many times. The poets like to call it the finder's passion.

I try to open the door, but I can't work the handle. *Haste.*

"Open the fucking door. Now. Now! *Kia, kia!*"

I feel sweat forming on my skin. Too slow the driver gets out, then he opens my door.

On the ground, in the dust, a piece of wood with one flap of a strap hinge attached, marker of a phantom door that leads nowhere. I fix on this briefly, then take exactly four steps forward. I turn on the spot in this desolate place. I kick the powdery dirt with my shoe. Something is different. I hunker down and swipe what I find with my left hand, rub between index finger and thumb. This is not dry earth, it is sawdust.

I look back at the car and notice the woman disembark, her dress flapping in the wind, a ghost snatching at her hemline. My tumescence shifts as I see her thighs.

I say, "I need a—"

"Shovel," says the driver. He is already walking to the boot. It is suspicious that he knows, that he already has a shovel handy. My urge to locate, to find, is overpowering and I will sink into the ground if it means I will know peace.

I dig in silence apart from grunts and heavy breathing. I keep a rhythm, knowing from my experience of manual labour when younger that this is the only way to get it done. I am shirtless now, having stripped when sweat drenched my clothes. The woman and the driver do not offer to help, but watch me without comment or apparent guilt, the guileless manner of the rich towards a serf fulfilling a role.

Four hawks land with thumps in the dirt all around me. They are cyborg observation beasts, COBs, recording information, spooling it to servers in the sky.

The shovel hits something more solid: a boot.

"There's somebody here," I say. "Someone's been buried."

I dig around and use my hands to gouge out chunks. My efforts slowly reveal that the corpse is ...

"Not alone. There ... that's a hand from ... This isn't ..."
I look up and see that the woman and her driver are not surprised at all. They stand like telephone poles in the wind, conveying secret information while seeming inert. "This isn't the kind of job I'm used to. Take me back, right now. I'm ... I'm not involved. Klaus was mistaken about the work I do. I don't work. I'm unemployed. The police will—"

"Calm down," says the driver.

"Have you found it?" asks the woman.

"The trance ends here. This is the person you were looking for, one hundred per cent. Or to be specific, one of these. But you already knew that, didn't you. You knew he was dead, and that he'd been ... God, I can't stop talking."

"Calm down." The driver looks around, then at his watch.

"Please, I beg you, don't kill me," I say.

"Why would we kill you?" asks the woman. To the driver she says, "They're late."

"If you let me go, you can forget my fee. I need to live because I have a family to look after," I say.

"No you don't. Now, shut up, please. You're starting to irritate me," the woman says. Both she and the driver keep looking around and up.

If I get out of this alive, I will kill Klaus. He is probably not even Belgian to start with. *Fucking German Nazi bastard scum-sucker!* I stand in the shallow grave not knowing whether I should continue digging or try to escape. There is no place to escape to. Desolation for miles around, which makes it perfect for getting rid of bodies in the first place. I can probably outrun the driver, and the rich woman isn't even in contention there, but there are other factors. The driver's uniform bulges in the right places to suggest a concealed firearm. I may be a low-impact variety of telepath, amazing in my own way, but I cannot run faster than bullets or deflect them with my skin.

"I usually find runaways and jewellery. This is ... Dead bodies make me nervous. Please!" If only I could make tears. Usually I am a good actor – the best scammers are – and when nothing is at stake I can make myself cry easily. This time the fear dries up my mouth and eyes.

I hear it: the whipping of rotor blades as they cut through air. Helicopter. I scan the sky and see it approaching from the west.

"About time," says the woman. She walks closer to the verge of the grave. From my angle I can see up her skirt, but both the finder's passion and my sexual interest are gone. "Did you know that we humans are probably the first primates to kill our own natural predators? We learned to use tools, and bam! Up the hierarchy because of opposable thumbs and big brains."

The helicopter is so close she has to squint from the dust it kicks up and raise her voice above the din.

"That's interesting," I say, uninterested. "I did not know that at all."

"Just listen. You were born with certain advantages that other people do not have."

So were you, I think, but do not say.

"Your mental abilities are like metaphorical thumbs. What do you think the lions and the panthers would have done if they knew the significance of emerging opposable thumbs? They would have wiped humankind out, uppity apes that we were." She has to hold her skirt in place now. "You are supposed to register yourself as a finder."

"Yes, I know and—"

"Just listen. You are the best we have encountered. Amazing, really. I had one woman from Ojota who wandered all over Lagos before settling here, but she could not pinpoint the grave."

"It's not an exact—"

"The men in there, one of them was my husband. The others were dissidents like him. I knew he had been liquidated, but my superiors did not tell me where he was buried."

"Why? What ... I don't understand."

"I'm from Section Forty-Five. We've been trying to find you, or someone like you, for a long time now. We're not going to kill you, although we could and nobody would know. We're not going to put you in prison, although we could because you're breaking the law. We have a job for you. Complete that task and not only will you walk free, but we'll pay you a handsome fee. It's up to you. Will you do it?"

She holds up an ID badge to confirm that she works for the secret police. The helicopter lands and disgorges uniformed armed men who spread like a plague to surround me. My options dwindle fast.

"Say yes," says the driver.

Fuck it.

"Yes," I say.

Chapter Thirteen

Rosewater: 2066

Now

I do not spend a long time in the hospital. A week is enough, although I am still stiff and my urine looks reddish. On my last day I ask where Shesan Williams is being held, and because of my S45 status they let me see him. He is hooked up to life support with his family around him. His second wife is enormously fat. She literally looks like a monument to greed. Beautiful face, though.

In the xenosphere, Shesan is surrounded by a featureless grey fog. He looks perplexed. I whisper his name and he looks about. I have hidden the gryphon form from him. I hesitate. What I am about to do isn't nice, but I remember my help-lessness when the floater held me, bullets flying past, and I remember the bones in the cell. I remember blood from the creature splashing into my mouth.

"Shesan Williams, you should not act with impunity," I say. "It is never a good idea to cause pain to angels."

I generate images of floaters, six of them, and set them on him.

The floaters swoop down and begin to take bites. I know this is only in his mind, but he will feel fear and he will feel the real pain of each tooth. When they finish with him, the whole cycle will start again, a fresh hell each time. In reality, Shesan's face is smooth and he seems restful, serene. His family is not alarmed because they cannot hear anything, but in his mind Shesan screams for ever.

When I get back to my bed, Aminat is waiting, having packed my stuff.

I have an optional cane, but I use it all the same. I have a fantasy of hitting any attackers with it. I need one of those disguised sword sticks. I'd draw it and slash my initials into the air. I'd swashbuckle.

"Bola wants to talk to you," Aminat says in the car.

"Okay," I say. I have that feeling of unreality that you know of if you've ever been in hospital. The outside world is odd to you, takes getting used to.

"She's really sick," says Aminat.

"She must be about to drop that child."

"She . . . ah . . . she lost the child."

"I'm sorry, what? How? When?"

"I didn't tell you because you had your own problems going on. Like I said, she's really sick."

I have a sinking feeling. "Take me to her."

"Sure. We'll drop your things at home—"

"No. Now, please. I have to see her now."

It is odd seeing Bola with a flat belly.

She is at home, lying on the sofa, covered, skin hanging loose on her frame. She seems older and her bonhomie is all gone. Beside her is a plastic tumbler of water with a straw, which from time to time she sucks. It is a child's straw with happy floral patterns that seem out of place.

"I don't understand," I say.

"Sit down," she says. Her voice is low, and words come with difficulty.

I sit on the centre table, which is uncouth but the other chairs are too far away.

I've had a cough since the parade. It got worse, then one day there was blood. The baby ... I had to go into labour. Devastating.

As she shares it with me in the xenosphere, I get a wash of her despair but also some shame. Bola is not a trained sensitive, at least not in the formal way that S45 trained me. She is more of a traditional adept who found her way by trial and error and plied a trade in peripheral towns and villages before the bank's headhunters found her. Powerful. I wonder what she would be like if she were trained. This, I think, is the only edge I have on her. In her sickness, that edge is not needed because her defences are down. Unbidden, I am awash in her images and sounds. She is or has been somewhere else in the xenosphere, with her dead husband, Dominic.

Bola ...?

You may.

Even though she is as accessible as any lay person on the street, I still have to ask permission. She wants me to, maybe even needs me to. Out of respect, I use my real self-image, not the gryphon.

Her mind is a decaying temple. The ground is putrefying meat and the columns are wet with spit, mucus and pus. The windows let in a jaundiced light, which is bile-filtered sunlight. The glass is made of crushed kidney stones. There are

154

no seats or pews, but a few tumour-like growths approximate the look of chairs. They are lumpy, but have depressions that a person might sit in. There is no altar, but two figures sit on the floor. One of them is Bola, her self-image as she was when in her early twenties. Behind her, sitting on his haunches, is a tall, skinny man I recognise to be Dominic. I can only see the upper half of his head, but his eyes follow me, shining with malevolence. His hands grip both her shoulders. Bola's mouth is slightly open, as if she can't get air in fast enough, but I see the rise and fall of her chest, and it is slow.

Dominic's grip is the opposite of a lover's embrace.

"Dominic, right?" I say.

He does not respond, but keeps tracking my approach. The give of the meaty floor is unsettling, but I push any sign of weakness far away. I stop in front of them, then I walk around and see why he does not answer. His mouth is attached to the middle of her back, teeth embedded in the muscles. A slow stream of blood drips down. I do not know what this means, but it cannot be good for Bola.

"Let her go," I say.

He does not respond. He does not move, although his eyes are on me.

I punch him hard, on the temple. His jaw loosens and Bola falls to the ground. He snarls and leaps up, facing me. His mouth, nose and chin are smeared with blood and snot. He looks feral, but is essentially human.

"Bola, memory, imagination or fantasy, this has gone too far, I think. I will have to—"

Do what you must, she responds.

Dominic loses interest in me and goes back to Bola. There is a wound on her back that corresponds to his teeth, but it is not anatomical. There is a pulsing blood vessel that I do not recognise; it spurts away Bola's life force or its equivalent in this place.

I transform into the gryphon and dig my beak into Dominic's neck. I grab onto his sides with my forepaws and flap my wings. We both soar, with Dominic struggling and leaking not blood but ichor. I use my hind limbs and kick against his flesh, ripping him apart with the claws. I am at the roof of the temple and I drop him, but follow, maintaining a distance of a foot. After he hits the floor, I lift him again, but making sure he faces me. This time I claw away his belly and chest. His organs fall out with a splat. He stops thrashing and is still. His eyes go out.

I hover for a bit, then I open my eyes and I'm back in Bola's living room. She is asleep, it seems.

Thank you ... so tired ...

Rest. I'll let myself out.

Aminat is waiting for me.

"What did you do?" she asks.

"A kind of exorcism," I say.

"She was possessed?"

"No, she got caught up in her own memories. A thought loop that she couldn't get away from. I broke the loop."

"Will this make her well?"

"It shouldn't have made her physically unwell in the first place. The two are not related." I thought of the decaying temple of meat. "*Should* not be related."

Something about the whole episode perturbs me, but I cannot put my finger on it. I am tired and just out of hospital. I ask Aminat to drop me at home. I call Femi Alaagomeji, but there is no response.

"I'll check on you after work," Aminat says.

"I don't know what you do for a living," I say.

"I deal with drugs," she says and raises both palms, splaying and shaking them, meant to convey spookiness. She kisses me and is gone.

My flat seems desolate. "Intrusions?"

There's a five-second delay before the flat responds. "None."

"Messages?"

"None."

"Music. Otis Redding."

I strip, and lie on the floor for what I mean to be only a minute, but fall asleep.

Chapter Fourteen

Unknown military base: 2055

Then

When I am frightened, my gift becomes erratic.

They fly me away from Lagos in a helicopter and take me to a military installation, but I have no idea where it is. This is not a problem, because I am a finder. I can always make my way back home, but that depends on distance and the need for a vehicle and whether I will have to steal, which seems likely given how long the flight takes.

They keep me in a white windowless room under armed guard. I have not been fed and by my estimate I've been here for seven hours. The psychotic woman and her muscle-bound driver do not travel with me, and the robotic military types assigned to me will not talk, no matter how obsequious I try to be.

"So this is Section Forty-Five?" I say. "Wow. It's full of lights."

The guard maybe shifts a bit. His eyes may have narrowed, or perhaps I imagine it. Either way, it is a reaction of sorts.

"I'm hungry, though. Ravenous. I would really, *really* like some food. How about it, soldier?"

The guard keeps still.

"Did you know that your stomach empties between ninety and a hundred and eighty minutes after your last meal? It's true. It's a fact." I push back and rock my chair until it stands on two legs. I balance this by putting my foot on the table. "I must have one of the ninety-minute varieties because ... whew! My belly just keeps grumbling. Maybe because I had beer for lunch. What do you think?"

The guard keeps still.

"What's your name?"

This time there is a definite wrinkle of the brow. Small sign of irritation, but a fine result all the same. I startle as the door opens. My chair falls with a clack.

The rich woman comes in, this time in a tight beige trouser suit. She holds a few sheets of paper, a flat rectangular tin container, and a lighter. My lust returns and it brings friends.

"Please tell me that's a menu," I say.

"Confidentiality agreement," says the woman. "You sign and you give a thumbprint."

"First opposable thumbs, now a thumbprint. You really like your thumbs, don't you?"

"Just sign the fucking document, Kaaro."

Klaus told them my real name! I will never work with that Belgian bastard again. Tintin and fruity beer can go hang. I scribble across the dotted lines where an "X" indicates that I should. I open the tin, dip my thumb in the ink pad and leave my print. I hand the paper back to the woman and clean my thumb against my thigh.

"Thank you."

"Who are you?"

"I'm from Section Forty-Five."

"I already know that. What's your name? What's your rank?"

She smiles, and even though it is mocking, my heart accelerates. "You don't know much about us, do you? We don't run this organisation on hierarchical principles, Kaaro. We don't hold ranks. Planar philosophy. That means flat."

"I know what planar means." A lie.

"Good, so don't go asking to speak to my supervisor or manager or anything like that."

"I won't. How do you run an organisation without bosses?"

"Surprisingly well. Much better than any other organisation in Nigeria, I'll tell you that."

"Tell me your name. Please. I can't just call you a number each time I need you or dream about you."

"You talk too much."

"I've been told. Name?"

"I am Mrs Femi Alaagomeji."

"Mrs?"

"Recently widowed."

Of course. Husband interred in mass grave. "Pleased to meet you, Femi—"

"*Mrs* Alaagomeji."

"Femi. As an act of faith, can I get some food?"

"Perhaps later." She places the lighter on the table in between us. "Tell me, have you heard of the Bicycle Girl?"

"Sort of. Wasn't she some girl who was murdered in Ibadan back in 2044, along with her entire village? Her ghost appears to people from time to time and they go all hysterical. It's an urban legend."

"It's not an urban legend," says Femi.

"It's an urban legend," I say. I suck my teeth, dismissive.

Inside, though, I'm churning. I remember my brief glimpse of a raised fist and a closing gap in space on a drunken night. "Listen, seventy-six per cent of urban legends are deliberately crafted, did you know that? It's a form of storytelling. Anyway, what's the significance of Bicycle Girl to you?"

"We want you to find her."

"You don't need me. You need that old actor ... what's his name? The American who snogged Scarlett Johansson?"

"Kaaro."

"I'm not a finder of ghosts. Actually, forget that. Feed me and I'll bust as many ghosts as you like."

"Kaaro, read the file. I'll get you some rice and oku eko." She pushes a button on the lighter and a holo screen pops up in front of me. "Then make up your mind."

The file is the written report of one Corporal Folashade Olomire, and most of the information is related to the police interrogation of a Professor Aloysius Ogene, expert in theoretical physics. The corporal explains in her report that Ogene's RFID chip has him as travelling from Lagos to Arodan on 28 February 2044. He goes missing from the grid until 14 March, when he walks up to a police checkpoint on the Lagos–Ibadan expressway, confused and asking for his wife. This would have been a simple missing persons issue, except that the entire population of Arodan had disappeared. The document also contains embedded photographs. Femi has been good to her word and I chew as I read. I am so hungry that I do not taste anything, just swallow. I don't even care that they serve me oku eko, which means "the corpse of Lagos", cheap mackerel that nobody likes to be seen eating. Hunger is the best spice, they say.

On the matter of the 1,175 civilians missing
from the village known as Arodan, the subject,
Aloy Ogene, had nothing to say. He insisted
he did not murder them, and indeed, no bodies
have been found. He continued to speak of a
young girl called Oyin Da, native of Arodan,
who sought him out at the university and took
him to the village to see a machine. See
attached JPEG image 478 for a sketch he made.

The sketch looks nothing like a machine. The man must
have been tortured within an inch of his life, because he could
not draw a straight line. I cannot decipher the symbols, so I
set the photo aside. There is a machine, if not real, at least in
Ogene's imagination. Move on.

Ogene would have us believe that the girl,
Oyin Da, activated this machine after he made
suggestions that could improve its function,
whatever that may have been. He claims she
disappeared along with all the inhabitants of
Arodan immediately afterwards.

A pop-up photo floats above the text showing Ogene. Round
face, flat on top, short hair, strands of grey in his eyebrows. I
have never been to university, but I think this is what a professor would look like. Which means a professor probably doesn't
look like this. I swipe away the image and continue.

Preliminary scouting and deep forensic exam-
ination did not reveal any such machine or

related schematics. I attended the site personally. My initial impression was that Ogene had a psychotic delusion. He said a colonial scientist called Roger Conrad had built the machine but returned to England around 1960, leaving the engine behind. Oyin Da had repaired it, according to Ogene. Curiously, he stated that Oyin Da spoke no English and communicated in Yoruba or in phrases from a Yoruba Bible translated into English.

Through contacts in the British Embassy and communication with MI5 in London, I was able to establish that a Roger Conrad did in fact exist, may have arrived in Nigeria circa 1953 and settled somewhere in Yorubaland to carry out some unspecified duties for the British government (Nigeria was a British colony at the time). He may have had a contingent of soldiers with him. He returned to London in 1961, spent seven years in a county asylum and was released under the Care in the Community programme. He committed suicide in 1975.

I come to an embedded audio file called "Interrog excerpt 11-10". I tap it. A male voice speaks, deeper than I would have expected for an intellectual, but hesitant, broken in parts and fearful.

"I woke up with a start, the notes I made on the schematics gone. The noise, the din from the engine, was impressive and frightening. I got countless pings from the cyborg observation beasts, the hawks. There were up to a hundred hawks outside, all facing the bicycle block, recording the event.

"The sound from the machine rose in pitch. Light flowed from the only entrance. The whine was all over Arodan, twinned with a Doppler stammer. Villagers staggered out to investigate. It sounded like it was reaching for a crescendo, after which something would happen. Smoke pumped out of the top, blacker than the night sky. Some hawks flew through it, as if to taste the nature of the soot. Oyin Da's mother yelled something at me, but I could not hear over the din. She ran off into the night.

"The hawks began to fall out of the sky. My glasses cracked. I fell to my knees. My entire brain was on fire with vibrations, and just before I fell unconscious, I was aware of a bright light."

Aloy Ogene pauses and sobs, then continues.

"When I woke, it was daylight and I was alone. It was two weeks later and I stumbled around until I came to a police checkpoint. They arrested me, charged me with murder."

"Actually, we're charging you with genocide because of the ethnic cleansing of the people of Arodan." A female voice now, confident, merciless. Probably Corporal Olomire. "You are Igbo. The people you killed were all Yoruba. It's tribally motivated."

"So now I'm a mass murderer." Sardonic laugh. "But where are the bodies?"

The recording cuts off abruptly.

The next part is labelled "Transcript from cell microphone". Various pop-ups state the highly classified nature of the material and threaten all manner of punishment. I dismiss them.

```
Timestamp: 26/04/2044 16.13:21
[Unknown sound on recording]
[Unknown sound on recording]
Prof A. Ogene: Oyin Da?
[Unknown sound on recording]
Prof A. Ogene: My work.
[Unknown sound on recording]
[Unknown sound on recording]
Prof A. Ogene: Thank you.
[Unknown sound on recording]
```

A fish bone gets stuck in my throat and I cough, drink some water, and cough some more. I gesture to the guard, point to my own back, but the man is a hologram or statue. When the bone dislodges, I give the guard the middle finger and continue my reading.

Now it is an audio file titled "Debrief excerpt 08-22".

"His locator chip was gone. We searched the cells, the surroundings, the nearest buildings, everywhere." This is Olomire speaking.

"Any blood or body fluids in his cell? I mean as signs of a struggle."

"There is always blood and shit … excuse me, waste material in the cells. It's a prison. Prisoners struggle all the time. The place is full of DNA, if that's what you mean, but from old struggles, bowel opening and masturbation."

"Did you ask his wife?"

"Did we … Listen, we are not amateurs, you know. Just because we lost a prisoner does not mean—"

"Corporal, please answer the question for the record."

"Yes, we asked the prisoner's wife. She was unable to help."

"Unable or unwilling?"

"She was catatonic with grief."

"Did she think he was dead?"

"No, but at the time he had been charged with mass murder. That can be upsetting if you are of a delicate disposition. This woman certainly was."

"I see. Then what happened?"

"I filed my report and awaited instructions. I received them and carried them out."

"And what were these?"

"Declare that Professor Aloy Ogene died in custody before he could be executed, and state that he had been buried in a secret location to prevent vandalism by the victims' relatives."

The recording ends.

I stretch and scratch my belly.

Ogene missing. The girl, Oyin Da, missing. Wife catatonic somewhere. And this was eleven years ago. Everybody knows about this ghost story, but only the superstitious believe it. Having read the file, I have some more questions, but cannot dismiss the story of Bicycle Girl as fiction, especially since I saw her, outside that nightclub in Lagos. Kind of. I saw a fist that could belong to anyone. And I was drunk.

Femi comes back in. Her make-up is perfect and I receive a fresh dose of her perfume. She sits opposite me and deactivates the holo screen. It shimmers in the air, then winks out.

"Well?" she says.

"Interesting," I say. "I have some questions."

"I'll answer what I can."

"Section Forty-Five receives all the data feeds from the hawks, right? The COBs?"

"I can't confirm that."

"Okay, I'll rephrase. I'm guessing S45 can access the COB servers. The report said there were many hawks around on the day the Arodan villagers and Bicycle Girl disappeared. What about that information?"

"All data retrieved from that area between 28 February and 14 March 2044 was corrupt."

"What happened to Ogene's RFID chip?"

"Missing. Deactivated. Nobody knows."

"Femi, I've listened to your fairy tale. While I admit it's rather entertaining, I'm not sure what you want me to do with the information."

"Isn't it obvious?" says Femi. She sits back in her chair and smiles. "Kaaro, we want you to recruit Bicycle Girl for us."

Interlude: Mission

Rosewater: 2057

I fucking leave it too long.

Taiwo is onto me. I trip on a plastic garbage can and go sprawling. I feel none of the scrapes and I do not bother to dust myself off. I keep running in the night. My phone polymer vibrates but I ignore it. I know who it is. Taiwo wants to taunt me or delay me while his Gujarat bot hunts me down. *Shitty fuck!*

At least the roads are better than a year ago. Many of them are tarred and graded. The skyline in Rosewater is spiked with cranes and the occasional skyscraper. The multinationals have finally moved in and all day, including Sundays, the sound of construction rings out. The Yemaja is cleaner because rudimentary sewerage systems are being built.

I run. I cannot hear the bot behind me, but that doesn't mean anything. Indian robotics are the best in the world and the engines run silently. The only noise I expect is detonation when it bombs me. My chest hurts and I can almost see my ancestors calling to me from the grave. I turn into a blind alley, spin, and run into an adjacent space.

It is a night without moon, and visibility is poor because it's Harmattan season. Dusty particles from the Sahara Desert suspended on a trade wind lower temperatures and threaten laundry and breathing everywhere. This will not slow the construct. It seems one of Taiwo's lieutenants hacked my implant and it's broadcasting a homing signal. I imagine the actual message.

I'm here, come and find me! I'm here! Yoo-hoo! Come get me, Indian robot of death!

I briefly consider digging out my implant, but dismiss it out of hand. It's deliberately too deep to get to without nicking a major artery and killing myself – this is supposed to help avoid identity fraud. I could get an underground hack to discontinue the message, but no time. I only have – *had* – a fifteen-minute head start.

I see a chute, narrow. I would barely fit in there, but I'm pretty sure the bot can't. I slide in. It's the entrance to a kind of silo. I find myself amid cobs of maize packed into burlap sacks. Dark. I stop breathing to force my heart to slow.

I am still connected to Taiwo. My distance reading has been reducing recently. Professor Ileri said this is because with increased construction there are more disruptions to continuous connections. The xenosphere is more broken up.

A crawling creature moves across my foot. There will be rats here, but I'm not worried.

Femi told me that over the last two years I have given S45 terabytes of information on the twins. I know this, I say. S45 has enough to put them away, I say. Just dotting i's and crossing t's, she says. Any day now, she says. Right.

I mine Taiwo's brain indiscriminately, sucking as much as I can through the tenuous link we have. I don't know what use it will be if I'm dead, but it's better than—

BLAM!

I hear the slam and whine. The Gujarat bot is outside, slapping against the entrance. Now I don't understand what I was thinking when I chose this enclosed space. It's an attack construct. It will decide to launch a grenade in a minute. One exit. Brilliant.

"Kaaro!"

Oh, this is just outstanding. Taiwo is talking to me through the robot's public-address system.

"Kaaro, I know you're down there."

"Hello, boss," I say.

"*Odale ni e,*" he says. You are a traitor.

"*Ta lo so yen fun yin, egbon?*" I say. Who told you that, respected brother?

"*Pa nu mo! Mo ti mo fun oshu meji.*" Shut up. I've known for two months.

The construct has a cutting implement and it is widening the opening. Fragments of cement and brick fall inwards and a cloud of dust rises. There are no weapons in here. I hear music. Is that asshole piping music through the killer robot? I can see the marketing campaign: *one hundred tunes to die to*. Oh God, don't let me die to Clayton.

From our mental connection I see that he does not want me blown up. He wants me slowly disembowelled, and he wants the event recorded.

"*Mi o nse olopa,*" I say. I'm not a cop.

He laughs. It rings hollow through the speakers. "*Okuro ati odale.*" Liar and traitor.

Cracks appear and the walls give way. I fear the entire structure will collapse on me, but it holds. The rats squeal with fear and I hear them scramble. The construct is eight feet high with a variable width. It adjusts for manoeuvrability. It looks like a tank, with no humanoid features at all. A squat vertical black alloy cylinder resting on a horizontal one. A force field glows around it, protecting it from debris and dirt and insults. Something whirrs and twists inside, a note becoming higher as if it is charging a weapon. A small cylinder, a muzzle this time, detaches from the frame and points at me. Even the floor vibrates.

"*Ile l'omo owa ti nmu 'na roko,*" I say.

The construct stops, powers down, reconfigures. The cylinders collapse into themselves, compacting the structure. My phone rings. I answer as I scramble over rubble to get out of the space, leaving the construct behind.

"Hello, Taiwo," I say.

"What have you done? That's an expensive piece of equipment!"

I am not sure what I've done, but I may have pulled out the back-door deactivate phrase from Taiwo's mind. I'm not about to tell him that, though. I don't know if he knows about sensitives. Less is more.

"I think you should ask for a refund," I say. "*Awon agba ni gbogbo oro lo lesi, sugbon kii se gbogbo oro laa fesi si.*" The elders say, there is an answer to every question, but it is not every question that we answer.

I hang up.

Outside, as I emerge, I find guns trained on me. S45 has finally heard my distress call. They tell me to keep my hands where they can see them.

"Fuck off," I say, and walk away.

Femi Alaagomeji calls and calls, but I am in no mood and ignore her.

I catch my own reflection in a shop window. I look hideous. I know that units will be moving in to capture Taiwo and his people. Simultaneously they will raid his businesses and arrest his brother. I hope they have adjoining cells. They hate each other, though I've heard Kehinde is more cruel. Perhaps he will kill Taiwo.

I wonder what the rest of my classmates are doing for the organisation.

I wonder about Oyin Da and I look to the biodome. The outline is indistinct, and I remember something Alhaji said during every Harmattan season in Lagos:

> *Fair is foul, and foul is fair:*
> *Hover through the fog and filthy air.*

It gives me no comfort.

Chapter Fifteen

Rosewater, Lagos: 2066

Now

A fortnight after my encounter with the floater, I am reasonably healed. I return to work in a black suit and wield my walking cane. If people noticed my absence they do not speak of it. I notice Bola's absence but do not speak of it.

I settle into my seat near the window overlooking the city. At the firewall table, to my right is an emptiness. We prepare to read *Orlando* by Virginia Woolf from the prompter. Just as the banking hours are set to start, I am interrupted from entering the xenosphere. A secretary type taps me on the shoulder.

"The management want to have a word," he says.

"Right now?" This has never happened. All previous transactions have been by email or phone.

The man nods and indicates that I should follow him. This is my first day back, and all the time I've worked here, nothing has required me to meet with management. They generally tend to stay away from the sensitives. Clement's eyes follow me as I walk out. I am a bit sad. I have read *Orlando* and was looking forward to reading it again.

I am ensconced in an office, air-conditioned, with an airlock separating me from a desk with three people seated. There is one of those starfish-shaped conference speakerphones on both sides of the glass.

"Mr Kaaro, are you well?" a disembodied voice says. The people don't move so I cannot tell which one it is.

"I'm fine. Who am I talking to?"

They are in the dark and are virtual silhouettes. One is shaped like a woman.

"We are people in authority. We make decisions," says one voice.

"Decision-makers in Integrity Bank," says another.

"Kaaro, did you see Bola while you were away?"

"Yes, I did." If they are asking, they know. There is nothing to hide, I don't think.

"What opinion did you form of her illness?"

"She lost her pregnancy," I say.

"You are being evasive."

"Okay, my opinion is that she did not feel well enough to work. I am her friend; I went over to support her."

"Is it your opinion that what is wrong with her is contagious?"

"Not to men. Or women who take birth control seriously."

"Are you taking *us* seriously, Mr Kaaro? Do you really think levity is the right approach?"

"I do not think her illness is contagious."

"What do you base that opinion on?"

Sweet fuck-all. "I am not a doctor; it's not my area of expertise," I say.

"Let's talk about your area of expertise. Did you form a mental or mind link with Bola?"

Lie. "I don't know."

"What do you mean?"

"The xenosphere is not … it is composed of multiple net-worked fungi-like organisms floating in the air. Links are formed and broken all the time, whether sensitives intend to or not. It is the reason you are talking to me from behind a screen. It is why we spend time rubbing on antifungal cream when we go out in public. So when I sat down with Bola, it is entirely possible that a connection formed. Or not."

They know something, but I don't know what. I do not, however, need to cooperate with them.

They are silent for a time while they consider the information.

"What?" I ask, all innocence and righteous indignation.

"Did you speak to any of the other sensitives today before work?"

"No."

"Other than your physical injuries, do you have any other illness symptoms?"

"No."

"Flu-like symptoms? Fever? Burning urine?"

"No. Nothing." *Burning urine?*

I know what is coming. Having offended the Irish House of Desmond, the eponymous Orlando is banished by the king from the English court.

"We would prefer it if you did not return to work today, or until we ask you to return. We will of course pay you for a full day's work today."

"How generous," I say.

"Don't be like that."

*

Home.

I am not sure if I have been fired or not, and I am equally in the dark as to what I did wrong. The situation does not apply since I am a contractor. I am not worried – fiscally, I am secure. I receive my S45 pay. I have various safety deposit boxes and protocols of escape, worked out with Klaus back when I was forced to become legitimate.

The suits at the bank are worried about contagion. I wonder if I should also be worried.

I have messages, some freelance work. Some junk. One official email from S45. It's so secure that it requires a password, my mother's maiden name and an eighteen-digit personnel number to confirm my identity. The message is from Femi.

> Dear Kaaro,
>
> After years of service, I have decided to step down from my role as divisional lead. Please join me to welcome Japhet Eurohen, who will be taking over my role.
>
> I trust you will extend to him the same spirit of hard work that you did me.
>
> Sincerely,
>
> Mrs Femi Alaagomeji

What?

I have not heard from Femi in ages, but I presumed she was busy. What kind of internal coup is going on? I dial her direct emergency line – never used before since it is for absolute life-or-death situations only. The line does not connect. I put my phone down and it rings. Unknown number.

"Hello," I say.

"You rang a restricted number." Male voice. "Identify yourself."

"Mr F. U. Asshole." I hang up. That was juvenile, but reflective of my mood. I grab my pre-packed emergency bag and my car keys. I strap on holster and gun.

I'm on my way to Lagos in less than ten minutes.

I have been to Femi's house once before. I was cocky and young and did not consider the consequences. It is evening when I arrive in Lagos, full night by the time I negotiate the traffic. Bats are returning to their caves and fruit trees in flocks that cover the sky. They make screeching sounds that remind me of electronic warning beeps.

Where do fired secret agents go?

The lights are on, there are no sentries and, other than the sounds of traffic, all is quiet. The weight of the gun is alien, a metallic tumour growing out of my chest into its holster. I drive slowly, examine all parked cars, of which there are few. In this part of Lagos the cars are behind high walls. They can afford complex security systems. I will not be breaking in. My hesitation is more to do with being welcome. Mostly I know that I will not be encountering open arms. Femi has always been difficult for me to read. She is not warm, but she has never been a bitch. She *has* been a dick, but mostly when I deserve it, which is a lot of the time. Whether I am welcome or not, I do know that she will not be happy.

You are always a complication, Kaaro.

How many times have I heard her say that?

I am a complication. I complicate.

My phone vibrates but I ignore it. There have been countless calls since I last used it. I power it down and get out of the car.

It's a warm night. If not for my weapon holster, I would wear something cooler, but I need a buba to cover up. I freeze when I hear a sound to my left. I see eight fingers appear on a gate, then an unshod foot. A skinny teenage girl hoists herself over the top and leaps down. A pair of shoes flies over after her, possibly thrown by an accomplice. She puts them on as a car comes around the corner. She notices me then, and her eyes enlarge briefly until she can tell that I am neither a robber nor her father. She places an index finger against her lips and silently shushes me. The car approaches too fast, burns rubber in coming to a halt, and zooms off with her.

I go to the house next door and ring the bell. I know Femi has surveillance cameras and scanners. I raise my hands to elbow level. I sport a benign facial expression, although I haven't needed to use one for a long time. The xenosphere is so silent, it's eerie. I cannot worry about that right now.

A voice comes back, distorted, neither male nor female.

"Kaaro? What are you doing here?"

"I have to see you, Femi."

"You don't work for me any more, Kaaro. And I have company."

I wait.

"Get in here. Walk around the back," she says.

Femi's back yard is the size of a football field. The grass is patchy, green and brown. She has two fowls, a peacock and a turkey. Odd pets, ill-tempered, always at each other's necks.

178

The turkey hates visitors and it attacks me three times until I kick it. I suspect both of them to be COBs.

Femi appears in the garden. I have not seen her in years. The shadow of who she was is there, but her waist is thicker, her hair is frosted with grey and her face is fuller. She is a beautiful, elegant and intelligent woman, but not the Femi Alaagomeji I met in '55. She is holding a digital clock, which is counting down towards something.

"Is that a bomb?" I ask.

"It might as well be," she says. "You will have been seen."

"No, I was careful."

"You are wasting seconds. Scanners, remote viewers, your implant – they know you're here. A team is or will be on the way. What do you want?"

"I got an email—"

"I'm out, Eurohen is in. Yes. Questions?"

"Why?"

"Performance. Internal politics. I could not deliver on a problem. Next?"

"What problem?"

"Your problem, Kaaro. Your people, sensitives like you, they're dying. I have not been able to stem the tide or find out why."

"Dying?"

"Lose power, get sick, die."

"How many?"

She hesitates.

"*How many?*"

"Classified. I cannot tell you this. Move on."

"I could yank it out of your thoughts."

"No, you idiot. Do you think I would meet with you if there

was any risk of that? Sterile environment here. Tick-tock, Kaaro. Wasting time."

"Theories?"

"They think the sensitives are diseased."

"We've always been diseased, Femi. That's how we do what we do. A benign infection."

"Maybe not so benign, maybe a different disease." She draws me to her and I think she will kiss me, but she taps my neck with a mobile phone. "Your personnel file and some classified info on other sensitives, I've sent it to your implant."

"What should I do?" I'm worried now, plus the clock makes me tense.

"I can't tell you that."

And then she calls me by my family name. She knows. Femi knows where I came from. I can't speak from the sheer surprise.

"What? You think you have any secrets from me?" She laughs. "I'm on your side, Kaaro. You should look up your parents, though. *O l'eko ile*." Bad home training.

"Tick-tock, Femi."

"Touché."

"What can you tell me about the new guy?"

"Better politician than me. New ideas."

"Like?"

"Sensitives on government payroll should be used to support the government in power, which the politicians love."

"Isn't that what we do?"

"Not exactly and not all the time. I have had carte blanche, answerable only to the office of the president at Aso Rock. They asked me to subordinate to Special Offices. I refused. They reassigned me."

"What's Special Offices?"

"Essentially, cloak-and-dagger related exclusively to re-election."

"It's two years to the next presidential—"

"*All* re-elections. They want us to be part of the team."

"Terrorism, crime, inequity, and this is what the administration prioritises?"

"Focus, Kaaro. You're losing perspective."

"What should I focus on?"

"Death. Extinction. People like you are dying. Find out why. Find out how to survive. Have you considered that this might not be a natural disease state? That it might be enemy action? An engineered biological agent? These are questions you should be asking yourself."

My heart speeds and each of her words clouds my thoughts. I still can't feel the xenosphere.

"Who's in there?"

"Excuse me?" She is taken aback.

"Your date."

"Nobody. A writer. He writes poetry and short stories excoriating the West for colonialism, lamenting the loss of America, and defining the 'African Identity', whatever that is. Tedious, tiresome stuff."

"But you're dating him."

"Writers are interesting to me. He's attracted to the money he sees in me, looking for a patron perhaps."

"Interesting exchange."

"Kaaro, I've always liked you. You're irreverent but you deliver on your tasks, most of the time. But you're a buffoon, not very bright." She strokes my cheek, then turns her back on me.

Tade Thompson

The turkey edges in my direction. The timer is closing in on zero and I think I can hear a car in the distance. I start to leave.

"One more thing," she says. "Ditch the Aminat girl. She's trouble."

"I'm not taking relationship advice from someone who used the corpse of her dead husband as bait."

She pauses, and I don't need the xenosphere to know I've hurt her, but I can't take it back, so I change tack.

"Thank you, Femi. For everything. From the start. I know you helped me and I've never thanked you properly."

"Get off my property, Kaaro. And it's Mrs Alaagomeji to you."

Chapter Sixteen

Unknown military base, Lagos: 2055
Then

It takes me a few hours, but I have an idea about how to find the Bicycle Girl for S45.

"He had a wife," I say.

"Who had a wife?" asks Femi.

"Aloysius Ogene. Professor of theoretical physics and the so-called butcher of Arodan. He was married, according to the records you gave me."

Femi sits down opposite me on the tiny table. "Okay, he had a wife. Why is that relevant?"

"Maybe I should let you think about it for a bit."

"Kaaro, I'm a busy woman. Get to the point."

"Remember how my abilities work? I can find anything as long as it belongs to the person who wants it found. Professor Ogene disappeared, so did Bicycle Girl and all the inhabitants of Arodan. It's a stretch, but Ogene and Bicycle Girl might be in the same place. Do you see what I'm thinking here, Mrs Alaagomeji?"

"I see. You want to use the wife to find Ogene." She smiles, and it hits me like a blessing from on high.

"I do. Except that there is no real identification here. It mentions that he was married, but ends there."

"Leave that to me," says Femi. "Do you want to go to her?"

"It doesn't matter. Put me in a room with her and I can find her husband. Assuming, er ... that he's not in a mass grave somewhere."

"You are not funny, but still, good job. Take a break."

"When are you taking a break?"

"Kaaro, you may be mistaken as to the nature of our relationship."

"Oh, we have a relationship now?"

They house me in a dank, poorly lit en suite room which is part of the complex and does not exactly seem like a prison but cannot be far off. Maybe it is a retro-fitted jail cell.

First off, I take a monumental nervous shit. My belly always indicates when I am tense. The light in the toilet flickers with uncertainty. There is a bed with a brown cover, no pillow, and a chest of three drawers beside it. I open each in turn and find scraps of paper, a rubber band, a New Testament Bible (*Not For Sale!*) and an old biro. I lie on the bed and fish out my mobile phone, which they have returned to me. Good signal. They are probably monitoring any calls from it, but then they seem to know a lot about me already. I call Klaus.

It rings twice before connecting. "Hello, you," he says, though it sounds more like "Hellow, yew." His accent can be confusing at the best of times.

"You low, low, bottom-feeding, oath-breaking, deep-fried asshole motherfucker. When I finish this job—"

"Calm down, Kaaro."

"When I finish this job, I'm going to drive a steak knife into your eye sockets and twist. Then I'm going to beat your eyes into scrambled eggs."

"Omo, relax."

"Don't call me omo, I'm not your child. And don't tell me to fucking relax. You gave me up to the authorities."

"Are you finished?"

"No."

"Enough with your whining, Kaaro. Have you not been paid well?"

I had. Femi did not take the initial advance away from me, and had promised more.

"See? Do you see who is looking out for you? Did you think to give Klaus his twenty-five per cent? No. Instead you hurl insults and hurt my feelings."

"Shut up, Klaus. The only reason you would have gone along with this is if they shat a lump sum in US dollars right in front of you. And it's fifteen per cent."

"I think after this job you should take a vacation."

"If I'm still alive!"

"Don't be silly. If they kill you, they have to kill me, and I am not ready to see the heavenly gates just yet."

"You're going to the other place, fat boy."

"Again with the insults. Listen, I have many jobs lined up. Finish with those people and let's make rich, okay?"

Let's make rich. Mad motherfucker. After hanging up, I contemplate phoning my parents, but I do not wish to link them to me just in case S45 decides to harass them. I go to the window to look outside. The view is fake. About a foot from the window the fuckers have erected a massive painting of a blue sky and clouds. I punch the glass in frustration.

I sleep for an uncertain time, but it is dreamless and restful.

I open my eyes to find Femi and the short, muscular driver in my room. I yawn and sit up.

"Don't tell me, you love to watch me sleep. That's very romantic, Femi," I say.

"Get up. It's time to go to work," says Femi. "We've found Aloy Ogene's wife."

The driver drops a suit on the bed. "Put this on."

"I don't dress like this, man. Thanks, but can I see what else you have?"

The driver's eyes narrow.

"I'm just kidding. How the hell do you guys make it through a working day? You're all so serious."

I haven't dressed formally in about five years, but they got the size right, and while it isn't a label, it does fit and the fabric feels good on my skin. I plan to make a greater effort with clothes after this caper. Nike Onyemaihe's wisdom twists inside me, contorts against the idea of clothing made expensive by a name. I suppress this.

Three in the morning. The professor's wife is called Regina. The driver and I park outside her house, waiting for her to return from a job as a cleaner. She lives in New Ajegunle, which is much like Old Ajegunle in being a haven for the poverty-stricken and the criminal. Open gutters run alongside each road with the effluvium of desperate lives refusing to budge and leaving a miasma in the air. Children walk about, even at this hour, running unknown errands and staring at the car with envy and malice. Groups of smoking young men investigate, see the number plates and move on.

Only one street light works, but even that gives a weak and jaded view. The driver whistles a tune. He has ignored all of my overtures. Perhaps they have been instructed not to talk to me.

"That's her," says the driver.

Regina Ogene is a gaunt shadow creeping in the night. She walks as if in pain, and one of her feet drags slightly, like that of a stroke victim. She holds a handbag and opens the house gate with the other hand. She lives in a face-to-face, which is a bungalow with one central corridor that runs from front to back, and a row of rooms with doors opposite each other. Bath stalls and other facilities are shared in an outhouse at the back, and while it is not the worst accommodation available in Lagos, it is close. Very close.

"Femi should have come along," I say. "Look at me in this fucking suit. I'm going to frighten the lady."

"Show her the badge. Everybody cooperates when they see the badge."

I leave the car and catch up with the woman as she tries to open the front door.

"Mrs Ogene?" I ask.

"I don't have any money," says the woman. "Don't hurt me. There is some plantain in my bag. You can have that."

"I'm not a thief," I say, but that is not true, so I rephrase. "I'm not here to steal from you. I'm here about your husband, Aloysius Ogene."

She stops fiddling with the door. "I haven't seen him in years."

"I know. I just want to speak about him."

In the end, she only lets me inside when I show her the badge, for which I do not blame her. Suit or no, I do not cut a confidence-inspiring figure. Something about my posture or how my hands don't stay still or how much I talk all the time.

At first we are in darkness, with very little filtered light from a window. Regina strikes a match and lights a kerosene lantern, making the room come to life. She has a single metal-frame spring bed by the window, made up with ankara, which is not a fabric typically used as bed linen, except when the poverty bites hard. Some books rest in neat piles, forming columns rising to three feet, but the light is not good enough to read the titles by. She puts the lantern on one of the piles, next to a spent candle. The room holds a muggy, moist smell, but the smoke from the lantern displaces it.

She exhales, and sits on the bed. "You have something to say about my husband. Tell it to me."

Despite the worn-out clothes and the defeated air around her, Regina is a beautiful woman. She looks like she is in her mid-fifties, but her frame is thin and her eyes sharp, though narrow. She has an oval face and a small mouth with a large lower lip but a thin upper one. Life has given her many lines, which fan out the angles of her eyes and mouth.

"Mrs Ogene, I need to find the professor," I say. "Do you have any information that can help me?"

She smiles, the most bitter expression I have ever seen, and I have seen many.

"You people." She shakes her head.

"What do you mean?"

"Aloy went to work on 28 February 2044. I have not seen him since. Your people informed me that he had been arrested."

"My people?"

"Police! You informed me that he was a murderer and that he was being interrogated, that I would see him soon. Then you told me he had escaped, then that he attacked a prison guard and was shot and killed. Then that he was executed. The stories never end! I have no body, I have no gravesite, I have no official letter stating that he was dead or guilty. A year later, a constable dropped this off."

She opens a small box and places a broken pair of glasses on the table along with a pen and a book. The glasses have some of the lens left on the right-hand side, and light moves and twists on the surface. I look closer and can see scrolling text. It is one of those lens displays that were popular a while back. Whole Nimbus feeds on the go. Variety of power sources. Remarkable that this one is still functional, if broken.

"I'm sorry for your loss," I say. This is the right time to touch her, now that I have her thinking about the professor. It will make her trust me. I need a pretext while I wait for the knowledge to come.

"You are not like them," says Regina. "I don't think you're one of them."

"Why would you say that? Are you trying to hurt my feelings?"

Again the bitter smile. "You're too meek. You seem nervous, afraid even. You don't have the arrogance or air of danger they have, like children given live ammunition instead of toys."

"I can be dangerous."

"Is Kaaro your real name?" she asks. "Are you a real agent of S45?"

I sigh, and move from my standing position at the door. I sit on the table. "Mrs Ogene, I do work for S45, but I'm not an agent. They call me in for special assignments. It is important that I find your husband."

"So you do not believe him to be dead," says Regina.

"I don't know. Mrs Ogene, I would like to hold your hand."

"What?" She shrinks back.

"No, no, sorry. That's not what I mean." I hold up both hands. "I'm a finder, Mrs Ogene. I can find your husband, dead or alive."

She scoffs. "I have tried finders, Mr Kaaro. Criminals, all of them. They took my money and sent me to places no decent woman should have to visit. And for what? I was almost raped once because I went ... " She gathers herself, takes deep breaths. "Finders are no help. People like you are frauds, and the ones that are not fake are thieves."

"I am a thief," I say. I decide to be honest, or as honest as I can be without implicating myself. "Or rather, I was. I stopped doing that a while back."

"What does S45 want with my husband?"

"They don't want him. They want someone they think he's with, someone who may have taken him."

"And you will bring him back to me?"

"I don't know if he's alive."

"If he is dead, will you bring me his body?"

I nod, and she holds out her hands. I take them, skipping the display I reserve for my customers and marks.

The room changes, the darkness sweeps in, and I feel myself lost in rushing winds as if falling from an aeroplane or rotating in a tornado. Regina Ogene is gone, nowhere. My body is gone, disintegrated in a thousand criss-crossing light rays. Not ordinary light. This light has swirls and curves, crayon marks made by a bored God.

What the fuck. What the fuck. What the fuck.

I cannot speak. It is not wind. It is I who am rushing. My ... presence, my consciousness keeps moving and changing direction too fast for me to think. Alternating light and dark, shadow and flash, a rainbow of impossible colours, extended spectrum. I want to stop, to get off, to find my bearings. The weightlessness, the lack of a single vector, the loss of control … is this dying?

What did Regina Ogene do to me?

I let go of the tenuous control I had and scream into the void. Without lungs you can scream for ever, and I do.

Chapter Seventeen

Lagos, Rosewater, Akure, Kano, Abuja, others: 2066

Now

There are three figures around my car when I emerge from Femi's house. It is dark and I can't tell their genders, but they examine my vehicle like ants around a sugar cube. They may be thieves, but more likely they are from S45. I spy an idling SUV about fifty yards away. It is similar to every other one used by the agency.

They spot me, which is not difficult seeing as I am just across the road. Running is not an option – I'm still stiff and slow from my injuries.

"There he is," says one.

I draw my gun from the holster.

"Gun!" says a second.

"No, he never carries."

I pull the trigger. I hear an almighty bang and the flash almost blinds me. The kick is so strong I drop the weapon. Deliberately.

"What the fuck?"

They take cover, surprised.

"I told you it was a gun," says the second man, in a plain-tive voice.

One of them likes strawberry ice cream and resents being out here. This is how I know the xenosphere is back. The shot still rings in my ears and it's difficult to concentrate, but I am desperate. My mind expands outwards – I am told that when in the xenosphere, my brain's electrical activity is like an epileptic seizure. One of the men is of the cult known as the Machinery and is thinking of pain as malfunction. I have no time to be gentle. I tell their nerve endings, the temperature receptors, that they are burning, that there is flame all around. The men begin to scream and roll around on the ground, thrashing about. If I had time, I could make their skin blister with partial-thickness burns, but I am in a hurry. I flee on foot, on the margins of pain.

I know that I can only evade S45 for a short time, but it's crucial that I download what's in my implant before they catch up with me. I first think of Klaus. He'll know a lowlife with the necessary technology and flexibility of morals. But then I think of my last visit to Lagos.

I cut through an alley and have to bat away the leaves of wild sugar cane. I can hear traffic, but it is muffled. I will never wear a gun again. What was I thinking?

I come to a road busier than Femi's. I wait, calming myself, looking for evidence of a defensive perimeter. I am not a pri-ority. If I were, there would be a drone tracking me. I look around for COB cats, but I see none. I pick a taxi out of traffic and pay him up front to take me to Olusosun. I tell him I will pay double if he will shut the fuck up.

*

Bad Fish fiddles with a machine. He works in a Celestial Church white robe. Olusosun used to host a thriving market with a tiny rubbish dump beside it. The dump grew and the market failed. As it covered a larger area, scavengers moved in – a growing local economy. The tech scavengers can be seen everywhere in Africa, picking bits and bobs of retrieved technology and repurposing laptops and implants, performing identity hacks, building illegal new configurations of what already exists.

With a lot of charm, money, and some xenosphere manipulation, I am given audience. The workspace is cloaked by bespoke scan jammers. It can only be seen by human eyes or directed satellite. Bad Fish and his cohorts are post-hackers, survivalist entrepreneurs. Olusosun Dump is his home and he is a Celestial in many ways. He is the best of a group of blindingly intelligent tech wizards who ply their trade here, in the twilight.

"You have an Ariyo chip," says Bad Fish.

"If you say so. Is that bad?"

"Be still. Not bad, just ... old. But old is good."

"Why?"

"Easier to manipulate."

Bad Fish hands me an old tablet. The screen is dark, a directory is open and there is a list of folders.

"This is everything on your implant. I can print—"

"No," I say.

"Do you want it uploaded to Nimbus?"

"No. Too dangerous for both of us."

"Don't worry about me. Where do you want the data?"

I think for a second. "Download the data to the tablet then block all connections so that it's a local device. Disable its ability to connect with anything. Delete the files from my chip. And clear any of your RAM that may contain it."

It takes him less than a minute. "Done."

"Bad Fish, I can read your mind. I know you intend to keep a copy and will attempt to extort money from me."

"I—"

"I don't blame you for trying, but I warn you: don't. I'll know if you do."

"I—"

"Thank you."

I hollow out a gigantic King James Bible and seal the tablet in it. I go to a courier service and send it to myself at Rosewater.

I am ready to be captured now. I take a taxi to the Bar Beach, buy some suya, and sit eating on a small sand dune until I hear footsteps.

I go quietly.

I have never been to any of S45's Lagos field offices. This is where I videoconference with Eurohen. I am treated well. I have a Diet Coke and shortbread biscuits on the table beside me. I enquire after the men I "burned" and am told they are well, but shaken. I send them apologies by proxy. The boss keeps me waiting for twenty-one minutes before the plasma field springs to life.

"Kaaro! It's a pleasure to finally meet you." Eurohen's voice is effeminate, but enthusiastic.

"Unfortunately, I cannot say the same."

"Ah, I see. Loyalty to Femi Alaagomeji. Good. Excellent. I like that."

I swear the guy has blond highlights in his hair.

"You like history, Kaaro?"

"Not particularly."

"I do. The Gulf of Gela, Sicily, 11 July 1943. A friendly-fire incident led to the shooting down of twenty-three C-47 aircrafts. One hundred and fifty-seven servicemen lost their lives, and over two hundred were wounded. Do you know this story?"

"No."

"It doesn't matter. What you need to learn, the takeaway message, is that a lack of coordination of resources costs lives."

There's an undercurrent of irritation here, so I stay silent.

"From now on, coordination. Laser focus. All parts working together. Agencies, arms of government, parties—"

"Excuse me," I say. "Sir, I am miles away from my home base. I'd like to go home tonight. What are you saying, exactly?"

"I want you to trust me."

"Then meet me in a room with contiguous air."

"Oh, I intend to. I have nothing to hide."

That's new. Stops me in my tracks.

"I have a whole new focus for you, for sensitives. Mrs Alaagomeji was ... competent, but she lacked vision."

"I have a focus, sir, an interrogation."

"That's not focus. It's an assignment. What I want is for you to join a church."

"What?"

"Do you not feel the love of our Lord and Saviour?" He smiles.

"Get to the fucking point," I say.

"Calm down, agent. You still work for me." He did not seem annoyed. I wish I had time to read the file they had on me before this meeting.

"I'm sorry, sir."

"Think nothing of it. In fact, think to yourself, what would Jesus do?"

"He'd say 'get thee behind me, Satan' under these circumstances. Sir."

Eurohen laughs. "I want you to join a church, a big one with a congregation of millions. I want you to gain their trust using your abilities, and when the time comes, I will instruct you on how to use that trust."

"A church outside Rosewater?"

"Might be, yes."

"So I'd have to leave the city?"

"You sound disappointed. I thought you didn't like it here. Weren't you ordered to stay in the first place?"

"That's true, sir."

"Good. Now we're ordering you to leave."

On my way back, I watch the street lights pass me like UFOs. I've been here so long that I've never contemplated leaving. After a few years of living around the dome, my antipathy eroded into apathy, but at some point even that turned into a sense of being home. I definitely don't want to start all over again in Lagos, Abuja or Kaduna, and there's Aminat to think of. My flat texts ambient conditions to me. Temperature twenty-seven Celsius, humidity eighty-nine per cent, wind two miles per hour. No intrusions.

The radio informs me that "Woo-woo" is now the number one single and Clayton is back in the charts. Back in the late 2050s, their style of free verse over atonal music was considered cool, but ... ugh. The whole shitty thing fits my mood. I switch to an oldies station.

I am allowed to finish my current case – the interrogation – before they get me doing God's work, which is fine, because I'm curious about what Tolu Eleja is hiding, and success will put me in a good negotiating position when discussing my next assignment.

If I live that long.

My night is full of guilty dreams and sex with Molara. The next day I take delivery of the tablet, with all the information Femi sent to my implant. I power it on and start to read.

I check my personnel file first because I need to know what they are holding over my head. I am relieved at the demographic data. It lists me as "last name unknown". This means Femi found out my surname but kept it to herself. There is the usual: home address, religious affiliation (none or unknown), height (5' 10"), weight (170 lb), race (black), ethnic group (Yoruba), date of birth (uncertain).

There is a free-text entry by Femi.

Kaaro started working for us in 2055. We sought him out because our sensitives were unable to find Oyin Da, aka Bicycle Girl, which was a priority for the administration at the time. Bicycle Girl had some uncertain involvement in the disappearance of all the inhabitants of the village of Arodan in 2044. Since then she has been a symbol of anarchy. In her talks, she appears to have a neo-socialist bent.

According to Professor Ileri, who trained him, Kaaro is the most powerful psychic operator known to us. He was able to grasp multiple

domains of function within a short time. Ileri
hypothesised that this was not due to Kaaro's
inherent ability, but to skills he seemed
to have been taught by someone called Nike
Onyemaihe (relationship unknown at the time of
writing). As a finder he is unparalleled. The
Bicycle Girl incident in 2055 was his greatest
triumph as well as his most dismal failure.
The subsequent creation of the do—

That hurts, and I skip ahead. I don't need to be reminded of
that fiasco, and I know how good I am with the xenosphere.

When suitably motivated, Kaaro can be a
valuable asset. That said, he is sexist, materialistic, greedy, insolent and amoral. When he
was young, he stole regularly even though his
parents were not struggling financially. He is
not violent and does not tolerate the threat of
violence well. To recruit him we used a combination of these factors, offering his freelance
rate of pay as well as exposing him to extreme
violence done to others.

He has not formed any long-term relationships and his psychological profile suggests
that this is related to a fractious relationship with his mother. Initially when I met
him he would use humour and garrulousness to
create distance between himself and others.
After the biodome incident he became withdrawn
and did things automatically, without passion.

> He lives alone, has no pets and no real
> friends, and as far as I know does not live for
> anything. He is considered a low to moderate
> suicide risk should the right conditions occur.

Suicide risk? Me? Meh.

I close my file and concentrate on the other stuff, the details of other sensitives and the information on what's causing the decline. I read everything three times, taking no notes, coming to no judgements.

Most of it is bland personal data: dates of birth, addresses and current assignments. Most important to me are the contact details for Professor Ileri. There are cursory theories about the problem of the dying sensitives, but it is all vague and diffuse, experts hedging to keep their own position. Nobody knows what is happening, but it seems to have started over the last five years. It took a while for them to notice and the statisticians had to account for local morbidity and mortality data.

Theories run wild. The sensitives are committing suicide. The Chinese sent an experimental virus to copy the xenoform variants on our skin with a view to creating their own synthetic strain. The sensitives were weak stock to start with and this made them vulnerable to the alien infection in the first place. Act of God. Act of Satan. Act of terrorism. Natural extinction of what was already a minor aberration. And so on.

I stand up and stretch. My phone has run out of charge and I am hungry. The stories of the dying sensitives swirl around in my mind. The one tasked with trying to get the truth out of a prisoner by monitoring dreams while pretending to be a cellmate. The one helping doctors research mental illness by exploring the xenosphere of patients. The team of twenty who formed a hive mind which worked well until one became unwell and caused a mental breakdown in all the rest. The undying sensitive whose personality pattern persists and haunts the xenosphere.

I definitely do not wish to cook. I have a hankering for street food, so I leave what I'm doing and take a walk in the early-evening light. The dome is dull today. I meet one or two of the reconstituted but otherwise just normal people wandering about, returning from evening shifts or hawking things on the street. Two armed soldiers walk by on a casual patrol. They wear desert camo and have implant scanners on their helmets. They both stare at me, probably because of my "do not impede" status. They are probably wondering who this soft old man could be; maybe he bribed someone to get the alteration on his chip. They are leftovers from the cull detail, although the government is still twitchy about terrorists.

To the east of the city there are tree-covered hills that rise out of the Yemaja valley. I can see the rises from here, above the skyline. I explored them once in '59, spent a week with the hardy, scraggly, tough but compassionate tribe that scratches out a living there. The people were kind to me, always offering me food or wine, looking after the helpless and hapless city person. Their thoughts were genuine too, no hypocrisy.

They use minimal technology, but are happy. They see the dome as a supernatural phenomenon and want no part of it. They told me of being harried by egbere who live within the forest. I suspect that these evil spirits are aliens who, like the floaters, have somehow found their way out of the biodome.

The tribe's rules are simple, but more evolved than the *lex talionis* that ruled Camp Rosewater in '55. Look at us now. We have road signs and parking fines.

A family of Machinery stride past with that regular gait of theirs, jerking me back to the present. Wankers to bring up a child like that.

I walk west along streets that are mostly residential. Palm trees line the pavements at irregular intervals, most of them bearing posters of Jack Jacques. Cars drive by, some blasting loud hip hop. I forgot to apply ketoconazole to my skin before leaving the house, and the xenosphere is ablaze with thoughts and emotions of random people. It takes a fair bit of concentration to maintain my goal. I come to a row of three stands on the side of the road. The first is a Hausa man who roasts spiced meat over an open flame. Suya. He serves it with chopped tomatoes, onions and a powdered spice that includes garlic, ground nuts and cumin. His name is Ahmed and it is his food that I seek. There is a bench beside him where one customer waits. I sit next in line. The other vendors sell fried yams and plantain.

Ahmed knows me and nods as he quietly goes about chopping meat and selecting strips, moving them around to get optimal flame and squirting groundnut oil on others. His daughter Kahlela, who is six, plays close by, talking to herself the way only children do. The way I once did. She has a whole pantheon of imaginary friends, but she would really prefer to play with her father. For a child, she has a complex understanding of interactions. Ahmed is concerned about his wife's fidelity. This is because of a Nimbus video that a friend of his shared. A naked woman bearing a striking similarity to Ahmed's wife inserting household objects into her most intimate parts, no charge to viewers. He does not know how to broach the subject. He has seen the video seventy-two times and is still not sure if it's her or not.

There is a radio on, battery- and solar-powered, used to entertain customers. It's broadcasting a programme about America, and the economic collapse of the 2020s. The man beside me is of the Machinery, and he sits stock still, like an automaton. He looks straight ahead and I know he will continue to do so until prompted by either myself or Ahmed. The Machinery are a bunch of fuckwits who believe that the human body is best conceptualised as a machine, and that if behaviour is stripped down to only what is functional, a higher form of humanity will emerge. This means actions that lead to the fulfilment of their basic needs only. Disease is a malfunction. You can see where this goes. They're boring as hell, they only speak to convey information, and they are more inflexible than actual machines. They are said to be good spouses and accountants. The one beside me has a distinct self-image, fully identified as a machine. He repeats to himself mentally, "You are a machine, you are a machine." Usually the Machinery are secular, but this one struggles with a separation from extended family and church.

While the aroma of open-flame-roasted beef tickles my nostrils I realise that I'll have to seek out Ileri and get some answers.

While I wait, Yaro the mongrel pads up to me. When my batch of suya is ready, I feed him scraps. He eats with enthusiasm and stares up at me wagging his tail, expectant. I scratch behind his ears.

"What's this, boy?"

There is a wound on his flank, infected.

"We need to get you to a vet," I say.

Ahmed says something about the dog being dead in a week. Yaro picked up the wound a few weeks ago when he got into a fight with three larger dogs while trying to protect me. He occasionally walks me from the station and believes I belong to him. I hope he doesn't die. I feed him a quarter of my food.

On my way home, three teenagers kick a reanimate who is stuck in the open gutter at the side of the road. They take turns and swing their feet like its head is a football. I think of intervening, but change my mind and keep walking.

By the time I get back to my flat, I have decided. I open my safe and take out what cash is inside. I have a car, but it's tagged by S45 and I ignore it. I've got the buggy I used to use back in '56, but it's so distinctive and old that people would stare. I change my clothes, pack a light bag, and leave again. I contemplate stealing a car. As soon as I think the thought, I see multiple pathways to opening three vehicles right on my street and I am tempted. Stealing is like alcohol dependency. I have to recognise that I will always be a thief, albeit one who no longer steals.

I can't steal a car. It will draw attention.

In the end I take an okada – a motorbike taxi – which drops me off at a rental place. I am not used to the car and have a minor collision with one of the carbon scrubbers that line the motorway, but nobody is hurt.

I start in Abuja.

Temi is posted in Aso Rock, her standing assignment having to do with foreign delegates. I park outside her house in one of the suburbs and wind the windows down. I taste the xenosphere, but there is no sign of the serpent she uses. This does not mean anything; she may have changed her avatar, although sensitives rarely do.

I press the buzzer at the gate, but nobody answers. Abuja's landscape has undulations, and you can see Aso Rock and the presidential villa from here. I'm staring at it when someone nudges me. I look down at a girl on a bicycle, hanging her elbows off the handlebars, smiling.

"Hi," she says in English.

"Hello," I say.

"Are you Auntie Temi's friend?"

"Yes."

She tilts her head to one side. "How come I've never seen you?"

"I'm an old friend. We went to school together," I say. Which is more or less true. "Do you know where she is?"

"Yes. She's in heaven. She died last week. There is nobody in the house."

"How did she die?" I ask, my palms feeling sweaty and uncomfortable.

The girl shrugs. "She was sick, my mother drove her to hospital, and she didn't come back."

I find what's left of John Bosco in a seminary in Enugu, to the east of Nigeria. He had been assigned to keep track of the thoughts of radical students in the universities. He has been dead for six months, given the honour of being buried in the military cemetery. His gravestone is a small, irregular bit of marble, with a smooth face stating his name. No descendants. Aside from Bola, I have not known sensitives to have children.

It occurs to me that I have never heard the call to bury an outstanding sensitive like I did when I was young. Are there not enough of us left, or are we just not notable?

I access the xenosphere. It is empty, barren and desolate. I marshal my thoughts and build a twenty-foot tombstone in a grassy meadow. I cap it with a statue of the monk-like avatar John favoured. I carve on the stone a simple message:

HERE LIES JOHN BOSCO.
HE SERVED HIS COUNTRY.

If any of our kind come this way, they will see it.

Ebun is a teacher in Akure, not on assignment.

She is in a coma.

I try to access her avatar, but I cannot decipher anything. It's as if even her conceptual self has dissipated. It is like trying to grasp wind. There is nothing in the xenosphere to respond to me.

When I find the grief in the atmosphere too overwhelming, I leave.

It takes two days of travelling and phone calls, but I track my targets down.

The class of '55, all ten of us, either dead or dying. Drake on a palliative care ward, dying. Ebun comatose. John Bosco dead. Temi dead. Kolawole, Nuru, Mojibola, Akpan deceased, unknown illness. Chukwuebuka missing, presumed dead on assignment. I leave xenosphere monuments for them all, as much as I can. Towards the end I am exhausted, and I cannot imagine anything more than a black monolith.

This is disturbing. I figure I will go through the contact details of the other sensitives, the ones I did not know, but I already see the pattern.

I come home tired, saddle-worn, afraid. I return the rental, get an okada back to my flat and start thinking of what's next.

When I get home Aminat is waiting. I have forgotten all about her and I start to apologise, but she silences me with a gesture.

"Bola's dead," she says.

Chapter Eighteen

Lagos: 2055

Then

I calm down. I do not know where I am, but I am not afraid of being lost. I am a finder, and the most basic skill of a finder is getting home.

Weightless. Weightlessness is never good. I know I am not in outer space. What have I been doing? A job of some kind. Around me are hundreds of light corridors of various colours and thicknesses. Each seems to radiate away from my position. The lights are akin to a laser show and are inconstant. They flick in and out. Some remain steady but move up and down, or describe arcs. Others appear only once.

Nice show. I flail my arms and set myself in a spin, head over arse over head, repeat ad infinitum. The only sound is this constant hiss, which is familiar to me. I keep turning over, although I am not nauseated. No gravity per se. I hope movement isn't by swimming motions here, because I cannot swim.

Am I dead? Is this the hell of people who cannot swim?

I remember being in Regina Ogene's house, trying to find her husband for Femi. As soon as I think this, the lights multiply and multiply again, increasing until they are too dazzling to look at. The hiss becomes louder. I close my eyes and cover my ears, but it makes no difference. I still *sense* the light and hear the hiss.

"Oh shit," I say.

I know where I am and understand the problem. I am locked inside my own mind. I am not sure why, but Aloy is in multiple places at once. Hundreds, maybe thousands of places. My ability is directing me to all of them, and it is too much input. How the motherfucker managed to do that does not concern me, but I need to find a way out of my crashed brain. Since this has never happened before, I have no idea how to go about it. One thing is sure: I can't think about Regina, Aloysius or the fucking Bicycle Girl.

I find a memory.

Spinning, spinning, spinning.

I steal a car, a Mazda hatchback, and drive it towards the lagoon, although the petrol runs out before I reach water. I stand on the road, waiting. A car stops.

Klaus.

Cigar-smoking Belgian motherfucker, who picks me off the road and asks me what I am good at.

"Stealing," I say.

Klaus laughs. "You don't smell like someone good at stealing."

"You have a total of fourteen hundred dollars in this car. Two hundred dollars on you in a hip wallet, and the rest in the boot in a bag," I say.

Klaus turns to stare, ignoring the road. "How did you do that?"

I shrug.

Klaus drives me to a hotel and shoves me into the lobby. "Do it again."

I pick people at random and describe what valuables they have and where they are hidden. I do this for twenty minutes, then Klaus asks me to steal something to prove it. I steal a gold watch, a wedding ring and a Transformers toy.

"Why the toy?" asks Klaus.

"It was valued by the child as much as an adult would value a Bentley. I was attracted to the intensity with which the boy loved it."

That is the start of my relationship with Klaus.

Except it wasn't, and I realise that this memory isn't mine. It's Nike Onyemaihe's. I didn't meet Klaus on a roadside. I met him when Nike died.

The Belgian recognises a niche in the twilight trade, the market where odd favours are exchanged and money is often an afterthought. I find money and people for him. On one memorable occasion I find a lost artefact in a museum, misfiled and dying under the weight of an overgrown bureaucracy. This makes the news, although only a photo of me makes it into the report. I grin beside the professor, who thinks I am the second coming. Later Klaus points out that the item is worth six million dollars.

My income is steady, but unimpressive. I try to reconcile with my parents, but they have moved and nobody will tell me where they went. I could find them, but they do not want to be found. I leave them alone to respect their wishes.

Klaus is my pimp, prostituting my finder's skill with verve. Like all pimps, he takes on a role that mixes paternalism and exploitation. I don't care as long as I can go to clubs and spend some cash from time to time. I do not save much.

"Have you ever read Seneca?" asks Klaus.

We are in one of his cars, a Honda this time, driving to Victoria Island.

I answer in the negative.

He quotes: "*No good thing renders its possessor happy, unless his mind is reconciled to the possibility of loss.*"

"So what are you telling me? I shouldn't buy shit?"

"You complicate the equation because people like you, with your abilities, you neutralise the possibility of loss," says Klaus. "I am wondering how much you neutralise happiness."

"Parents are happy when I find their lost children," says I. Except my mother and father, but I keep that to myself.

Klaus wags his finger. "Children are not possessions. That's what most parents do not understand. They are custodians, not owners."

"Fine, whatever."

"I have a client for you. Quality."

"Where?"

"Seven Sons Beer Parlour. Tomorrow. Do not fuck this up, Kaaro. She paid cash just for me to set up the meet."

"Okay."

"Listen, you can't go slobbering over this one. Keep your torpedo in the tubes. This is upper crust, my friend. Icing. Not the dregs you're used to."

"How does she look?"

Klaus takes a deep breath and exhales noisily. "She looks like an angel walked into your dreams and fucked the perfect girl you have wanked to since you were twelve until the perfect girl got pregnant, had a daughter and brought her up on milk and honey until she finally left your dreams and materialised in front of you."

I whistle.

"Indeed. Believe me, her shit does not stink."

When I think of Femi, the spinning shifts gears, slows down. I remember her perfume and the lift of her breasts, and the silly pout around her mouth. The tubes of light resolve into one tunnel.

I aim for it and am born into more light.

I wake in a hospital. White walls, white sheets, white ceiling with a ventilator above me. Phallic rubber tube down my throat. I attempt to remove that, but find my arms tethered with an IV tube on one side and a monitor clip on the other. To my left, a fifty-inch display screen pulsates with knowledge about my condition. It seems to throb with an excitement at every peak and trough of my vital signs, which makes me very uncomfortable. I remove the tubes, monitors and intravenous fluid lines. I don't bother looking for clothes. I do not hesitate. In the hospital gown, I leave the room, knowing that the single guard has taken a nature break. I go down the corridor barefoot and unerringly end up in a changing room, where I pick up a bunch of keys that someone has dropped. I put on theatre scrubs from the freshly laundered pile, pick up a lost wallet, and leave the building wearing the equivalent of green pyjamas. In the car park I walk right to the Volvo, use the key from the found ring to open it, and drive away.

I am in a daze, and part of me suspects I might still be in that dream, that contaminated coma world. I think only of Femi, and speed up. I discard the vehicle fifty yards from her home, engine running, door open. Let the area boys joyride it.

I ring the bell outside the forbidding fence and stand in the light so that the cameras can pick me up. After a minute, a door cut into the metal gate swings open and I pass through. I walk down a short palm-tree-lined drive and she meets me at the front door. She has her right wrist to her mouth as if she is smelling a perfume sample, but she is talking. Probably has a phone implant. She is casual, wearing sweat pants and a loose white pullover, with a colourful scarf binding her hair.

"You have just got someone fired," says Femi. "You shouldn't have been able to walk away from the hospital."

"Can I get a hug?"

"No."

"Come on. I've been sick."

"You still are if you think I'm going to hug you. How did you escape?"

"I'm a finder, Femi. I can escape from anywhere."

"Come inside."

She steps aside, and gestures towards the interior of the house. As I pass her, I steal a kiss. It lands on her lips and her knee lands right in the centre of my crotch. I fall to the marble floor and clutch my genitals, curled up into a foetal position and resisting the overwhelming urge to vomit. The pain is a visceral thing, shooting up and down my body in successive waves. I lick my lips through the red haze and smile at how she stares down at me.

"Totally worth it," I say in English.

Later, I sit at her dining table sipping Hennessy.

"This *is* the quality. Klaus was right about you," I say.

"And I'm starting to think he was wrong about you," says Femi. She sits opposite me and seems to have forgiven my indiscretion. "You haven't done the job you were contracted to do."

"Yeah, I've been thinking about that. Where's Regina Ogene?"

"Safe."

"Can we get to her?"

"I can have you at her location in fifteen minutes."

"Good. I've been thinking about what I read in the files and some rumours I've heard while drinking or at work. Do you know what the Lijad is?"

She shakes her head.

"Neither do I, but I've heard tell. It appears and disappears today in Enugu, tomorrow in Lokoja. It's never in the same place longer than an hour. It moves so fast sometimes that it is thought to be in two places at once." I act like I know, but it all comes second-hand from Alhaji.

"What does it look like?"

"Nobody knows." This is not entirely true. I remember my drunken encounter with the Bicycle Girl outside a bar.

"Then why are we talking about it?"

"Because I think your Bicycle Girl is in the Lijad."

Interlude: Mission

Rosewater: 2059

All hail the Ocampo inverter!

I am waiting to be picked up.

Kaaro ... Kaaro ... diphthongs. Dip your tongue.

I shake the thought out of my head. I am standing in the shade of a kiosk, watching the launch of the North Ganglion Power Station. There is a canopy, and a stage where a few official muckity-mucks pontificate. The feedback from the PA system is horrendous. It worsens my headache. There is a small crowd, maybe a hundred people. A few stands are interspersed among the people, bearing scale model reproductions of the power plant. There is one right beside me. There are bottles of champagne up on the stage, and some fizzy shandy drink for the hoi polloi. I am tempted to drink but I don't want the bubbles to worsen my headache. I have to concentrate to keep other people's thoughts out of my head.

These days I use ketoconazole. It seems to work better than clotrimazole. The problem is the thick layer on my skin makes me sweat in the afternoon sun. And I think I smell.

This close, the biodome looms over everything, and

everybody in Rosewater glances at it every hour, as if it has apotropaic powers. I look at the model station. A team of scientists finally figured out how to exploit electricity from Wormwood's ganglia in order to power the city. This time last week the air would have been split with the din of petrol and diesel generators. Fights occasionally broke out when people discovered that neighbours had tapped electricity from them by means of extra-long extension cables.

Until now, the most construction we've seen around both north and south ganglia has been elaborate warnings and fences. Both ganglia are skirted black with carbonised flesh from the dead. Animals and birds know to keep clear, yet even though we are at the top of the food chain, humans don't have enough sense to avoid the area.

Nobody has been able to explain why Wormwood would leave two pylons of nervous tissue out in the air. Some say it uses them to broadcast thoughts; others that it harvests the thoughts of people. Speculation within S45 is that they serve as sensory organs and weapons. Me, I think Wormwood wants us to exploit the electricity the way we are now. It's not really malicious the way humans are, but you need to have met it to know this.

I remember a drunken night when I tried to link with the South Ganglion, to see if I could find Oyin Da or Anthony or anyone on the other side of the biodome. I got no humans, but in the thought stream there were entities made of electricity, elementals, friendly. They were sentient, I think, but we did not understand each other. They had no physical form, but moulded their charges to mimic my body. I was surrounded by eight of them frolicking around. They projected imagery that I did not understand, although occasionally there was an asteroid or a space station and a moonscape covered with countless machines. Of Wormwood's thoughts I understood nothing at all. The nature was too alien without Anthony to translate.

The scientists use the Ocampo inverter and all of a sudden we can connect to the national grid, right voltage, right frequency. DC to AC. You can still see the ganglion, but nobody unauthorised will get near it since there is a building around it as well as security.

Kaaro ... Kaaro ... diphthongs. Dip your tongue.

I look at the people milling about. They will be getting their first ever electricity bills because, hey, Ocampo inverters don't come cheap. On the other hand, self-drive cars might become widespread.

Estimated population, three million. Come for the healing, stay for what exactly? What unites the citizens of Rosewater? The lure of the alien? I even ask myself. I am ordered to be here, stationed here, but it has the emotional pull of home. I am a Lagosian. I do not miss Lagos, but I am from there. At some point, between 2055 and now, I lost the affinity for Eko Ile.

Dip your—

Dip.

Detonator. Check the detonator.

I stand straighter. That is a clear determined thought from someone in the crowd. Shit, it's a fucking suicide bomber. I check the time. My pickup isn't here. I hate suicide bombers. Their heads are always full of mushy rhetoric, faulty logic and grim fucking resolve. Just after they activate the detonator there is some regret, but still. I fucking hate suicide bombers. I briefly wonder if I can just wander away, ignore this and change the rendezvous point, but I know that won't work. My implant tracks me, tells them where I've been. It won't do for the record to show that I was here minutes before some fanatic detonated a load of C-4.

Where the fuck are you, piece of shit?

I don't have my gun. Brilliant, Kaaro.

Fuck are you . . . ?

It's disorienting doing this with my eyes open and while scanning the crowd visually, but I can't take any chances.

Got him. He's wearing a crash helmet and agbada, working his way towards the stage. He wants maximum carnage. I can't stop him from here, but I phone dispatch.

"Identification?"

I give it.

"Situation?"

I can't remember the code.

"There's a bomber, a vest."

"Caller, I need—"

"Yes, a code. I can't remember, but a whole bunch of people will die if you don't act right now." I speak in an urgent whisper. In my mind I can hear the batshit suicide bomber rhetoric warming up.

"I'm on your location."

"Is there a bird?"

"Affirmative. Localise."

"Blue crash helmet, grey cotton fabric."

"I've tagged the target. Neutralise in three."

"Roger, dispatch. Out."

It's not quite three seconds. My arm isn't even by my side when the drone shoots a high-speed, high-impact adhesive round. The shock wave throws most of the people around my bomber into the air like bits of chaff. At the centre is a brown congealed mass, like a frozen splash of water. Four people including my bomber are caught in the trap, sealed, unable to move. I'm fascinated. I've never seen this before, although I've been briefed about it.

All the celebrants rush from the stage, and people disperse, stampeding. Except me. I walk in the opposite direction, towards the adhesive trap. There are no thoughts coming from inside, perhaps because even xenoforms can't survive in there.

Kaaro . . . Kaaro . . . diphthongs. Dip your tongue.

Like this?

Mmm.

My pickup arrives. Dayo. Ferrying me is beneath her, but she volunteered because we have history, and in this game you take whatever pleasure you can get, wherever you can find it.

She's driving an old jeep, internal combustion. She smiles as she pulls up, and she remembers what I remember.

"That was very heroic," she says.

"I don't do heroics," I say. "You kept distracting me by thinking that stuff at me. That's not what the professor trained you for, you know, and it could have been risky for me."

She laughs. "You can walk and chew gum. Are you in a hurry, or do we go halves on a room like last time?"

I'm definitely going to be late for debriefing. "Ah, fuck it, why not?"

Later, when Femi finds out I didn't report on time, she is incandescent with rage. I switch off my phone for twenty-four hours to make things worse, and because I like it when Femi uses colourful language.

Chapter Nineteen

Rosewater: 2066

Now

"Where have you been?" says Aminat.

I do not answer at first. I open my apartment door and let her in. She is shaking, though whether with anger, cold or grief I am yet to find out.

"Dealing with some work stuff," I say. I lead her to the sofa.

"I called and called."

"I had to ignore my phone. I went to Lagos," I say. "What can I get you to drink?"

"I thought ... you and I ... "

"I was busy, Aminat. Calm down."

"Do not tell me to calm down." She snaps off each word, each consonant crisp with the force of her rage.

"I know you're upset, but I've had a weird time and I'm getting a drink. Do you want one?" She is wearing a sleeveless top, but even from where I stand I can see the goose flesh on her shoulders. I get us both Jack Daniel's because ... well, it's what I want and she's not saying a damn thing. She holds the glass, but does not sip.

"How did Bola die?" I ask.

"She got up briefly after you visited her. Walked around the house, chatted with her kids, did some paperwork to do with finances, asked to see her will. It's as if she knew she was going to die. She phoned me, or I phoned her. I can't remember which. We talked and she joked with me, told me she loved me, asked about you. I got a message the next morning that she didn't wake up."

She blurts this out and there is a lack of inflection to her words, a blankness to her face. She's in shock, almost entranced. Her forehead glistens.

"I'm really sorry—"

"Stop. Don't even say that. What did you do? What did you do to her? Did you kill her?"

"What? No. Why would I—"

"Then what did you do?"

I sigh. "Aminat, you know what we do, right? You know something of what Bola and I are. Were. I mean . . . you know about sensitives?"

"You're psychics. You can tell if there's an attack on the bank."

"Well, yes, sort of. Bola developed an illness that only affects our kind. The idea of a deceased person, a loved one, especially if this person was a spouse, it takes root and becomes a persistent memory pattern." I don't know how much to tell her. Most people have some idea that there are people like me, but do not understand the full extent. The details of the xenosphere being composed of alien microorganisms is classified. From a lay person's perspective, psychics were once unreliable and have been more reliable since 2012 or thereabouts. I have to be careful what I tell Aminat.

"And?" she says. She finally samples the Jack.

"I helped to remove that pattern. It was of Dominic. There is no reason for her to have died from my actions, so it must have been something else." I do not say that whatever it was may be causing the death of many like me.

She stares at me with bloodshot eyes. I do not expect her to cry, as she has probably done a lot of that already. Emotion from her is pawing at the xenosphere, but I resist the temptation. Upset people are the easiest to read.

"Why don't you get some rest," I say. "Sleep a bit. Do you have to phone your office?"

"I already have." She drains the drink and lifts the glass in my direction. "Another."

I oblige.

Soon she is asleep on the couch. I consider taking her to the bedroom, but I don't want to wake her. I just remove her shoes, adjust her legs and cover her with a wrap.

Bola is dead. I allow that to hit me and I feel the grief. We all loved her a little, and she was always pretty decent to me. Then self-preservation kicks in: I have been exposed to her. Do I have what she had? Am I even now incubating the seeds of a destructive pestilence that will kill me? I need more information. I decide to check what psychic residue Bola has left behind.

"Double lock," I say, and the apartment seals the front door and windows with steel bars. I go to my bedroom, to the dresser, and open the bottom drawer. I have an ancient pack of Benson & Hedges and a lighter. I sit at the foot of my bed, on the floor. I quit smoking years ago, but what I am about to do is difficult and dangerous. In order to make it work I need a ritual, and lighting a cigarette is part of that.

"Sound, bedroom only, Marvin Gaye, 'I Heard It Through the Grapevine', low volume."

As soon as the percussion hits, I select a cigarette, push it slowly between my lips and light it. Reality eddies as I view it through the haze of cigarette smoke. I take two lungfuls, then put the cigarette out in my empty glass. I exhale, focusing on the billows of smoke rising to the ceiling.

I recall snatches of Professor Ileri's voice.

What we call the xenosphere is larger than we think. What we use is the tiny periphery that connects us and the people in our immediate environment. You've heard of how photosynthesis involves quantum physics? This lattice of xenoforms connects throughout Earth's atmosphere, but not just at the present time. It is in the past and the future, and in alternate versions of our planet. It is an easy place to get lost in.

I am about to enter the wild, the open sea, the drop-off, the full xenosphere.

At first I see green. This is expected. I am in a maze, walls of hedge, well kept, tall. Above me the sky is blue and clear, free of clouds. The walls of the maze will always be this height. I am the gryphon. If I flap my wings I will fly, but never higher than the wall. That's the way I designed it. The way in is the way out. If an entity can make its way through this maze, I will be vulnerable to it. Working the maze is not just a matter of direction. There is texture, there is the temperature and ambient sound, which changes every ninety seconds. There is the smell, which varies in a specific order from floral to cut grass to manure and back. At predetermined intervals I say certain phrases, seemingly random. It's a more complex form of what I developed in my student days.

Andare in gondola fa bene alla salute. A ride in the canoe is good for your health.

Getting any of these wrong results in a transformation of the environment into a diamond cage.

At the end of the maze there is a guardian, a fearsome sixty-foot version of a Hawaiian carving I own. It is dark brown, with a gigantic head, large eyes, teeth all around its mouth, and relatively small, muscular limbs. It's more of a place marker, a milestone. Beyond this is wild country. *Here there be monsters.* The first thing I see is mirrors, too many to count, each showing a reflection of a different me, the real me and not the gryphon. Each represents a different thought pattern taken to its logical conclusion. There is fat me, short me, Chinese me, steroidal superhero me, and so on. Or maybe this represents different quantum realities, different worlds.

I also have to be careful what I think. This is a psycho-field, a thoughtspace, essentially unstable. While most people conceptualise thinking as this straightforward, linear thing, I see ideas spreading out into alternatives before one is selected. In this place every notion can potentially become reality. It is inherently unsafe and only the greatest need drives me here this time.

After the guardian, I encounter hundreds, thousands of people suspended unmoving as if in amber, eyes rolling here and there or not at all. This is everybody who carelessly thinks or does not think. They exist here in the unprotected state, passive, oscitant, uncritical, naive. Navigation can be difficult here, but I beat my wings and soar. I fly through the school of human souls, trying not to disturb them. Perhaps some of them will dream of an eagle-lion tonight. They are not arranged with any regularity. Clumps here and there, then empty space with mathematical formulae and infinity symbols and catalogue price tags, the interpretation my mind puts on this place.

I fly higher than the highest floating person. I notice some quill feathers in my wake. I don't moult and I wonder why this happens. I've never lost feathers before.

I make a rookie mistake and think briefly of Aminat, and I am taken to her, awash in her jumbled memories. Oddly, there is fire all around her, a black fire with dark tongues of flame that burn. I soar away from this, disconcerted. I do not want to know what she thinks unless she wishes to tell me.

There is detritus of the nation's communal consciousness that I have to navigate. The blood and sweat of slaves in a stew of their own anguish at being removed from their motherland, the guilt of slavers, the prolonged pain of colonisation, the riots, the CIA interference, the civil war, the genocide of the Igbos, the tribal pogroms, the terrorism, the killing of innocents, the bloody coups, the rampant avarice, the oil, the dark blood of the country, the rapes, the exodus of the educated class ... If I were untrained, this would bog me down.

I see multiple lynched politicians, burned in Operation Wetie. It reminds me of my near miss. I see the execution of armed robbers by firing squad on the Bar Beach, men tied to cement-filled barrels and shot to death, spilling blood, shit and piss, taking bizarre postures in death. I see our dictators, overwhelming our lives with want and need and despair. When Wormwood surges into awareness, we are unimpressed, even in our knowledge that it is the most significant event in Earth's history. We've seen colonisers before, and they are similar, whether intercontinental or interplanetary.

I see—

"Where are you going?"

I look around. A white man in a navy-blue cassock stands on air in front of me. His self-image is tall and muscular, and I wonder if he is like this in life, or if this is a compensation for a deficiency.

"I asked you a question, creature," he says again.

"I'm lost," I say. It doesn't pay to be too forthcoming in the xenosphere. You never know who you're communicating with. Besides, this man seems too confident.

"That's not true," he says. "You're an adept. I can see it in you clear as day. Perhaps I'll follow your spoor and occupy your physical body. Perhaps I'll kill you here."

I did not expect to get into a fight so soon. Is this man responsible for killing the other sensitives?

"I wouldn't like either of those options," I say. I am careful not to beat my wings too vigorously so as not to alarm him. It is difficult to lie in the xenosphere. You are more naked than when you are in your physical body, where you can control your breathing and fix your eyes to maintain contact. Luckily lying in the psyche is part of my training. Thieves must lie well to survive. Government agents must lie even better.

"There are threads reaching out from you like spider's silk, but not from a spinneret near your anus. From all around you. I'd say you're a finder, which means you know the way to everywhere."

"Who are you?" I don't like how easily he is unpeeling me or the way he looks at me, like I'm a rasher of bacon.

"My name is Ryan Miller. Or it was. I've been called many things. Sometimes the Invisible Monk. Sometimes Father Marinementus."

"You're the immortal," I say. "I studied you. I was at one of your funerals. At Esho."

"How is Esho?"

"It's been years, but they still paint the time on the clock face."

This is not reassuring news. I studied this guy way back when I first found out about my abilities. Ryan Miller was the first person to encounter the alien microorganisms, and the first to enter the xenosphere. He was born in the seventeenth century. His natural body and life ended long ago, but his personality and memories are stuck here. He is a ghost, but also a demon of sorts, because he can and does possess people. Nobody can manipulate the field like he can, and his capriciousness is legendary among sensitives. In fact, many think he serves the xenoforms or is controlled by them. I fear him.

He is tall, muscular, and in that twilight age of about sixty upwards where nobody can tell. His eyebrows are slightly bushy, and tiny green veins play about under the skin around his eyes. While we regard each other, we drift into a cluster of floating souls and he casually bats them away. They bounce off each other and spin off into the strange light that illuminates this place.

"What is your path, little finder? What are you here for?" He sniffs around my head, actually sniffs. Then he reaches out and plucks a feather from my wing and eats it, all with a puzzled expression on his face. His body splits in two and the newer version of him flies away without a backwards glance. I do not know how long my defences will hold against one such as him.

"I am going to help a friend," I say.

"Indeed you are. I think I will come with you," he says.

"You're helping me?"

"I didn't say that." He powers upwards and I am pulled along behind him.

I tell myself I will never return to this place, but I have said so in the past and here I am. You never know what life will throw at you. We fly past a cliff face where sheets of rock break off and fall to a ground I cannot see. At intervals Ryan Miller splits off into duplicates, faded versions of himself that drift off while becoming more solid, like newborn snakes' fangs. Colours swirl around us, lilac mostly. and some yellow.

"We're here," says Miller. "Your friend."

Except it is not my friend at all. It isn't Bola.

We land on a floating platform of earth, surfaced with asphalt, two telephone poles with wires stretched between them in a haphazard fashion. It is a fragment of street. I even know which street. Miller lands in front of me and spreads out his arms like a welcome party. In the centre of the platform is a lump that used to be human. It is a burned mass, flesh almost carbonised, in a sitting position, with the legs folded, skull grinning, lower jaw detached. The femur points to the sky because it has separated from the knee. There are about a dozen thin metal rings around the neck of the corpse. There is a stench, there are flies, and there is the crawling of my skin.

"You know where the rings come from?" Ryan Miller asks.

"When you burn someone alive with a tyre, the metal rings remain after the rubber is consumed."

"And do you know who that is?"

"No." It can't be.

"That is Fadeke."

My former girlfriend, whom I condemned to die by escaping.

"No," I say.

"Yes. It's interesting. Until just now, I found you completely lacking in guilt."

"It wasn't my fault."

"Wasn't it? If you hadn't stolen your parents' and neighbours' money, would she be dead?"

I want to cry, but the gryphon seems lacking in tear ducts. A part of me wants to attack Miller. I can tell that he senses it, because he looks at me.

"Don't," he says.

He sets off again in a burst of lilac, and I am sucked along. Fadeke's body fades to a dot, but not the weight it leaves in my heart.

"Why are you doing this?" I ask.

He twists around in flight and looks at me. "Maybe I'm bored, Kaaro. Or maybe I'm your Magical Negro on this journey, although I happen to be white. Or maybe I'm looking for a reason not to kill you."

"You may not find killing me so easy," I say. Careless, but right now I'm losing my traditional fear of pain.

"*Macho!* Listen, I don't think you could have done any harm to me even before I entered this space. I was proficient in many fighting styles. Stick fighting from Barbados, wushu from a number of Cathay monks. Speaking of Cathay, here's your friend."

A Chinese woman I do not know stands before me, her head twisted at a forty-five-degree angle. A reanimate, perhaps? There is nothing around her, no street, no context. Her eyes follow me and blink with disconcerting regularity.

"This is not a friend of mine," I say.

"Oh? Odd. Why are we here then? Oh, I know. Her name is Zhang Wang. You stole her money in Lagos. She got into a taxi and thought she could pay. She could not. The taxi driver threw her out in a rough part of the city and she was knocked down by a truck and killed."

"I didn't—"

"Oh, but you did, Kaaro."

He continues like this for a time, takes me to different people, some whom I remember faintly, others who are lost to my memory, to all of whom I've knowingly or unknowingly done wrong. I start to think this is a hell of some sort. Kaaro's Inferno, but instead of Virgil, I have a psychopathic failed priest.

We end up at a replica of my father's grave.

"What are we doing here? This has nothing to do with anything," I say. It rings false even to me.

Ryan Miller is implacable. He sits on the gravestone.

"Get off that," I say.

"Why are you pretending to care?" he says. "You did not attend the funeral."

"I was busy."

"Killing insurgents."

"I've never—"

"Intelligence you provided has led to the killing of insurgents. Your talent is used for death. Just like in your father's case."

"My father died of natural causes."

"At sixty-two, of a stroke brought on by your felonious exploits."

"Stop."

"Your mother will die too, and it will be your fault. Your entire family line wiped out."

"Why are you doing this? Where's your human kindness?"

"I lack humanity, Kaaro. I am a construct of electrical impulses and monoamine neurotransmitters. I might not even be that. I might be in your mind, a manifestation of your own guilt. Maybe this is the only path to your destination."

And at once I am standing in the courtyard of Bola's

defences, unsure if I have met Ryan Miller or not, but still shaken. I am in a temple that I remember as being made of muscle and bone. Now it is putrefying flesh. Every step I take sinks in, and pus wells up around my paws, soaking my fur. I decide to hover. The walls stream with mucus and serum; red fluid sweats from the ceiling. Everything wobbles and undulates. I block out the overpowering smell and fly towards the altar, which is barely recognisable. If Bola has left me a message, it will be there, but the muscle fibres are broken, stripped down and folded back. The floor around it is scored. The bone core of the altar is exposed. The former rectangular structure doesn't look to be decayed, like the rest of the temple. The breaches look like bite marks. It looks like it's been eaten.

No, *being* eaten.

I am slammed by something and go into a spin, hitting the wall so hard I sink into the muscle and feel the bone crush me. The pain is exquisite, and I feel the tug of my physical body in Rosewater trying to wake up. I orient myself, beat my wings, ruffle my feathers to appear larger, breathe and listen. My claws pop out automatically, and I give out a shrill that I hope sounds fearsome.

My first instinct is that it's a robot of some kind. It is about eight feet tall, a male humanoid with a metallic sheen and cubic metres of malevolence. On closer inspection it's a kind of iron golem; equally impossible, but we're in the realm of the mind. It can be whatever the imagination of its owner wants it to be. Neither does the size matter, which is why I launch at it. I hit it in the sternum with the full weight of my anger, guilt, grief and fear. The impact shakes it and I claw through, stripping off shards of metal, digging a hole. I pass to the other side and hear its inhuman screams.

I soar higher and wrap my tail around its neck. I don't know if the simulation breathes, but a humanoid image may have humanoid weaknesses. My fur and feathers are covered in its constituent metal, and the bits melt and move like worms. I see them sink into me, and pain follows. The large construct is on its knees, but I am falling, held briefly by my tail before it loosens and I hit the ground. I swipe at its thigh and gouge out a chunk of metal, but it's desultory and I feel myself weakening. It is like being covered by angry fire ants who drill down and eat from the inside out.

I am going to die and I won't even know why. Aminat will find me dead or comatose. After Bola, that'll be fucking traumatic and unfair. My mother. I would have wanted to see her before dying, to say I'm sorry for Dad and everything. I abandoned my family, my responsibilities. I do not want to die. No, not just that. I want to live.

"Then you will," says the voice of Molara.

She hovers, her wings beating faster than the eye can follow, and her blood leaks from her eyes, ears, nose and mouth, dripping on the metal man with a hiss, melting him. I sense pain in my mind, and the metal retreats out of me into the source, but it's too late. It is reduced to a puddle of gunk, steaming with psychic residue.

"Hello, Gryphon," she says.

Chapter Twenty

Lagos: 2055

Then

With an elegant gesture, Femi hangs up and returns to the table from the window where she has been whispering. I cannot stop staring at her; I am sure I have never seen anyone as beautiful, even on television.

"We can't access resources yet," she says. A small vertical crease between her eyebrows.

"Why?"

"Something to do with the COBs on a farm. Some guy got killed, but I don't know all the details. They're still collating the data, but what it means is we can't get to Regina Ogene at the moment."

"You're lying when you say you don't know all the details, aren't you?"

"Yes. I just can't tell you."

"Can you access records from here?" I ask.

"Some of them."

"You left something out of the pack you gave me. What exactly has Bicycle Girl been doing to irritate the president?"

"It's not in our remit to know," says Femi. She sits, reaches for my glass of cognac, and takes a swallow before returning it to me. Her lips leave a lipstick stain.

"But you've said she's some kind of anarchist, right? That means public displays of, I don't know, civil disobedience, vandalism, that kind of thing?"

"Not necessarily. What do you know about anarchism?"

I shrug.

"It's not the equivalent of chaos. It's actually a kind of socialism. Some of them can be violent and disruptive, but not all."

"Is Bicycle Girl violent and disruptive?"

"No. But she does ... preach. Can't predict where she'll turn up. She gives little speeches whipping the populace into a frenzy, then she disappears."

"We need to correlate dates of those events with rumours of the Lijad. If I'm right, there will be overlap."

"The moving village. It's hard to believe, you must admit."

"It doesn't have to mean the movement of the buildings, roads, wells and so on. It could be conceptual movement. I never paid much attention to it before."

"What's conceptual movement?"

"It's nothing. I just made it up when I said it. What I'm trying to say is it may be that the idea of the village moves around."

"I still don't get it."

"Okay, imagine villages X, Y and Z as fixed points. Then there are three different days of the week, say Monday, Tuesday, Wednesday. On Monday, X is the Lijad, on Tuesday X reverts back and Y becomes the Lijad—"

"And on Wednesday Z is the Lijad," says Femi.

"Yes."

"But what about the people?"

"Yeah, well, like I said, this is just me floating ideas. I need Nimbus."

Femi taps a spot on the underside of the table and I sense a brief hiss as ionised gas fills the space in front of me and forms a holo screen. The surface lights up and a QWERTY keyboard appears. There are sixteen free Nimbus portals and a few secure tunnels.

"Smooth. Did you know that West Africa has the highest population of Nimbus addicts in the world? No running water in some places, but Nimbus is present."

"How can we afford it?" asks Femi. She doesn't sound interested.

"The networks provide several pay-as-you-go deals. I think about a third are unauthorised links by Junk Jockeys."

I touch the tunnel I want. The holo screen expands to accommodate my destination, a clearing area that looks like an atrium with several ornate doors. When I hover over each one, info pop-ups tell me how many users are plugged into that path, how much it will cost, whether I have been there before, and a list of possible cyber risks I will be exposed to. There are no advertisements – Femi can obviously afford the good stuff. I go into a search alcove where a 3D graphic of a steampunk robot awaits. I type in "Lijad". A pop-up message asks if I would like audio output, to which I answer in the affirmative. A second warning tells me it will be insecure if another person is in the room or if a listening device is monitoring them. I dismiss these with a brushing motion.

Sixty thousand results come up for the Lijadu Sisters. I push one with my left hand and use the right to bat stray malapps, malignant applets caught in Femi's security trap. I reset the cyber security to destroy without notification.

The Lijadu Sisters were Nigerian jazz singers active from the late 1960s to the 1980s. Photos blossom around me and an audio clip provides a gentle background. Their music is of its time, but their harmony works well and the arrangements are influenced by rock; in addition to bass, they often have an electric guitar accompaniment. In their photos they smile the same smile. Toothy grins, deep clefts in their cheeks, real smiles that reach their eyes. These are happy, beautiful girls. As is traditional for twins among the Yoruba, they are named Taiwo and Kehinde. Twins are mystical to the Yoruba, and even the word for twins, "ibeji", is derived from the name of their patron god. They sing in both English and Yoruba. I summon a trawler from my Nimbus shack and task it with gathering their songs and sending them to my phone.

Interesting though it is, I am no closer to Bicycle Girl unless she is a fan.

Lijad is a Spanish word, a verb, meaning "to sand" or "sandpaper". I dismiss that thread. The Lijad that interests me is a noun.

I reach for the cognac, only to find it gone. I shoot Femi a questioning look.

"I need you sober. I've put coffee on."

"I need alcohol for the ... for the finding process."

"No you don't. Don't forget, I'm the expert on finders."

"Fascist," I say.

I go to a portal called Irohin, which is the Yoruba word for "news", then push past all the cul-de-sacs until I get to Amebo. Amebo means "gossip", but it is an example of the dynamic nature of language. The actual Yoruba word for a gossip is "olofofo". Amebo used to be a proper noun, and was the name of a character in a popular television show, *Village*

Headmaster. In the show, the character was a prodigious gossip; thus her name passed into the Nigerian lexicon. A small part of my brain notes that the Lijadu Sisters recorded a song called "Amebo".

Amebo has one stream on Lijad. A lone voice, it seems. These places are the domains of conspiracy theorists and paranoiacs.

Have you seen Oyin Da? Have you heard her message of light? The Science Hero of Arodan lives!

I wonder what a science hero is.

"What's a science hero?" I ask.

"No idea," says Femi.

"Is Oyin Da a religious nut?"

"Not that I know of. I know she didn't speak any English, but picked it up later."

There are eight posts, all by the same person, who amazingly leaves his phone number as a signature line. There is also a ... is that SHTML? Isn't SHTML an Internet language or code? The Internet was the precursor to Nimbus but has been overrun by pornography and other oddities. If I understand this right, the posts should direct me to websites, which are text-based and 2D graphics intensive. Flat. This motherfucker is a flat-Earther.

"Can this equipment parse Internet?" I ask.

Femi says, "I don't know. I've never had to. Come and get your coffee."

"You can't bring it to me? You're coming over here anyway."

"Not your serving girl, Kaaro. Get it yourself."

I burn my tongue on it as I read a post titled "The Problem of Arodan".

What the authorities are suppressing is interesting to any student of history or the paranormal/esoteric principles! They say this disappearance was an isolated freak event. Indeed, towns and groups of people in vehicles have disappeared before. The Roanoke Colony, the *Mary Celeste*, the 1956 B-47 Stratojets, all mysterious in their way. Arodan presents a unique case, in my opinion. My research has shown that it has been repopulated THREE times. Three!!! Let that sink in, reader.

Arodan was a village that existed in ancient times but was first destroyed by the British in 1894. They burned the buildings and killed the men, women and children, scattering survivors. It is not clear why, but some British scouting soldiers may have been killed in the weeks prior. It slowly repopulated and rebuilt on the same site, but was destroyed again in 1956. (1956!!! The same year as the Stratojets!!!) This time the villagers were killed and mutilated; in some cases there were bite marks on the bodies. We are to believe cannibals came for them in the night!!! Finally, in 2044, the most recent catastrophe was visited upon Arodan. It simply vanished.

Clearly the gods do not wish for this town to exist, yet people are attracted to the site. Why?

The answer is in the Lijad.

"We have to phone this guy," I say. "He's not well, but he has done some research and it would be a mistake not to exploit that."

"Go ahead. You have your phone," says Femi. She drinks a coffee of her own and peers at me over the rim behind rising steam.

"I thought you'd need to trace him or something." I block caller ID, then dial, but the number is disconnected. "Well, that's that, then. We still need to get to Regina." I think I know what went wrong the last time and I want another shot.

Femi tries again, but she informs me that there is a major operation going on. It will be hours before they can find their way there. She seems exasperated. "Someone used a fucking particle accelerator weapon. Why would they—"

She stops abruptly when she sees I am not paying attention.

I pick at the crusts of my wounds, the spots where the IV went in.

"Do you want to tell me about your husband?" I ask.

"Oh, I see. You'll get me talking about him, feeling the loss, feeling the guilt, then I'll get all teary and you'll come and put your arm around me to comfort me, and one thing will lead to the proverbial other, right? We should get one thing straight, Kaaro, there will be no sex between you and me. Is that clear?"

"Relax, Mrs Alaagomeji. I wouldn't dream of such a thing." A lie, but I have to put her at ease. "I just wanted us to pass the time is all."

"I'm sure you did. I'll put the television on for you." Femi leaves the room.

I can see her husband still, cold and on a slab somewhere, in darkness. One part of being a finder that most people do not know about is that once I have found something, I will always know where that thing is, like a psychic tag. It takes deliberate and sustained effort to push it to the back of my mind, and if I give even the slightest thought to something, I can see what is current about the found object or person. I know that a brooch belonging to a rich but rather forgetful woman that I found eighteen months earlier is lost again, stuck between two

239

wooden items of furniture and gathering dust. I see the faces of a number of children.

I take a last sip of the coffee and move away from the table. I marvel at the cleanliness and shininess of the surfaces. I have never seen a kitchen so sterile, so devoid of the smell of food. The ghosts of meals past usually make a kitchen the most welcoming room in any home. I sit on the floor, on tiles that smell of pine. I rest my back against the cabinet under the sink and close my eyes. Both my back and buttocks are against cool, hard surfaces, and they ground me in place. Pine is a third anchor. The aroma of coffee is a fourth, though I would prefer a cigarette. The distant hum of air conditioning is weak, but I still register it as number five.

I think of Regina Ogene, and the moment I touched her. The sensations come rushing back in an instant, but this time I am ready and braced for them. I welcome rather than resist the light tubes. I take control of my breathing and say to myself, "You are in the kitchen, on the floor, near the sink, smelling Brazilian coffee beans." I repeat it till the anchor beats back the tide of panic induced by too many possibilities.

I have never experienced this before and want to study it. The ends of each tube present themselves to me, shoving openings forward and pulling back when another becomes dominant. I pick one of the larger tunnels at random and my mind rushes through, with a sinking, falling sensation.

You are in the kitchen, on the floor, near the sink, smelling Brazilian coffee beans.

Even before my awareness reaches the destination, I know Bicycle Girl is not there. It is an area beside a stream, near a clutch of green bamboo, with a beige raffia mat on the grass. There is no human being within fifty yards of the spot. I already feel my consciousness returning to the starting point, but I have an idea.

A second ostium leads me to a market scene bustling with activity. Hawkers, butchers, grain traders and palm-oil farmers negotiating, and rich housewives trailed by servants create a confusion of presences, but no Bicycle Girl.

You are in the kitchen, on the floor, near the sink, smelling Brazilian coffee beans.

A third leads to Tafawa Balewa Square in Lagos, easy to recognise with its shop-bound complex and buskers outside. A fourth leads to a desert, another a car park, a dense jungle, a waterfall.

These are places Oyin Da has visited. The possibilities are multiple and multiplying because she never stays still, never lingers long enough to leave her psychic mark on a place.

You are in the kitchen, on the floor, near the sink, smelling Brazilian coffee beans.

The light tunnels change and their paths warp. I can study them, try to determine which are more recent, maybe with time predict—

My phone rings and jars me out of the finder's trance. For a minute I am groggy, and I stagger when I stand up. The phone vibrates and whines next to the coffee mug.

"Hello?"

"You called my number." Unfamiliar voice, male, slow speech.

"A message said it was disconnected."

"Yes, it is a subroutine I have in place for barred calls. I can never be too sure. The government is always watching."

"Who are you?" I ask.

"I beg your pardon, sir. You called me. And since you used this number, I can only assume you are interested in Oyin Da."

"That is correct. No names, then. Do you know how I can find her?" I am going to change my number this very day. Can't have this guy owning my contact details.

"Have you heard her message of light?" asks the caller. He drags the sibilants, giving the unsettling mental image of a diglossic tongue.

"No, I have not, but I want to," I say.

"She wants us to share with one another. Petty feuds are to be put aside, and so should all malice, greed and sexual impropriety."

Sexual impropriety?

"She wants us to follow her into the new places, the places where there is a new heaven and Earth."

"Are you her priest?" I ask.

The man pauses. His breath sounds heavy, but it seems more that he holds the receiver too close to his mouth. "I am not worthy of such a position."

"Then what—"

"I had the opportunity to go with her and I could not."

"Why? What stopped you?"

"I . . . I hesitated. I was not pure in my conviction. The window closed."

"What window?"

Silence.

"Sir, what window? The window of opportunity?"

"The window!"

"I—"

"She wanted me to come through the window and I hesitated. Others went, but I hesitated. Do you see? I hesitated."

"The window to the Lijad? A portal? Is that what you mean?"

The man pauses. "I see you are hesitating too. Goodbye."

The line goes dead.

I redial the number from the site several times, but get no response.

Chapter Twenty-One

Rosewater, Lagos: 2066

Now

Molara stops bleeding and helps me up. I am both grateful and concerned that she is powerful enough to subdue the metal man. I can read her lust, but there is no way I'm going to have sex in a rotting meat temple. She has saved my life, and she knows it, but my recent run-in with Ryan Miller makes me more aware of the moral aspects of my behaviour. Aminat is in Rosewater, in the same apartment as me. Is what I do with Molara cheating? Does being in a relationship mean she owns my mind as well as the fidelity of my body?

Ryan Miller noticed the old one inside me, the dead one, Nike Onyemaihe.

The liquid metal pools, and then soaks into the muscles that make up the floor, without mixing with the pus. I dip my finger into the puddle before it's gone. I taste it, and feel the familiarity immediately.

Clement. From the bank.

"You know him?" asks Molara.

"You can tell?"

"It's on your face."

"He is someone I work with. Used to work with."

Puzzling, but at least I know where to find the motherfucker. I return to the altar and touch the bone, stroke its surface.

"What are you looking for?"

"A message from my friend. Something. A warning, perhaps."

"There is nothing here but rot, Gryphon," she says. "Come and make love to me."

I turn on her. "There is something wrong with you, Molara."

I recite the first of many phrases that take me back to my maze, and presently I open my eyes in my room.

I have wet myself.

I stand up and stretch the stiffness out of my joints. There is still pain from my injuries, but it is mild. I strip off my clothes and walk naked to the bathroom. Aminat has not changed position, and only forty-six minutes has passed since I entered the room.

"Shower. Twenty-seven degrees."

I wash away my fear and residual lust for Molara, but my guilt remains. Fucking Ryan Miller. Although that might have been just my own mind creating order out of the chaos of the xenosphere. Ryan Miller is a sensitive's fairy tale. I was freaked out and my subconscious threw something my way.

Aminat opens the door and her anguish washes over me.

"You want to go on a road trip?" I ask.

"What about Bola's funeral? The family needs support and I—"

"I'll support *you*. You're family by marriage and you're upset. You need cheering up and I need to go to Lagos."

"Why?"

"To see my family. My real family."

*

Alhaji's house has changed. The structure is the same, but the paint is peeling, fungus rises along the sides in a dry black tide, and weeds overtake any semblance of order that I remember from over a decade ago. Alhaji always took such care of his garden. The windows are intact, however, and this fills me with hope. There is no movement.

"What's here, Kaaro?" asks Aminat.

"A friend, I think. Someone who saved my life many years ago." I turn to her and smile. "*Musulumi ododo bi tie*." A true Muslim like you.

"*Mi o kii n'she musulumi*," she says. I am not a Muslim.

"Your name—"

"Is an Arabic name meaning 'trustworthy', but I'm named after the legendary fifteenth-century queen. Nothing to do with religion. Not all Arabs are Muslims, you know."

"Oh. Okay then."

"Are we going to see your friend?"

"In a minute."

Lagos is hostile to me, but not because of the people. My employers like to confine their agents to specific cities unless there is a reason for movement. This time I asked for and got permission to travel, but that doesn't mean they aren't tracking me by drone. I feel a need to remove my implant altogether, but it is embedded close to the spine. The surgical skills required are not available on the street. Still, if S45 does not know about Alhaji, I don't want to expose him. I've also been timid since my last foray into the xenosphere. I apply extra-thick layers of ketoconazole all over my body and it gives me that chemical taste in the mouth.

Alhaji, are you there?

Alhaji, are you there?

Alhaji, are you there?

It flows out from me like a beacon. It should be no problem for Alhaji to pick it up. He and Valentine didn't have a problem hearing my distress call all those years ago. On a whim, I try something else.

Valentine, are you there?
Valentine, are you there?
Valentine, are you there?

After a few minutes, I sense that someone is listening.

Valentine, it's me, Kaaro. I was—

I know who you are. You've grown quite a bit since I last heard you. You can come in.

Valentine meets us at the door, but I get the sense that he has not been on his feet in a long time. He is withered. Where his skin used to be smooth, there is a crumpled, papery parchment lined like a medieval map. He is hairless. Even his eyebrows are gone, which makes me wonder how he deals with sweat from his forehead.

Where's Alhaji?

I'll take you to him. "Who's this lovely creature?" he asks.

"This is my girlfriend, Aminat," I say. My hand is in the small of her back.

Valentine hugs her. "What are you doing with this reprobate?" he says, a little too seriously for my liking.

"I'm just using him for sex," says Aminat.

Valentine laughs, but it ends in a cough. *Cheeky, this one. Also, nice ass.*

"You can't objectify women, Valentine. You're gay."

Aminat looks from one of us to the other.

"He is appreciative of your anatomy," I say. *Take me to Alhaji. It's important.*

And her?

She can hear what I can hear.

"I just want to say that this is a very frustrating conversation for me," says Aminat.

She is joking, but I take her hand, feel the skin of her palm, then flip it so that the back of her hand is in my palm. I look her in the eyes. I do not believe I have ever been this close to anyone.

Valentine takes me to a room in the house, and before Aminat and I cross the threshold I already know what is there. There is a small gravestone in the middle of the room with *Memoriae sacrum* and Alhaji's true name carved on it.

A grave inside a house is not unusual in Nigeria, although I've mostly seen them in courtyards or atria. As is traditional for Muslims, the stone does not rise above thirty centimetres. It's marble, veined with black streaks, and squat. It is surrounded by murals of various flowers, and the light from the single window shines directly on the grave, which is depressed to a depth of a foot.

"I could not attend the funeral because ... homosexuality is still a crime and the family would rather not hold that discussion. I exhumed the body and had him reinterred here."

"How did he die?" I ask.

"He got distracted, he got sick, he decayed and died." *I have the same sickness. I feel my life slipping away each day.*

"I'm sorry to hear that." *What can I do to help?*

Valentine shrugs, and even the air appears to be the weight of the world.

"Come to Rosewater," I say. *The Opening will heal you.*

"No, my place is here," says Valentine. *It didn't help your friend Bola and it hasn't healed you.*

"I can make space for you, just like you did for me." *I'm not sick.*

"Long time ago, that was." *Aren't you? I can see Molara, you know. You see a butterfly, but I see a shroud flying through thoughtspace, harvesting ... I don't know what. She is rot and decay, yet you see her as a goddess of love and slake your lust. How long has that been going on? Does Aminat know?*

I—

You're sick too, Kaaro. Find the cure or die. I'm going to stay right here with my love. You should tell Aminat the truth.

"How do you know them?" asks Aminat.

"They took me in when I was a wayward teenager." I am driving away. "I ... Aminat, I have something to tell you."

I pull over to the side of the road because I do not trust myself to drive safely. Normally I am afraid of physical confrontations and the pain of a broken nose. This feels worse. My heart beats so hard that my words come out with tremulousness.

"What's wrong?" she asks. She leans forward slightly and the seat belt presses into her.

"I am not the kind of guy you think I am. I've done many things that I am ashamed of."

"But this is one specific thing, right? What have you done?"

I tell her everything. I tell her about Molara, about the sex, about the gryphon, about the nature of my job with S45, about Klaus and my stealing. I tell her about the agama lizard I killed for no good reason when I was eight. When I can't think of anything else to confess to, I trail off, breathing heavily. And cough.

She doesn't say anything. Just stares straight ahead at the cars and trucks that pass us hissing on the asphalt.

"Say something, Aminat. What are you thinking?"

"I don't know, Kaaro, why don't you read my mind?"

That hurts, and I recoil, sure that I have fucked up this relationship beyond redemption.

"I'm not like other people, Aminat. I . . . I don't feel the way other people do. My parents disowned me and I didn't care. I take that which doesn't belong to me. I know that my morals are broken in some fundamental way. But if I didn't care about you, I wouldn't be telling you any of this and—"

"I love you, Kaaro." She says it in a matter-of-fact way, still not looking at me. "I am in love with you. I was afraid of telling you before now."

I don't know what to say to this. I have never been in love. I had a gargantuan infatuation once. One time. It got me into big trouble. My throat tickles, so I cough again.

"Aminat—"

"I'm a big girl. I know there is a difference between being in love and having a relationship. I know there is a difference between love and trust."

"I—"

"Do you still want me?"

"Of course I do."

"Then you will have to earn my trust." She looks at me now. "You have never been with this woman physically?"

"Never. I wouldn't even know what she looks like."

"Have you been with anyone else since you've been with me?"

"What? No. Jesus."

"Drive, Kaaro. When we get to Rosewater, take me to my office. I forgot something."

"I don't know where your office is," I say. I start the engine. "Come to think of it, I still don't know what you do."

"There's a lot you don't know about me, Kaaro. It's a good thing my brother likes you."

I think of the black flames surrounding her mental image in the xenosphere, but I do not ask.

We stop at a motel and spend the night.

A sound jolts me awake. The sheets rustle and Aminat shifts against me but remains asleep. We are in bed and I feel a sense of unfamiliarity and displacement, but it passes quickly. She breathes into my temple and I turn to her to inhale her exhalation, to confirm that she is here.

Love.

This is an unfamiliar state of mind for me. I used to search hospital wards for a reason to get up in the morning. I went to the terminal wards and I saw and listened to terminal thoughts. Whatever the dying person regretted not doing, this I aspired to, even though a lot of what I read was impractical for me.

I was a ghost in the hospitals. It was another kind of stealing. I steal dreams, I steal hopes, I steal entire lives.

Thoughts are different in hospitals. There is a primal life-affirmation thing going on. It is the perfect antidote to my apathy. Was. Since Aminat, I have not needed to go.

I walk into St Joseph's or the Omojola Clinic, and I sit in Casualty. I do not even need to access the xenosphere at first. The conversations are angry, fearful, anxious and often incoherent.

"Why are they taking so long?"

"What were you thinking?"

"So much blood."

"What's taking so long?"

"Stay here. I'm calling your mother."

"I swear, it was an accident."

"Why is it taking so long?"

"You think they're just in there playing?"

"I'm bleeding to death here."

"God, this hurts."

"*Walahi talahi*, I will kill someone unless I get help."

"I need some attention here."

I can only really stand this for five, ten minutes at most. In Casualty, the inner thoughts tend to match the outer and there is no need to go into the xenosphere.

I drift into the corridors, avoiding stretchers accompanied by rapid-talking, scrubs-wearing professionals, lazy, random mentations from the anaesthetised patients. Children's thoughts blasting out of the paediatrics floor, energetic, hopeful, brightly coloured, as soon as they are recovering. The sick ones are muted, but no less hopeful.

The palliative care wards are usually out of the way, in a quieter part of the hospital. The xenosphere is full of ghosts here, shades of the thoughts of people long since passed on. Repetition keeps the pathways alive within the network. Their self-images do not see me, but drift. They are information clots in the worldmind. Not alive, although they are capable of interaction. Their responses are exactly what they would have been when alive. I can and have talked to them. They tell me about their lives, what they did, what they didn't do. Hospital spectres look diseased or injured, bleeding, leaking pus, coughing despite having no lungs, still manifesting the symptoms of the disease that took them.

Many of the people here will die too quickly, before the next biodome Opening. Hepatocellular carcinoma. Six months to live.

Regrets wash over me. I should have called her. I should have said sorry. I wanted to see Olumo Rock. I have never been out of this country. I should have had children. Why did I kill him? I worked too hard, and for what? I wonder what happened to her? I wonder what happened to him? I shouldn't have … I want … I need … there's still time …

I leave. I can only take so much, but what I do take energises me for the next month. I exercise more, eat healthily, phone friends, go out. I go to the holo museum and there I visit Venice, Taiwan, Niagara Falls. I cook an unfamiliar meal and fuck it up. I resolve to be happy, and force myself to see what is good in my life. I stare at the lush vegetation that surrounds the dome, the illegal farms that try to tap into the hyper-fertile soil, and the cursed government officials who turn up to clear the foliage from time to time.

This works for a while, but the apathy always creeps back in. I wake up and I do not exercise. I drag myself into Integrity Bank. I look at but do not see the wild roses and hibiscus that flourish on my way to work. Life greys out again.

Sometimes I mine the memories of people I've encountered, but it doesn't help, because when I'm in this mood, only the negative aspects of their lives bubble to the surface. I see only black.

I touch Aminat's cheek. She opens her eyes immediately. Light sleeper.

"Hi," she says.

"Hi," I say.

Sunbeams play across her flank. At this moment I buy into whatever the love songs and poems say. I believe the wispy, whimsical feelings and the waking up together in the dawn sunlight.

She reaches out to touch my hand, then guides it to the warm place between her thighs.

"Wake me up," she says.

Here we are. We return to Rosewater in silence for most of the journey. It is good when feelings are formless and left unsaid, but Aminat says she loves me. Expression weighs passion, both measures and limits it. We both know that I am spending the silence assaying my own heart.

We arrive outside her office and she tells me to wait in the car. I ache all over because of my injuries and because of the driving. She does not kiss me when she leaves the car, but she gives me a look that I feel all the way from my eyes to my loins. She loves me. Do I love her? I have never loved before, but I have never felt as strongly about someone as I do about her. I watch her walk away.

There are no signs, so I do not know what the office block is. I am too ashamed about not showing interest in her work before now, so I do not ask.

Just before she gets out of earshot I say, "I love you."

"What?" she says, turning.

"Nothing. I'll see you ... we'll talk when you get back."

It's daytime, but outside working hours. There is only a guard. He smiles and laughs at something Aminat says to him. He lets her in.

Some kids play football on the road and squeal with delight whenever the ball flies past the two rocks they use as goalposts. The ball bounces off the windscreen and loses momentum on the ground. The boys holler at me. I step out of the car and line the ball up with my foot. I swing my foot back to kick, but I never get to take the shot.

The blast from the building throws me against the side of the car. I hear nothing but ringing. Debris everywhere. Black smoke stains the air and spreads through the sky. Flames roar and frolic around what is left of the structure.

I can't move. The car alarm goes off. I see a burning child. I wish I had not looked.

Aminat.

Aminat, I love you. Come back.

I burst into the xenosphere and see the black flames immediately.

Interlude: Mission

Kainji Dam, Niger State: 2057

Ah, the anger, the suppressed rage. It amuses me, though I keep this to myself. I try to work a piece of stock fish from between my incisors with my tongue.

We are in a control room in Kainji Dam. I am the only sensitive. With me are six special forces men from a unit so classified they won't tell me its name. They wear ultra-light body armour, carry ultra-light, ultra-destructive weaponry, and are tensed for action.

"Kaaro, anything?" the CO asks.

"It's still raining. I can't help you. I need clear weather, remember? Unless you have access to Shango or any other thunder gods, we're stuck." I stick my finger in my mouth, using my nail as a toothpick. It doesn't work.

A narrow rectangular slit shows dark grey skies that are occasionally illuminated by lightning. The rain is torrential, unending. Lake Kainji must be engorged by now, and the turbines should be working at full capacity, except not all the turbines are functional. They never have been since the Italians finished building it in the 1960s.

Insurgents have threatened to blow up the dam and S45 has loaned me out for this mission. I am only required to detect if and when the insurgents arrive on site. The brutal men of war around me will do the rest.

I look at these guys. Motherfucking Danladi could eat them all for breakfast without getting out of bed.

The CO pulls a knife and bites the blade. "I don't know Shango, but this iron is Ogun and I swear that nobody's blowing up this dam tonight. You're coming with us."

"What? No. I'm not a field agent." Now I'm angry too. And afraid.

"You are tonight. Boys, let's go."

We trot off into the downpour.

First chance I get, I intend to run away.

Chapter Twenty-Two

Lagos: 2055

Then

Gun.

As soon as I think it, as soon as I know that I need to escape, I see the path to the gun. It's a girl's weapon, a .22. Pearl-handled. Silvery, high-sheen polish, elegant case. Loaded. In Femi's handbag.

I have no intention of firing it, but I need her to believe I will. I left the hospital to confront Femi at her home, yet she wants to return me to the S45 facility. I can't let that happen. Mass graves and disappearing villages are a bit too much for me.

I am back in the kitchen before she returns. I am confused by something I saw in my reverie. A conversation. I am sure it is from the future. I have never been able to do this, but I have heard of sensitives who can. Over the years I have had flashes of other abilities, and this is a flash of prescience. The conversation is between Femi and a woman I do not know.

"Did you sleep with him?" asks the strange woman, who is seated at a desk and writing on sand that has been smoothed out on a ceramic tray.

"Who?" asks Femi.

"The shift. Kaaro."

"No."

"Hm. You should have. You were meant to."

"First of all, ew. Secondly, ew. That's all I have to say on the matter."

"If you had ... well, that was our last chance to control him."

"What do you mean? He's a mercenary. Money controls him."

The woman raises an index finger like a schoolteacher. "No. He only thinks money controls him, but in fact it does not."

"What, then?"

"Love."

"Love of whom?"

The woman shrugs. "You won't find Bicycle Girl through him. That thread is dead now."

The vision ends there.

I don't know who the woman is, but sand-pressing or sand-writing is a form of divination known to the Yoruba. It is similar to geomancy. Jesus is said to have done it when he saved the adulterous woman from a mob. I've never seen or heard of a woman performing it, but I suppose anything is possible.

I push the revolver into my waistband at the small of my back. No matter what happens, I can't sleep with Femi. The vision was a clear warning against that. I do not know how she would control me, but I do not care to find out. I don't know what the love business is all about, but since I am not in love with anybody, I won't worry about it. Besides, love is for pussies; real lovers get pussy.

I find the coffee cold and fire up a fresh brew. I feel uneasy, partly because guns make me uncomfortable, but also because of the vision and a general aura of apprehension. This jumble of emotions makes me jittery, and I drop a mug on the floor by mistake. I'm picking up the pieces when Femi comes back in.

"I ... there's a 'copter coming for us," she says. She either looks worried or I am picking the vibes up from her.

"I'm not going," I say.

"Don't be ridiculous. I have to go, therefore you have to go. I'm not leaving you here."

"I'm not staying here, but I'm not going with you either."

"Kaaro, I don't have time for this."

I pull out the gun.

"Have you lost your mind? You're not going to kill anyone," says Femi. "I don't know what you think you're doing, but you don't need to threaten me. I thought we were getting along."

"We were not getting along. You were getting what you wanted, but *we were not getting along.*"

"Calm down and put the gun down, Kaaro. That pistol is an antique and it's worth a lot of money. It was used by the Oyenusi gang in their crime spree in 1972. It's probably faulty and will misfire if you pull the trigger." Femi has a complete lack of fear, like she can reach out and take the gun from me, but she wants to see where this scenario leads.

"I'm only borrowing it. I just want to get off the boat, Femi." I smile at her, because who wouldn't? "You're the prettiest girl I've ever kissed."

"I'll be the last girl you ever kiss if you don't stop pointing an offensive weapon at a federal agent. It is a crime, you know."

"I'm sorry, but I don't trust you, Femi. I don't trust what you did with your husband and I have no wish to be involved in the extrajudicial killing of Bicycle Girl."

Femi sighs. "I'm going to have some more coffee." She moves without paying me any attention. A part of me thinks I should shoot once, to make her afraid or something, but I do not have the will. Besides, I've never used a gun outside basic training from my mad Belgian. Classical music plays through the house. "That's Mendelssohn. This violin concerto always makes me sad. My husband liked it, particularly the first movement. I'm a Ludwig person myself. Symphony No. 9 is one of the highlights of human civilisation."

"That's nice. I'm not a fan."

"No, you wouldn't be." She pours some coffee into a mug and offers it to me, but I ignore it. "I can't tell you everything, but my relationship with my husband was complicated."

She tells me that Wande Alaagomeji was her one indiscretion in S45. He was a pretty-boy guard she had noticed and fucked. It turned out she enjoyed having sex with him enough to want him around longer. By this time her family had given up hope that she would ever marry. Her mother said she was "too strong-headed", while her father said she was "too much like a man". Wande was from the right tribe and family, and stupid enough to know his place. It was convenient to get married.

Femi and Wande had one year of endless cavorting, with brief interruptions by work. Then Wande started getting restless about his career, wanting to rise in the ranks and hinting that Femi should use her influence. Nepotism didn't work in S45, but the boy wouldn't believe her. She pushed for him slightly, abutting on the boundary of propriety, and eyebrows were raised. It affected her in some ill-defined way, and the relationship lost its lustre. The sex became less fantastic, more mundane, until it ceased to exist. She knew he was dipping his wick elsewhere, but did not care. Their house had twelve-foot ceilings and was large enough for them to live separate lives. "I once went six weeks without casting eyes on him," she says.

They settled into a nice, destructive routine of each pretending the other did not matter or even exist. Twenty-four months of that dulled her instincts with him. It came as a big surprise when the surveillance jockeys brought the footage.

Wande as insurgent. Wande as distributor of seditious literature, as collaborator with enemies of state. Wande as composer of leaflets for Bicycle Girl, conspiracy theorist and searcher.

Femi pauses to drink coffee. "There were clumps of followers of the girl here and there. She popped up like an alien, abducting some, preaching her version of utopia, a version with which the president emphatically did not agree. I did not blame him; it was nine months to the election.

"I had been kept informed of the progress of tracking Wande's cell, but could not be involved for obvious reasons. For a time even I came under suspicion and experienced a rash of subtle surveillance and interdepartmental innuendo. I endured it like a bout of herpes and continued to work with customary diligence. If there is nothing to find, there is no reason to fear the observing eye. I treated it as a minor irritation and it went away."

She found out from reading a classified bulletin. Six dead, arms tied, shots to the back of the head, unknown perpetrators, one Wande Alaagomeji identified as a victim. Femi did not react, though she felt sorrow. The death squad wasn't S45's style and it probably came from an entirely different department that had access to the information.

She had been drawn to the extra-natural elements of S45 at the time, learning fragments about various aspects of her work: the reborn, the witches, the psychics, especially shifts. In-house psychiatrists thought it was a displacement of the mourning process. An interest in the occult after a death in the family is almost a cliché, they said. Weeks after Wande's burial, Femi had the idea to create a mass grave for the purpose of testing finders.

"Which brought me to you, Kaaro. Possibly the best finder in Nigeria and hence the world, but a plebeian who loves the good things of life, a wine biber and satyr, filthy and completely lacking in probity."

I giggle. "One day soon, you're going to change your mind about me."

"That is *an honour that I dream not of*," says Femi. "Will you stay and help me find Bicycle Girl?"

"Sorry, Femi. I'll find the girl and hear her point of view. I still don't trust your organisation."

"We don't exterminate."

"Maybe. Maybe you don't, but other branches of government do, and they have access to your data. I'm sorry." I return the gun to my waistband and start to make my way out.

"This is unwise," she says.

"Like most other things I've done in my life," I say.

At first I think Femi will organise people to follow me, but she doesn't. There are other crises on her mind. I do not fool myself; I know she will get around to me at some point.

I know where to find Bicycle Girl. I know where she will be.

A danfo bus drops me, literally. It is still moving when I step off. It is early in the evening and people are milling about the market. I wait for a gap in the traffic, and cross to safety. The square is lined with shops that all face a cast bronze statue of Oduduwa, the founder of Yorubaland. Most are simple wooden structures with corrugated-iron roofing. Some traders have gone home for the day. Others sell savoury snacks and food, especially boli served in paper and garnished with fiery-hot pepper sauce. Boli is roasted plantain, and it is usually sold with roasted peanuts. The aroma dominates the air. I have no money, so I ignore my watering mouth.

The occasional constable walks a beat, but with no expectation of action, as violent crime is virtually zero. The local newspaper, *The Clarion*, reports domestic spats, contamination of the water reservoir by pranksters, visits by national dignitaries, and the release of the latest implant technology. Most people get their news from Nimbus on their phones and ignore the highly censored and pre-digested bulletins.

There are paper bills on several telephone poles; they hold a sketch of a young woman with Afro puffs. *Have you seen Oyin Da? Have you heard her message of light? The Science Hero of Arodan lives!* Beneath this a phone number blazes in red marker. I kick myself for not memorising the number of the crazy man I spoke to before for comparison.

I walk among the citizens, return the greetings of those who greet me. A stray dog barks at me and charges in a fitful way before finally breaking off. Up in the sky there are early stars and the ungainly blob of the Nautilus, that failed space station.

A gaggle of teenaged girls giggles past me. Their fingers are chest height and they depress each digit as if on invisible keyboards. They have dactylo implants and text with a linked keyboard only visible on their contact lenses or glasses. Too much metal in them for my liking. I hate implants.

I find an empty stall and wait. I am uneasy. Something is

going on inside me, inside my mind. I am getting flashes of ... images, impressions, smells, tactile phenomena. They last seconds, but are distinct from the wide array that led me to the market in the first place.

I see them after twenty minutes. Two men, three women. They do not exactly glow and I do not hear the Hallelujah Chorus, but I know them as distinct from the other shoppers and straggler traders. They do not mill or window-shop. They have lists and buy what they want without haggling. Their fashions are about a decade out of date. The fabric is that thermal-dissipation shit, with seamless cuts, that people used to wear around '47. I can't believe I used to wear that. They are furtive, but trying not to appear so. They never lose line of sight to each other, I notice. It's as if an invisible thread connects them. They root, looking up after buying to be sure the others are within reach.

I am careful about watching them. It seems to last for ever, but on giving and receiving an unseen signal they converge and leave the market area. I follow behind at a safe distance. I have no bag of goods, about which I am irritated because it makes me obvious. I grab an abandoned green beer bottle and slow down, try to give the impression of a drunk, but I'm sure I'm fooling nobody.

They pass down an alleyway between two houses. It opens into a field denuded of grass by local kids playing football. They walk diagonally across the pitch towards nothing at first, but I can feel a convergence of possibilities. This is it.

A brightness appears and they do not hesitate, but aim for it. I do a quick calculation and realise I won't make it. One by one they start to disappear into the light. I start to run. There are only two of them left, now one. Before the light swallows the last one, I leap, catch hold of one of the bags. It feels cold and bursts open, showering me in cutlets of beef. I lose balance and end up on the ground.

The ground is now concrete and all five of the people surround me. I pick meat off my face. A woman stands in front of me. She wears overalls and has her hair in Afro puffs. I know who she is and she does not seem surprised to see me.

"Wait right here and remain still," she says.

She turns, darts to the side of a machine panel, reaches into a scabbard and draws a double-barrelled shotgun. She points this at my face and speaks to the others.

"Move away from him. This will make a mess."

Chapter Twenty-Three

Rosewater: 2066

Now

I'm seated on the road a metre and a half away from the burning building. My hearing is back, sort of.

As usual, the fire brigade has engines but no water. The firemen are in uniform and do not seem embarrassed at all by the empty hoses on their truck. Their expertise is directed to organising the numerous local men and women who turn out with containers of water and white sand. Between them they put the fire out. The smouldering mess is the embodiment of hopelessness. The walls are still standing, but the roof has caved in and all windows lack glass. I am coughing from the smoke, but uninjured. About fifteen COB hawks rest on cars, walls and ledges close by, observing, sending information to servers. Two more circle overhead. A few steps away from me the security guard who waved Aminat in sits staring at his shoes. A line of blood trickles from his left ear, his uniform hangs in shreds, and his skin is dotted with broken glass. In his hand is the burst football the street kids were playing with just before the blast. The dead are lined up on the ground, uncovered. Most of them have lost one or both shoes and I find that puzzling. Even more puzzling is that I cannot locate Aminat.

In the xenosphere there is no sign of her, but that does not necessarily mean she is dead. The explosion may also have burned off the xenoforms in the air, so the network may be growing back slowly. Her telephone goes to voicemail.

People make attempts to look after me, and I am overwhelmed by the kindness of strangers, but I do not need or want it. I am not a sentimental person generally, but I feel deep sorrow at Aminat's luck. Why was there a bomb at her office? Was this aimed at me? *God, Aminat, what the fuck?* My chest actually hurts, and I think I might be having a heart attack, until I realise it's just grief. My heart is beating as if I have a small bird in my chest, but it feels as heavy as lead. I need a drink or something. I breathe, and the pain abates.

"Mr Kaaro?" says a voice.

I look up to see a young local militia man standing over me. Three other armed men in uniform stand behind him at parade rest.

"It's just Kaaro. What can I do for you?"

"You're to come with us to the Department of Agriculture, sir. Orders."

"My girlfriend just died," I say.

"Which one is she?" he says, pointing to the corpses.

"Her ... She hasn't been found yet."

"Then I'm sorry. We have to take you with us. It's orders. I promise I will come back to get her for you."

When I don't move, he grabs my upper arm to steer me away, but I twist free and take a clumsy swing at him. He ducks under it and gently trips me while holding my upper torso. He kneels on my chest to keep me down, though I am fighting him and shouting something incoherent.

"Sir, calm down. Be calm." He repeats this until it gets through to me. I think he shushes me like a baby at one point. When I feel stupid, I stop struggling and go limp.

"Let me up," I say.

He does and apologises. He even makes an attempt to brush dust off my clothes.

I take one last look at the ruined building. As I follow the man, I think again of quitting S45. It's easier for me to accommodate rage than grief.

There's a new guy at Ubar. His name is Badmos and he sweats a lot. His handshake is wet. He says he is my new handler. I find him obsequious, slick, smiling. I will no longer have direct access to the director.

"It was an anomaly, really. The only reason Alaagomeji had contact with you was because you were there when she got promoted."

"She didn't get promoted. Everyone senior to her got—" I try to say more, but cough instead. It comes from deep inside my chest.

"You better do something about that cough," he says, smiling, but with a hidden edge that says it's not a suggestion. "It's important to, eh, to finish up this business."

He means the interrogation. "Why? Why is it important? Do we now know what he's up to?"

"Do you want to be thought of as lazy?"

"I find that the older I get, the less I care what people think about me. I only care what a small number of people think, and that number is dwindling daily."

"Eh, you are talking about Aminat, your paramour. Well, you'll be pleased to know her body was not recovered from the debris. She was not in the building."

"Were you starved of oxygen at birth? I saw her walk in, Badmos. I was right there."

"Twelve deaths, three minors, all accounted for. Your girl, Aminat Arigbede, is not there. We've queried servers for her implant information, but that will take time."

What?

"For now, I need you to finish up here. Find out what this guy is up to."

I pick up nothing from this Badmos, but that doesn't mean much. He may have scrubbed with medicated soap and moisturised with ketoconazole. Why else would he be meeting me unprotected?

"I'm not of a mind to do this right now, Badmos."

He places a sweaty proprietorial hand on the back of my shoulder. "Not optional, Kaaro. I've read your file and heard good things about you. I'm sure you can wrap this up in a single session."

I enter a room with my mind in turmoil because of Aminat. Tolu Eleja is seated with the white-noise headphones on. He is dressed this time, and his wounds have had time to heal. I feel kinship with him since I am healing too. He has not been beaten in my absence. I indicate to the agent that the noise should be stopped. Eleja licks his lips nervously, like he knows what's coming.

I start. Nothing happens. I hear the whirr of a climate-control device somewhere in the building and the rushing of my own blood in my ears, but I have no access to the xenosphere. I try everything. Deep breathing, forced hyperventilation,

mindfulness meditation, fantasy image flooding, distraction ...
Nothing works. In desperation, I try to call Molara mentally.
She does not answer.

"I need to have a shower," I say to the agent, and this may
even be true. Sometimes with prolonged use ketoconazole builds
up on the skin to such an extent that the xenoforms cannot
form links. Theoretically. This has never happened to me.

Washing makes no difference. I use scalding hot and ice-cold
water, but all is, as they say, vanity. The mirror is frosted over
and I clean it with my forearm and stare at myself. I slap my
own cheek. "Come on, fuckface. What are you playing at?" I
head-butt the mirror, checking whether it will jar my abilities
into working or shake something loose.

I slide to the floor.

I could pretend. I could write up a bogus report. I already
know that Eleja is up to something, and that he's trying to hide
it from anyone poking around in his head. I can make up a paragraph or pages of shit and leave. Problem is, it might conflict
with whatever concrete information they have. So what? This
isn't an exact science. It isn't even a science. I cough and I can
taste blood in the phlegm I swallow. I'm sick.

I doze off and find myself with Professor Ileri in the classroom where he taught me and the other raw sensitives. Or
maybe in sleep whatever blocks me from the xenosphere is
removed. It feels like a dream. Ileri stands in front of the class.
I sit in the front row because I'm older than the others and I
have no time for their classroom antics.

"You are dying, Kaaro," says Ileri.

"No I'm not. I have smoke inhalation."

"You were coughing before the explosion, remember?" Ileri
is patient, always has been.

"What is killing me?"

"The same thing that killed the others," he says, and points to the rest of the class.

I look and see that all the other students are dead. Their corpses are posed in the seats, but they are all in various stages of decomposition.

"What can I do?" I ask.

"Call in your favour," he says. "And wake up."

I'm on the floor of the bathroom and an agent is shaking me. "Thank God, I thought you were dead," she says.

"Wait around a bit longer. Your thoughts might be correct," I say, and get up.

In the end I tell Badmos the truth, or a version of it. I say I'm feeling unwell, so I can't read Eleja. I allude to grief about Aminat – if she's not dead, she's missing – and since this is true, I am convincing. He releases me. If I lose my abilities, who knows what S45 will do? I won't be useful to them any more, and it's easier to keep secrets when you're dead. As soon as I leave, I think of contacting Ileri.

Professor Ileri has retired, of course. He must have been about sixty back in '55. He is probably under milder surveillance than others. The address I have places him in Ilesha, Osun State. Ilesha has existed since just before the 1700s. The city is known for cleanliness and order; not civil, but geometric regularity. That's for outsiders. People from Ilesha are also known to be stubborn and hard-headed, exemplified by the statue in the town square of the hardest motherfucker you have ever seen, wielding a machete and garlanded with charms. That statue says: *if you fuck with us, we will fuck you up*. It definitely is not there to welcome visitors.

Ilesha is an hour from Rosewater. I hope to be in and out before S45 notices I'm gone. I have to speak to Ileri. I'm driving along Iwo Road, five minutes to Ileri's last-known address, when a quadcopter appears in front of me, matching my speed, not doing anything. I'm trying to decide a course of action when two more appear at the sides of my car. In the rear mirror I see one more. I slow to a halt. I've pushed my luck too far.

I hear noise now, and the grass on the side of the road bends under invisible weight. A larger aircraft, a helicopter.

I start to come out of the car, but an alarm goes off.

"Stay where you are, Kaaro, or we will kill you."

Here we go again. What did I say about Ilesha? They do not fuck around. I stop breathing just in case my movement is misconstrued.

Three hours later, I'm back in Rosewater, in my flat, an official reprimand on my record. I'm staring out of the window when I see four reanimates happening along my street. No matter how efficient the Special Detachment, there are always reanimates, all year round. They don't hide, they are just ubiquitous. Not all are dangerous. Some people swear they are harmless and only reflect the emotional states around them. I know that to be bullshit, but what's more ridiculous is movies that have them eating brains or raw living flesh. Why the fuck would they do that?

I'm drinking tepid water. I've been coughing, but not bringing up phlegm. The water helps, but not much. My wrists are bruised in a circular fashion from the handcuffs those Ilesha cops put on me. It'll pass. It's not the first time I've been bruised from fetters.

My phone rings, unknown number. I'm not expecting any calls.

"Go dark," I say, and my apartment hides itself from

273

surveillance by sending out virtual chaff, nonsense information based loosely on how I protect the xenosphere by reading classic literature into it. The windows vibrate gently. The apartment emits subtle wavelengths that discombobulate cameras.

"Hello?" I say.

"Are you secure?" Familiar voice.

"Yes. Who is this?"

"I heard you paid me a visit today," says Ileri.

"Prof!"

"It's odd speaking to you like this. I had a dream a few days ago that you and I were working on a machine together. In the dream I knew what the machine did and we were both happy creating it, but I woke up and the details faded."

"How are you, sir?"

"I am more dead than alive, my boy. There are still enough people in the organisation that feed me information, which is how I heard about your stunt today. What were you thinking? Nobody's going to allow you and me to be in the same airspace. I know more about S45 than they are comfortable with you knowing right now."

"Desperate times, sir."

"I see. And what has made them so desperate?"

I tell him everything, though in shorthand, and edited to remove culpability on Femi's part. After all, nostalgia aside, it's been more than ten years since I last saw Ileri, and I have no idea where his loyalties lie.

"Nobody from my class is unaffected," I say. "Wild strains are diminished, maybe gone, I don't know." I fall silent as I think of Molara.

"Son, the real mystery is why this is only happening now. Get something straight, Kaaro: nobody likes you."

"Why does everybody keep telling me this?" I'm irritable.

"You sensitives, I mean. Because it is true. Nobody should be able to do what you do. The mind is supposed to be the last sanctuary of a free human. Even prisoners are not meant to give up the sanctity of their thoughts. Then people like you come along. There is bound to be resentment. Resentment in human populations leads to both chaotic and organised attempts at destruction of the object."

"Prof, I get it. I've learned a little bit about human behaviour in the last decade. What I want from you is insight. Who wants us dead? Who is killing the sensitives?"

There is a beat where he says nothing and I have the impression that he either shrugs or takes a drag on a pipe or cigarette. "I do not know, but think in terms of candidates, Kaaro. I am trying to avoid a prolix dissertation here, but consider what you have found out from the Americans. No country on the planet has had more time or resources devoted to the study of xenoforms. They had a budget of millions, maybe billions, while in comparison Nigeria had just me, a mycologist and a dendrochronologist. The American response to all this study? They ran and hid.

"Think about that for a moment, then think about this: the religious people don't like the idea of you because you challenge the concept of their various gods. Only gods and prophets are supposed to know the hearts of men, so look out for the Jesuits or Jesuit-like zealots. Examine your own house. There is a definite group within the government that does not support the use of sensitives, or any study of xenoforms for that matter. They have, over the years, used pretty incendiary language and asked for deracination of our department. Considering the fact that we report all information upstream, and that we have no information on them coming downstream ... well, we have always walked in the shadow of death.

"Consider, also, nature. The xenoforms are unnatural. I personally consider them biological machines, biotechnology rather than living organisms. Machines get instructions from somewhere. Maybe the owners or designers set timers that are winding down. Or maybe your bodies have finally recognised them as alien, and in the process of shutting them down, a massive autoimmune process has been triggered."

"Which is it, Prof?"

"Pay attention, Kaaro. I said I do not know. I have only theories for you."

"Right. Fantastic. Now I'm supposed to do something heroic, right?"

"Please. For one thing, you're not the type. Second, I am tired of women and men of destiny. The idea of a singular hero and a manifest destiny just makes us all lazy. There is no destiny. There is choice, there is action, and any other narrative perpetuates a myth that someone else out there will fix our problems with a magic sword and a blessing from the gods." Ileri coughs after talking.

"Are you sick?"

"No. Not in the way you are. I am just old, Kaaro. My own biological clock is winding down. Entropy catches up with us all."

"I was never really sure if you were one of us," I say.

"I am not. I just know how to move information around. From study into my brain and from my brain into others'. I am going to hang up, Kaaro. I think I am being traced. One thing is most important to me. You were not my best student – that honour goes to Ebun – but you were the most skilled, and the most respectful. I have no children of my own, and I would not like you to die before me.

"Goodbye."

He clicks off. The reanimates have shuffled out of sight.

I go back to Ubar to take another run at interrogating Eleja, but it doesn't help. I leave again before my employers can notice I'm stalling.

As soon as I clear the protected building, my phone messages come in. Clement has sent me a text:

Why are u trying to kill me? What did I ever do to u?

What the hell is wrong with the world? What does he think I have done or am doing? He's the one who tried to kill me with that iron golem thing. There is a voicemail and I guess it's from him, but I get another surprise.

"Kaaro, it's me. Don't worry, I'm fine. I know this seems strange, but I'll explain. I'm all right, my love. I did lose my phone function, though. I'll see you later tonight."

Aminat. Alive, just like that idiot Badmos said. I dial her phone, before I remember that she's lost the use of it. Then I call Clement.

"Why won't you leave me alone?" he says by way of greeting. His voice is hoarse. "I'm not a threat to you. I never have been."

"Will you shut up? What is your problem?"

"My problem? My problem is you've been attacking me for weeks!"

I get a bout of dizziness.

"I tried appeasing you at work. I bought you coffee, snacks, everything. I tried to be your friend. You did not stop."

"Clement, I have no idea what you're talking about."

"Stay away from me!"

He hangs up.

*

277

The world has gone mad, Clement has definitely gone mad, and I have to chart and quantify the madness for my own safety. On the train back to my flat in Atewo, I access the news. There is perhaps a paragraph on the explosion. The building involved is described as belonging to the Drug Authenticity Directorate and has been the subject of many threats since inception of the organisation. Huh. Aminat is a drug inspector, or at least works in the same building as drug inspectors. Fake drug manufacture in Nigeria is an industry in itself. Almost every hospital has found some of its injections to be river water and its pills to be chalk. Inspections are a public safety concern. Bombings of inspectors is an old tradition dating back to the early 2000s. Not a very popular job and, if some exposés are to be believed, rife with corruption.

Passengers are congregated at the windows on the right. The dome is throwing off what we tend to call reverse lightning. Shards of blue electricity puncture the night sky and disappear beyond, like the world's most expensive firework show. Power supplies, phone coverage and Nimbus will suffer tonight. The ganglia will be firing at the dome and the dome will be firing at the sky. Wormwood is having a nightmare. A warning will go out to air-traffic controllers. I try to listen to my fellow commuters, but all I get is elation and half-realised *Schadenfreude*. They stay away from me because of my cough.

I come off the clockwise train at Atewo. Yaro is there licking a discarded food wrapper. He catches my scent and follows for a few steps, but I am busy and he is held back by his wound, which is teeming with maggots. I have no food to give him, so I speed up. I receive a text from my flat. It tells me someone is in there. This is not an S45 agent. My flat is configured not to register their presence. Is it Clement? I'm two streets away. My first instinct is to rush over there, but I have almost no access to the xenosphere, and I have no gun. I can call in S45, but if it is Clement they'll know that my abilities aren't working and bring me in for a medical overhaul. Is that such a bad thing? The way I'm coughing ...

On the other hand, they might take the opportunity to place a more sophisticated implant in me. That palaver I do not want.

I call a neighbour. I tell him my flat sent a text detecting gas and ask can he please go and check. He calls back.

"There's no gas leak. Your girlfriend's making pancakes, and it must have been the smoke."

I thank him and enter the flat just as Aminat baptises the pancakes in honey. She has a glass of red wine in the other hand.

"You know, I think this wine has acquired an edge. How long has it been open?"

I am in her arms, and I am kissing her. "How did you escape?"

"You smell of smoke," she says.

"I thought you were dead." I look at her. My people would pour sand on her, which, if she were a ghost, would make her disappear according to Yoruba folklore.

"Yes, about that ... "

"Hello, Kaaro."

Layi stands in my bedroom doorway wearing a towel around his waist, with three or four chain links left on the manacle around his ankle. The last one is deformed.

"How are you here? I thought you don't ... How is he here?" I look from Aminat to Layi and back. What I don't mention is the absurd thought that I always seem to see him in a state of undress.

Aminat says, "He saved me, Kaaro, but don't ask any questions. Please. Just ... I'm just grateful to be alive."

I kiss her again.

Layi does not say anything. He is in good humour as usual. He claps his hands. "Shall I have some wine?" he asks.

"No, definitely not. You are not allowed alcohol." Aminat extricates herself from me. "The car will be here any minute. Are you ready?"

Layi spreads out his arms. "It's not like I have anything to pack."

I am puzzled, but I don't ask. I take another shower, because I did not change my clothes at Ubar and I feel like the smell is on me. I probe for the xenosphere and I experience a slight turn, some vertigo, and a non-specific sense of dread that is not from me. I feel what might be Aminat, but nothing from Layi. It's a start. It's better than the last time I tried.

I call S45 and ask for a home address for Clement. They give it to me without asking for authorisation or reasons. I put on a suit, although each time I cough I feel unworthy of it. When I emerge, Layi is hugging his sister goodbye. From her left shoulder he looks at me. He is wearing my clothes, although the trouser cuffs are at mid-calf and his muscles bulge out of my shirt. I do not mind, and he knows this. He smiles at me. I almost want a hug myself, looking at his beauty. I hear a car horn from downstairs and he runs off, chain rattling like a cowbell.

Because of my gratitude that Aminat is alive, I decide to pay the taxi fare. I read off the registration number, enter it into my financeware via my mobile and give instructions. It registers an error. I think nothing of it; I've probably punched in the codes wrong. I'll do it later.

Aminat turns to me. "You look good in a suit."

"Don't try to distract me. What the fuck, Aminat?"

"Can we at least sit down? Is there any more wine any-where? I have decided I like being alive."

When the new bottle of Merlot has finished breathing, I pour her some and sit opposite. I do not want any alcohol. The xenosphere returns in pulses of alien mentations and I don't want to delay it.

"Layi is only my half-brother," says Aminat.

"Which half?" I ask.

"We share a mother."

"I didn't know your mother was married before."

"She wasn't. Layi is between us siblings. She had him ... well ... "

"An affair?"

"No. Not exactly. My father believes it to be a rape, but a few years ago my mother told me the truth. She went with a friend of hers to some kind of tent revival on a beach. There were rumours that an angel had landed there."

"Seriously?"

"You know how Lagosians love their prophets. Thus, there was Brother Luke – the only true vessel of the Lord, mon-strously fat, with six wives at last count; there was Jesu Bariga, a paranoiac who thought he was Jesus and had hundreds of followers, none of whom had ever cracked open the Bible; there was Guru Maharaji; there was Omotola of the Nine Bells – obvious charlatan, civil war veteran, twitchy doctrine; and there was Joachim of the Lord's Flame, who claimed to have access to an angel of the Lord. Which maybe he did."

I sigh. I remember that Aminat has books on talking to God.

"Just hear me out, okay? Joachim of the Lord's Flame used to be known as Joe-Joe Abbadon, also known as Junior Agbako. He ran a gang of armed robbers who operated the Lagos–Ibadan expressway for eighteen months until they accidentally shot and killed an off-duty police constable. It was not an accident to shoot the man; they just didn't know he was a policeman. As such things go, the Nigerian police rained its righteous fury upon them and most of the gang ended up tied to stakes and steel drums on the sands of Bar Beach, executed on live television. Joe-Joe evaded capture, shaved his head and moustache, lay low for some years, and reappeared on the same Bar Beach as a white-garment prophet calling himself Joachim of the Lord's Flame.

"He built a bamboo beach hut, veiled and painted with gaudy red crosses and orange flames drawn in crayon by a five-year-old. The prophet himself wore a dazzling white gown and a hood that covered most of his head. This might be because he did not wish to be recognised, given his larcenous past, but he claimed to have been burned in the fire of the Lord. He preached in the open air and carried a bell tied to his sash like a leper of old. His message was garbled, incoherent and punctuated with swigs from a bottle of holy water. There was speculation that the bottle was filled with an entirely different kind of spirit, and the smell of Beefeater gin hung around him even in the early hours of the morning.

"Joachim was an obvious, desperate and inebriated charlatan to be sure, but there was something real in the hut. A few choice members of his congregation had been allowed to enter – six in total, the only ones persistent enough to endure the required purification rituals. One of them was struck blind. Another went insane and was in the mental hospital at

Aro for countless years. Two could feed on fluids and pureed foods from then on. One was so badly burned that she died within hours. A butcher from Ajegunle survived. In a manner of speaking. He did not talk much any more, but when he did speak he said, 'Joachim is a true prophet of the Lord.'"

"Of course," I say.

"The message turned out to be some grandiloquent pap designed to move the crowd to empty their pockets into the collection bowls. Joachim himself was a lanky cadaver in a red-lined white robe. He spoke with the scratchy deep voice of a constant smoker. After his message and the offering, he directed my mother into the hut."

"And he raped her in there?"

"No. He apparently stayed outside. Her memory of it isn't good, but she was sure of one thing: she did have sex. She said she couldn't guarantee that it was non-consensual, and that the angel in there was on fire, but that the flames were black."

This makes me stop. I remember seeing Aminat surrounded by black flames in the xenosphere. It could be an image she manufactures from her mother's story.

"She came back to herself wandering the beach. The revival had packed up and moved on. Later she found herself pregnant with Layi. He was beautiful—"

"He still is."

"Oh, I know. I know. You can believe he was ... his father was an angel. We found out early, though: he burns."

"What do you mean?"

"He ignites, spontaneously combusts, explodes, I don't know, something. He never does it when anyone is watching, but we see the aftermath. That's why there are fire extinguishers and sprinklers all over our house."

I remember seeing all the safety equipment when I visited.

"He's burned the house down once, as you saw."

"Why the chain?"

It is her turn to sigh. "We . . . we also think he flies."

I start to laugh, but it turns into a cough, and then I see that she is not joking.

"I'm serious."

"Has anyone seen him fly?"

"No, but he escapes, and not by the doors. We see a hole in the roof, and scorch marks. You saw the melted chain."

"Aminat, has anyone asked him?"

"What do you think? Of course we've asked him. He doesn't talk about the fires or his escapes. He just doesn't answer."

She drains her glass. I think of Femi telling me to keep away from this family. At the time I thought she was talking about Aminat's husband, but this . . .

"How did you get out of the building alive?"

"I have no memory of it. I was there, furious with you, going inside. Next thing I knew, I was here, on the floor, and Layi was standing over me grinning, naked as the day he was born."

"I don't believe in angels, but I suppose it's possible that an alien was in that tent. I've seen a few species in books and encountered some over the years. Your husband had one and it almost killed me. The problem is they aren't genetically compatible with humans and many of them died after the Visitation."

"I'm just telling you what my mother told me, Kaaro." She leans back in the chair. "And I'm alive when I should be dead."

I stand. "Go easy on the booze. I'm going to pay someone a visit. I won't be long."

"I have to retrieve my online files anyway. Do you mind if I stay here?"

"Just don't blow the place up." I kiss her, and leave to go and see Clement.

Interlude: Adrift

Rosewater: 2065

The Yemaja cult walks its route through the streets, south-bound. They are led by a priestess in white wearing clear beads, with acolytes carrying carvings and statuettes of the goddess. They lead a bull and seven rams along with them. The procession is half a mile long, and at the tail end is a two-foot statue of Our Lady of the Leaking Breasts.

I know why this is happening and I'm ambivalent. In June, the Yemaja overflowed its banks and flooded the poverty-stricken districts of Ona-oko and Idowu. Fourteen people died; many were rendered homeless. Yemaja is the goddess of rivers, so if there's a flood, she must be angry. Hence the procession. I follow because ... well, I don't know. In legend, Yemaja's husband was Orunmila, the second most powerful of the Yoruba gods and the father of divination. There are those who say that what sensitives do is like divination, and I know that at S45 there are sensitives who use Ifa geomancy.

Which means nothing, but I still feel an affinity to the goddess, and a part of me wonders if the gods are aliens. So I follow all the way to the banks of the river we named after her.

They dance and chant and pray, legs dirty with spattered mud. They slaughter the rams one after the other, then the bull, and the acolytes enter a convulsive possession trance. The priestess is the only one in apparent control, as she listens respectfully to the message from her goddess.

By dusk it is over and everyone goes home. I scan the xeno-sphere for traces of the goddess, but other than the fading memories of bystanders ... nothing.

Chapter Twenty-Four

The Lijad, unknown military base: 2055

Then

"Err ... " I say.

I am staring down the barrel of a shotgun in what is undoubtedly the Lijad. I am only slightly confused and disoriented. This is exactly what I want. Well, maybe not exactly. The girl with the gun in my face is Oyin Da, the Bicycle Girl. Behind her is the professor, Aloy Ogene, who led me here. None of the scenarios in my head involve being on the ground wondering if a shooter can miss at this range.

"He has no weapons, Oyin Da," says Ogene.

"I have no weapons, Oyin Da," I say. I maintain eye contact with her like I've heard animal trainers say, because I have no idea what she may or may not do to me.

"Who are you?" she asks.

Her name means "spilled honey" in Yoruba. Her mind churns like a choppy sea, but with clarity. I don't know how I know this. Something has changed in me, or in my abilities.

I have shown occasional flashes of this before, but it's more consistent all of a sudden. I know, for example, that she is not going to kill me, that she has never killed a human, though she is good with the shotgun.

"I am going to stand up," I say. I tell her because she still seems twitchy.

"No, you will stay there until I am satisfied," she says.

"He is unarmed," says Ogene again.

"Can I at least pick this meat off myself? It's a bit disgusting and this shirt is expensive." I pick the contents of the shopping bag off one at a time. I get an image of my father teaching me how to butcher a goat, cutting the belly open lengthwise and identifying all the parts. Except my father never did that. The memory belongs to one of the other men standing around. With other people's thoughts in my head I am distracted, can't concentrate. This is not going to be easy.

"You will tell me your name," says Oyin Da. She speaks oddly, as if she is reading from a book.

On impulse, I tell her the truth. "I will. My name is Kaaro. I am a thief and I've been asked to find you." I tell her everything, partly because I'm tired of carrying it all around with me, partly because she seems to lack guile, while I am full of it, partly because I want her to trust me and I'm going to need a place to land after I fuck over S45. While I talk, I am amazed that I can pick thoughts out of her brain like ears of corn. They float on the ether, visible tasty morsels with weight and character and odours. It's difficult to explain if you have never experienced this. I can feel her relax. No, that's someone else, off to the right of me, one of the women with the shopping. She owns the bag of meat cutlets. Owned. She is wondering if any cutlets can be salvaged. There are

289

children in the Lijad and there has been some difficulty keeping them all fed.

I sample the others, but I am addicted to Bicycle Girl's
thoughts. There is a clarity, a lack of deception, a beauty mixed
with an untamed playful expansion of possibilities and alternatives. She has four trains of thought going at the same time. She
is truly egalitarian and holds Ogene in high esteem.

The place I find myself in is just the antechamber of the
Lijad; a rectangular space half filled with a grotesque machine.
It's a true Frankenstein's monster, with parts cobbled from
different eras and swapped out from pilfered components. It
works, but only with frequent intervention from Ogene, Oyin
Da and some other men and women, which I sense is a kind
of joyful labour for all of them, filling them with a sense of
achievement that emanates throughout the room. The area is
surprisingly dark, although some of the control panels glow in
warm green and red hues. I absorb the Lijad in a combination
of what I can see and what I derive from the thoughts of the
people around me, and the information arrives in a mishmash
of knowledge that I have trouble sorting.

In spite of the gun, I detect no malice in Oyin Da. Quite
the opposite. It seems she thinks of the threat as a kind of
screening for new inhabitants, although she is undecided about
what to do.

"Why does this Section Forty-Five want me?" she asks.

"I do not know, but I don't think they want to give you a
medal," I say. She is unafraid of the government. Not even a
twinge of anxiety.

She tilts her head to Ogene. "Have you heard of this
organisation?"

"Not Section Forty-Five, but I've heard of what might have

been the parent department back when ignorant people were killing children they called witches decades ago."

There is more, but Ogene keeps it to himself because he does not want me to know what he knows. I pluck it out of his head anyway.

What became S45 started in the mid-noughties as a rescue operation, of all things. By 2006, there had been several lynchings of children and teenagers. They were either beaten to death by a mob or necklaced. The killings were instigated by church pastors who declared the children witches. In some cases, the only sign of witchcraft was albinism. The pastors could not be arrested because they were popular in the community, and popularity equals votes, even in a country with widespread election rigging. The world watched mobile-phone footage of mob action with horror, and Nigeria was once again a laughing stock in the international community. The president wanted something done.

The first actions were simple church surveillance assignments. Agents were placed in or recruited from the congregations and the messages from the pulpit analysed. Overt interest in spirituality was not enough; such beliefs were ubiquitous in Nigeria. An interest in exorcism, particularly the violent variety that tried to beat or starve a demon out, was the kind of thing Section Forty-Five was tasked to root out. A potential child in danger would be identified as possessed and targeted by the pastor with the cooperation of parents. Section Forty-Five agents would whisk the child away in the night.

This operation was so successful that local superstition laid the blame at the feet of Satan. The Devil was a thief, stealing away the children instead of allowing God to cast out the demons. This did not matter. Deaths were down, children were saved, and nobody suspected government involvement.

Then the departmental focus shifted to other anomalistic phenomena.

Ogene loves Oyin Da like a daughter. He also seems to love his wife Regina, even though he is fucking one of the Lijad women. One of the other women in the room thinks I might be a danger to her daughters and mentally urges Oyin Da to shoot me. She does not.

Oyin Da swings the barrel up, eyes still on me. She is interesting to watch. At first glance what you notice about her is her massive Afro puffs, which look like twin dark moons frozen in orbit behind her head. I'd put her age at about twenty, definitely no older than twenty-five. A neat parting bisects her hair in the exact middle. But there's more. Her eyes are restless, alighting on everything in the visual field several times, but at the same time able to focus on me. She has a large mouth, but thin lips. She is skinny, and her body movements are a mixture of complete stillness interspersed with bursts of hyperkinetic activity, as if she takes time to contemplate, then acts decisively. She also talks like she's reading text from a book. Precise, correct, but strangely without affect.

She thinks it must be uncomfortable on the floor and wants an excuse to let me up. I smile. I decide I like this thought-reading business.

"What's funny?" asks Oyin Da.

"Nothing. I just thought there would be Lijadu Sisters music piped all through this place," I say. I sing a few bars of a song I heard on Nimbus.

Oyin Da gives Ogene a look, and I know that the name was his idea. "Search him," she says.

As they manhandle me, I note that there are no windows

here, and as well as the lights of the machine there are fluorescent tubes at various intervals. There is a strong smell of burning metal, the kind you get in welder's shops, although nothing is on fire.

"There are no weapons on him," says one of the men who search me. He is disgusted by the meat stench.

"I told you," I say.

"Yes, you did," says Oyin Da. "What am I to do with you?"

"If there's a threat, we need to move in a direction away from it," says Ogene.

"Shall we not understand the threat first?" asks Oyin Da.

"I'm not a threat," I say.

"Not you. Section Forty-Five." Oyin Da's mind is as elegant as a French horn, thoughts moving in whorls. "Take the shopping in. The children will be getting hungry soon. And get me the implant scanner."

They sit me down and place a black device shaped like a toilet seat around my neck. It makes me shiver, a reminder of when the mob put a tyre around my neck. It beeps when it crosses my chip at the root of my neck. Oyin Da sits across from me looking at a holo-field display. "At least you've been where you say you've been," she says.

"Will you people stop looking at me like I'm some variety of snake then?"

"You *are* some variety of snake," says Ogene. "You're the first uninvited person who has ever been here and you confess to tracking us for the federal government."

"Yes, but I'm here now and I don't want to expose your location."

"You could not even if you wanted to," says Oyin Da. "We are not in a location per se." *More like a potential of location,*

293

the different spaces between various heres. The Lijad exists with Schrödinger's cat in a dimension of several unknowable probabilities.

She leaves the panel and starts pushing com controls. Ogene moves to her side and whispers. This is so easy, this thought awareness. He is concerned that she might be walking into a trap and that it would be energy-expensive keeping a window open for as long as it would require to find out. She says it will be all right, but what she is thinking is that being a finder, I will guide them and help them escape when the time comes. She has granted me a limited amount of trust. This fills my belly with warmth.

"Give him a change of clothes," says Oyin Da. She code-switches into Yoruba, where her speech is not so devoid of emotion. "I'm not going to meet running-dog government lackeys smelling of meat."

"Touch these clothes and you die," I say. "Meat or no meat, this shirt is Pierre Cardin. I'd rather stink."

There is a flowering of thoughts from all of them following my comment, each of them wondering how I came to be so absurd. I *feel* absurd; then I realise that actually I don't, but I'm aware of emotions from around me. I am confused, but in a good way.

"Let's see what the council thinks," says Oyin Da.

They march me out of the control room into what should be open air, but isn't. It's dark, but not like night. I look up and see that the sky is artificial. About a hundred feet up there appears to be a vault of some patchy material held up with metal ribs. Both the material and the ribs are variously coloured, like found material. The ribs end on both sides of the horizon, but are held up with poles sunk into the ground at intervals. I wonder what is outside the vault, and when the people walking with me think of the sky, there is an undercurrent of trepidation. There are light bulbs at intervals on the ribs, but they are not lit.

Behind me, the building that houses the portal machine is an ugly block of concrete with some slit windows near the flat roof. What is unusual is that there are scores of bicycles sunk into the concrete, wheels removed, chains linking pedals to small generator devices, cables trailing into the roof like artificial cobwebs. There are so many that the roof looks hairy from a distance.

"The cycles," I say. "Is that art?"

Oyin Da snorts. "An earlier version required a kick-start of power at a time when we were not connected to the national grid."

I see a succession of images from her. A black-and-white photograph showing a shirtless white man in the foreground with several black men behind him, and the block in the background. The flip side of the photograph has the words *Bicycle Boys* on it. The image shifts to Oyin Da working on both blueprints and the manifest machine. There is an image with all the boys riding the bikes to infinity, generating some current, firing up the machine.

I see a catastrophic explosion after which there is no blue sky, nor clouds, but a kind of warped space, a twisting, churning abyss that drives people mad and necessitates the building of the vault.

Oyin Da nudges me. "Are you all right? You seem preoccupied."

"I'm ... fine. It's just a lot to take in."

"It's best if you don't see this place like a village. Think

295

of it as a vehicle," says Ogene. In his mind he worries that I will go berserk if I happen upon a gap in the vault, of which there are many.

Along the path there is a brightly lit area for growing crops. This farm is untended right now, but I can see the work that has gone into it. Not a weed in sight, and tight ridges and furrows. I smell fertiliser and compost, although I am unsure if this is the memory of the smell picked up from someone around me.

We pass empty schoolhouses, the buildings locked. From several people I receive the image of virtual-reality pods for each pupil, scavenged and retrofitted. The people here are proud of the education they offer their children. They have a version of local Nimbus, limited by their lack of consistent connection to the world, but Ogene and others have servers that are updated when the Lijad reality intersects with ours.

There are gymnasiums, again empty. My sense is that I have arrived at their agreed night-time. The ersatz day lasts for sixteen hours, and they turn on the lights, which nobody in the Lijad really likes.

We come to a village hall. News of my arrival has spread by gossip. I can literally feel the wave of information, a data front spreading throughout the village. There are about fifteen hundred people here, all curious about me. At least they aren't thinking of killing the stranger.

They have a council of thirteen elders and Oyin Da puts a case, my case, to them patiently. It is possible that one of the elders is her biological father, but this does not come as a clear thought, perhaps because she is concentrating on convincing them to let her go with me to confront S45.

They ask me a few clarification questions, then I am sent

outside while they debate. I make friends with some free-range livestock. I idly wonder if it ever rains here, and some children stand a yard away and stare at me, one boy sucking his thumb and smiling around it. It takes the council twenty minutes to decide.

"Well?" I ask Oyin Da.

"We're going," she says.

Oyin Da and I arrive through one of her time–space gaps into the room where I was initially ensconced at S45. I can only hope that Femi Alaagomeji is in the building somewhere. The room is empty and dim. There are no documents on the desks. Neither Oyin Da nor I can activate the workstations on the tables. I read from her that she would be able to do it, given time, but she is curious about other things. The door is unlocked, and unsurprisingly there are no guards outside like the last time I was here. The corridors hold silence close like a sick child. It's like the kind you get in really high-level banks, the result of expensive soundproofing.

"How do we go about finding this Alaagomeji person?" asks Oyin Da.

"I can think of two ways. We can keep walking along these corridors until someone accosts us and takes us to her. Or I can find a fix on her and lead us."

"Is she here?"

"I don't know yet. It's taking me time to acclimatise after the journey in the Lijad. Let's just walk. It'll kick in soon."

She has many questions about me, about my abilities. She does not ask them, because she is focused on the matter at hand.

"You can ask," I say. "I know you're curious."

"So, you can find anything?"

"Not anything. If an aircraft breaks apart above a jungle, I can't find it because a person did not leave it there. There has to be some thought behind it. It's the thoughts that I find, not the object."

"And do you know how?"

"No. It's the usual supernatural stuff. Psychics have always existed."

"That is nonsense," says Oyin Da. "There is what exists and what does not. There is what is known and unknown. What you call the supernatural is just the intersection of what exists and is not known. Once it is known it becomes less magical, trust me. It just needs more observation and the application of rigorous scientific method."

"Do you know how I can do it? The science of it?"

"No." But she has ideas. "When you do whatever it is that you do, it is clear that you are accessing data of some kind. That means that the data or information exists somewhere in a place that not everyone has access to. In fact, only a tiny minority are aware of it, those we call psychics or witches. The two lines of enquiry I would pursue would be how the data is stored, and how you access it."

I am about to respond to this when I sense Femi. I know exactly where she is with such certainty that I experience the finder's passion again, although it is difficult to tell if what I feel is because of my sexual attraction.

"Let's go," I say.

I take us through passageways and up flights of stairs. These have locks and access pads in some cases, but are open at the time we reach them. We pass some people, but they are not soldier types and appear to be preoccupied with their own troubles. They barely spare us a glance. I start to move faster and resist the temptation to grab Oyin Da's arm. She keeps up and keeps quiet. The first soldier we see is outside the conference room that is our destination. I watch from the end of the hallway.

"She's in there," I say.

"Then we must go in," says Oyin Da.

"They might take us into custody."

She turns to look at me. "You do realise that I got Professor Ogene out of Kirikiri prison, right? Do not worry. I cannot be held and you can find your way out of anywhere." She smiles, and with her wide mouth it reminds me of something I read in a book. If the ends of her smile reach all the way around her head, will the top fall off? *Through the Looking Glass*. Lewis Carroll. I am definitely through the looking glass here.

We walk to the soldier, who tags us as soon as we round the corner and unsubtly swings his rifle to cover us. This is the second time I've been threatened with a gun today. His thoughts radiate to me. He does not consider us threats. He thinks we are visitors to the Department of Agriculture who got lost. He thinks Oyin Da's hair is daft and he is puzzled by the asexuality of her dressing. His tastes run to that of the commercial sex worker, in any case.

"Halt!" he says.

"We're here to see Mrs Alaagomeji," I say. "She's expecting us."

"I received no notification of that. Remain still," he says. He speaks into a mouthpiece and listens.

The double doors of the conference room swing open and Femi emerges.

"Where's my gun, you fucking klepto?" she says.

299

Chapter Twenty-Five

Rosewater: 2066

Now

Clement lives in a crowded high-rise in Kinshasa. The best thing to be said about Kinshasa is that it's close to the South Ganglion. The uninterrupted power supply does not make up for the density of population, the crime, the social deprivation, and the general nastiness of the area. There are illegal aliens there, extraterrestrials, owned by locals, used for whatever advantage can be extracted. Fight clubs, illegal betting, intimidation, getting rid of inconvenient bodies – all are rumoured to happen here. It's cheap to live in the rise, though, and Clement is a young man just starting out, without the benefit of rich parents. There's a high rate of eru use too, and the authorities can't keep up. Eru is a shadow currency, loosely based on barter and used when the naira seems to benefit the rich more than the common man. Eru is a glorified IOU slip. There's a Goodhead store on the ground floor. The walls are covered with graffiti like cheap make-up.

My xenosphere awareness is coming back, enough for me to want to suppress it. The sense of desperation and despair from this block is overpowering. The elevator is out, so I take the stairs up twenty floors. There is a kid on the seventh floor sitting on the stairs, head lolling, stoned, unaware of me. His shorts are wet with liquid shit and his mouth hangs open. I move on. I am not fit so I am breathing hard by the time I get to the floor I want. The corridor is full of buckets attached to rainwater-collecting devices. I have to pick my way between them.

I knock on the door of Clement's apartment. There is no response, so I phone him. I can hear a cheesy ringtone from inside. I knock harder.

"Clement, I know you're in there," I say.

The door sweeps open and a woman as tall as me and wide as the doorway stands there. She's not black, but appears dark enough to be mixed race. Before I can say anything, she punches me in the face. It lands right on my nose and I see stars. My knees buckle. I fall back, but she grabs the front of my shirt and drags me into the flat.

"What's that noise?" I hear Clement shout from inside somewhere.

"Baby, get the police," she yells. "He's here."

While she's distracted, I clap both hands over her ears, though not hard enough to rupture her eardrums. She lets me go and clutches her head. I am about to follow through when Clement pops out of a door.

"What are you doing?" he asks, but it is unclear if he means me or his ... friend?

I'm dripping blood from my nose to my shirt. I like the shirt. She lurches away towards whatever front room they have, wailing. Clement pats her shoulder and steers her towards a bedroom, but looks back at me.

"Go to the lounge. I'll meet you there. You want a tissue?"

The sitting room is a shrine to Jesus and professional wrestling. There is the usual reproduction of *The Last Supper* and some Raphaelite Gethsemane scene. Here and there garish bumper stickers persist on the walls like barnacles of poor taste. It looks like Clement's partner used to wrestle. There are several framed photos of her in tights hurling some other poor woman about. There is one with her balanced on the turnbuckle; one with her lifting a belt. In these she looks younger, lean, muscular and sexual. Her hair is cut short. There are no pictures of her in her current stature.

Clement comes in.

"You've met Lorna, then."

"I've met Lorna's fist," I say.

"I'd like to say I'm sorry, but I'm not. She's just protective."

"Bully for you."

"You are not welcome here, Kaaro. Why are you trying to kill me?"

"I'm not trying to kill you, you fucking idiot."

"You can't anyway," he says. He unbuttons the ankara shirt he has on and thrusts his bare chest at me. "I have protection."

"What are you doing? Put your shirt back on."

"I figured out how to block you!" His torso glistens almost white with a thick layer of ketoconazole. I can smell it from where I sit. It's a chemical, sulphurous smell so strong that I taste it in my mouth immediately.

"Clement, why would I need to kill you? *Cui bono*, motherfucker? Who benefits?" I cough slightly, and the blood spurts from my nostrils. I feel it trickle down the back of my throat.

"I . . . I . . . Why have you been attacking me?"

302

"You attacked *me*. In Bola's flesh-temple thing. You laid in wait and tried to ambush me with your stupid iron golem."

"Only because you've attacked me almost every day since I came to Rosewater. I saw how you stared at me. You're trying to get rid of a rival."

"Clement, I do not give a shit about you. I don't give a shit about your job. I'm not in competition with you for anything. Get this shitty idea out of your head. I never even thought about you until the day you tried that cack-handed attempt to kill me." I cough. "And if you think a layer of cheap antifungal cream would stop me if I wanted to kill you ... " The tickle in my throat won't stop. I cough again, and feel something viscous coming up, although it seems to need convincing. I hack, I change posture, stand up. My eyes start to water. I look at Clement and mime a glass of water, but he is staring at me in horror.

Lorna bursts into the room wearing a T-shirt and what look like a man's boxer shorts. She stares too.

Have they never seen someone coughing?

I sense a tearing in my chest and I can feel the edge of something coming up my throat. I cough, but then it's like vomit and it flows on its own. My vision becomes misty and I am mindful of the lack of tears on my cheeks. Whatever is coming out of my eyes falls upwards.

Oh fuck, it hurts.

The effluent from my mouth rises and joins the vapour from my eyes in a continuous flow.

"Let's get out of here," says Clement.

"It's our house. I can throw him out," says Lorna.

I raise a hand as if to say, *wait*. I can feel the lower edge of it now, the end of it, flowing like a mollusc, leaving a trail of pain and disgust. When it's out, I fall to the ground and look up at it. It swirls close to the ceiling, as cheerful as a shroud, opaque, yellowish here, there off-white, thick. What the fuck is it?

It is not just a cloud. It roils, but with purpose. It moves towards Clement and he's too frozen in place to move away. I try to tell him to run, but I cough instead. The xenosphere is there, but it's full of electric noise; interference or deliberate blocking, I cannot tell. When I see the miasma entering Clement, with Lorna screaming like a horror-flick soundtrack, I recognise it.

Ectoplasm.

The real kind, with neurotransmitters and xenoforms.

Strands of it enter his eyes and his nostrils and his open mouth. He starts to choke. Lorna hugs him and I want to tell her to do the opposite.

Lay him down and pump his chest!

Help him breathe!

I am too weak to help. I can barely breathe between coughs.

Clement moves intensely, jerkily, and then goes still.

I back towards the door. Lorna has not been the most stable of hosts and I don't want to negotiate peace with a professional wrestler. I have to escape while she is disoriented by grief. The ectoplasm drains out with vermiform fingers from Clement's orifices. Lorna sees them and lumbers out, charging past me into the corridor and out of the flat. Her screams die away.

I should not be here.

The ectoplasm speeds up and is back in me before I can think. I am in the xenosphere and Molara is there, aroused, nipples sharpened to pinpoints, poised above me, hovering with her wings. She licks her lips and descends and begins to fuck me. Her tongue is long enough to flick against her own chin. We are in a place of multicoloured mist that swirls in different directions as we buck against each other.

"You are ... the last ... one, Gryphon," she says, panting. "Soon, now. Soon, you ... "

She climaxes violently and disappears, leaving me lying in a room with a dead body, blood on my shirt, a broken nose, and sexual arousal. Not a vista that speaks to my innocence.

What does she mean, soon?

I get up. Clement's eyes are open and seem to accuse me, and not without reason. I did bring death to his home. I feel shame and guilt. I try to close his eyes like I've seen done in movies, but for some reason his lids seem too small and they keep retracting back to the open position. I cover his face with a tea towel. I have to escape, not because of the police. Thanks to my bleeding nose and maybe the ectoplasm, my DNA is already all over the flat and my implant will tell them I've been here. What I'm worried about is Lorna whipping the neighbours up into a murderous frenzy. I've already done the mob scene and I'd rather not repeat it. Better to call the police myself than get necklaced.

The door is ajar. I hear no unusual noise that might indicate ructions beyond. I feel for the xenosphere. It is full of a mixture of Lorna and Clement's thoughts. They are not what I expect. I anticipated disorganisation bordering on psychosis, but what I get is rationality. Clement's safe thoughtspace is a school and a police station. It shifts constantly between the two. I find out that his mother was a police officer and his father was a teacher. I am walking in the hall of the school and then into a classroom. I sit at a desk and read the exercise book in front of me. Now it is a folder, an old-style police record.

Hatred is gained as much by good works as by evil. Machiavelli.

Why did this man hate me? Or at least fear me?

There is nothing written in the folder, and when I look up I see a new door. When I open it, I am looking at Clement on the day he joined the bank. I see myself. It is a strange feeling. *I don't look like that. When did I get so old?*

Clement feels intimidated. In the background someone drones on, telling him the names of the others who make up the psychic firewall. He does not listen. It is I, glowing radio-active, who distract him. He has heard that I have been here since the old days, since the first days. Later, when he recounts it to his lover in the midst of sex funk, all he can talk about is meeting me. In their copulation she is the aggressor, penetrating him with fingers, which he loves. He practises his drills in the xenosphere, trying to keep his skills honed for the firewall. There are tubes of ketoconazole all around him, a mountain of discarded, twisted, empty containers. Lorna helps him. She feeds him random bits of information to use as white noise against personal attack.

"Did you know that Ernest Hemingway patrolled the East Coast of the US on his personal yacht looking for U-boats during World War II?"

That night, even after making love, he is too excited to really sleep, but too exhausted to stay awake. He dozes and finds himself in the xenosphere. And there, in the swirling mists, he sees me, Kaaro, dressed in all black, grinning. I don't ever grin in real life. Without talking, we begin to fight, him and this mental image of me. In his xenosphere we trade blows, and I beat his iron golem to a bloody mess. I produce a dagger and he flees. He wakes beside his lover, breathing heavily, comforted by her snores.

I shift and move more swiftly through his memories,

remembering that I am in a room with a dead body, and that either a mob or the police or a physically powerful and trained lover will come for me.

There are multiple encounters with my doppelgänger. Clement never wins. In the daytime he tries to appease me by using the usual primate signs of surrender. He smiles, he defers to me, he flatters me, and he never disagrees with me. Since I am unaware of the violence he experiences, I behave indifferently. At night, every night, he fights what he believes to be me, and it is exhausting.

He tells his lover. With Lorna's help he begins to increase the size and skill of his avatar, but it makes no difference. The fake Kaaro is too powerful. Finally, Clement stops going into the xenosphere outside work. When Bola dies, he hides in her safe place, operates from there. Which is fine, until I appear, a terrifying gryphon attended by a succubus. After his giant avatar is destroyed, he spends all his hours under a thick layer of antifungal cream. Then I turn up at his doorstep and belch ectoplasm into his face.

I exit the xenosphere.

"I'm sorry," I say to his corpse.

I listen and hear nothing, then I leave the flat and close the door behind me. It will lock automatically. I wonder where Lorna has run to, but I don't dwell on it until I hear her say the three words I have been dreading.

"There he is."

Interlude: Health Check

Ubar, Rosewater: 2061

Annual mental-health check.

Assholes throwing questions at me from behind airtight screens or teleconferenced in. What they don't know is that they have an imperfect seal and the xenosphere link is spotty, but present.

"Are you religious?"

"No."

"But you had a religion when you were young?"

"My parents were nominal Christians; my mother took it more seriously than my father."

"Do you go to church?"

"No."

"Do you attend mosque?"

"No."

"Do you practise African traditional religion?"

"No."

"Are you a satanist?"

"What?"

"Are you a demon?"

"Please."

"Answer the question."

"No."

"Have you ever been possessed or been diagnosed as being in a possession state?"

"No."

"Have you ever participated in an exorcism?"

"Yes."

"Tell us about this."

"You know the answer because I told you last year. Every year we have to go through this. Every single year."

"Answer the question please."

"An S45 agent went on a mission with a sensitive called Bakare. The mission was a success. On their way back to debrief, they became close and had sex. It happens sometimes in high-stress situations. Unfortunately Bakare wasn't a very experienced sensitive. While coupling, he left a version of his mental image in the agent's mind. By accident. The agent first lost his own personality and then became catatonic. The psychiatrists said it was a possession state and recommended an exorcism based on the agent's religion. My supervisor, Femi Alaagomeji, invited me to observe. Ordered, more like. During the ... ceremony, I saw the problem: Bakare's multiplying avatar. I intervened. The agent got better."

"What do you mean by 'intervened'?"

"I entered the xenosphere and killed the avatars."

"How many were there?"

"I stopped counting at six hundred and twenty-four."

"How did you kill them?"

"Does it matter?"

"Answer the question."

"Slashing, decapitation, blunt force, suffocation, burning, eating."

"Eating?"

"Symbolically. Look, my avatar's a gryphon. It isn't cuddly. Both the eagle and the lion part are pretty predatory. They like to kill and eat things. I absorb the avatar into myself and digest it."

"Have you ever killed a human being?"

"No."

"Have you ever eaten human flesh?"

"Is that because of the eating comment?"

"Answer the question."

"No."

"Do you feel any remorse for killing Bakare?"

"Have you been listening? The guy is still alive."

"Was this accident really an accident?"

"No."

"Why did Bakare duplicate himself inside the agent?"

"He was trying to wipe the agent's memory of the sex."

"Why?"

"Because some assholes in government have not been able to overturn homosexuality laws for decades, that's why."

"Are you a homosexual?"

"No. But if I were, I wouldn't tell you."

"Are you human?"

"What?"

"Are you a human being?"

"Yes."

"Is any part of you controlled by an external agency?"

"Yes. S45 controls me."

"I mean other than employers. Is your volition your own?"

"Yes."

"Are you controlling anyone else?"

"No."

"Do you feel life is worth living?"

"Sometimes."

"Are you ... "

"Do you ... "

"What is ... "

"When will ... "

"Why ... "

"Why not?"

Chapter Twenty-Six

Unknown military base, the land that would become Rosewater: 2055

Then

"Has everyone calmed down?" asks Femi. "Good. Pay attention."

In the conference room we all have screens on the table as well as a giant one on the south wall. The guard who was outside is now in with us. Femi seems to think differently from when she sent me out, inviting Oyin Da and me to sit, offering water. I'm tense, but the thoughts in the room are heightened anxiety with no impending violence.

Other than Femi and Oyin Da, who is seated beside me, there is a white man called Bellamy in the room. I do not know if this is his first or last name and nobody clarifies. He is British and seems to act as a kind of consultant.

Femi says, "You are all aware of Wormwood, the extraterrestrial that landed in London back in 2012. You know that it has been travelling in the Earth's crust. It contaminated the biosphere with alien microorganisms that we call xenoforms. We have not been able to track its movements, but we've always speculated that where there is an unusual concentration of xenoforms, Wormwood can't be far away. About a month ago, S45 scientists detected rising levels of xenoforms. The elevation was too sharp to be a statistical fluctuation. Wormwood was here. It burst through here."

She points to an empty spot on the map of Nigeria in the west, close to Ilesha, and near a small town.

"We sent Tactical to investigate, but it seems like they misunderstood their orders. They lost contact. A second team went in, with two of my superiors taking a more direct part in the field operations. They thought it would be a good idea to have decision-makers on site. Lost contact again. The observation cyborgs aren't sending any information back from there, neither the hawks by day nor the cats by night."

"You want me to go in for you," says Oyin Da.

"Yes," says Femi.

"Why? What do you want with Wormwood?" says Oyin Da.

"It's not just us. Everyone, every nation wants a part of it. There's a theory that the Americans went into seclusion because of its existence. If we could befriend it, there's the scientific data, the contact with unknown species, the health benefits, the defence applications ... it could help us clean up the environment. We, Nigeria, can be the first nation to engage it. Think of what it would it mean."

"But you have to be careful," says Bellamy. "It's a different type of civilisation, different intelligence—"

"Wait," I say, "didn't you guys fuck it up? In London? It was engaging with humans until you introduced the military option or something."

"Mistakes were made, yes, but we've learned. We have the experience to—"

"Stop," says Oyin Da. "We have more experience than any Western country in dealing with first contact. What do you think we experienced when your people carved up Africa at the Berlin Conference? You arrived with a different intelligence, a different civilisation, and you raped us. But we're still here." She turns to Femi. "Make sure this one does not speak any more, or we leave."

I notice the "we" but I don't comment. It is interesting having Femi and Oyin Da in the same space. It confuses the hell out of me. I feel drawn to them both.

Femi is smiling. "This is going to be delicate. Bellamy does have experience with the aliens."

"So do I," says Oyin Da. "You have no idea how many entities I have interacted with, how much knowledge I have gleaned in how many dimensions of time and space. I know how to do this."

"This can't have been why you were looking for Oyin Da, though," I say. "You were looking for her before any of this alien escalation." I relish the wave of gratitude I feel from Oyin Da.

Femi gives me a look. "I don't question my orders. I answer to people. They told me to find her. I tried. Now that I'm in charge, I think a woman who seems able to enter and exit high-security installations at will is a useful asset since going in hard has failed."

"What's in it for me? Why should I help you get into Wormwood?" asks Oyin Da.

"We're willing to let bygones be bygones. You do this and the slate is wiped clean. No treason. You must stop spreading your venom and kidnapping Nigerian citizens."

Oyin Da laughs. "I don't kidnap them."

"We're wasting time," says Bellamy.

"I told you not to talk," says Oyin Da.

"You have no authority here," says Femi. "Take the deal or leave it, Bicycle Girl."

"You've already failed. What will you do if I walk away? Continue to hunt me down and accuse me of sedition?"

"I don't believe in using the stick to motivate people."

I raise my hand as if I'm in school. "You used the stick on me."

"That's different. I was taking orders from others when I recruited you. Besides, you're an idiot." She sniffs. "And why do you smell of spoilt meat?"

I slump in my seat, cowed. I'm not going to give her that antique revolver back.

"Oyin Da, when I woke up this morning I was a lower-level section head in S45; now I'm in charge. Believe me when I say we will make do. So tell me, little girl, will you help?"

Bicycle Girl tinkers and fiddles with the innards of our workstation while I do the hard work of studying the material S45 has supplied us on Wormwood and other "activities of non-terrestrial origin".

"What are you doing?" I ask.

"Cannibalising. These jokers have high-quality components, although they have no idea what to do with them. I need what they have to build and repair. Everything we have in the Lijad is made from cast-offs and scraps." She doesn't look up, but pride emanates from her. She thinks this is justified. So do I.

"Don't you think you should be reading this stuff? You're the smart one."

"No, what I'm doing is more important. Besides, what I really need to know is where Wormwood is. After that, it's just communication. You can tell me if I break protocol."

"There is no protocol. Nobody knows—"

She holds up her hand. "I do not wish to know. You read. I will scavenge."

"Don't we need the components for this to work?"

"No, these dummies use a lot of redundant stuff. I can easily run bypasses ..." Her words fade and she begins to think in engineering shorthand, with which I can't even hope to keep up.

I start to read. The initial material is a jumble of words on the biology of non-terrestrial organisms. Most of it I do not understand, and I remember that I hate biology.

"I don't understand any of this," I say. "I know damn well that I won't remember it either."

"Read it out loud," she says. "You can read, yes?"

"You're very funny," I say, but I return her smile. A joke. She made a joke. I wonder what it would be like to see her smile more often. "Okay, this is ... exen ... ex ... I can't pronounce the word." I spell it.

"Xenobiology."

"Yes, that. 'The macroorganisms show the same general complexity as terrestrial flora and fauna. The microorganisms are different from this. They appear to have the characteristics of both plant and animal cells, including a chloro ... chlor ... chloroplast-like organelle that aids in C3, C4 and CAM photosynthesis depending on where the sample is from. These microbes have more in common with human stem cells in that they have the potential to adapt to almost any function. Their versatility is responsible for their healing action, for example. They have been shown to mimic all known variants of animal cells, including human cells. They are capable of replacing damaged or diseased cells without stimulating either type I or type II immune responses. Osteoblast mimicry has led to repair of fractures but also secretion of macro-structures as powerful as and indistinguishable from human bone. The exploitation potential for these xenoforms is incalculable, but dependent on the directing intelligence.'"

As I read and Oyin Da corrects, my understanding increases. I cannot always understand the thoughts she has, but they augment my intelligence while I read.

Wormwood was an amoeboid blob of alien organic matter that fell to Earth in 2012. It was the size of a small town and it initially seemed like a comet that wiped out Hyde Park in London. It contaminated the biosphere with xenoforms and macroorganisms trapped within Wormwood itself. Information from the Americans was that there had been three previous incursions of similar alien organisms, but they were smaller and dead on arrival. There is a list of seventy plants and animals now existing on Earth but thought to be of alien origin. The British damaged Wormwood with non-nuclear explosives, but it didn't die. It sank into the Earth's crust and disappeared from view for a time, though it soon became obvious that it was travelling a subterranean path without discernible pattern.

There is speculation that the Americans went silent when they felt Wormwood was uncontrollable. A whole section of the material is devoted to theories about what is going on in the former United States. America is preparing for war. America is preparing for mass exodus off-planet. Wormwood isn't extraterrestrial; it was grown in American labs. Nothing definitive.

Wormwood itself is thought to be of at least human-level intelligence. It appears to direct at least some of the xenoforms. Some reports say it consumes humans whole. Others say it merged with one human and produces duplicates of that body.

It is peaceful in some articles, but warlike in others. Many say it is unknowable.

"This is rubbish," says Oyin Da. "All the information is available on Nimbus and in textbooks."

She rises and plugs a device into an opening that she has created, then presses a few buttons. A Nimbus portal opens. It shimmers in the air, imperfect, makeshift. She moves her fingers within the low-power ion field. She murmurs as she works. "Just like I thought. Their security protocols are attached to the local machine ... If I just ... Yes ... Sloppy, sloppy, who does your security? ... Is that a Pix firewall? Haven't encountered one of those in years ... Now ... Yeah, here we ... go ... "

A three-dimensional diagram blossoms in the air in front of her. It's four feet in height, about two wide. The top third is trees and a small hill. Oyin Da traces a path from the outside, into a cave in the hill, down into a tunnel. The tunnel leads into a series of caverns. I think it's a cave system at first, but then I see that we're looking at a living organism. It reminds me of an iceberg, with most of it below the surface, but it's also like a tumour, budding and infiltrating. This is Wormwood.

"Now I know where it is," says Oyin Da. She dismisses the diagram and starts to type on a virtual keyboard. I cannot follow her thoughts.

"What are you doing?"

"Looking for the cells so I can free the prisoners." She glances at her watch briefly.

"That's not why we came," I say.

"I freed the professor from a place like this," she says. "And he was innocent. The people he supposedly killed are alive and well in the Lijad. They tortured him."

"That wasn't these guys."

"They work for the same government." She starts to disconnect her machine just as an alarm goes off. She is packing up, but every few seconds she looks at her watch. "Are you ready?"

"For what?"

"Prepare to become theoretical," she says, and smiles.

The air changes, wavy lines eddy together a few feet from us, and reality surrenders. She dives in and I follow.

In the between, in the uncertainty, we talk. I think.

What do you do when you're not saving the world?

What do you mean?

Do you guys ever relax in the Lijad?

We have people from all over. Of course we relax. These people bring all kinds of unwinding.

All over Nigeria?

The world. We even have some Americans.

Really?

Yes. We have about six. They'd been moving north from Zimbabwe through Cameroun. Ended up drifting across the border and living in Lagos. I found them and took them in.

You take everyone and anyone?

Anyone as long as they do not harm others and will contribute what they can.

Would you take me?

It depends. Are you harmful? Do you bring anything with you?

Well—

We have arrived, Kaaro. Let us see to the alien . . .

We're in woodland now, and I learn quickly that mosquitoes love the smell of raw meat.

319

Oyin Da seems fine with our new surroundings and just starts walking away from me. For me, the travel turns my guts inside out and I retch but cannot bring anything up. The nausea comes and goes. I have a headache and it feels like all the blood has rushed to my head. I can't walk just yet, and the mosquitoes find me fast. For a moment I cannot sense thoughts, but then my ability becomes heightened.

When I recover, I look up again. The nausea dies away and Oyin Da cocks her head, generally wanting me to grow a spine. We are near a forest and it is close to evening. The light is dying. There are clusters of people crouched over naked flames. They look at us, but seem unsurprised and unperturbed that we appeared out of nowhere. They seem vaguely pleased, truth be told. I can say I've never been here before, but it is a standard forest with mostly palm trees and tangly undergrowth. There are clearings here and there, but they appear recent, tool-made rather than poor growth from the steady stamping of feet. Some of the people are praying.

"This is odd," says Oyin Da.

"How so?" I ask.

"They're not really praying. They're calling out."

"That's what praying is," I say. "Are we where we should be?"

"Yes, give or take a few dozen yards."

"A lot of them are sick," I say.

Indeed. The ratio of visibly sick to apparently healthy is like fifty-fifty.

My *would you take me?* echoes in her mind. She wonders then if I have a girlfriend. The next moment is unreal. I know, for example, that I am having a premonition. I know I am about to make a monumental mistake, but I am unable to stop myself. It feels like my future self is watching me fuck up, but has come to terms with the inevitability of the instant.

"W . . . wait," I say, weakly, but she does not hear me. Her brain is brilliant, and she is barely aware of me. She sees herself as a landing party and her mind is spooling through variables at an unbelievable rate.

WAIT!

She cries out and falls to her knees. I have caused her pain. She turns back and stares at me in the dying light. "What did you do to me, Kaaro? Were you in my head?"

"I—"

"I felt different all day, something worming away at the edge of my awareness. That was you," she says, standing slowly. She is mostly curious at first. Not really angry. She is interested in the biology of the thing. I am a specimen.

We are interrupted by a bright lime-green light bursting through the gloom, a column of it up ahead, accompanied by a gasp from the camping people. It is at least fifty feet tall, thick as an iroko tree and bulbous at its tip like a giant matchstick. It thrums with a kind of electrical vibration and I feel a resonance in the back of my skull, as if it activates something.

"What *is* that?" Oyin Da says, forgetting my invasion of her thoughts for a minute.

When the initial dazzle fades from my eyes, I see that there are several such columns of light, perhaps four. The groups of people stop their singing and rise in silence, walking towards the light. Oyin Da moves with them, and I can feel her impatience. She wants to run, but a sense of caution holds her back.

"Is this wise?" I say. I am not curious, I am not an explorer. When I see something I don't understand, I run in the opposite

321

direction like any good living organism. This is just good survival strategy, in my opinion. I notice that I am feeling better. I no longer have a headache, and my feet are not wobbly.

There is a boy, nine, ten years old, who was limping before. I see him standing up straight and walking towards the light. Oyin Da takes photographs on a handheld device of some kind. Looks like a smartphone, but probably customised. The closer we get to the lights, the healthier the grass and trees seem. The gathering people also seem to be filming with their phones. Nobody coughs.

"There's healing going on here," I say.

"I agree. Let's get closer to—"

"Hello," says a voice behind us.

A man stands about a yard away, hands by his sides, a benign look on his face. He is black, but the shade of his skin seems artificial, like a person who has been bleaching his skin with low-quality products. His skin is light brown, but it seems painted on. He wears dungarees, and they appear to be cast-offs because they are too large. They are baggy on him, and the long trouser legs are rolled up. He wears no shirt, shoes, or other clothing or jewellery of any kind. His nails are bitten to the quick. This is the only person who shows any curiosity about us.

"Who are you?" Oyin Da asks.

Without thinking, I put myself between her and the stranger and he seems to focus on me. I pick up Oyin Da's disdain for my gesture, which she interprets as sexist. It's sexist to protect a girl? Really?

"Oh, you brought a quantum extrapolator. How interesting," the man says. "My name is Anthony. Was. Is. I don't know. Am I still Anthony?"

"What's a quantum extrapolator?" I ask.

"You are," says Anthony. "You can extract real-time information from our bio-network and extrapolate backwards and forwards. You can know things you weren't told, and things that haven't happened yet in your conception of time." He seems amused and non-threatening. He looks at me as if I am an interesting specimen of insect, just like Oyin Da did. There are no thoughts coming from him. He is not really there, or he is immune to my abilities.

"If you are not Anthony, who are you?" asks Oyin Da. "*What* are you?"

"I'm a space invader," says Anthony. "Your people call me Wormwood."

323

Chapter Twenty-Seven

Rosewater: 2066

Now

There is a mob of twenty-seven people outside the flat. I can feel their minds along with that of Lorna, who is set to avenge her lover. Even in death, Clement is still fucking me. The mob does not care about me or Lorna. They think in terms of violence they can deal, pain they can dole out without consequence. This is the mob mentality, a suspension of whatever fragile social contract is in place. Endorsed brutality. If you kill someone within the context of mob action, you are absolved of sin. *It wasn't murder, we all did it.*

I am in pain. It seems to me that every part of my body hurts and my lungs can no longer process air. It hurts to draw it in. Not just my ribs are bruised; the inner surface of my lungs is raw too. It is as if the ectoplasm peeled away a layer from my insides when it came out.

I stay just inside Clement's apartment, out of sight of the mob but connected to the air so that the xenoforms can link me to the xenosphere.

I've only ever done this to one person at a time.

I am inside all of them. The man who uses his flat as a boxing club. He has chained reanimates for his fighters to train on. *Punching bags are not authentic. You must know what human flesh and bone feels like against your bare knuckles to be a true fighter.* The woman who sleeps with her son-in-law and feels no shame. The man whose girlfriend has been missing for a month, him the prime suspect in her murder though his thoughts say he is innocent. The reconstructed sex worker with two phalluses, which he hoped would mean he could charge his clients double but instead disgusts them.

All of them, saints, sinners, in between, I hold in my mind and I send a single signal. When I emerge from the flat, light from the sun will hit me and bounce off. This reflected light will hit the retinas of the people watching. The cells of the retinas will transform the photons of light into electrical energy, signals to the brain. If the brain interprets it correctly, the people perceive me.

I tell the brains of all these fine people to ignore the signal. I will be invisible, to all intents. Some of their thoughts bear malice and petty angers that hurt as they pass through me. I contain this shit.

I walk.

I see them waiting, impatient. They do not see me. Lorna is stretching her neck and rolling her shoulders, preparing for a fight. They hold rocks and planks and iron bars. I have been here before and the déjà vu is disconcerting. I am swimming through an acid pool, a river of venom. I am down the first flight of stairs, the second, the twelfth, stepping over the drugged kid, to the ground floor. They are staring up waiting for me. I pass between them in the courtyard. I can smell the stink of their sweat, their acrid bloodlust, and hear their heavy breathing. I feel stoned. So many minds, so many thoughts. If not that my life is in danger, I would enjoy this. There are now four people between me and my exit.

Then I cough. It bursts out of me like a hatching parasite, too sudden to suppress. It throws my concentration off.

I am seen.

My control does not slip so much as slide, carried away. I lose all of them. They see me instantly. There is an interval of shock where nobody does anything. They stare, I stare. I consider, in those seconds, if I should run. The nearest person to me cries out, and I hear a swing, a slice through the air. It hurts, a flash of pain that spreads from my temple throughout my body. I fold up like a millipede and wait for the rest.

It does not come. Instead, there is a dry, hot wind, howling like a wolf. I open my eyes and do not believe what I see. There is fire in a cylinder all around me. I stand. Blood drips from my temple and I'm unsteady.

"I am the light, I am the flame, I am the shining one. No one may hurt the ones I love."

O-kay. This is a hallucination.

Layi zooms off into the sky and I am yanked off my feet after him in a kind of flame-free backwash. It reminds me of hanging onto the floater that belonged to Aminat's husband. I see Layi's feet. He pedals and kicks them as if he is swimming. He is barefoot and naked. Flames burst on his skin here and there, but these only provide pockets of modesty. His fleshy baton flies free. I lose sight of him as the world turns upside down. I am spinning.

I hear his voice fading in and out. "I am sorry, Kaaro, but I have burned the clothes you gave me."

The buffeting reduces and I am cushioned to the ground, a gentle landing. I do not know where we are or how far we have travelled from Clement's place. We are on a flat concrete roof. Layi stands naked in front of me, no longer burning. I take off my shirt and hand it to him.

"You know, we are going to be arrested as homosexuals," I say.

He shrugs. "Thank you for the coals."

"Coals?"

"I said 'clothes'."

"Really? That's odd. I heard different ... "

A gust of wind almost blows me off my feet. This must be a tall building, because I see no other rooftop. Just clouds and blue sky. Sparks form playfully on Layi's skin, but die out. There is a tower poking into the sky and communications dishes attached, but otherwise the roof is featureless. For a while I feel stronger, but it's only the exhilaration. I'm still sick.

"I feel stupid asking this, but are you an angel?"

He laughs. "My sister has been talking to you. Which is good. It means she must really like you. This is, I'm told, a family secret."

"It does explain the chain and the fire extinguishers and why they don't let you out."

"Ah, it is not that simple. I consent to the fettering. Sometimes I sleepwalk. Sometimes I burn while I sleep. I have burned the house down in the past. These are necessary precautions."

"So what are you?" I ask.

"I am like you, Kaaro. I am infected with alien cells."

"Aminat says your mother had sex with an angel."

"I think she had sex with an alien, or someone infected

with these cells. I am my father's son, at any rate. I know this because I have matched our DNA. My skin is infected with the same xenoforms that grow and multiply on yours."

"I don't produce flame," I say.

He places a hand on my shoulder. It's hot, but I do not flinch. "You could. From what I see, the xenoforms you carry about look like neurones, elongated nerve cells. The truth is, they can be anything. The ones I carry are adapted to be intensely catabolic and shear off me, burning up."

"Do you sense the xenosphere?"

"The what?"

"The thoughtspace, the communal place created by the xenoforms. That's what I call it."

"I don't know what you're talking about," he says. "Let's get you downstairs and home. I don't think this wind is helping your cough."

"Where are we?"

"The roof of a Goodhead store."

A Goodhead store? For a minute I think he knows, but it isn't so. He has brought me to the store for practical reasons. We buy new clothes for him; or rather, I buy them while he hides. Not out of modesty. I'm the one who tells him to hold back. I once fed myself for a week by stealing off the shelves of a supermarket like this one, just opening packets and eating things. People stare at us, or rather at Layi. Men and women are enthralled by his beauty and his otherness. I notice this, but blood still drips from my head and I'm fading. I feel that awful fluid in my chest, but I can't even cough it out any more.

"Shall I take you to the hospital, Kaaro?" asks Layi in a voice that is too loud.

My vision eddies, reality wavers.

The floor approaches.

Molara stands before me, but this time without her aggressive sexuality. We are in a park, and none of the Goodhead aisles with canned fish for 4.99 is visible. I feel good, euphoric. I have been told that when you are drowning, one of the last feelings is euphoria. I am drowning in my own bodily fluids somewhere, so it is apt.

"We've come to watch you die," she says. Her face is expressionless, but there is a smile in her voice and a sense of accomplishment around her like a body odour.

"We?"

"We. I. Do you know that part of the Christian holy book, the Bible, where God refers to himself as us and I at different times? Well I, we understand it better than you."

"It isn't hard to understand. One God, different aspects. A Sunday-school kid could tell you that."

"You are not afraid of me any more."

"Not really. I feel quite good actually."

"And you are not afraid to die."

"Not any more. Everybody gets a turn at living and dying. When it's your turn, you can't go to the back of the line. I feel my connection to my body loosening by the minute. I'm curious as to what comes next."

"You can live on in here, you know. At least a form of you. Your body will die."

"To become a ghost? Like Ryan Miller? No thank you."

"Don't be hasty. You can live here as you want, luxuries limited only by your imagination."

"Why would I want that? Why would *you* want that?" I wonder how it benefits her.

She sits down beside me. "We want your home, Kaaro. Your planet. We have been studying it for a long time without the need for that bothersome interstellar travel. We're here. We have all your knowledge, your eccentricities, your emotions and your petty little naked-ape motivations. Simplistic. We did this by seeding space with what you call xenoforms, synthetic microorganisms programmed to multiply and change form as necessary, to infect the local species and gather data neurologically, to find out how the planet is run, to be warned of the pitfalls. Our infections answer many questions for us. Is the style of politics generated by the environment or can any system work? Can the climate change be reversed? What will we do with the nuclear stockpiles? Is *Homo sapiens* useful for anything, or will it be a nuisance? We had to answer these questions. Some of you had a different reaction to the infection. You became sensitives, quantum extrapolators. You had some access to our information store. That's over. The Earth is ours. We no longer need you."

"So you killed all the sensitives. All of my kind. Some of them were my friends, the people I worked with, trained with. You just wiped us all out." I think of Clement's paranoia, Bola's grief, my lust. "You intruded on our darkest thoughts and used them to finish us off, like personalised thought poisons."

"Yes. But it will cost nothing for some of you to live on in the xenosphere to remind us. Cautionary tale, maybe. It will have all the comforts."

"It will be a zoo."

"If you want to call it that."

"You want me to live as a performing fucking monkey in your zoo for eternity? Are you kidding me? You think this is a life I'll gladly consent to? Me as entertainment?"

"You humans can be so sensitive."

"And you aliens are so—"

"I'm not an alien, Kaaro, at least not in the way you're implying. You'd understand me better if you think of me as a programme coded into the xenoforms. I'm one of many, activated as conditions dictate. I've been here from the start."

I feel disgust for myself that I ever ... with her ... and ...

I hear voices.

Oh-two sats dropping.

I have IV access.

He's blue. Get a tube in him.

Febrile, forty-five.

"They're trying to save me. Layi must have got me to a hospital."

"It won't work. Many of the others went to hospital as well."

"You say you know everything about Earth, about us. What is dying like?"

"There are as many ways to die as there are humans. Some are snuffed out like an extinguished candle. For some it's like dusk, light slowly going out and darkness conquering all senses until there is nothing left. Others experience the opposite, where reality is bleached of meaning and becomes a whiteness." She gesticulates as she speaks, a teacher. She seems strangely gentle.

Beside me, the leaves of a plant are covered in aphids. I flick one away and it generates a chemical smell just like in real life. "So you kill us all and move in."

"There is no consensus on that. The humanity question is undecided."

Undecided?

He's in respiratory failure.

No he's not. You're reading it wrong. Get Ola in here.

Molara's face is like a carving. All the lines are smooth and strong, unblurred by the partial erasure caused by ageing. Her skin is polished. Her mouth pushes forwards from the rest of her skull and her big lips pucker outwards, exposing redness on their inner surfaces. Her eyes are sharp and pick me apart as she watches me die.

"Where is Aminat? I do not wish to look at my tormentor as I die."

Then I'm out of the xenosphere, in the hospital room, and Layi's face is heavy with concern.

"I am sure she wishes she could have been here. She is pursuing those who blew up her office," he says.

"Weren't they after me?"

"No, Kaaro. Aminat has her own story; she is not a supporting character of yours."

"Am I dead yet?"

"I hope not," says Layi. "Look. From your window I can see the Nautilus. Do you ever wonder if the scientists resorted to cannibalism in the end? Nobody ever speculates on this. Stuck in geosynchronous orbit, money for the Great Nigerian Space Programme dissipated, astronauts trapped, and nobody wonders if they ate themselves."

Why the fuck is he talking about the Nautilus? Dying is confusing enough, but Layi's speech is weird at the best of times.

"I am not sure if I am awake or sleeping." I close my eyes.

"Every year on New Year's Eve I am allowed out. I fly around in the open because it's fireworks night. People expect strange lights in the sky. I am free."

"I have never seen a man-shaped firework."

"You would have if you lived in Lagos, my friend." He goes silent, and I hear movement. "You have a visitor, Kaaro. Open your eyes."

I do. Layi is by the window, leaning against the sill, watching, still wearing ill-fitting clothes from the Goodhead store.

I see the visitor then, standing in the centre of the room, at the foot of my hospital bed. He is wearing clothes, but I know them to be organic. Cellulose-based, biodegradable, something he will shed like a snake's skin when he returns to his home. The clothes are for the sensitive eyes of humans, who are apparently offended by their own genitals. He is immensely powerful, but quiet. He has power over life and death to an extent. He is the god of the biodome.

I know him as Anthony or Wormwood, and he owes me his life.

"Kaaro," he says.

"Space invader," I say. My voice sounds weak, even to me.

He chuckles. "That was a long time ago, wasn't it?"

"Give me your hand," I say.

When he reaches out, I remember something that happened on the day we met and pull his sleeve to my mouth to taste it. He is physical, with mass, not a dream, not a part of my near-death delirium, not in the xenosphere.

"You're real," I say.

"Yes," he says.

"What are you doing here?"

He comes closer along the side of the bed and moves the IV stand out of the way.

"I felt your light go out," he says. "I came to find out why. I've kept track of you, since I owe you a life debt."

"Don't you read the alien *Tribune* or look at the alien

333

Nimbus or whatever the fuck you lot use to keep in touch with each other? Your people have decided to execute me."

"We are not all the same, Kaaro, and there will be no execution. You are coming with me."

Chapter Twenty-Eight

The land that would become Rosewater: 2055

Then

Oyin Da pushes past me towards Anthony and he focuses on her again, tracking her with his head but otherwise remaining still. Behind me there are gasps and declamations as the people of the woods become healed. I am used to the vibration from the columns, but aware of its steady presence. Mosquitoes hum and dive-bomb me. Underneath all of that, the sound of crickets and the moving pinpoint lights of tanatana, fireflies.

"Can I touch you?" asks Oyin Da.

Anthony smiles. "Often people feel this religious—"

"I want to touch your skin. It looks weird, unreal. I want to know how it feels – the texture." Oyin Da promptly begins to prod Anthony; smart people are strange.

It is true that Anthony's skin rings false. He smells of crushed vegetation, like a field immediately after a plough has been through. Oyin Da squints, bends at the waist and sniffs at his clothes. Then she licks his dungarees.

"You're wearing plants," she says, a hint of surprise in her voice, and in her thoughts.

"I grew them myself," says Anthony. Still no thoughts come from him. "Will you tell me why you have come here?"

I say, "The government sent us to find you. They want us to make friends with you—"

"Speak for yourself, Kaaro. I am here to see how you live in harmony with these people," says Oyin Da. "I do not work for the government."

"Come then," says Anthony. "I'll show you how we live and where your missing representatives are."

"Are you really an alien? From another planet?" Oyin Da asks.

"Technically I've been on Earth longer than both of you. By the time you were born, my organisms were already part of the biosphere. It calls into question your concept of alien, does it not?"

Oyin Da is quiet, but I sense the thoughts in her head churning, too fast for me to follow.

Guided by the electric light from the columns, he leads us up a hillock. A black attack helicopter lies on its side, twisted rotor half buried in the soil. I see no bodies. Dots of light blink on in the gloom beyond our path, all around us. They flicker, and it takes a minute for me to realise they are eyes reflecting light. In the bush there are living things with short, stocky bodies trailing us. They make no sound. Their bodies glisten. Oyin Da slows down and I sense her curiosity.

"Don't touch them. That mucus on their bodies is a neurotoxin," says Anthony.

"What are they?" I ask.

"We called them homunculi when I was in London. They were with me from the start, lived inside me, like all of the

336

plants, animals and other non-native creatures I came with to recreate the biodiversity I'm used to."

Though they are humanoid, the homunculi have no real thoughts, although I do feel some impressions of instinct and emotion from them. There are no words that I can pick up, but hostility and fear are pretty easy to parse. They are of various heights and ages. There are babies suckling at the pendulous breasts of their mothers. They groom each other. They fuck. They do this while silently keeping their eyes fixed on us.

There are dead hawks on the ground here and there. They both bleed and show exposed, damaged machinery. They are the COBS, dozens of them. I poke them with my foot, but Oyin Da picks one up, drops it, picks up another, until she comes to one that is more or less intact and stashes it in her pouch. I notice some have bites taken out of them.

Further along the path we come to four men. Three of them stand stock still, while a fourth frantically runs, shaking, hitting and yelling obscenities at each of his comrades, trying to get a reaction. They are clad in military garb, dark camouflage. The clothes are torn, burned in places and bloody, though none of the men appears wounded. The active man sees us approach and rails.

"You, alakori! This is your doing!"

He attacks Anthony with fist and boot. Anthony does not avoid the blows or fight back. He does not flinch or appear to feel pain. The military man exhausts himself and collapses at Anthony's feet. The expression on Anthony's face is kindly, pitying.

"I am sorry, Olabisi," he says.

Oyin Da goes to the men and examines them. "Who are these men?"

"Helicopter crew. They were sent to kill me. Or try to kill me."

"What did you do to them?" asks Oyin Da. She shines a torch into the eyes of each.

"I healed them. They crashed. I mended their bodies, restarted their hearts. I can bring the bodies back, but once the brain has died it is impossible to do more than reanimate the corpses."

"I do not trust your answers," says Oyin Da. "How am I to believe this?"

Anthony points to me. "Ask him to confirm. He's your quantum extrapolator, after all."

"He's not mine," protests Oyin Da.

"What ... how can I—"

"Look in my mind. See and share the truth." He places a hand on my shoulder.

I can.

He is suddenly open to me, and his memories wash through my mind.

There is a farm, there are farmers, animals, lush crops that Anthony has helped to grow. There are people, smiling, supplicating, asking the alien for healing, and Anthony obliges. They bring him offerings, votive foodstuffs, bolts of clothing, anything to show devotion. They know he is strange, unearthly, and they love him for it. For this, Anthony and Wormwood love them back.

Then the sound of helicopter blades. There is a brief orange light, then all around ash floats like snowflakes. Trees and telegraph poles are sliced through at a height of five feet, and though there are a few minor fires, the cuts are neat, surgical. The farmhouse looks like the plaything of a giant. It has the same tidy cut edge as all the other tall structures. The stump smoulders, and looks like a joke, a playhouse, an incomplete building. The roof, the upper floor, parts of the ground floor, all gone. The walls stand for a while, then cease to exist. Windows, furniture, lamps are intact, as long as they weren't too tall to start with. Anthony hopes his friends are safe, but is not optimistic. Behind the house the barn, the shed and the poultry are similarly sliced and vaporised. The chickens are gone, not even leaving carcasses.

Anthony wants to check on his friends, but finds himself floating above it all, noting a circular patch of incineration a mile wide like a demented crop circle. He experiences a moment of confusion as he sees an ephemeral red outline where he stood seconds before. Then the wind snatches the thing and scatters it to the four corners.

Anthony is dead. Again.

His anger is a cold fire.

His consciousness returns to the body of the alien and he feels everything, knows everything. He absorbs nutrients from the soil and rock, both minerals and dead organic matter. Anthony/Wormwood grows, spreads deep within the ground and in all directions. He pushes out pseudopodia of nervous tissue and projects them towards what is left of the farm. Sparks flee in their wake as they grow along the ground, and some trees are destroyed by land-based lightning.

Anthony senses the small animals and the insects scurrying away as they intuit the oncoming storm. He senses the cyborg birds riding thermals in the sky and annihilates them with bolts of electricity as he encounters them, reducing each to blackened feathers.

At the border of the farm he sees the aftermath of their

weapon. The farmhouse is flat, with malignant mechanical gadflies maintaining formation above. One is a helicopter, but two float in silence, spheres with a multitude of cables and antennae, gondolas on the undersides where tiny people move and machinate and control.

The pseudopodia split, and split again until they have surrounded the area, then each takes a ninety-degree turn and grows upwards like a vine, creeper plants without trellises. Just before Anthony electrocutes them, he becomes aware of a heating-up of the air, a preparation, a building of charge. Sensors have picked him up. They are going to fire the weapon again.

Humans, thinks Anthony.

Humans, thinks Wormwood.

His rage flashes across the giant neurones as bright green lightning, which starts from the tips and meets where the floating ships hang in the air. First one then the other darkens, ruptures, then falls to the earth, where they begin to smoke. He turns his attention to the black helicopter. Electric charge jumps between the nerve columns and escapes in a yellow and white flaming sphere-ball lightning. It engulfs the helicopter, which spins and crashes into the ground, rotors digging in. This craft is manned and the humans cease to function. Except one.

Anthony clothes his consciousness in electricity and appears to the survivor. The man is trying to crawl away on scorched grass. His left leg drags behind him, twisted awry at the knee. It must be painful.

"You. Human," says Anthony. "Stop moving."

The man's eyes widen and he starts to scream. Anthony wonders how terrifying he must look to the soldier, like constant ongoing lightning, vaguely shaped like a man, electricity arcing off every few seconds. It must hurt his eyes to keep them open like that. He must fear sudden death from electrocution.

"Sorry, I had something else to wear, but you disintegrated it," says Anthony. At the same time he manipulates the soldier's hormones and calms him with endorphins and anandamide. "I want you to go back to your masters. Tell them I want to talk to someone with authority. Do you understand my words? I've never tried to speak to someone in this form before."

The soldier tries to shy into the ground. His lips quiver.

"Just nod if you understand."

The soldier nods. Anthony leaves him crawling away from the farm, towards the road, and floats over the remains of the compound. The only sound is the constant vibration from the giant neurones, which stand like pylons. The helicopter has ignited and burns with a brisk flame that pushes black smoke into the air.

I disconnect myself from Anthony and feel light-headed. It takes a few minutes for me to establish that I am Kaaro, not Anthony. Not Wormwood. At the same time, I feel as if I have tasted the power and inhabited the mind of a god. His memory is now my memory, just like Nike Onyemaihe's, though hopefully not all of it. There are thousands of years in there, aeons drifting in space. I fear madness. If I continue like this, to read people, I'm going to need to anchor myself as myself somehow.

"He is telling the truth," I say to Oyin Da.

We come to a camp. The homunculi keep pace with us in the background, but stay away. There are probably twenty or thirty people here, all ages, calm and content. They greet us cheerfully, handing us freshly squeezed juice in wooden flagons. There are families and loners. Most treat Anthony like a holy man or god. Oyin Da darts forward and engages some women in conversation, firing questions like bullets. She misses nothing. In her mind I read that any community can be assessed by the way it treats women, not something I have thought of before.

There is trouble in paradise, however. There are rifles and handguns here and there. Grenades. People who have the look and manner of sentries about them.

I sit with Anthony on a wooden bench. A tall, muscular man walks over and squats in front of us.

"This is Dare," says Anthony. "He's the farmer who took me in. He and his family."

"Who are these people?" asks Dare, pointing at us.

"The government sent them to negotiate," says Anthony.

"Really?" says Dare. "I'm a bit confused. If they wanted to negotiate, why did they try to destroy you to start with?"

Anthony shrugs. "Humans always try to destroy things."

"I did not try to destroy you," says Dare.

"No, my friend. You welcomed me." Anthony smiles. "The British tried to destroy me when I was in London. I did not know the Nigerians were the same."

"The Nigerian government is not the Nigerians," says Dare.

"There was a British guy there when we were being briefed," I say. "Bellamy. He's a consultant."

"So this is still a British agenda," says Dare.

I think about Femi Alaagomeji. "I don't think so. I think the organisation, S45, really wants to be allies with you."

"Then you're a fool," says Dare. "The Nigerian government takes its cue from colonial masters always. Today they used a particle accelerator weapon. Tomorrow, who knows? Nuclear weapons? Tesla ray from the Nautilus?"

"Stop being paranoid. The Nautilus is decommissioned," says Oyin Da, suddenly in our group. She looks to Anthony. "How much space do you have here? What's your capacity?"

"Why do you ask?" Dare seems puzzled by Oyin Da's manner.

"I have some refugees who need a home," says Oyin Da.

"How many?" asks Anthony.

"One thousand one hundred and seventy-six."

"That's very specific."

"Could you take on that number of people without running out of food or—"

"Yes," says Anthony.

"Wait, who *are* these people?" asks Dare.

I tune out of the conversation because I sense a change in the homunculi. Their affect switches from calm contentment to anxiety and fear. In many cases, the feelings stop abruptly as if a radio has been shut off. Then I get a few random mentations.

There, beside Kaaro.

Steady. Get it right.

Weapons free.

Oh shit!

"Anthony, look out—" I say. Simultaneously I dive and tackle him to the ground. I feel a hard kick to my chest. I know I've been shot before I black out.

Interlude: Mission

Maiduguri: 2055

I am in the library, looking at a video of a lattice-sheet microscopy of the xenoforms, what xenobiologists now call *Ascomycetes xenosphericus*.

At first it looks like a yeast cell, round, with a nucleus, cell wall, and plasma membrane. It is inert and just lies there suspended in whatever fluid they found it in. Apparently it cannot be grown in culture.

I am alone. More and more I walk alone these days, my peers either eclipsed by my performance or frightened. I care, but I cannot help it.

We know that the nuclear material is genetic, but none of our microscopy methods can penetrate inside. Pores form and there is congress between the cell and the nucleus for protein synthesis, but the metabolism suggests that a lot more is happening than what we observe.

A section of human skin is placed in the proximity and the xenoform is galvanised. Nutrients in the vicinity are used up at an amazing rate. Intracellular filaments grow into microtubules through the xenoform cell membrane and snake towards the human skin. They penetrate the epidermis and dermis towards a structure that looks like a lollipop but is really several capsules folded over each other with a core that terminates in a neurone. It breaks through to the centre with ease and breaches the human neural tissue, becoming one with it.

The xenoform shows no interest in any other organelle of the skin. It preferentially seeks out the mechano-receptors in the skin. Shown here is a lamellar corpuscle, concerned with vibration, but xenoforms are promiscuous with neural tissue. Once connected, it sets up duplex communication, despite the fact that mechano-receptors are afferents, i.e., they take impulses in the direction towards the central nervous system and not from it.

The xenoform changes form, extends pseudopodia like an amoeba, moving towards the skin and flattening itself against the epidermis, maintaining the connection to the neuron like a drill pipe from an oil rig. It projects a filament from the opposite side that casts about the fluid.

Once it forms a connection, the xenoform looks for other xenoforms around it to build a network and share information. It is quite extraordinary how far this data can travel. Some commentators also suspect that there are two forms of communication between xenoforms. Adjacent cells use direct microtubular links, but there appears to be a quantum-based entanglement-style distant communication employed under special circumstances. The—

"Kaaro."

I take off the headphones and push away from the desk.

Professor Ileri stands with two other men. I can tell from their bearing that they are agents.

"Studying?" asks Ileri.

"I just want to know more about how I do what I do," I say.

"Good, good."

Ileri says that a lot. He spends extra time with me, honing me to an edge, wanting me to be a sharper instrument than the others. He teaches me methods of focusing concentration, meditation techniques, mind clearing, breathing, and certain time-boxing strategies that clear mental clutter. He teaches me deprivations that weaken the body but sharpen the mind. Fasting. Sensory isolation. I feel like an Olympic athlete. Processed food laden with extraneous chemicals weakens my ability. Entheogens could go either way.

"Kaaro, these men would like to ask you something."

I notice he does not bother to introduce them. This is standard procedure when students are visited by agents. We are forbidden from reading them, but in my hyper-alert state I cannot help picking up impressions. One is bearded, and the psychic smell from him is mouldering, festering guilt and humourlessness. A closer look at the other surprises me, because he is rather androgynous and I cannot tell from his slim figure and smooth skin whether he is really male.

"You've had a direct encounter with Wormwood," says the beard.

"With its humanoid avatar, yes," I say.

"We'd like to debrief you," says the other.

"I've already been debriefed by Mrs Alaagomeji."

"We'd like to debrief you under hypnosis," says the beard.

I look to Ileri.

"They think when you linked minds there may have been information passed into your memory that you are unaware of. It may help us know more."

"It won't hurt," says the androgynous one.

Right. I've never heard that before.

I am patient and silent. I've been taught to let other people fill silences and I have no reason to make these agents uncomfortable.

"Let us repair to the drawing room," says Ileri in a faux English accent.

This isn't so far-fetched. I have all of Nike Onyemaihe's memories inside my mind and I get snatches of images and sounds from God knows where or when.

Still.

I have greater awareness right now. I feel all the people in the building. My fellow students. The guards. The instructors. Everybody. I know how to keep it all in check so that I can get rest. Sometimes I have to use clotrimazole. There are some sterols in the cell walls of the xenoforms that make them vulnerable temporarily to antifungals.

Still.

The "drawing room" is calming. The paintings are non-representational neutral shit. I'm sitting in a dentist's chair. I am alone in the room, but I am sure there are cameras and an audio feed.

I begin to entrance myself, using breathing techniques. I feel, then isolate everybody else. I briefly remember the time Akpan masturbated and caused all our class to climax at the same time. I giggle, then screen it out.

I dig into my memory. No, I excavate, slowly peeling back layers and finding my encounter with Wormwood.

I go beyond what the avatar Anthony tried to show me. I look for after-images, déjà vu, memory watermarks.

I . . .

I remember being in a place with siblings beside me. I cannot see them, but I sense them, innumerable, floating in zero gravity, embedded in individual rock casings, all of us enclosed in a hangar. I am awake because my masters need to check how alive I am, what sort of commensal organisms live within me, and the likelihood of my surviving a trip into deep space. We are called footholders, and our function is to descend on planets with fauna and flora from our home world and see if we survive. It is a wasteful colonisation technique, but the masters can no longer go back home. They live in space now, but would love to live on a new planet.

I have no memory of travelling in the Milky Way. I am designed to wake when I breach atmosphere. When this happens, I realise I am on fire, bits of rock and ice sheared off by the friction of this planet's protective envelope. It is unimaginably painful, especially when the rock encasement is gone.

I land in a city, London, right on a park, Hyde Park. Scores of humans die on impact. Some survive and live within me. Footholders only live in symbiosis with a sentient organism, so I find a human, Anthony Salermo, homeless, full of regret, emaciated, in an alcohol stupor, ashamed to return to his family.

I do not know human anatomy, so I have to ... dissect him, body and mind.

I start with the body. Unfortunately, I do not know about human pain until it is too late, therefore Anthony Salermo suffers. I strip off the skin first, examine hair, nails, organelles, sweat glands, pores, bacteria on the skin, patches of fungal disease, scars, sebaceous glands, tiny blood vessels, tattoos, melanocytes, fat cells, all of it. I look at muscles, stripping them individually off the bones, examining the striations and how they work, ligaments, tendons, myoglobulin, everything. I look at cartilage, bone, marvel at the mixture of rigid calcium hydroxylapatite combined with collagen generated by osteocytes. I look at internal organs (it is at this point that I realise Anthony Salermo has been screaming all along. It stops when I take out his lungs). Thyroid, thymus, heart, bowel, pancreas, liver, kidney. Brain. I take my time on the brain.

I make thin threads of neural tissue and connect with his nervous system, the cortical layer that forms higher consciousness: the amygdala and hippocampus for primitive functions, and the medulla, cerebellum and midbrain for automatic functions.

When I have taken Anthony Salermo apart, I put him back together again, after a fashion. I have him at the heart of me. I have imprinted his DNA. I even grow myself a brain just for the fun of it, though I do not have a central nervous system. My thoughts are modular. The humans think they can kill me by destroying the brain, but of course they cannot. It is good to be aware that they want me destroyed.

I build organic duplicates of Anthony and place part of my consciousness inside them. I send these duplicates out into the world, to Earth, to gather information and interact with humans. I enjoy this. Not all humans wish me dead. Many of them are, in fact, quite pleasant.

While this happens, I take the measure of Anthony Salermo's mind. His family's genetic material has only been in London for two centuries. Before that it was on the Italian peninsula. He was trapped in a cycle of poverty in London when I first arrived.

I—

I come out of the trance.

"I'm done," I say. I get out of the chair, endure a little vertigo, but it passes.

"Why, Kaaro?" asks a voice, possibly the bearded guy.

"I'm just done. Leave me alone." I leave the drawing room.

The truth is, I felt myself submerging, my identity in question. I made myself come out of the trance.

I will sacrifice none of myself for S45. Fuck them.

I have a headache for days afterwards, and I have nightmares of being dissected alive by Wormwood for months. When I wake, I usually think I am Anthony Salermo.

But I am not.

I am Kaaro.

Rosewater, biodome: 2066
Now

I am moving.

I am on an uncomfortable platform, and I am being wheeled. A gurney. Lights passing overhead.

Layi says: "I didn't know you had friends in such high places."

I am outside, at the dome. There is a small crowd around. I can sense their thoughts, their awe. There are about sixty people saying prayers to ward off maledictions. The dome glows as usual, but a dark spot is forming and I feel the wind change. I feel the hope of the people of Rosewater when Anthony, Layi and I begin to enter the biodome. *What is this impromptu Opening? Will there be healing? Will we be healed more frequently than once a year now? What will happen to my gout? Who are these people?*

"This is where I stop, my friend," says Layi. He does not enter the lip of the opening. He has his hands raised half-mast in a slow wave to me. He looks uncertain for the first time since I've known him. Anthony doesn't seem surprised. I wonder why. What taboos prevent Layi the angel from entering paradise?

"Thank you," I say. I sound weak even to myself.

"Make sure you come back for my sister," he says.

The opening closes just as I begin to feel stronger. I sit up, and Anthony is pushing the gurney along. He smiles. I feel health rush into me like a drug. I feel the air in my lungs and the contraction of my muscles.

"I can walk now," I say. I slip off and land on something velvety. It's moss, or something akin to moss.

I am in the dome. When I first came here, it was little more than a tent settlement with a few dozen people, and even that was under threat from the federal government. The air here is fresh and sweet, though there is no wind. There are motes floating about akin to dust or pollen, but different. They glow faintly. I turn around and around; I'm feeling healthier by the minute and I can sense the xenoforms in my system running through my lungs. The dome reaches higher than I thought, easily two hundred feet. At the apex, wild floaters cavort. When they make contact with the dome, there are sparks. There are only footpaths here, no roads, nothing harsh on the eye, although there are straight lines. The dome is over thirty miles wide when measured from the outside, and I wonder how these people navigate such a space with just footpaths. There is art lining the walkways, Yoruba deities, orisha: Obatala, Ifa, Yemoja and the like. They are rendered in wood and bone and are twice the height of a human. There is a large wooden panel suspended it seems by growing vines and covered with nsidibi ideograms.

The paths lead off into a maze bordered by trees, some out of season, some evergreens, many not native to Nigerian shores. The predominant smell is floral and vegetation. I remember that Anthony's clothes are made of cellulose.

I scrunch my toes, picking at the moss. I feel happy, like I must laugh. I feel the xenosphere open up to me.

"Be careful," says Anthony. "You've never—"

It's too late; I am connected. The rush of information is dizzying and feels like I have left my body. I feel the xenoforms leaving the dome and returning with information about the weather, about people outside, about soil pH, about flora and fauna. I feel the people in here, who all seem to be connected. Families, individuals, children playing, couples fucking. Too late I experience the sexual congress and feel my penis stiffening and erupting. I feel the homunculi, which have multiplied beyond imagination and live as feral cats among the humans, who are immune to the neurotoxin thanks to the xenoforms.

I feel the people trapped in the prison. Prison? There is a prison here and people do transgress. People live in pods grown of vegetation or houses of wood, rock and Wormwood's bone, or in the open air. The temperature is always mild. There is technology, and several ganglia line the inner surface of the dome.

I feel Wormwood itself, not through Anthony, but the leviathan itself nested in the Earth, growing the city above, protecting, nurturing. The size of it surprises me. The city is like a pimple on its surface. It is more far-reaching than I could have imagined.

The Lijad is in here, merged, the dome dwellers mixed together with Oyin Da's people, integrated, indistinguishable. Something twists in me when I remember her.

The dome does not have a uniform appearance. There are glyphs on the inside, writing from an unknown language or culture. Unknown to me, at any rate. There are drawings mixed in with the ideograms. These are not static. They shift, sometimes scrolling, sometimes disappearing. They are both beautiful and grotesque, but always strangely comforting.

Light does not refract through the dome. It produces its own illumination, and I can feel the crackle of energy. This is not alien to me. It feels familiar. I am part of this. I have been for a long time.

I see the people, the men and women with cellulose clothing, some decades out of fashion, others experimental. Here and there is nudity, and living tattoos slither across skin. Some people stop what they are doing and smile; they smile at me for they are aware of my scrutiny. A woman smiles and feels aroused at my orgasm. She picks the information out of the xenosphere here. She wills me to read the writing on her skin; it is something from Soyinka's *The Interpreters*. I pull back from her after reading for a time. I do not understand the complicated feelings that this brings. My usual manner of reading people does not involve them reading back, and I feel exposed.

For nourishment there are different options. They have thick xenoform layers and can, if they wish, photosynthesise and draw electrical power from Wormwood's abundance, but humans have centuries of adaptation to guide them, and they farm for food crops or garden for beauty. Everything grows easily here. There is no code of behaviour for them to be vegetarian, but there's no livestock or desire for it. Some eat insects that make their way in from the outside.

There are stations, places to receive bursts of xenoform spores, which have coded information from outside the dome. Music plays, some from recording devices, but some emanating directly from memories and into my sensory cortex. There are composers here, and the fragments of their work jar and disturb my harmony.

There is a monument constructed from dead COBs, flesh rotted away or dissolved in acid, machinery welded together.

As I observe it, I am aware of the history. COBs flying close to the dome are electrocuted and absorbed. Nearby is a weapons museum, all the weapons destroyed or taken from the Nigerian government's attempts to get in. Tanks, RPGs, handguns, Gatling guns.

Every few yards there is a mound of hard flesh, tumours, extrusions from Wormwood isolating toxins that the xenoforms cannot neutralise. The tumours are safe, but I did not believe there was anything Wormwood could not render harmless and recycle. It introduces uncertainty.

I follow the ganglia, I descend, and the elementals follow me. They are welcoming and curious and friendly. There are thought parasites in the neurotransmission stream, which the elementals trap and consume. I feel again that Wormwood covers a wider area than I initially assumed. It extends beyond the margins of the dome, beyond Rosewater city limits. It is deeper than when I was first here, neither is it stationary. It moves with the Earth's crust and the shifting of tectonic plates. It is like a tick on the Earth. I follow the ganglia to what I think is the brain of Wormwood, but I am surprised that there is no central function. There are no grand thoughts or instructions issuing forth. I used to know this.

"It is not like us, Kaaro," says Anthony. "It grew a brain to be like me, but it does not need or use one. I am the grand translator, the codebreaker."

His words bring me back to the surface. I am standing by the gurney, Anthony in front of me.

"This will be uncomfortable," he says.

He just stands there, but I know he is doing something. I feel it like drowning in reverse. The ectoplasm surges up from my lungs into my throat and for a while I cannot breathe.

It doesn't come out in one smooth go. It corkscrews gently, shearing parts of my respiratory tract, although it emerges in one piece. Ultimately it is less like a cloud than a clump of floating jelly, slightly translucent and projecting pseudopodia from time to time. Anthony sticks his hand in the gelatinous mass.

Molara is in there, all over the xenosphere, a fearsome creature with blue-black butterfly wings in full spread, her fury spraying against both me and Anthony.

What are you doing? This does not concern you, she says.

Fly away, says Anthony.

There are negotiations to be had. You cannot just—

Do not question me, you insignificant infection, says Anthony. *Go.*

Molara detects threat and leaves.

I cough, but otherwise I'm fine.

"What now?" I ask. "Will you tell it to leave?"

"I cannot just tell these xenoforms to leave. We are not all the same. We are similar, but do not always agree or even speak the same language."

"That's insane. Don't you come from the same planet?"

"Do you speak Bantu?"

"No."

"Polish?"

"No."

"And do you come from the same planet as people who do?"

"Touché."

"We need to negotiate."

"For the human race?"

"For you. The human race is already lost."

"What do you mean? The world is still—"

"Look at me. This body is one hundred per cent alien; the only part that remains from the human called Anthony is the specific electrical pattern of my brain, and even that is entangled with Wormwood. This body dies, I just build a new one. Some of the people in here vary from ten to forty per cent xenoform because their internal organs or limbs or some part of their body has been slowly replaced. This is not only happening in here – think of Opening Day, the healings. Ultimately, all the bodies will be replaced. Kaaro, the human race is finished. It's just a matter of time, and we are very patient."

"I thought you were on our side."

Anthony raises his arms by his sides and then lets them drop. "Some of you will live."

"You owe me."

"That's why you will live, Kaaro."

I am not a brave man, neither am I heroic. I suppose cowardice evolved in humans to ensure survival. Some must fight, others must fear and use flight. I do want to survive and I do want to see Aminat again.

"Let me out," I say.

"Kaaro—"

"Let me the fuck out of this place, right now. Let me out. *Let me out!*"

Layi is not waiting when I return to Rosewater. There is a small crowd of about fifteen or twenty people, and they stare at me as if I am Lucifer cast out of heaven. There is hunger in their eyes. They rush forward and mob me. I flinch and am about to defend myself when I realise they want healing. They touch me, pull at me, lick my sweat, beg me.

"I can't help you! I'm not a healer," I say, but maybe that's not true, because the xenosphere starts to tell me a man's gall-stones just dissolved.

I am not the same. I don't look at the dome in the same way. It's now a stye or a boil, swollen with purulence, waiting, biding its time. I don't know what my healing has cost me. How many native cells have the xenoforms driven out? Ten, fifteen per cent? How human am I? I see the people touching me and the ones at the periphery staring as dead people. Conquered and killed by invaders, walking around carrying their own death, but they don't even know it. I want to scream at them, but it does not matter. I stop struggling. The cellulose clothing Anthony grew for me is torn, but still they come.

Emi! Emi! they keep saying. Me, me. Or it might be the word for spirit they are saying, distorted by the shouting. Maybe if enough of them are healed, the xenoforms themselves will be depleted, diminished. But I am not fooling myself.

I know that rather than healing, I am seeding these people with their own destruction. I am a Typhoid Mary, a Patient Zero, a Pale Rider.

Perhaps that's what humanity deserves.

So, this guy, this titan, Prometheus, he steals fire from the gods and gives it to mankind. His punishment? They chain him to a rock and Zeus, in the form of an eagle, eats his liver every day. Since Prometheus is a titan, his liver grows back overnight, only for the eagle to eat it again. This continues for ages until Hercules comes along and kills the fucking eagle, which is Freudian as hell because Zeus is his father, but that's beside the point.

I've known this story since I was young.

I've been thinking of Shesan Williams, Aminat's husband,

trapped in the xenophere, eaten by floaters, then regenerating, then being eaten again. I was clearly thinking of Prometheus when I designed the punishment. Now, though, now I feel guilty, a result of being confronted with my past sins by Ryan Miller perhaps. I am not a judge, or a god; I should defend myself, but not mete out punishment. It isn't my place to offer this kind of retribution, and cast the first stone and all that shit.

I go to the hospital. I see him. I see the floaters tearing his neuro-flesh, all the more painful. I see blood leaking, I see the creatures bickering. There is a head buried in Shesan's belly, excavating his bowel. His scream is constant. I take no pleasure in it.

Fuck it. I dismiss the floaters.

Nothing happens.

What?

I try again. No effect. I suspect that the images I left in Shesan's brain have been there so long, his mind has accepted them as real. If he thinks they are real, my contribution is extraneous. Fantastic. I have many shitty ideas and this one is classic.

The floaters notice me and two break off to attack me. I click my beak and let out a screech. They are undeterred. I extend both fore and hind claws and beat my wings to gain height. They follow, but I can manoeuvre better. I slash at them, cutting through their dorsal gasbags. One bites me on the leg. I am going about this wrong. I shake it loose, fly higher, beat my wings until a mighty wind results. It blows all the floaters away, leaving Shesan standing there frightened. I descend, land in front of his bleeding mental image. He trembles, but does not run.

"Shesan Williams, do you know me?" I ask.

He shakes his head, but then he thinks about it.

"You're the one who's fucking my wife," he says.

I swipe him across the face, though I have withdrawn my claws so he isn't cut. He falls to the ground on one knee, then gets up. I can hear the susurrus of floaters flying. They gather around us, gaining courage.

"Make them go away," I say.

"I can't."

"You can. This is all you. I have nothing to do with it."

"You're lying."

"Fine. Stay here and be eaten alive over and over."

"Can you take me back with you?" he asks, voice laced with hope.

"That's up to your body, Shesan. It's too damaged. Unless you want to come out of the coma, I can't help you. Do you have a message for your family?"

He thinks for a moment. "Tell them I'm sorry I caused them pain. I'm not sorry for the life I chose. God knows they benefited from it. Aminat benefited from it, then she stabbed me in the back."

"What do you mean?"

"She hasn't told you?" He starts to laugh, just as the floaters move in and begin to nip at him.

"Told me what?"

"She's an undercover cop."

Twenty-four hours later, I give my report to Badmos, the S45 section chief. For the first time since I joined, I type up the whole issue: the sickness of sensitives, Molara, Wormwood, Bola, the xenosphere, the role of the dome, and what Anthony told me. I recall everything verbatim where I can. I add context and my own conjecture. It is the best work I have ever put to paper. I expect it to galvanise the department into action. It does not.

Badmos nods and makes the appropriate *well done* noises for positive reinforcement, then puts the encrypted memory device away. I know it will get filed and lost. He warns me not to share my experience with anyone else and suggests that I do not leave town. No, I cannot see the boss, but my message will be passed on. I miss Femi. I know that if she were here, I would have a direct audience. Eurohen is probably too busy schmoozing politicians.

It seems to me that they already know what I have told them. They also do not want me to be part of the solution. They do not trust me. They have never really trusted sensitives, but this is more than that. I am seen as an agent of the invaders because of what I carry and what I can do. They won't even let me continue my interrogation of Tolu Eleja, which is kind of sad because I've been thinking of atonement lately. I wanted to find him innocent and get him released, even though I've already incriminated him. At least there's nobody else to probe his mind. The section chief is too blasé when he dismisses it and me. I don't think I'll be able to live with myself if they execute him, but I have no idea how to prevent it. It weighs on me like an unpaid phone bill as I leave.

Aminat comes back after a week. I get a request on my phone to allow tracking and I see her ID. I allow it, my heart thumping with anticipation and resentment. I am sitting on a low rise overlooking the Yemaja. It is an abandoned park. I have just finished a phone call when I smell her perfume.

"Who were you talking to?" she asks. "New girlfriend?"

"In a manner of speaking. I may have a new job in the National Research Laboratory."

She sits next to me, leans on my shoulder and looks out at the river. Some poor fool is trying to fish in a canoe in the sluggish flow. He will catch nothing but mutants and disease.

Aminat looks beautiful and is wearing tight jeans that show off her powerful legs, but I sense a weariness in her, and her left wrist is in a plaster cast.

"Are you all right?"

"Yes."

"Do you want to talk about where you went?" I ask.

She shakes her head.

"Do you still love me?"

She nods.

"Was there someone else?"

She shoves me lightly. I swing back like a pendulum.

We sit there in the evening light, watching the silly fisherman, loving ourselves in silence.

Chapter Thirty

The land that would become Rosewater: 2055

Then

Coming back to life seems familiar, and it takes me a second to realise why. I have Anthony's memories from when I looked into his head, and he has returned many times before. I feel the alien cells replacing my damaged blood vessels, repairing the shock-wave damage to my heart, knitting the bone back together, extruding bullet fragments and soil, sealing the muscles, the subcutaneous tissues and finally the skin. My hearing comes back and the world judders with gunfire. My eyes feel gritty, but I open them all the same. My body is one-third buried in soil and there is sand over my face. The soil is wet. I move tentatively, and there is no pain. I look at my chest. Though my clothes are torn ragged, there is no scar on my skin. In addition to gunshots, there is thunder. The ground seems to heave, though it might be dizziness.

"Fuuuuuuuuuuuuuck!"

"Are you okay?" says Oyin Da.

"I've been shot. Hurts like a motherfucker! Well, it did. Doesn't any more."

She is crouched over me and looks anxious but not really afraid. Anthony is behind her, facing the other way.

"He's fine. Better than new," says Anthony.

The ground undulates. "I don't think I'm fine. The ground seems to be moving."

"No, that's not you. It really is moving," says Oyin Da.

"What?" I stand up. The ground surges gently, not like an earthquake, but with definite soil displacement. "What's happening?"

Anthony turns and holds me by the shoulders. "Your employers attacked us. You misguided fool, you tried to save me and got shot in the chest. Thank you for that. I will not forget, though in truth I was never in any danger."

The guy's face is emotionless, but his voice is kind. Why the hell did I jump in front of the bullet for him? I don't even know him. Was I trying to impress Oyin Da? Fuck, I've been shot. I died. Are my new abilities making me take on the qualities of others? Maybe Oyin Da had an altruistic impulse to save Anthony, because right now I can read from her that she thinks he is important.

"Kaaro, you have to decide," says Oyin Da. "Anthony is going to raise a barrier between us and them. You can stay here or you can go back to your old life."

"I—"

"Come with me," she says. It is the first time she has shown any interest in me, and her eyes bore directly into my soul. There is promise, but I don't know of what. She is not sexy in the way I am used to, not like the girls in the clubs in Lagos. She makes no effort to be beautiful. Her mind is on science and predictive values. I am drawn to her, but also afraid of her. But she is also afraid of me, of being rejected. I sense the uncertainty within the intensity. Lightning flashes and brightens the night to day, illuminating her face and hair. I discover that what I think is dry lightning is actually electricity bolts from the ganglia striking invaders.

I like Oyin Da. I like what she stands for, too, but I can't commit to staying. I can't give up the life I have. I am ashamed to think of Femi and her beauty and the remote possibility that I might have … something. The glamour of being a government agent. Femi's car. Femi's house. Femi. I am young and fickle and do not know my own mind. At this age, sexier is better than anything at all.

"I am bringing the Lijad here, to stay with Wormwood. It's safe here and there is food, shelter, and an entire new ecosystem that I want to study."

"I can't," I say.

Her mind closes like a shutter, with finality. I wish, at that moment, that I had said something else.

I am not the only one who stays out. The concept is too frightening for dozens of people – some from the Lijad, some of Anthony's followers. We stay all night watching the thin membrane rise and form a dome, then the gaps filling out. I do not know where they go afterwards. I will never see any of them again.

At the end, Anthony shakes my hand and passes something to me. It's slimy and difficult to keep in my hand, like a slippery version of putty.

"For when your back is to the wall," he says. "Put it on your head. Only if you have no other choice."

"What is it?"

"A decoy."

With that he is gone.

In the morning light, the dome grows, becomes less translucent. Flashes of electricity sometimes crackle towards the husks of military vehicles and set them on fire anew. None of the people around me are harmed. Those who have phones record the event. The air smells of freshly tilled earth, cordite and ozone.

I walk back towards civilisation, hoping to catch a ride to Lagos or steal a car, but I am arrested by some army boys instead. The gift Anthony gave me now looks like a smear of mucus on my palm. While in detention, I cannot wipe it off. I wonder if I am going to be left in detention for years before someone from S45 remembers to look for me. I ask to speak to Klaus, but they are not interested. After two days, I am taken to Femi Alaagomeji.

My father visits me while I'm in detention. I am sitting on the bunk reading the Book of Ezekiel, because the King James Bible is the only book in the cell, when a rookie yells, "Get up."

I am taken to a room and seated. There's a second empty plastic chair, but that's it. No windows, camera in one of the corners, a faint smell of quicklime that tells me someone might have died in here. I can get out of this prison if I want. I can see the route out, but I'm not quite ready yet, and to be fair, I haven't been treated ill. I think Femi's here to visit, but the door opens and my father walks in.

Ebenezer Goodhead. *Chief* Ebenezer Goodhead. Our real family name was Orire, which means "good head" in English if you transliterate. In actuality it means "good soul", but nobody cares. He owns all those Goodhead stores you see in every town centre. Yes, he met two successive presidents and is courted by prospective candidates. Yes, he is richer than God now. He looks slight, and he is not muscular or tall, but his voice is surprisingly deep. It resonates through any room and people listen to him. He has grown a beard. His lodge ring is still in place and he wears an agbada, which makes him seem larger than usual. I know he doesn't like wearing them, but he must have wished to project power when coming here.

I greet him in the traditional Yoruba way, by prostrating myself on the floor in front of him. I've never done this, and he knows I am in some way mocking him by doing it now.

"Father."

"Son."

He sits, right opposite me.

"What do you want?" I ask. "Are you here to say you told me so?"

"What use would that serve? You're a thief. I knew you'd end up in jail."

"Point of correction, Father, I've not been charged with anything."

"You will be."

"I doubt it."

"Come home, son."

"What? Why?"

"Is it not enough that I am inviting you back? Your mother—"

"Delivered me to a slavering mob to be killed. Do not speak of her."

"But it turned out okay. You're here now."

"Father, that mob murdered Fadeke. They burned her alive and she had nothing to do with anything."

Fuck this. I burrow into his mind. I am new at this, but I know that it hurts, even though I only probe for about three seconds. I know why he wants me home. He is afraid. I see his business interests and his hidden things, the mistress, the affairs. I see that he fears I will bring shame on him and he will not have enough money to—

"Just get out of here," I say. "I will never use your name. Don't worry about your precious life. I'm staying out of it."

"Kaaro—"

"*Fuck off!*"

The first thing I do before basic training in Maiduguri is vandalise a Goodhead supermarket.

Interlude: Mission

American colony, Lagos: 2066

I am curious in spite of myself.

This America mystery has been going on since I was a child.

Nobody has heard anything from North America for forty-five years. Around the world there are colonies where Americans are granted protected status, but nobody can get into or out of the States. This is because of what other nations have called Drawbridge, the ultimate Trumpian fuck-you to the world.

Wormwood is not the first of its kind to arrive on Earth. It's the third that we know of. The first was on 12 January 1975 in Lagos, Nigeria. It was reported as a meteor by the CIA station chief at the time. A living, spreading biological organism lived underground for 106 days before dying and decaying. The head of state at the time, Murtala Mohammed, struck a deal with the US asking for help with analysis. The organism was shipped off, but Mohammed was assassinated in 1976 and it is unknown whether the Americans got back to him before his death.

In 1998, in Hamburg, Germany, a fiery object smashed into a railway line, derailed a train, and sank to a depth of forty-nine metres before NATO allies extracted it and sent it to a research lab in Atlanta, where it survived for eighteen months before dying.

In 2012, Wormwood devastated London. Given the size of this specimen, the failure of the British to either tame or terminate the visitor, and the inability of their own scientists to come up with a credible counter-measure, America elected to pull the drawbridge up.

At the time, there were 294 US embassies and consulates in the world. Within a week, they were all closed, consular staff recalled with no explanation. The American staff in the ISS were pulled.

All communications to or from the US ceased, and no sensitive could find them on the xenosphere. I tried. Drone fighters turned back commercial flights. Satellite imagery showed a gigantic black patch, an electromagnetic anomaly with full absorption of all spectra. The Middle East ignited and burned with violence for years. The UK, already isolated and politically unstable from leaving the European Union, could no longer count on US military might. The country quietly ceded the leadership of the world to Russia and China, while fighting to retain Scotland. Ireland did not exactly return to the Troubles, but the political infighting tore entire regions apart.

No spycraft could reveal what the fuck was up with the Americans. Theories were like assholes: plentiful.

The one I presently favour is that having studied the two previous Wormwood siblings, the Americans knew no defence would work and either took off to Lord knows where or pulled a turtle – withdrew into an impenetrable shell for protection.

Which brings us to these guys. They say they just left America last week.

They've been debriefed by regular agents. Femi wants me to see what I can find in their heads. It's not an interrogation per se. For one thing, they know I'm going to be poking around and they know what I am. They have agreed to this. The thing about Americans is that they want to go home. None of them want to live in the refugee camps that we call American colonies. If this will help, then they'll do it.

They stand up to greet me when I walk into the lounge. They both wear hippyish beards and have long hair. They look skinny and wind-blown. We speak in English.

"Hello, Mr Kaaro," says the first.

"It's just Kaaro," I say.

"I'm Chuck O'Reily and this is Ace Johnson."

"Ace? That's a real name?"

"We're from—"

"I don't really need to know. I mean, I will know because of what I'm about to do. My understanding is that you consent?"

"Yes," they say in unison.

"All right then."

"Should we close our eyes, hold hands?" asks Ace.

"If you want to. Makes no difference to me. Look around the room, read a magazine if you want. I'm going to sit here. Do whatever you want, but don't disturb me."

"Do you need quiet?" asks Chuck.

"Nope. You can have a party for all I care. Just don't leave the room."

I enter the xenosphere.

I see both of them, but it's all wrong. Neither of them reads like human. Their self-images are amorphous, protean. I should see outlines that look like Ace and Chuck, but what I see resembles dark miasma. I probe around it, test the edges,

371

see if this is some kind of trained mental camouflage to defend against people like me. It is not. In the xenosphere, I can expand what I see to microscopic level. If this were training, there would be regular, recurring patterns in the smoke. This is as random as they come.

I stretch a wing and bat the smoky tendrils. They warp around the gust, but re-form quickly.

Shit. I know what I have to do, but I don't like it. It's risky, especially since I don't know what I'm dealing with here, but fuck it.

I trot into the area occupied by these two phantasms and inhale.

Immediately I know this is one of the more difficult excursions I've ever made into the psyche of others. My ego becomes unstable. I am both of them, Ace and Chuck, and I am Kaaro, from S45.

We are on a rubber raft, barely staying afloat on choppy seas. I don't know what ocean this is. Come back to that. We are lashed to the raft, and are afraid. The inflation isn't great, and we have no paddles. Ace is asleep, but Chuck worries enough for both of us. It is morning and there is miasma clinging to the surface of the water. We do not know why we are attached to the raft; we do not know how we got here. All we remember is the raft.

No. *I am Kaaro and I need more than this, more than you can remember.*

I go further back than their memory can take me.

I am here, and here is America. The new America.

I don't know what state or city I'm in, but the streets are clean. No cracks in the sidewalk, no potholes anywhere, no litter. No cars either. There are blocks of flats everywhere I look, arranged in that grid pattern that Americans favour. They stretch into the sky, each one of them. The sky, right. The sky is not our sky. No clouds, no sun, moon or stars. An artificial darkness broken by strings of lights lining up from horizon to horizon, crossing each other, reticulate. I know, as does anybody, that when it is the day cycle, the lights will brighten enough to read by, but the older folk know that the sun was much brighter. This, in comparison, is sickly. Most younger people don't mind. I have seen this kind of thing before, albeit on a smaller scale.

At this time of night most everybody is asleep or at least in their flats. There are no longer any suburbs. The price of safety. Spheres patrol the streets, silvery, high sheen, silent flight. One passes close to me, but there is no sound.

The trees lining the boulevard I find myself on have no leaves underneath them. I investigate them, and find plastic bark, synthetic leaves, hallucinatory soil.

There is too much sameness here, too much repetition. The street on both sides goes off into oblivion. I try to enter one of the blocks. I cannot. I imagine the doors work by the same implant-recognition security that we use in Nigeria. No, wait, this is where I live. The air is clean, cold, artificial-tasting. The door should be opening. Am I Ace or Chuck? Ego integrity check.

I am afraid. Why? Something Ace and Chuck have done or are about to do. Ah, breaking quarantine or segregation. This is City 151. They/we are meant to stay within our cities. We went to the borders, to the sixteen portals. We are young, we know there is more to our world, to our universe. We want to see it.

We circumvent security. This plan is two years old. We have done dry runs, we have protective suits. We have the balls.

You also have the stupids. There's nothing wrong with your lives, dummies.

We have not covered our tracks well enough. I am arrested outside my apartment. I am arrested in my room. We are interrogated by machines. Our rulers and overseers do not make contact in meatspace. In the end, we tell them everything, because there is no other option. It is always a matter of when, not if.

We are exiled. Exile is usually a euphemism for death. They throw you/us/we out of portal seven. It opens above the sea.

We are lucky. There has been a plane crash, debris all over the sea. Raft. No paddles. Wait.

Why do you not remember? What happened to your memories?

Maybe something the machines did, the androids who interrogated them? Maybe a side effect of the portal?

I come back to myself.

We leave the Americans in the Lagos colony. They don't know anything and are not a danger.

I tell Femi what I think. America is in hiding, in a constructed place, with at least 151 cities all kept apart from each other. Ghettos.

"One other thing: I don't think there are any xenoforms in these cities. They've found a way to keep themselves uninfected."

I get no medal, and a hero's welcome does not wait for me in Rosewater.

Chapter Thirty-One

Rosewater: 2066

Now

My new orders arrive and I am asked to read as much as I can from a politician, covertly. I immediately decide I'm not going to do it. It's a Sunday, so I play football on the field that is about a mile away from my flat. I haven't done this in a long time, and I do not know any of the kids, but as soon as I'm allowed to play, they recognise my skills and we're like lifelong friends. The game is brisk and it helps take my mind off the events of the last few days. As I expected, the police tried to question me about Clement, the mob and the whole wahala that happened. I waved my S45 identification around and they let me go.

The goalie is feeling sick, so I do a stint between the posts. I am terrible at this and I let three goals in before I'm swapped out. I don't know how long we have been playing, but I am out of breath and I ask to be subbed. Someone is at the touchline, a woman. She seems to be waiting for me, staring at me. I walk closer, and I can see who it is. She's older, and much thicker around the waist and arms, but she's unmistakable. It's Oyin Da. Her eyes are no different from the day we met.

"I heard you visited us," she says.

"Yes." I stop a foot short of her. "Why are you here, Oyin Da?"

"To see how you are. To ask you, again, to join us. When I learned you came into the dome, I was curious."

I shake my head. "Things are different now. I'm not infatuated with you any more. I know what the whole thing is about. What percentage of your cells has been replaced by xenoforms?"

"Sixteen."

"That much?"

"Yes, but by body weight, I'm twenty-nine per cent machine. That doesn't make me part of the robot uprising that has been predicted but will never come to pass."

"It's not the same thing."

"We are all part machine, Kaaro. Your phone is a polymer under the skin of your hand. You have a locator chip in your head."

"What do you have?"

"No apathy."

"What?"

"I have micro-electrodes to regulate my mood. I have a microfiltration system to augment my fluid balance in case there is no water. I have a portable link to the Lijad in my left forearm, backup power supply in my right—"

"Okay. Enough."

"The apathy part is important. Nobody cares that an aggressive alien species is slowly taking over indigenous human cells. It does not matter."

"So you zap yourself with your magic electrode and you don't have apathy. I get it."

"No you don't. They know, Kaaro. They have known for

a long time. They are not resisting it. Did they welcome you when you told your masters about Wormwood?"

"No, they sent me to perform some shitty political intrigue."

"I see." She does a half-turn to her right, although her feet remain in position. "I have a daughter."

"I'm pleased for you."

"Sarcasm?"

"No, I really am. What's her name?"

"Nike." I never told her about Onyemaihe. Strange synchronicity.

"Lovely name. What is she like?" I start to walk and she joins me.

"Stubborn. Brilliant. Unrelenting." She smiles as she says it. I cannot bring myself to ask about the father, which makes me feel I might not be completely over her. But there is one thing that has been on my mind for a while that I think she can help with. "Come with me."

"Oyin Da—"

"Or stay. I had to try, had to talk to you. I'll figure something out."

"I'm not the world-saving kind."

"No, you're not."

"But . . . but there is something I'd like to ask."

Aminat is uncertain about this. I can tell from the way she shifts this way and that, causing a whisper from her summer dress. The sound makes me want to stop, kneel in front of her, and stick my head between her thighs.

"Are you sure about this?" she asks.

"Nope. Not at all."

I am standing in front of my safe, she behind me so close

that I can feel her breath on the back of my neck. The safe is in a wall, and open. There is no combination. I instruct the flat and it disengages the lock. There is cash, some medicine, insulin if you must know. No, I am not diabetic, but I have had the notion for a while that if I were to suffer from a chronic illness, I would like to take my own life in my own way. There are contact lenses that link to Nimbus, as was fashionable some years back. They still work, but there were a few cases of phlyctenular conjunctivitis that put people off using them. There is a bronze mask of a Benin woman that I stole from my father. It is the only item of stolen property I keep.

There is a sealed cylinder, transparent, about six inches in height. It is on its side and the slime seems inert, lying like a water level taking up a third of the volume of the container. I unscrew the cap.

Some of the slime sticks to the cover, draws out, and snaps back to the parent mass. I tip it into my palm. Rivulets of action begin on its surface, though I do not know if it reacts to the oxygen or to the heat from my hand.

Aminat takes a step back.

"This is not one of your smartest ideas," she says.

"Actually, none of my ideas is smart," I say. "At least I'm consistent."

I struggle to remember what Anthony said about this when he handed it to me. Something to use when I'm in trouble? I'm not in trouble, although I am about to start some. The last time I attempted to use it, I freaked out and thought it was going to kill me. I feel that same emotion churning my belly right now, but I tamp it down and rub the slime on my head. It is cool to the touch and spreads like shower gel. It moves in all directions, dripping over my forehead. This is the part I don't like. It initially splits over both of my eyebrows and tracks down, but it makes up for that and covers my eyelids, which I snap shut just in time to keep it out of my eyes.

"Are you okay?" asks Aminat, voice frayed with creeping alarm.

"No," I say. I know how to put a stop to this, but I don't.

The slime covers my nose and enters my nostrils, coating the inside. I sneeze, but it does not dislodge anything. I open my mouth to sneeze again and there is slime in my mouth, coating my teeth, my tongue, the insides of my cheeks and a short distance down my throat. I am reminded of Molara's ectoplasm. Of Clement. Of Bola. Did they feel like this before they died? I struggle against it. I heave and retch, but do not vomit. It is a hundred wriggling maggots in my mouth with a slightly salty taste.

"Kaaro!"

"I'm fine," I manage to say, but I'm not.

The material keeps going, down my chin, around my neck, coating my chest, back, arms, groin, thighs and feet, including the soles. My clothes disintegrate and fall off. I cannot breathe. My nostrils are blocked and my throat spasms. I try to pick my nose or remove the slime from my mouth, but the growth is too profuse to stop.

"Kaaro, I don't like this. I'm going to get help."

"No."

Calm down. Think. Relax.

I'm not breathing, but my brain is not screaming for oxygen and I do not feel faint. I am alive, my heart still beats. I stop struggling. I am in mild pain because each minute ripple of the slime seems to stroke a nerve ending. My eyes are closed, but I am aware of my environment. The xenosphere is cut off, but I suspect the slime is sending information directly into my nervous system and drawing oxygen from the air.

"Kaaro?"

"It's . . . I think it's all right, baby. It's strange."

"You *look* strange. You look like a sculpture made of mucus."

"Don't say that. Meanwhile, I'm hungry." I walk to the fridge and start eating.

I wake up feeling cold. I do not remember when I fell asleep, but I open my eyes. The fridge door is open and every item of food is unwrapped and gone. All around the kitchen cabinets are open and there is a supreme mess although the vacuum robot is whirring around cleaning the floor. There is no sign of the slime. I am naked. A pool near me suggests that I may have wet myself.

"Aminat!"

"In here," she says from the living room.

I join her and see what she is looking at. Anthony's gift to me.

"I was worried about you going off on an adventure with your ex-girlfriend, but now I'm not," she says.

Okay.

Oyin Da comes to me at the appointed time in the appointed place – my suya spot. I'm offering the dog Yaro strips of meat, but he's so ill that he won't eat. His flank wound heaves with maggots and Ahmed has been trying to shoo him away, saying he's bad for customers.

"I'll come back for him shortly," I say. "I'll get him fixed up with a vet."

"Kaaro, we don't have time," says Oyin Da.

I say my goodbyes to Ahmed and his customers and walk with her.

"I analysed the different coordinates from your chip and I'm sure I can get us into the facility."

"Good."

"Your career with S45 will be over after this. Even if we get out in time, they will find out that it was you."

"Let me worry about that. I should be concerned about you, though. Last time you and I went on a mission, you went native."

"That won't happen with a government agency." She stops, looks around. We are in a secluded spot. It's dark. Nobody who is not using night vision can see us. "Remain still."

As we transition, I'm thinking about how she no longer has Afro puffs. I'm expecting nausea, but it doesn't happen. Instead, a sense of being stretched out over an instant, and time dilation, and a wrenching of the spirit.

It's dark where we arrive at our destination and I feel for the xenosphere immediately. I find it. They are not expecting a sensitive and have not suppressed it with antifungals. Maybe. There is static from Oyin Da. She's found a way to block me, which is unsurprising given how long she has had to work with and against the xenoforms. There are no guards in the immediate area, but I can pick up the remnants of their thoughts, neurotransmitters still buzzing around with the old patterns in the same pathways. I search for any references to my unfinished interrogation – Tolu Eleja or his appearance. I see the beatings and casual brutality and his panicked thoughts and fatalism. I see where he is held. I nod to Oyin Da, but we do not speak as agreed. Places like this have sonic recognition and I don't want to announce our presence. I set off, and she follows.

We're still on level minus four in the Ubar complex. I am moving swiftly, like a rumour. I have never been this fast, even when young. I am at the age where you have to work for the physical gifts you take for granted in your twenties, yet I move like my body is weightless. It is like playing a video game. I use the cognitive schematic I put together from the residual patterns in the xenosphere to guide myself, discarding wrong turns and experiencing false familiarity, borrowed déjà vu.

I am outside his room. There is a keypad, but I do not have to use it because there is someone inside with Eleja. The door is unlocked; I know this before I touch it. I know that there will be an alarm as soon as I enter the room. I am miffed that I can't tell what Oyin Da is thinking. I discharge an interference pattern inside the room. Nobody in there will be able to think. I also instruct their brains not to see me or Oyin Da.

The room is sparse: a bunk, a chair, a commode. The prisoner is on his knees, hands cuffed, with the guard standing in front of him holding a doubled-up belt. There are welts on Eleja's face, neck, shoulders and arms. I see in the guard's mind that this is not a sanctioned interrogation and that he is just bored on a night shift. I make him take the handcuffs off Eleja and fellate his own sidearm. He will continue to do this as long as he is awake. What I initially plan is for his dreams to be full of this action, and to continue when he wakes, but I remember the mistakes of the past and end the compulsion with falling asleep.

There is a camera, but I think this brutality would have made the guard kill the feed or ask a buddy to look the other way. I expect an alarm any second regardless.

I go to Eleja and use everything I know to strip back his

defences. I am aware of the slime's effect, enhancing my abilities, making this all so much easier. It is like swimming, not laying siege. It is easy. I get past the red herrings and the false memories and the crude conditioning.

I have no time for games. Who are you, and why are they interrogating you?

And just like that, I know.

Before I can speak, the alarm sounds. It is silent, but I feel a pulse in the xenosphere, a thrill of panic and an awakening flow of adrenaline and dopamine. No longer any need to be silent.

"Oyin Da!" I say, startling Eleja. He's been unaware of me until now, pondering the odd behaviour of the guard, relieved that the beating has stopped.

She walks into the cell. "Well?"

"Take him. Time to go."

I sense them coming with weapons and sealing exits. They can see us, and Oyin Da's image has triggered a primal frenzy since she is a known dissident. It takes her a minute or two to load her transporting program. I wink at her and leave the cell.

"Halt!"

How many times have I heard that?

Bright lights shine, and I can see nothing. I send out a wave of disorientation into the xenosphere, but nothing happens. These guards must be protected against sensitive attacks. I hear something rolling on the floor and I know to cover my ears. I cannot warn Oyin Da, no time, and she's wearing some white-noise device. I hope she's gone. The flash-bang does what it does. I am deaf as well as blind. I feel very few of the rifle butts that converge on my head.

I feel far away, removed from it all.

The last thing I am aware of is the disappearance of Eleja from the xenosphere.

Yaro sleeps the guiltless drugged sleep of anaesthesia while the vet debrides his wound. There is a kidney dish beside the surgeon and it is full of maggots. The vet incapacitates the maggots with chloroform and flushes them out, then uses a suction tube on the copious amounts of pus. He removes the dead skin and muscle and exposes viable tissue. I know all this because he gives a running commentary while he works. The stench is overwhelming.

"I'll have to keep him overnight to inspect the wound again tomorrow," says the vet. He is washing his hands while Yaro twitches with canine dreams. "Sometimes the maggots may be dead but still in the wound. I think I got them all, but—"

The door flies open and two uniformed, armoured militia people come in.

"Kaaro, put your hands in the air," says one. Her voice is artificial, electronic. She speaks from behind an airtight helmet.

I obey. "I am not armed and I am not resisting," I say in a calm voice. I'm scared because these are not thinking people and I do not know their orders.

"Where is the prisoner?" asks the militia.

"What prisoner?" I ask.

"The one you liberated from Ubar."

"What? I haven't—"

"Don't play games. Tonight you infiltrated a secure facility and liberated a suspect."

"Officer, I have been here all evening. Ask the good doctor. I brought my dog for surgery."

The vet has his hands up and water drips down his forearms,

wetting his scrubs. He seems as frightened as me and he nods his head vigorously.

I say, "I do not have your prisoner."

This is true, I don't.

It's six hours before they release me. During this time they carefully reconstruct my day. They check surveillance built in to my apartment. They check the GPS logs of my implant. They question Aminat. They show me a video of the breakout. I see a person who looks like me, but there is no corresponding signal from my implant. The timestamp on my implant states that I am nowhere near Ubar at the time. The doppelgänger disintegrates while being clubbed. When the mist clears, there is nothing left. Not even a smear on the floor. I almost feel sorry for them, because they have an empty cell, a soldier giving oral sex to his gun, and video footage of a ghost. Jobs will be lost over this, but not mine.

"That's not me," I repeat. "Did you find any of my DNA? No, you did not. Because that is not me. No, I don't know who it is or what it is."

When Aminat picks me up, I assume we are under surveillance and we only speak of our outrage at the unlawful detention and harassment. We live our lives as if nothing happened.

I take Aminat into the xenosphere while we sleep. I am my true self, not the gryphon. I show her my maze and we walk in it, holding hands.

"It worked, then?" she asks.

"Yes. The slime duplicate dissolved into the constituent cells and dissipated. S45 is confused, and they think maybe Wormwood created the duplicate after my jaunt into the dome."

"Are you in trouble?"

"Not really. Maybe. I don't know. I play the victim. I don't care. They suspended me with pay, which is fine. I don't want to work with them anyway."

"Who was he?"

"Eleja? He was a guy with a theory. He and a group of others figured out the invasion – that the aliens are taking over our cells – but more than that, they figured America's draw-bridge is related to that. It's a way for America to stay human. They formed a group that is trying to get into the American colony in Lagos. They were going to capture some of the Americans and force them to reveal the secret. They thought they were saving the world."

"So what have you done with him?"

"Oyin Da will take care of him, maybe use his knowledge, get into the colony, find something to reverse the replacement."

"And why won't you do this?"

"Because I am not the saving-the-world type. I am not a hero, Aminat. I'm just a guy in love with a girl. I'm the last sensitive. They don't need me at the bank, because there are no more attacks. I've been made redundant by the death of all the psychics, but that's okay, because I don't really care about the job. All I want is to spend my days with you. Nothing else."

"Is that a marriage proposal, Kaaro?"

"This memory will self-destruct five seconds after you wake up," I say.

I pause for a minute, unsure.

"Baby," I say.

"Uh oh, tone change," Aminat says. "Must be serious. What have you done this time?"

"I saw Shesan."

"Why?"

"I wanted to free him." I pause again. "Baby, I don't know how to say this. He told me you're a cop."

"Did you?"

"Did I what?"

"Free him."

"What? No ... er, no, I couldn't. He's ... No."

"Thanks."

"Well? Are you an undercover police officer?"

Cherry blossoms float in the air, disdainful of gravity. We are at the edge of my zone of the xenosphere. My giant guardian is patrolling, his long braids dragging on the floor in his wake. Scattered here and there on the grass are miniature tanks, five feet long, three high.

"Are those toys?" Aminat asks.

"No, they're Goliaths. Hitler's mini tanks, designed to halt the advance of the Allies in World War II. I saw them in the newspaper. My mental detritus washes up here. And you're trying to distract me from the question."

"That's not it. I'm trying to organise my thoughts."

"It's a binary, yes-no kind of question, Aminat."

"Do you want to read my memory?"

"No," I say. "I'm never going to do that."

"And nobody can hear us here?"

"Speak freely."

"I work for S45."

"*What?* How could you keep this from me? You know how I feel about—"

"Calm down."

I take a moment to reassert control, because I almost throw both of us out of the xenosphere. "Are you assigned to watch me?"

"No, just relax and listen, Kaaro. Years ago, in Lagos, my brother ignited and burned our entire house down. You know this already and you've seen him aflame. The debris was still smouldering when S45 agents came and took him away. He was young, confused, naked and crying. They took blood and skin samples from me, my father, mother, our entire family. My younger sister was away, but otherwise, everybody had to give samples.

"They didn't release Layi, so I made several legal challenges. One night, in the midst of it all, I was walking home when a car pulled up alongside me. I was prepared to take off my shoes and run. There were a lot of abductions in Lagos at that time. The driver was this stocky, muscular type. There was a beautiful woman in the back who knew my name and asked me to get in."

"Femi Alaagomeji," I say.

"The same. She asked me what I was hoping to achieve, and I said I wanted my brother home. She asked me pointed and reasonable questions about public safety. I said I would look after him. You've met Layi. He can't hurt people. Nobody even got singed when the house burned."

"So she got you to join S45."

"Not at first. She said I would need a specific skill set to be able to safely look after someone with my brother's abilities. She proposed to provide me with training."

"Yeah, that sounds like her."

"I trained for six months in Maiduguri."

"Did you get Danladi?"

"Motherfucking Danladi? No, he's left, but his legend lives on. After training, Femi said they might as well give me honorary S45 status. She outlined the perks, and said I'd be doing the work of an agent anyway. I came up with the adaptations that keep Layi safe. Femi modified them slightly, and my brother was released into my custody."

This must have been why Femi was against the relationship from the start.

"When Shesan started courting me, I had no idea about his criminal enterprises. After we got married, Femi summoned me and handed me a new brief. Layi had been stable for years. She ordered me to spy on my husband. I was very effective before I got tuberculosis."

"And me? Am I your next assignment?"

"No, Kaaro. Our meeting was a chance occurrence. Femi Alaagomeji did everything to discourage me from being with you. She's never asked me anything about you. Nothing secret, anyway. As we both know, there are other people watching you, and besides, she knows more about you than I do."

"Why were you blown up?"

"I can't tell you."

"Aminat—"

"You'll have to respect the integrity of my job, Kaaro. I cannot, will not tell you about my assignment. I can say it has nothing to do with you, but that's as far as I'm willing to go."

I nod.

"Wake me up. Get me out of this place," she says.

Back in the flat, she holds my face in both her hands and kisses me.

"Kaaro, I love you. I will never let you come to harm. I will always protect you. Do you understand?"

"Yes."

"Do you believe me?"

"Yes."

She kisses me again, and does not let go.

We live our lives, Aminat and I. She takes absences from time to time, but she does not explain and I do not ask. She is unknowable, or rather she prefers not to be known, and I will never open her mind. *I too am untranslatable*, she often says, quoting Whitman.

I take Yaro in after he recovers and he keeps me company when Aminat is away. He finds it difficult adjusting to domestication, but I am hopeful. He follows me to the pitch when I play football.

Silently, inexorably, despite the efforts of people like Oyin Da and Eleja, the invasion continues. Humanity dies one cell at a time. I don't know what will happen when we all become full xeno, but it's like climate change or that asteroid that will collide with the Earth and wipe us out. We all think we'll be dead and gone by the time the carnage begins.

The alien in me says that is delusional thinking. For this disaster we will all be present. For this we will all have front row seats.

Look out for the next instalment in the Rosewater trilogy:
The Rosewater Insurrection.

Acknowledgements

A book has the name of the author on the cover, but there is a multitude behind the scenes.

People I want to mention: my agent, Alexander Cochran; editors Jenni Hill (look how kind I am!) and Sarah Guan; my writing massive: Aliette de Bodard, Zen Cho, Cindy Pon, Victor Ocampo, Pat Ocampo, Vida Cruz, Karin Tidbeck, Alessa Hinlo, Nene Ormes, and Mia Sereno; Nick Wood for reading the earliest draft of *Rosewater* and saying it didn't suck; Jide Afolabi my constant reader, it's a Lagos ting; Kari Sperring, Liz Williams, Athena Andreadis, Laura Mixon, Kate Elliot; Pat Cadigan, who is a champion and an absolute bad-ass; early reader Rob White; Chikodili Emelumadu for listening to me moan; Carmelo Rafala, Milton Davis, you know what you did; Sue Atkins for the title; and my family for leaving me alone in the attic.

extras

extras

about the author

Tade Thompson is the author of *Rosewater*, a John W. Campbell Award finalist and winner of the 2017 Nommo Award for Best Novel. His novella, *The Murders of Molly Southbourne*, has recently been optioned for screen adaptation. He also writes short stories, notably "The Apologists" which was nominated for a British Science Fiction Association Award. Born in London to Yoruba parents, he lives and works on the south coast of England where he battles an addiction to books.

Find out more about Tade Thompson and other Orbit authors by registering for the free monthly newsletter at www.orbitbooks.net.

interview

Hi Tade, and welcome to the Orbit list! We have an easy question to kick off this interview: what are you reading at the moment?

I'm happy to be here! I'm reading *From Bacteria to Bach and Back: The Evolution of Minds* by Daniel C. Dennett and the Norton Critical Edition of Mary Shelley's *Frankenstein*. I always have at least two books on the go at the same time and I'm a Shelley fanboy.

Did you always want to be a writer?

No, I started out wanting to be Spider-Man. I was dead serious about it too. Around age six or seven I realised this was not going to happen (damn you, Nicholas Hammond, you were the lamest of the family von Trapp!) so I figured being a comic artist was the next best thing. In my early teens I switched to prose.

What inspired you to write Rosewater*?*

This is difficult to answer because I think there is a cloud of inspiration that worked directly and indirectly. There are two prominent things I can think of. I read Michael Crichton's *The Andromeda Strain* from a second-hand bookshop and it both scared me and stuck in my head. I think I was ten. I squirreled away some homage to it in *Rosewater* for the sharp-eyed.

The second thing was a fall I had when I was fourteen or fifteen. I fell into a pit and some scaffolding fell on me. I was trapped for about half an hour before help came, but in that time I wondered about an alien dropping from space as an actual meteor, incubating in the soil, having some internal nuclear fission with which it discourages predators while it grows. It first manifested as short story, but I wasn't interested in the pyrotechnics. I wanted to know what the effects would be on people. Like many speculative fiction writers I was obsessed with Fortean stuff growing up. Yuri Geller and Russell Targ, remote viewing, telepathy, spoon bending, I could not get enough of that stuff, especially where it intersected with CIA experimentation.

Who is your favourite character in Rosewater? *Who was the most difficult to write?*
Aminat, by far. I just think she's cool, accepting, sacrificing (for her family), serious, but at the same time fun. She deals with vulnerability well.

Oyin-Da was the most difficult to write because her intelligence meant her thoughts were at times difficult to parse, and her English was odd because she was self-taught. She's loosely based on a kid I once knew whose parents isolated her for religious reasons.

What's one thing about either the world or the characters of Rosewater *that you loved but couldn't fit into the novel?*
I cut about 50,000 words of the book because of Vonnegut's injunction to "start as close to the end as possible". I would have loved to get into the actual first contact, the events in London's

Hyde Park ... wait, I'm drifting from the question. The one thing is the first contact because that was more directly inspired by my fall into the pit.

If you could spend a day with one of your characters, who would it be and what would you do?
It would be Layi. I'd go to his house and ask him questions about life, the universe and everything. I have a fondness for people who have lived lives in relative isolation because they have perspectives that are slightly out of whack.

Can you tell us a bit about the research you did for this novel?
Most of it didn't get to the printed page, but I read *Planet Earth: Underground Worlds* by Donald Dale Jackson for the design and reality of the alien underground; *The Truth about Uri Geller* by James Randi; Ganzfeldt Experiment documentation; declassified MK Ultra documents; pretty much everything I could find on Bobby Fischer and so on.

I should point out that for me, research is a thing I do after the first draft otherwise I'm susceptible to getting lost in various rabbit holes.

*Which scene are you most proud of writing in **Rosewater** and why?*
Two words: Meat temple. Because? Meat temple.
The scene was based on a nightmare I had where I was stuck in this hall that looked normal, but was made of meat. Beef, specifically. My feet sank with each step, and blood would ooze into the indentation. It was disgusting. I think the scene captured the sense of disgust I had when I woke up.

You've peppered Rosewater *with lots of Yoruba words – do you have a favourite word or phrase?*
There's this scene where Kaaro is being chased by a killer robot and at some point he says, *Ile l'omo owa ti nmu 'na roko* which is a saying that applies to people from Ilesha (which is where my ancestors are from). Literally, it means the child of Owa (king) takes fire from home to the farm. It's part of a longer phrase, but any Yoruba person will recognise it and know exactly where I'm from.

Which I think is pretty neat.

When you aren't writing, what do you like to do in your spare time?
Reading, painting, mixed martial arts. Not to say I'm great at any of them, but . . .

Who inspires you as a writer?
I take inspiration from people of excellence in all fields. I think there's a unified field of excellence that involves hard work, concentration, discipline and the pursuit of perfection, regardless of the area of expertise. I think success comes from the intersection of all of that with luck. I don't think luck is all that rare; I just think most people aren't prepared for it when it arrives.

I'm talking about Serena Williams, Wole Soyinka, Prince, Lorrie Moore, Akira Kurosawa, Leonardo DaVinci, Stephen Hawking, Rebecca Solnit, Chiamanda Ngozi Adichie, Jake Weidmann, Jack Kirby, and so on.

Can you tell us a little about what we can expect from the rest of the trilogy?
Rosewater was an extreme close-up on one person's experience of the aliens. *The Rosewater Insurrection* explores the wider effects,

particularly when in-built controls start to break down within Wormwood. *The Rosewater Redemption* is humanity fighting back, but the odds are monumental, stacked against us. Is there hope, or is the sun setting on homo sapiens?

if you enjoyed

ROSEWATER

look out for

AUTONOMOUS

by

Annalee Newitz

Earth, 2144. Jack is an anti-patent scientist turned drug pirate, traversing the world in a submarine as a pharmaceutical Robin Hood, fabricating cheap medicines for those who can't otherwise afford them. But her latest drug hack has left a trail of lethal overdoses as people become addicted to their work, doing repetitive tasks until they become unsafe or insane.

Hot on her trail is an unlikely pair: Eliasz, a brooding military agent, and his indentured robotic partner, Paladin. As they race to stop information about the sinister origins of Jack's drug from getting out, they begin to form an uncommonly close bond that neither of them fully understands.

And underlying it all is one fundamental question: is freedom possible in a culture where everything, even people, can be owned?

1

Pirate Ship

JULY 1, 2144

The student wouldn't stop doing her homework, and it was going to kill her. Even after the doctors shot her up with tranquilizers, she bunched into a sitting position, fingers curled around an absent keyboard, typing and typing. Anti-obsessives had no effect. Tinkering with her serotonin levels did nothing, and the problem didn't seem to be dissociation or hallucination. The student was perfectly coherent. She just wouldn't stop reimplementing operating system features for her programming class. The only thing keeping her alive was a feeding tube the docs had managed to force up her nose while she was in restraints.

Her parents were outraged. They were from a good neighborhood in Calgary, and had always given their daughter access to the very best pharma money could buy. How could anything be going wrong with her mind?

The doctors told reporters that this case had all the hallmarks of drug abuse. The homework fiend's brain showed a perfect addiction pattern. The pleasure-reward loop, shuttling neurotransmitters between the midbrain and cerebral cortex, was on fire. This chemical configuration was remarkable because her brain looked like she'd been addicted to homework for years. It was completely wired for this specific reward, with dopamine receptors showing patterns that normally emerged only after years of addiction. But the student's family and friends insisted she'd never had this problem until a few weeks ago.

It was the perfect subject for a viral nugget in the medical mystery slot of the All Wonders feed. But now the story was so popular that it was popping up on the top news modules, too.

Jack Chen unstuck the goggles from her face and squeezed the deactivated lenses into the front pocket of her coveralls. She'd been working in the sun's glare for so long that pale rings circled her dark brown eyes. It was a farmer's tan, like the one on her father's face after a long day wearing goggles in the canola fields, watching tiny yellow flowers emit streams of environmental data. Probably, Jack reflected, the same farmer's tan had afflicted every Chen for generations. It went back to the days when her great-great-grandparents came across the Pacific from Shenzhen and bought an agricultural franchise in the prairies outside Saskatoon. No matter how far she was from home, some things did not change.

But some things did. Jack sat cross-legged in the middle of the Arctic Sea, balanced on the gently curving, uncanny invisibility of her submarine's hull. From a few hundred kilometers above the surface, where satellites roamed, the sub's negative refractive index would bend light until Jack seemed to float incongruously atop the waves. Spread next to her in the bright water was an undulating sheet of nonreflective solar panels. Jack made a crumpling gesture with her hand and the solar array swarmed back into its dock, disappearing beneath a panel in the hull.

The sub's batteries were charged, her network traffic was hidden in a blur of legitimate data, and she had a hold full of drugs. It was time to dive.

Opening the hatch, Jack banged down the ladder to the control room. A dull green glow emerged in streaks on the walls as bacterial colonies awoke to illuminate her way. Jack came to a stop beneath a coil of ceiling ducts. A command line window materialized helpfully at eye level, its photons organized into the shape of a screen by thousands of projectors circulating in the air. With a swipe, she pulled up the navigation system and altered her heading to avoid the heavily trafficked shipping lanes. Her destination was on a relatively quiet stretch of the Arctic coast, beyond the Beaufort Sea, where freshwater met sea to create a vast puzzle of rivers and islands.

But Jack was having a hard time concentrating on the mundane tasks at hand. Something about that homework-addiction story was bugging her. Mashing the goggles over her eyes again, she reimmersed in the feed menu. Glancing through a set of commands, she searched for more information. "HOMEWORK FIEND CASE REEKS OF BLACK-MARKET PHARMA," read one headline. Jack sucked in her breath. Could this clickbait story be about that batch of Zacuity she'd unloaded last month in Calgary?

The sub's cargo hold was currently stacked with twenty crates of freshly pirated drugs. Tucked among the many therapies for genetic mutations and bacterial management were boxes of cloned Zacuity, the new blockbuster productivity pill that everybody wanted. It wasn't technically on the market yet, so that drove up demand. Plus, it was made by Zaxy, the company behind Smartifex, Brillicent, and other popular work enhancement drugs. Jack had gotten a beta sample from an engineer at Vancouver's biggest development company, Quick Build Wares. Like a lot of biotech corps, Quick Build handed out new attention enhancers for free along with their in-house employee meals. The prerelease ads said that Zacuity helped everyone get their jobs done faster and better.

Jack hadn't bothered to try any Zacuity herself—she didn't need drugs to make her job exciting. The engineer who'd provided the sample described its effects in almost religious terms. You slipped the drug under your tongue, and work started to feel *good*. It didn't just boost your concentration. It made you *enjoy* work. You couldn't wait to get back to the keyboard, the breadboard, the gesture table, the lab, the fabber. After taking Zacuity, work gave you a kind of visceral satisfaction that nothing else could. Which was perfect for a corp like Quick Build, where new products had tight ship dates, and consultants sometimes had to hack a piece of hardware top-to-bottom in a week. Under Zacuity's influence, you got the feelings you were supposed to have after a job well done. There were no regrets, nor fears that maybe you weren't making the world a better place by fabricating another networked blob of atoms. Completion reward was so intense that it made you writhe right in your plush desk chair, clutching the foam desktop, breathing hard for a minute or so. But it wasn't like an orgasm, not really. Maybe it was best described as physical sensation, perfected. You could feel it in your body, but it was more blindingly good than anything your nerve endings might read as inputs from the object-world. After a Zacuity-fueled work run, all you wanted to do was finish another project for Quick Build. It was easy to see why the shit sold like crazy.

But there was one little problem, which she'd been ignoring until now. Zaxy didn't make data from their clinical trials available, so there was no way to find out about possible side effects.

Normally Jack wouldn't worry about every drug freak-out reported on the feeds, but this one was so specific. She couldn't think of any other popular substances that would get someone addicted to homework. Sure, the student's obsessive behavior could be set off by a garden-variety stimulant. But then it would hardly be a medical mystery, since doctors would immediately find evidence of the stimulant in her system. Jack's mind churned as if she'd ingested a particularly nasty neurotoxin. If this drug was her pirated Zacuity, how had this happened? Overdose? Maybe the student had mixed it with another drug? Or Jack had screwed up the reverse engineering and created something horrific?

Jack felt a twitch of fear working its way up her legs from the base of her spine. But wait—this shiver wasn't just some involuntary, psychosomatic reaction to the feeds. The floor was vibrating slightly, though she hadn't yet started the engines. Ripping off the goggles, she regained control of her sensorium and realized that somebody was banging around in the hold, directly behind the bulkhead in front of her. What the actual fuck? There was an aft hatch for emergencies, but how—? No time to ponder whether she'd forgotten to lock the doors. With a predatory tilt of the head, Jack powered up her perimeter system, its taut nanoscale wires networked with sensory nerves just below the surface of her skin. Then she unsnapped the sheath on her knife. From the sound of things, it was just one person, no doubt trying to grab whatever would fit in a backpack. Only an addict or someone truly desperate would be that stupid.

She opened the door to the hold soundlessly, sliding into the space with knife drawn. But the scene that met her was not what she expected. Instead of one pathetic thief, she found two: a guy with the scaly skin and patchy hair of a fusehead, and his robot, who was holding a sack of drugs. The bot was some awful, hacked-together thing the thief must have ripped off from somebody else, its skin layer practically fried off in places, but it was still a danger. There was no time to consider a nonlethal option. With a practiced overhand, Jack threw the knife directly at the man's throat. Aided by an algorithm for recognizing body parts, the blade passed through his trachea and buried itself in his artery. The fusehead collapsed, gagging on steel, his body gushing blood and air and shit.

In one quick motion, Jack yanked out her knife and turned to the bot. It stared at her, mouth open, as if it were running something seriously buggy. Which it probably was. That would be good for Jack, because it might not care who gave it orders as long as they were clear.

"Give me the bag," she said experimentally, holding her hand out. The sack bulged with tiny boxes of her drugs. The bot handed it over instantly, mouth still gaping. He'd been built to look like a boy in his teens, though he might be a lot older. Or a lot younger.

At least she wouldn't have to kill two beings today. And she might get a good bot out of the deal, if her botadmin pal in Vancouver pitched in a little. On second glance, this one's skin layer didn't look so bad, after all. She couldn't see any components peeking through, though he was scuffed and bloody in places.

"Sit down," she told him, and he sat down directly on the floor of the hold, his legs folding like electromagnetically joined girders that had suddenly lost their charge. The bot looked at her, eyes vacant. Jack would deal with him later. Right now, she needed to do something with his master's body, still oozing blood onto the floor. She hooked her hands under the fusehead's armpits and pulled his remains through the bulkhead door into the control room, leaving the bot behind her in the locked hold. There wasn't much the bot could do in there by himself, anyway, given that all her drugs were designed for humans.

Down a tightly coiled spiral staircase was her wet lab, which doubled as a kitchen. A high-grade printer dominated one corner of the floor, with three enclosed bays for working with different materials: metals, tissues, foams. Using a smaller version of the projection display she had in the control room, Jack set the foam heads to extrude two cement blocks, neatly fitted with holes so she could tie them to the dead fusehead's feet as easily as possible. As her adrenaline levels came down, she watched the heads race across the printer bed, building layer after layer of matte-gray rock. She rinsed her knife in the sink and resheathed it before realizing she was covered in blood. Even her face was sticky with it. She filled the sink with water and rooted around in the cabinets for a rag.

Loosening the molecular bonds on her coveralls with a shrug, Jack felt the fabric split along invisible seams to puddle around her feet. Beneath plain gray thermals, her body was roughly the same shape it had been for two decades. Her cropped black hair showed only a few threads of white. One of Jack's top sellers was a molecule-for-molecule reproduction of the longevity drug Vive, and she always quality-tested her own work. That is, she *had* always quality tested it—until Zacuity. Scrubbing her face, Jack tried to juggle the two horrors at once: A man was dead upstairs, and a student in Calgary was in serious danger from something that sounded a lot like black-market Zacuity. She dripped on the countertop and watched the cement blocks growing around their central holes.

Jack had to admit she'd gotten sloppy. When she reverse engineered the Zacuity, its molecular structure was almost exactly like what she'd seen in dozens of other productivity and alertness drugs, so she hadn't bothered to investigate further. Obviously she knew Zacuity might have some slightly undesirable side effects. But these fun-time worker drugs subsidized her real work on antivirals and gene therapies, drugs that saved lives. She needed the quick cash from Zacuity sales so she could keep handing out freebies of the other drugs to people who desperately needed them. It was summer, and a new plague was wafting across the Pacific from the Asian Union. There was no time to waste. People with no credits would be dying soon, and the pharma companies didn't give a shit. That's why Jack had rushed to sell those thousands of doses of untested Zacuity all across the Free Trade Zone. Now she was flush with good meds, but that hardly mattered. If she'd caused that student's drug meltdown, Jack had screwed up on every possible level, from science to ethics.

With a beep, the printer opened its door to reveal two perforated concrete bricks. Jack lugged them back upstairs, wondering the entire time why she had decided to carry so much weight in her bare hands.